ST. MARTIN'S PAPERBACKS TITLES BY
DONNA GRANT

THE DARK SWORD SERIES

Dangerous Highlander

Forbidden Highlander

Wicked Highlander

Untamed Highlander

Shadow Highlander

Darkest Highlander

THE DARK WARRIOR SERIES

Midnight's Master

Midnight's Lover

Midnight's Seduction

Midnight's Warrior

Midnight's Kiss

Midnight's Captive

THE DARK KING SERIES
(e-book series)

Dark Craving

Night's Awakening

Dawn's Desire

MIDNIGHT'S CAPTIVE

DONNA GRANT

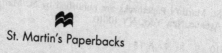

St. Martin's Paperbacks

This is a work of fiction. All of the characters, organizations, and events portrayed in this novel are either products of the author's imagination or are used fictitiously.

MIDNIGHT'S CAPTIVE

Copyright © 2013 by Donna Grant.

All rights reserved.

For information address St. Martin's Press, 175 Fifth Avenue, New York, NY 10010.

ISBN: 978-1-250-01727-7

Printed in the United States of America

St. Martin's Paperbacks edition / July 2013

St. Martin's Paperbacks are published by St. Martin's Press, 175 Fifth Avenue, New York, NY 10010.

10 9 8 7 6 5 4 3 2 1

For my readers.
Thank you for going on this
incredible journey with me.

ACKNOWLEDGMENTS

As always my thanks go first to my brilliant editor, Monique Patterson. I'm so very blessed to be working with such a wonderful person and talented editor. Thanks for all you do!

To Holly Blanck and everyone at St. Martin's who helped get this book ready, thank you.

To my remarkable agent, Louise Fury. You always know what to say and when to say it. Thank you.

A special note to my assistant, Melissa Bradley. Thanks for everything you do. You make my life easier, and for that, I owe you so very much. Thanks for the laughs, the long talks, the ideas, and just for being such an amazing person. Love ya!

To my kiddos, parents, and brother—thanks for picking up the slack, knowing when I'm in deadline that I might be a tad absent-minded, and for not minding having to repeat things.

And to my husband, Steve, my real-life hero. Thank you for the love you've given me, for the laughter you brought into my life, our beautiful children, and the happily-ever-after life I always dreamed of. I love you, Sexy!

ACKNOWLEDGMENTS

CHAPTER
ONE

Ferness, Scotland
May 2013

Charon slowed his car as he pulled off the main road into a strategically hidden drive. He eased his charcoal gray CL65 AMG Mercedes cautiously over the dirt road until he came to the rock-lined parking area behind the pub he owned.

He put the car in park and shut off the engine. For several minutes Charon sat silently, contemplating the previous hours.

The game had changed.

Again.

Charon released a long breath as he rubbed through the hole in his shirt where he'd been injured. During the entire drive from MacLeod Castle to his little corner of Scotland, he'd thought over the encounter that took place at Wallace Mansion.

So many times he'd battled evil, but always he and the other Warriors came out on top. With every battle, however, it seemed the danger continued to escalate.

As did the chances of their deaths.

For over six hundred years, he'd lived without fear of death. He was a Warrior. With a primeval god inside him that not only gave him immortality, but power as well, there wasn't much that could harm him.

Anyone could take a Warrior's head and end their life. If they ever discovered who was a Warrior. And if they could best a Warrior in combat.

Charon and the others kept what they were a safely guarded secret. Still, that didn't stop the unease that plagued him ever since discovering a new evil had taken over.

Jason Wallace.

"How many more?" he murmured to himself. "Were Deirdre and Declan no' enough to fight and vanquish?"

In his heart, Charon knew there couldn't be good without evil, but he was tired of fighting, weary of always looking over his shoulder, wondering when the next strike would come.

It was made worse because he'd had four centuries of peace. All because Declan had brought Deirdre forward in time.

Charon, like the rest at MacLeod Castle, had worried about when Deirdre would finally show up and unleash her evil once more. The MacLeods had even sent Warriors forward into the future as well, with the help of the Druids.

Charon hadn't been one to travel through time, and for him those four centuries had been paradise. Pure, unadulterated bliss.

It was easy to push aside the monster he'd become while locked in Deirdre's prison deep in her mountain of Cairn Toul. He even managed to get through several days at a time without calling to mind what Deirdre forced him to do to his father.

In the end, however, Charon had to face the fact that he was still the same monster.

Better clothes, money, and owning most of the small town of Ferness hadn't changed anything. They were a shell to cover the man he really was. A brute. A beast.

A fiend.

Charon pulled his key from the ignition and opened the car door. He stepped out of the Mercedes and inhaled the fresh, clean air around him.

He'd taken a chance in returning to Ferness after escaping Deirdre's prison, but it was his home. Too many decades had passed for anyone to remember him when he came wandering up those centuries ago, but it wouldn't have mattered if they did.

There was nowhere else he'd wanted to go. It hadn't taken long to begin transforming Ferness into a prospering town. He lived among the mortals without them ever knowing anything.

Until a year ago when Ian Kerr walked into Ferness with his Druid, Danielle. Charon had known trouble would follow, but there was no way he could turn away a fellow Warrior.

And just as he expected, trouble had come. He hadn't hesitated in transforming into a Warrior to protect his people and help Ian defend Dani.

He could still remember the way his men had gaped at him for a moment before diving into the battle. No one had spoken about seeing him or Ian change into their Warrior forms.

Maybe that was for the best. His men who had survived that awful night stayed by his side, which was all he could really ask for.

Charon gazed at the building before him. The inn dated back to the twelfth century, and had held up well, thanks to his constant care. The first floor had been transformed into a pub. Above that on the second floor was his office, and on the third floor, his home.

The inn wasn't his only acquisition. He'd bought several properties around town, but his major investment was land. He owned hundreds of acres around Ferness. It kept people from settling, but its beauty brought in tourists by the busload, which equaled profits to everyone in the small Highland town.

Charon put his hand in a pocket of his jeans and drew out the small bullet he'd recovered from the battle. The slug itself was nothing special, but the red liquid in the small see-through chamber was the unique part.

The liquid was blood, but not just any blood. It was *drough* blood. One drop from the blood of Druids who gave their soul to Satan to practice black magic could kill a Warrior.

That was bad enough. Declan Wallace first used the X90 bullets a year ago. They wreaked unimaginable damage, keeping the Warriors from getting close to their enemies, where they could use their strength, speed, and deadly claws.

With the death of Declan, Charon had assumed knowledge of the X90s would fade into oblivion. But somehow Jason Wallace, Declan's cousin, had not only managed to manufacture the X90s again, but also made them more powerful.

It wasn't just the X90s, as Charon himself had learned. He'd taken the blade meant for Arran. The instant the dagger tore through his skin, he'd felt the sting of *drough* blood.

There had been an inferno inside him that ate away at his bones and shredded his insides. The soul-crushing, gut-wrenching agony had been too much to bear. He'd known he was going to die.

Many times he'd craved death, but as it sat staring at him, Charon realized he wasn't ready to die. He wanted to live, if for no other reason than to kill Jason Wallace.

Charon looked down at the cut in his ruined navy pullover and flattened his lips. It was the other Warriors, the ones he'd kept his distance from who had saved him.

No one knew how or why another Warrior's blood could counteract *drough* blood, but it did. They used their blood to help him hang on to life until they could reach MacLeod Castle and Sonya, a Druid who had amazing healing magic that could help him.

He owed her a debt that could never be repaid. Just as he owed Phelan, Arran, and the others for saving him.

Charon wasn't the only one disturbed by the turn of events with the *drough* blood. Phelan's blood, that could heal anything and anyone of any affliction, had no effect on Charon's wound.

He'd seen Phelan's worried frown. But Phelan departed MacLeod Castle before Charon had a chance to speak with him. Neither felt they belonged with the Warriors at the castle, which had formed a tight friendship between them.

It was an odd friendship, one neither Warrior could have seen coming, but they were bound together. And not just because they were immortal.

Charon knew Phelan would eventually show up to discuss what might have gone wrong when Charon hadn't been healed by his blood. He wanted answers to give to Phelan, but what could he say when the power of the gods within them couldn't help?

He ran a hand down his face and turned away from his building. There was too much on his mind for him to face those within. Especially Laura with her pale green eyes, eyes that pierced him to his very soul.

Charon walked down the hill, following the path he'd worn over the years. It meandered through the thick forest, dozens of other paths branching off along the way. He had many trails he'd used over the centuries, but there was only one place he wanted to be right now.

He came to the sixth fork in the path and turned left. Another three hundred yards and he halted, his gaze taking in the valley below him. It lay nearly untouched by time. Beautiful and serene.

The trees stretched high into the sky, their thick limbs heavy with leaves. Even now he could hear them rustle as a breeze swept through the dense foliage. The sun broke through the clouds, its rays shining brightly on the small loch. The water dazzled like golden fairy wings with the reflection of light.

This was his haven, his sanctuary.

The one place he could let down his guard and allow the horrors of the world he lived in to show.

Laura Black watched Charon from the offices on the second story. She'd rushed to the window when she heard his car pull up. The instant the tires crunched on the gravel, she'd known it was him.

Even as she knew she shouldn't, she stared. Through the

windshield she could make out his strong jaw and the chocolate-colored locks of his hair that fell just past his chin.

She knew from her many hours of covertly observing him every contour of his face, from his razor-sharp cheekbones to his high forehead and square chin. She knew how his lips could look soft and inviting when he wanted something, but if he was angry, they were hard and thin as he pressed them together.

In the two years from working closely with Charon, she'd seen all his emotions. None had made her stomach knot like the one on his face now.

The way he looked at the inn as if he were in another time or place made her skin tingle with some emotion she could neither name, nor explain.

Her mouth went dry when his tall, muscular frame unfolded with liquid grace from the car. She never tired of looking at him. He was utterly virile, wonderfully male.

Completely, wickedly gorgeous.

His dark, seductive eyes, which she had seen promise other women sin and satisfaction, now appeared haunted. Troubled.

Her gaze raked over his frame that lounged nonchalantly against his car with one ankle crossed over the other. He wore his jeans low on his hips, as if they had been custom-made to show off every wonderful angle of his trim hips, firm butt, and long legs.

Laura bit her lip as her eyes traveled up from his narrow waist to the wide *V* made by his impressive chest and shoulders. She might not be able to touch him, but she knew every inch of his upper body from watching him move huge barrels of whisky.

In the summer he'd remove his shirt while working, and that's when it took every ounce of her willpower not to ogle his striking body and honed sinew like some love-struck teenager.

As drawn in to his body as she always was, Laura didn't miss the way his jaw was clenched. He stood strung tight as a bow, so tense he appeared as if he might crack into a million pieces at any second.

There were many secrets her box had, and she respected them. Yet, she found she wanted to go to him and wrap her arms around him. To give him the comfort it seemed he so desperately needed.

It was silly. Charon didn't need anyone. At least not usually. This was the first time she'd seen him look so . . . ravaged . . . by whatever ate at him.

He was rarely alone. If one of the men about town wasn't with him wanting something, there was a beautiful woman on his arm. Women flocked to him, but then who could resist such confidence and carnal sexuality combined into one man?

Thankfully, he didn't bring the women back to his rooms. It was one of his own rules. No woman he dated had ever seen his office, much less his home or the inside of his bedroom.

Laura didn't know why he kept to that rule, only that it saved her from having to see women with that pleasured look on their faces as she came into work.

She was used to the Charon who always had answers, the Charon who fixed any and all problems. The Charon who nothing seemed to affect.

But he was affected now. That much was obvious, and it worried her, settling into her chest in a tight knot.

She wished she didn't care about him—or long for him. But she did. At night when she closed her eyes, it was his arms, his eyes . . . his body that held her captive, his mouth that kissed her into oblivion.

If there had even been a hint he was interested in her, she'd have let him know her interest. Charon, however, was her employer and friend. Nothing else would come of the longing, the . . . need she had for him.

Laura narrowed her eyes and turned her head to try to see what it was he pulled from his pocket. It was small and he studied it as if it held the answers of the world.

All the while, he rubbed his chest where it appeared his

shirt had been cut. Concern spiked through her that he might be injured.

The only thing that stopped her from rushing down to him was that she didn't see any blood on his hands.

She put her hand on the window when he turned his head to the woods. As if hearing some silent call, Charon pushed away from the car and started toward the forest.

His strides were quick as they ate up the ground. Long after he disappeared into the thick trees, she stood there, thinking of him, wanting him. She knew that look upon his face. He always went into the forest when he was unsettled.

Laura turned away from the window. He could be out there for hours. Still, she'd seen the tear in his shirt. She hurried into his office, where he kept spare shirts for when he had to break up fights in the bar.

There had been a time she hadn't wanted to walk into his office. It was so very . . . male. So Charon. She loved the dark furniture, the gray walls, and all the wood, but it made her take notice of her handsome employer when she couldn't afford to.

This time she ignored the desk and large leather chair and pulled open a drawer in the filing cabinet. She took the shirt on top and draped it over her shoulder as she headed to the small half kitchen near her desk.

Just a few minutes before, she'd put on water for tea, which she now poured in a large carafe and added tea bags. She dunked the bags three times, then added one teaspoon of sugar before screwing on the top.

She unlatched the sliding glass door that opened onto the second-floor deck and stepped outside. Laura positioned Charon's shirt near the top step on the railing, and then set the carafe on the small table in case he came back sooner than she expected.

Once inside the office, she closed the door and found herself looking through the dense trees for a glimpse of Charon.

It was the ringing of the office phone that took her away.

CHAPTER
TWO

Jason Wallace took slow, deep breaths through the pain, but it didn't help to dull it. Nor had he been successful in finding a Druid with healing magic. Which meant he'd most likely have the five gashes along his left check as scars.

All thanks to Arran MacCarrick. But Jason's revenge on the Warriors would happen sooner than any of them realized.

He reached for his mobile phone and dialed a number. There was a muffled hello on the fourth ring.

"Is everything in place?" he asked.

The man on the other end of the phone grunted. "Oh, aye. The wench is almost too easy."

"I wouldna say that. You've no' even managed to get her to agree to go to dinner with you, Ben."

"Oh, doona worry. She'll be yours to do with verra soon, Wallace. I've given my word."

Jason squeezed the phone. "And I've given mine. If you fail, your life is forfeit."

"I willna fail," Ben declared.

Jason ended the call and looked out over the kitchen sink to the long drive overgrown with low-hanging trees limbs in desperate need of trimming. Any moment, Dale, his only remaining Warrior, would return with Mindy.

Mindy would be furious she'd been left behind, but she had to know getting out had been his only priority. It was up to everyone else to find him. Just because they were lovers didn't afford her special privileges.

Mindy was a hellion in bed. Her white thighs would part for him with just a smile as she waited for him to tell her how he wanted her and when she could come. As fun as she was to fuck, it was her propensity for evil that drove him wild.

As he watched, a small dark green car came into view. A moment later it parked and Mindy bounded out of the car, shouting Jason's name.

He turned to the door as it was thrown open. Mindy's eyes glared daggers at him, and her lips—coated with her usual red lipstick—were flattened in fury.

"You left me," she stated.

"You didna keep up."

"I could've been killed."

He leaned a hip against the kitchen counter and shrugged. "Aye. But you were no'. You're alive."

She took a step toward him, and her feet faltered when she caught sight of his face. The anger drained away, replaced by concern with a hint of disgust. "What happened?"

"The damned Warriors happened. Arran, point in fact."

Mindy closed the distance between them and put her hands on his chest as she gazed up at him adoringly. "Have you tried to heal yourself."

"Aye. Nothing works."

"We'll kill Arran together, and then we'll take his woman and make her suffer. No one harms you. No one."

Jason pulled her into his arms and smiled.

Laura rolled her head from side to side to stretch out the tight muscles from sitting at the computer all day. She saved her current spreadsheet after entering in the week's total sales before pulling open another document to place an order for the alcohol they were running low on.

Four orders later, she glanced at the clock to see it was half past six. Charon still hadn't returned.

She worried her bottom lip with her teeth and clicked her

e-mail instead of leaving. Upon seeing a message from Dreagan Industries, she quickly opened it.

Dreagan had the best scotch in all of Scotland, but they were choosy about who they allowed to sell their liquor. She had been writing them for over a year now proving how well Charon's business was doing and why the sale of Dreagan scotch would be a boon for both of them.

So far they hadn't bothered to answer. So why the sudden response now?

Laura was too excited to care. She opened the message and hastily scanned it. When she didn't see a refusal, she paused and read the message more slowly.

"Good," she said as she leaned back in her chair and let out a sigh. "I've finally got some great news for Charon."

Laura looked behind her to the deck where the shirt she'd set out and the tea—replaced three times already—still sat untouched.

Charon had to be deeply bothered to stay away from work so long. He rarely left, and when he did, it was usually for something important.

Though he kept his whereabouts a secret from her, if she called him, he always answered the phone. Except for this last time. She'd called to let him know there had been a brawl in the club with several broken windows.

When he hadn't answered, she'd grown concerned. When he didn't return her call, she had almost phoned Scotland Yard. Charon always kept in touch with her.

Always.

She hadn't realized how worried she was until she looked out the window that morning and saw his car. The brief glimpse she got of him had been enough to know something wasn't right. Was it regarding the business or personal? She didn't know.

At least when he returned she could tell him the news about Dreagan. The fact they wanted a meeting could only mean great things. Their first hurdle was over with. Now, all Charon had to do was charm them as he did everyone, and the deal would be sealed.

Laura rose from her chair and walked to the row upon row of CDs lining the far wall. Charon's offices weren't like most employers'. Few people ever had the opportunity to come upstairs, and when they did, they were treated to a spectacular sight.

The office was an extension of Charon. The floors were a dark wood, the walls painted a soft, muted gray. There were highly prized—and coveted—swords and shields dating back to the fourteenth through seventeenth centuries. A vase from eighteenth-century China, paintings from British artists during the nineteenth century, and other highly prized items.

Mixed with the historical items were photos of Scotland in varying sizes around the room. The rugs, drawing in the various shades of green, bronze, burgundy, and navy only helped to accentuate the warm feel of the room.

There was a cream-colored leather couch sitting near the hearth but facing the windows looking out over the forest. Charon sat there often, sipping on his favorite scotch, Dreagan.

Laura's desk was situated in a corner so she could see anyone coming up the stairs. The way her desk was arranged, it also prevented anyone from peering into Charon's office unless she allowed the visitor.

She looked at the closed door to Charon's office. The door was the same color wood as the floor and moldings. It was one area she rarely ventured into when he wasn't there.

He'd never told her she wasn't allowed, but just like the rooms above used for his residence, they were private. And she kept them that way. It just seemed wrong to venture into the places that were his when all it made her do was think of how it would feel if he would look at her with desire, as he did other women.

Laura looked back at the rows of CDs and let her gaze wander the titles. Charon had eclectic tastes. He loved hard rock, classical, soft rock, rap, and everything in between.

Last night she listened to Beethoven, and she was in the

mood for something faster, something she could jam to while filing the mound of papers on her desk.

With a smile, she pulled out *Whitesnake's Greatest Hits* and put the CD in the player. In seconds, the riffs of "Still of the Night" filled the room.

She kicked off her heels and sang as she picked up the stack of papers and walked to the filing cabinet behind her desk.

Charon watched the sun make its way across the sky. The bright ball of light turning from yellow to a huge orange sphere as it sank into the horizon, casting the clouds to shades of tangerine and lavender.

Even as the darkness began to descend, he wasn't concerned about finding his way back. He knew the lay of the land like the back of his hand, and the god within him allowed him to see in the night as easily as he saw by day.

He wasn't ready to leave the peace of the woods. It was stunning during the day, but once night fell, a different kind of beauty took hold. There had been many nights he'd slept under the stars, listening to the night.

Yet he knew the time had come for him to return. Slowly, he stood and after one last look at the valley, turned on his heel to make the trek back to town.

Before he could see his building, his enhanced hearing picked up the strings of music from the tavern as well as his nightclub next door. There was a third set of music. This one he knew came from his office.

Laura loved music, and he had given her access to his collection. Every day she picked something different. He had long ago stopped being surprised by her love of vastly diverse music. It nearly matched his own.

Her choices also told him how she was feeling on any particular day. There were days when he knew she was troubled by the slow, soulful melodies she chose. Whether she was in a somber mood from missing someone or just lonely, he didn't know. And never asked.

He wanted to, and there were times he'd almost looked

into her past. But a past was a past. If she wanted him to
know, she'd tell him. The days her green eyes took a faraway
look were the hardest for him to keep his distance.

Charon liked her, but he knew better than to get too
close. He'd made that mistake too many times before and
watched friends grow old and die. Now, he did everything
he could to keep his distance. From everyone.

She was an enticement he'd sensed the first time he saw
her. Still, he'd been unable to turn away from her. The next
thing he knew, he was offering her a job. She was depend-
able, reliable, and so damned pretty there were days it hurt
just to look at her.

He paused as he reached the clearing behind his building. His gaze was drawn upward to the second story, where
he heard the unmistakable rhythms and lyrics of Whitesnake.

Without meaning to, his gaze sought out Laura. She wore
a dress of sapphire that hugged her form, outlining every
wonderful feminine curve. Her wavy dark hair was pulled
away from her face with a Celtic silver clip at the back of her
head while the rest of her long locks fell down her back.

With the chorus starting, she closed her eyes and did a
little spin. There was a bright smile pulling at her delectable
lips when she opened her eyes.

He had often found himself wanting to trace her mouth
with his finger. With eyesight as sharp as a falcon's, Charon
let himself look at his leisure.

Laura had the look of nobility about her, as if it were bred
into her DNA. She walked with confidence women rarely
had. Every move she made, every action she did was done
with unconscious elegance.

Her smile was infectious, her laugh irresistible. She had a
stubborn streak he recognized by the way her nose scrunched
a heartbeat before she said anything, as if she was debating it.

But her eyes, her striking pale green eyes, were the windows to her soul. One minute she let him see every emotion,
and then the other it as if a wall came down, shutting him
out.

She was stunning, but that wasn't why he hired her. Her

beauty had almost made him turn her way. But then he had seen something in her eyes. Hope.

And sorrow.

He'd wanted to know what gave her such sadness, and how she kept a hold of the hope. Instead, he'd learned how intelligent she was. Laura was far too clever to be in such a job. Yet, it was her love of the town that had ultimately gotten her the offer.

Charon hadn't regretted it either. Laura worked hard, sometimes too hard. He would have to send her home some days. But no one had ever kept his books, and the accounting, in such impeccable order. Not to mention vendors, other employees, and customers alike melted at the sight of her smile.

He found himself grinning as she danced across the room to gather more papers only to dance back to the filing cabinet, the swing of her hips drawing his gaze and making his balls tighten in response.

His hands curled into fists as he imagined walking up behind her and grabbing a hold of her hips as he rocked his aching cock against her.

"Are you only ever going to just watch her? Or are you going to take her as you want to do?"

Charon stiffened at the sound of the voice. He'd been so caught up in thinking of Laura, he hadn't heard Phelan walk up. He hated when Phelan sneaked up on him.

In his present mood, Phelan deserved the tongue lashing Charon wanted to give. Instead, he kept his gaze on Laura. Even if his mind released his brief fantasy.

"She's my secretary."

"They're now called executive assistants," Phelan said as he came to stand beside him. "And here I thought you were the one more in touch with the times than any Warrior. I'm going to have to rethink things."

Charon stuffed his hands in his pockets and fingered the X90 he couldn't seem to toss away. He cut Phelan a look for his sarcasm. "She's more than that. She does the work of three employees."

"And why have you no' taken her to your bed? It's obvious by the way you watch her that you want her."

"I doona mix business with pleasure," Charon said and looked away from Laura.

There was a pregnant pause before Phelan said, "You have no' changed your shirt."

"Thank you, Captain Obvious," Charon said sarcastically.

When he started to walk away, Phelan's hand clamped on his shoulder, stopping him.

"Are you no' all right?" Phelan asked as he peered into his face. "Does it still hurt?"

"You mean do I still feel the *drough* blood inside me?" *Aye.* "Nay."

Phelan visibly relaxed as he dropped his arm to his side. "You had me worried for a minute. Why have you no' changed?"

"I had some thinking to do."

"Aye. That's why I'm here. This battle with Jason, it was . . ."

"Different?" Charon supplied when Phelan paused.

Phelan nodded. "He was prepared for us. Better prepared than Deirdre or Declan ever was."

"I know." Charon ran a hand through his hair. "Deirdre knew us the best. She knew each of us individually because she watched us in that hellhole of a mountain. Some better than others."

Phelan snorted. "You mean me, because she kept me chained from the time I was a lad? Or because she drank my blood every day after I became a Warrior?"

"Both."

Charon knew Phelan hated to speak of his time in Cairn Toul Mountain, and rarely did. But there had to be a reason for Jason Wallace to know so much about them.

"Aye," Phelan said and walked a short distance away before turning back to Charon. "It was as if Jason knew exactly how we would attack. Could Ronnie have told them?"

Ronnie, also known as Dr. Veronica Reid, had fallen in

love with Arran, another Warrior. As a Druid, Ronnie's magic allowed her to find magical items in the ground. Which made her a very popular archeologist.

"Nay. I doona believe it was Ronnie. She might know Arran, but she had no idea of how we would attack. Besides, I drove her from Edinburgh to her dig site after that first attack. She wouldna betray Arran in any way. She loves him."

"Then how?" Phelan asked and threw up his arms in frustration.

"Another Seer, perhaps?"

It was a shot in the dark, especially since the Seer they had at MacLeod Castle, Saffron, was the first in ages.

Phelan shook his head. "Nay. He *knew* us. Knew things only someone who had spent time with us would know."

"There's no way. We were with the other Warriors and Druids after Declan was killed. We went through every book in that mansion and destroyed it. There is no possible way for him to know anything."

"Yet he does. He no' only knows us, but he knows black magic. In order for him to become *drough,* there has to be a ceremony. Someone had to know the ceremony. Which means we missed something."

The music coming from his office changed to a relaxed, sensuous beat as Whitesnake began belting out "Slow an' Easy."

"I know Gwynn already did a background check on Jason through the computer." Charon rubbed his chin. "But I think I'm going to do my own digging into Jason Wallace's past. Maybe we'll find something."

For the first time that evening there was a ghost of a grin on Phelan's face. "Just what I wanted to hear. Shall I return tomorrow?"

"Give me a couple of days. Where are you going?"

"No' far. I'll be around," he said and vanished into the trees.

Whereas Charon had set up a home in Ferness, Phelan was forever wandering. Everything he owned was in a small bag on the back of his Ducati motorcycle.

Charon rubbed his hand over his chest. The wound might be gone, but he couldn't stop remembering the feel of the blade inside him or the *drough* blood methodically shutting down his organs.

He hadn't spoken of it to Sonya after she healed him. Mainly because he hadn't been the only one injured, but more importantly, because no one else had said they continued to feel the poisonous blood once Sonya had worked her healing magic.

Charon hoped it was only because he'd had the *drough* blood inside him for so long, and not because there was something different about him.

He started up the stairs leading to the deck outside his office. Just as he reached the top step, he spotted the shirt.

Hesitantly, he put his hand on the plain black tee. Without a doubt, he knew it had been Laura who put it there. Had she seen him? Was that how she knew his shirt was ruined?

Charon picked up the shirt and turned to where a carafe sat on the table. Steam still drifted through the space in the lid. He bent to retrieve it, and found his gaze locked on Laura.

Her eyes were closed as she swayed enticingly to the music. He had wanted her from the first moment she walked into the pub and asked him for a pint of ale.

He figured with her English accent she was just a tourist passing through as everyone did, but when she asked for his help in locating a room, he knew she saw the beauty of the town as he did.

The next day, he learned she was looking for work. Two years later, and Charon still didn't know what had brought her to Ferness.

She didn't pry into his life, and he didn't pry into hers. Even though he was insanely curious at times. Especially when she would look at a locket she kept in her purse.

Suddenly, Laura stopped and opened her eyes. Their gazes clashed, and as always, Charon found himself arrested by the pale green orbs that stared at him.

It was a good thing she wasn't a Druid or Charon might

give in to his desires. With every Warrior at MacLeod Castle finding their mates with Druids, it was difficult not to think about doing the same.

But he was better off alone. Not to mention, no matter how hard he tried to feel any kind of magic around Laura, there was none.

She wasn't a Druid, and he had seen enough death in his long life. Not even the lust that burned through his veins could change his mind and have him slack his body with hers.

He knew it would be glorious to have her in his arms, to taste her kisses, and hear her cries of ecstasy, but he couldn't stand to lose one more person in his life.

So, whatever pleasure he might find in her arms would have to be forgotten.

The glass door slid open and she greeted him with a soft smile he'd come to expect. "I was getting worried."

Charon glanced at the deck. How much longer would she worry about him? There would come a time he would have to leave Ferness behind forever. The people he knew, the friends he had would stop thinking of him, and he would fade to nothing.

Maybe that's why Phelan didn't put down roots anywhere and why the other Warriors kept hidden at MacLeod Castle.

He thought he was doing something good for himself. In reality, he'd only made things more difficult. At one time, things had been so easy, so uncomplicated. Where had it all gone wrong?

CHAPTER
THREE

Laura didn't miss the misery on Charon's face, and even though she usually kept her distance, she found herself reaching out to him.

Her hand rested on his arm. Beneath her palm she felt the steel of his muscles, the warmth of the man himself. She sucked in a startled breath but didn't release him.

"Are you all right?" she asked when his dark brown eyes jerked to her face.

"Aye. Thank you," he said and lifted the arm that held the carafe and the shirt.

She reluctantly dropped her hand, instantly missing his warmth. "No problem."

Silence lengthened between them until she grew uncomfortable. She glanced down when she felt the cool night air on her toes and realized she had forgotten her shoes inside.

"The day ran smoothly," she said as she turned to walk back into the office. Work was always a safe topic.

"That's good."

She heard the door slide shut and the lock click into place as she put her feet in her heels. "By the way, I sent another e-mail to Dreagan last week."

His chuckle, deep and soft, filled the room. "You doona give up, do you?"

"No." She found him standing in front of her, and that's

when she noticed the stains on his shirt. The material was dark, but the stains were obviously blood. She reached out to him again. "Are you hurt?"

Before she could touch him, Charon took a step back and tossed the tee over his shoulder so that it covered the torn section of his shirt. "Nay."

Laura cleared her throat, wounded that he would lie so blatantly. "Um . . . anyway, I received an e-mail from Dreagan. They want to meet with you next week."

"You're worth your weight in gold. I really doona pay you enough."

"You pay me plenty," she said, but preened at his praise. "I told you I'd get you that meeting."

"I think you need to come with me, then."

She blinked. This was something knew. Charon always took these meetings himself. "You never take anyone."

"I'm taking you this time. You need to learn that side of the business. I'm no' always going to be around to take these meetings, and I need someone I can trust."

She shook her head emphatically. Her stomach clutched, not at the thought of the meeting, but the idea that Charon wouldn't always be around. "Oh, no. I'm much better drafting e-mails and letters than in person. Find someone else."

"You doona see your own worth. Have you no' noticed how men stare after you?"

"Me?" she asked with a frown. "Charon, no one looks at me."

"They do."

His words were softly spoken. The way he held her gaze told her he wasn't lying, but she still couldn't quite believe him. Because the one man she wanted to notice her, didn't.

She looked away and reached for her purse. "I prefer to sit behind a desk for a reason. I'm really not good in front of people. I'm too shy, and some people think I'm rude or cold because of that shyness. In truth, they frighten the crap out of me."

Charon's snort had her lifting her gaze to him. "You can no' even curse, can you?"

"I can."

"Prove it. Say something."

She adjusted her purse on her shoulder. "I have to be in the right mood," she hedged.

"Bollocks. You doona like to curse."

"Well, no. I think the point can come across using other terms."

"I hate to tell you this, but there are times when 'gosh darn' and 'crap' just doesna cut it, lass. A good curse word solves the problem every time."

As usual, Laura found herself entertained when she was around Charon. He had an affable way about him that had immediately put her at ease, something she thought she'd never feel after what her family had done.

Whereas it used to take her weeks to get up the nerve to talk to people, she had begun talking to him within an hour of arriving in Ferness.

The pint of ale might have helped as well. Mostly it was his charm and easy smile that had won her over as no one else ever had.

Regardless, Charon always made her cheery.

The smile faded when she caught another glimpse of his torn shirt. "I tried to call you."

"I'm sorry," he said, and set down the carafe. "I lost my mobile. Was it important?"

"Nothing I couldn't take care of. I just like to keep you informed. I'll be sure to get you another mobile tomorrow."

With a nod, Laura turned and walked to the stairs that would lead her to the pub and out the front door.

"What am I going to do without you?"

Charon's words halted her on the first step. She swiveled her head to him and saw the sadness in his dark eyes that he couldn't always keep hidden.

"I'm not going anywhere. I've told you. I love this place. It's my home."

"One day you'll leave. Everyone leaves."

She opened her mouth to deny it again, when he walked

into his office. He quietly closed the door and, in the process, shut her out.

For several seconds, she stood rooted to the spot, debating whether to go to him or not. Had there been a double meaning in his words? Charon rarely showed this side to himself, but whatever it was caused the hurt to go deep inside him.

Laura recognized it because she felt it within herself. Even after two years. It had faded, but it was still there. It would always be there.

Just as her family was always there.

"Good night, Charon," she whispered and started down the stairs.

"Good night, Laura," Charon whispered when he heard her words with his enhanced hearing.

The sound of her heels on the stairs faded as she opened, then closed, the door at the bottom of the stairs. He wondered what she would do when she hadn't immediately left, and he found himself wanting her to come to him.

He'd needed her. After her touch on the balcony, it had taken every ounce of restraint he had not to pull her against him and just hold her.

Holding her wouldn't be enough. The few times he'd found himself touching her, all he'd wanted was to bend his head and take her lips, to kiss her until she was panting and clinging to him.

He wanted that tonight. He wanted to rip the dress from her body, sit her on his desk, and plunge inside her. Maybe then the horrors of the night before would be pushed from his mind.

It was only because he felt sorry for himself. In the light of day, he would regret taking her to his bed.

Charon rubbed his eyes and walked to his desk. He pulled off his ruined shirt and tossed it into the garbage. Just as he was about to tug on the clean tee, he caught a glimpse of himself in the mirror across from his desk.

He didn't regret taking the blade for Arran. In his mind, taking a thousand blades covered in *drough* blood wouldn't be enough to make up for spying on Arran, Ian, and Quinn for Deirdre.

Was it just a year ago that Charon had found Ian and his wife, Dani, in Ferness? Charon hadn't known Ian was pulled through time along with Deirdre by Declan.

But seeing Ian had been like the four centuries hadn't happened. It still felt as if it were the fourteenth century and they were running from Deirdre.

So much had happened since then. Deirdre had killed Duncan, Ian's twin. Deirdre, and then Declan, had been killed by the Warriors and Druids.

And Charon had told Ian why he had spied for Deirdre. He hadn't done it for Ian's forgiveness, but as an explanation of why Charon didn't feel as though he belonged with the others at the castle.

Even now when those at MacLeod's called, Charon felt odd going to them. He would never tell them no, but he wasn't part of their close-knit group.

He, along with Phelan, were outsiders.

That was all right. Charon deserved no less. He would do his part in the fight against evil, but in the end he would return to Ferness. Alone.

Charon shoved his chair into his desk and strode toward the door. The phone rang just as he put his hand on the doorknob to open it.

With a sigh, he turned and answered the phone. "Charon here."

"You left early."

Charon squeezed his eyes closed as he recognized Arran's voice. "Aye. I've businesses that needs my attention."

"I wanted to say thank you again."

"You said it once. That was enough."

There was a loud sigh through the phone. "Nay, Charon, it isna. I blamed you for what happened to us in Cairn Toul, but you were just as much a part of Deirdre machinations as we were. You were trying to stay alive. I'd have done the same thing you did."

"I doubt it."

"Ian told me what happened with your father."

Charon dropped his head back and looked at the ceiling. "I didna share that story for sympathy."

"That's no' what you're getting from me. You're getting an apology for my attitude," Arran said. "You shouldna have left. The girls cooked a big meal. Malcolm even stayed."

Malcolm. Charon thought his life had been hell. It was nothing compared to Malcolm's. He'd been mortal helping his cousin, Larena. Larena was the only female Warrior and married to Fallon MacLeod, but Malcolm had done everything he could to keep Larena from Deirdre.

In the end, Deirdre sent Warriors to kill Malcolm. Sonya had managed to save him, but could do nothing about the scars or the loss of the use of his right arm.

Malcolm remained at the castle for a while, and then left. Only to be captured by Deirdre and his god unbound. In exchange for doing as she wanted, Deirdre promised Malcolm Larena would never be harmed.

But even that hadn't saved Deirdre, for it had been Malcolm who ultimately served her the killing blow.

"As I said, I had things to do," Charon stated to Arran. "I'll stay next time."

"Nay, you willna. And neither will Phelan. I understand though. If you need anything, you call me. I'm serious."

"I know."

Charon hung up and made his way up the stairs to the third floor. He shut the door behind him and listened to the silence.

It had cost a fortune to make sure the second and third floors were soundproofed from the pub. But the silence was deafening tonight.

He tossed aside the tee Laura had gotten for him and pulled open the glass doors that led to his deck. In one jump he leaped over the railing. He landed with one foot in front of the other, knees slightly bent.

Without looking back, he took off for the woods. He had to find peace before the sun rose.

No matter how far he ran through the dense forest, there was one thing that kept calling him back to the village.

Laura.

CHAPTER FOUR

Aiden MacLeod adjusted the strap of his messenger bag on his shoulder and eyed the building in front of him. He stepped around a couple standing on the sidewalk as his gaze surveyed the area.

It had taken some talking to convince his father that he didn't need to have someone with him. Quinn MacLeod had given up a bit too easily in their argument.

Somewhere among the huge buildings of the university, his father stood watching him, Aiden was sure of it. He also knew his father wouldn't be alone. He'd probably brought his uncles, Lucan and Fallon, as well.

But that's what happened when a person grew up in a castle hidden by magic filled with Druids and immortal Warriors.

For four centuries, Aiden had been protected because he was immortal only in the magical shield surrounding MacLeod Castle. He'd watched his parents and family go off to fight the *droughs* while he stayed at the castle, worried and frustrated.

No longer would he allow that to happen.

As a *mie,* or good Druid, he had magic. It was time he contributed to the cause everyone else was fighting.

The evil they fought had taken things up a notch, and it was only fair that the MacLeods do the same.

Aiden pulled the heavy door open and stepped into the building. He stopped and looked at the stairs that would lead him to answers he desperately needed.

Someone bumped into his shoulder, sending magic skidding along Aiden's hand, ready to use as defense. When no threat appeared, he sighed and lowered his hand. He took one more look around before he started toward the stairs.

Finding just the right person to help them had taken tons of research from him and the resident hacker at MacLeod Castle, Gwynn. Gwynn didn't consider herself a hacker, but her skills with the computer were unmatched by anyone else there.

She was from Texas, but as a Druid she found sanctuary—and love—at the castle. Gwynn and Logan, like the other couples at the castle, only made Aiden realize how lonely he was.

Others might call him fortunate because he had lived four hundred years. What they didn't know was that each time he left the protective shield over the castle, he put his life on the line.

Yet he didn't fear dying. He yearned for a family of his own. It was something he knew he'd never have, not that he blamed his parents.

They had done what they could to ensure he was kept with them and allowed to mature. What they didn't know was how he craved to go out in the world alone and experience all the wonders he saw on the computer and TV.

That wasn't possible, not with the new threat of Jason Wallace. Aiden knew Wallace could find him and use him against his parents if he was able.

So he remained at MacLeod Castle, venturing out into the world when he could. And when he needed to clear his head.

This time was different. This time Aiden decided he

could help solve one of the problems plaguing the Warriors. He took the last flight of stairs two at a time until he reached the landing. He looked down the brightly lit hallway and the numerous rooms on either side.

"Gwynn, I hope you're right," he mumbled as he turned to the left and searched for the room numbers.

He was beginning to wonder if Gwynn had texted him the wrong room as he reached the end of the hall. And then he noticed a door slightly ajar to his right.

A glance at the numbers confirmed it was the room he searched for. As he approached, he recognized the music of Godsmack coming from within.

Aiden leaned around the door and peered inside to find rows upon rows of tables filling the entire room. Each table had at least one microscope on it and numerous vials and other equipment whose use he couldn't begin to guess.

His gaze fell upon a woman in a white lab coat leaning forward as she looked into a microscope and jotted down notes on a pad of paper beside her.

Her golden blond hair was pulled back in a ponytail at the base of her neck and loose curls flowed to the middle of her back. It seemed at odds with the picture of Dr. Barbara Smith he'd seen on the computer.

He shrugged, figuring the good doctor had changed her hair in the hopes it helped to soften her middle-aged look.

Aiden knocked once on the door, but Dr. Smith didn't turn around.

He sighed and said, "Excuse me."

"Go away," came the muffled reply.

He narrowed his gaze on the woman. He'd expected it to be difficult to get her help, but he hadn't anticipated this. "Nay."

When she ignored him, Aiden walked into the lab and leaned his hip against the first table he came to. "I've got all day to sit here and bug you until you at least look at me."

She fiddled with the microscope for several minutes before she said, "I'm busy. Bugger off."

Her accent, muffled before, was clear to him now. He

didn't remember reading anything about Dr. Smith being from America, not that it mattered. She was the only one who could help him, and he wasn't leaving until she did.

Aiden decided words weren't doing the trick. He made a great show—and lots of noise—when he removed his messenger bag, set it down, and then pulled out the stool. He ensured the stool scrapped the floor long and loud before he took his seat.

There was a loud sigh before Dr. Smith slapped her hands on the table and lifted her head.

Aiden's breath caught in his throat. It wasn't Dr. Smith staring at him, but some siren come to seduce him into doing her bidding.

Her bright blue eyes blazed with fury, which was so at odds with the strands of loose curls framing her cheeks. Her heart-shaped face tilted to the side as she lifted one golden brow.

"Well?" she demanded. "I'm looking at you. What else do you want?"

"You."

The word was out of his mouth before he realized it. What was worse was that it was the truth. He wanted her. Wanted her as he had never wanted anything in his life.

Her lips compressed as she rolled her eyes. "Really? That's the best you could come up with?" She turned back to the microscope and murmured, "I need to start locking the damn door."

"Wait," Aiden said as he jumped off the stool and started toward her.

Her blond head swiveled back to him, her eyes suddenly wary. "Look. I don't know who sent you up here, and I don't care. Just leave, and no one gets hurt."

Aiden couldn't help it, he smiled.

"You think that's funny?" Her brow furrowed as fire blazed in her blue eyes. "Shall I show you what I can do?"

"I've no doubt you can handle yourself, lass. I'm just surprised is all. I thought I was meeting Dr. Smith."

"Ah. Well, she's on sabbatical for the next month."

Aiden squeezed his eyes closed for a moment. "Bloody hell." As much as he wanted the woman, he couldn't waste the time talking to her when the lives of his family were at stake. "Thank you," he said, and turned to grab his bag.

"What did you need Dr. Smith for?"

Her words halted him in his tracks. Aiden slowly turned to her. "It's . . . confidential."

"You expect me to believe that?" she asked, and leaned an elbow on the table. "We're microbiologists. What could be so secretive?"

"Forget I came." Aiden pulled his messenger bag back over his head. "Do you know another microbiologist with pathology experience?"

"Yes."

She answered without hesitation. A shiver went down Aiden's back as he looked into her bright blue eyes. They were the color of a summer's sky, brilliant and bottomless. He knew he should walk away, but he couldn't. Nor could he stop his next words from falling from his lips.

"Who?"

"What's your name?" she asked instead.

He glanced at the door. "Aiden MacLeod."

"Wow. A real Scottish name. Well, Aiden MacLeod, I'm Britt Miller. Dr. Britt Miller, actually. I've got my PhD in hematology and my undergrad in microbiology."

"Hematology," he whispered.

She grinned. "Yeah. You know, the study of blood disorders."

"I know." Could this have worked out any better? Aiden was almost afraid to even think that question. "I thought you were too busy."

Britt shrugged and crossed one jean-clad leg over the other, dangling one of her gold flats by her toe. "I'm offering to help. Not something I do all the time."

"So why are you?"

She gave a bark of laughter and shook her head. "I'm not sure. Perhaps it's the disappointment I saw in your face when I said Dr. Smith wasn't here."

"Look," Aiden said and walked closer to her. "I need help. I want to accept your help, but in doing so, you need to understand that there are things I can no' tell you."

Britt studied him for a long minute, as if weighing his words. She pushed one of the curls behind her ear and touched the small gold orbs that dangled from her earlobe. "Can you tell me anything?"

"I can tell you the information I need is to help family and friends."

"Why not go to a hospital or a real medical doctor?"

Aiden had to be careful in what he told her. "They're no' sick. Well . . . damn. I can no' answer that correctly."

"So you can't tell me much of anything, in other words."

"Aye."

Britt looked at her microscope. "What will I be looking at?"

"Blood."

Her gaze jerked back to his. "Blood. Why?"

"There are special properties in the blood I need determined. I need to know what could affect them adversely."

She held out her hand. "Let me see a sample?"

Aiden prayed he was doing the right thing. Instead of getting the blood, he reached for his phone and called Gwynn's mobile.

With his gaze locked with Britt's, Aiden gave Gwynn her information to see if there was any connection to Jason Wallace. When Gwynn gave the all clear, Aiden ended the call.

"Well, then. Why do I suddenly feel like I've been scanned by the CIA or MI5?"

Aiden inwardly winced. "I apologize. There are things going on that you're better off no' knowing for your own safety. And I needed to make sure you were no' working with Ja . . ." He trailed off and hoped she didn't ask more.

"The blood?" she asked, her hand once more held out.

Aiden pulled out the small vial. There were several tests he needed done. The first blood she would see was his. He grabbed a slide and pulled out the vial. With the dropper, he put two drops of blood and covered them with another slide before handing the slides to Britt.

"Nothing abnormal here. This blood comes from a healthy individual," she said as she looked through the microscope. She then leaned back. "Next?"

Aiden repeated the process with his father's blood and waited as Britt stared into the scope for several quiet minutes.

She finally sat back slowly and looked at him. "Where did you get this?"

"It doesna matter. What do you see?"

"I . . . I need to run some tests. Come back in an hour."

Aiden shook his head. "Nay. I'm no' leaving the blood with you."

"You don't trust me."

He grinned slyly. "Nay. As I said, my family and friends are at risk. I willna put them in more danger."

"This could take hours, days even. Are you willing to stay here that long?"

"As long as it takes."

"I work alone."

"No' this time," he retorted. The idea of spending so much time in Britt's company was more than agreeable to him.

She tapped a finger on the table, her nail softly clicking in the silence as she regarded him. "I'm curious now. I need to know all the properties of this blood and why it's so different."

"Then get to work, Doctor."

She eyed his bag. "You have more blood for me to look at, don't you?"

"Aye."

"Let me see."

Aiden pulled up the nearest stool and opened his bag.

CHAPTER
FIVE

Laura straightened from putting up the new bottles of gin from beneath the bar. Brian, the bartender, had needed to leave early to take his son to soccer practice, so she stepped in to cover the bar in his absence.

She turned when the door opened, flooding the pub with sunlight and blinding her from seeing who had walked in. The pub quieted as each patron turned to the newcomer.

Ben gave a bright smile when he spotted her and hurried to the counter. "I was hoping I'd catch you here."

"Hello, Ben." Laura was flattered with how much attention he paid her. And it wasn't that he wasn't good looking, he just wasn't Charon. "What can I get you?"

"You."

She smiled as the door to the pub opened again. Finally the door closed, allowing Laura to see again. And in the entrance stood a gorgeous man with hair black as midnight. It was parted down the middle and fell to just brush his shoulders.

He stood tall and a bit wary, while his eyes scanned the pub as if he were a predator looking for prey. Laura's skin prickled as his gaze stopped when it reached her.

He said not a word as he walked with long, sure strides to a far back corner. Somehow she wasn't surprised when he moved a chair so that it was situated in the corner and then sank into it.

The patrons in the pub went back to their drinks and conversation. Laura cleared her throat and returned her attention to Ben.

"I mean it," Ben said. "I'm going to keep asking you out until you agree."

She licked her lips as Ben's blue eyes held hers. "Let me see to this customer," she said and hurried to the newcomer.

"Hi," she said when she reached his table. "What can I get you?"

"Your best scotch," he replied in a rough voice, as if it hadn't been used in a while.

Laura went to the counter and grabbed the bottle of scotch and a glass. She went back to the table and poured the scotch before scooting it across the table in front of him with a smile. "You're in luck. We have one bottle of Dreagan left."

The man began to laugh as he looked at the glass and amber liquid inside it. "Of course it would be Dreagan," he muttered.

"I'm sorry?"

His gaze lifted to her, and she found herself held by the eerie light of his golden eyes. "What's your name, lass?"

"Laura," she answered.

"Well, Laura, life is nothing but one ironic thing after another," he said as he lifted the glass in a mock salute.

Laura went back to the bar, unnerved by the man's response.

"Well?" Ben urged. "Let me take you to dinner. One dinner. If you doona want to see me again after that, just say the word."

She'd been putting him off with one excuse after another for weeks. The excuses had run out. He was nice enough. He sent her flowers and called often to talk. He'd done a good job of wooing her, and it wasn't his fault that she was interested in someone else.

It had been so long since she'd been on a date that she wasn't sure she knew what to do. But she also didn't want to spend the rest of her life alone. Life was too short. She needed to have some fun.

"All right," she agreed. "Dinner it is."

"Perfect. I'll call you." Ben lifted her hand and kissed her knuckles. "You've made me verra happy, Laura."

She was still grinning when he exited the bar. It slipped, however, when she saw the black-haired man staring at his glass of Dreagan as it sat untouched.

"If you don't like it, I can get you something else," she said as she walked to him.

"Dreagan is the best. I asked for the best." His voice was flat, as if just saying those words had cost him untold torture.

"Yes, but why do I get the feeling you don't want that particular brand?"

A half grin tugged one side of his mouth slightly upward, giving him a devilishly handsome appearance. "A perceptive one you are. What are you doing in this place?"

"I like it."

"Aye, but neither of us belongs here. You should be in England."

"And you?" she prompted.

His golden eyes darkened a second before he looked away. "Nay, I'm no' meant for this place. Let me give you a piece of advice I wish I'd adhered to: Watch the decisions you make, sweet Laura, because they'll change your life in a second."

He drained the scotch in one drink. Laura tilted the bottle and refilled his glass.

At his questioning look, she shrugged. "I know when I see a man who needs a drink."

"And your price?"

"What makes you think there's a price?" she asked with a grin.

He leaned back in his seat, one arm on the table and the other dangling over the back of his chair. "Nothing is free in this world. Ever. What do you want?"

"Your name."

He looked away and inhaled deeply, a muscle jumping in his jaw. "You'd be better off no' knowing."

"What does it matter if I know your name?"

His head swiveled back to her to pin her with his gold eyes. "Ulrik."

"It suits you, I think." She nudged the glass at him again. "Now, take your drink."

She started to walk away when he said, "Leave the bottle."

Laura turned back to find two hundred-pound notes on the table. "That's too much."

"For your trouble then."

She looked into his golden eyes as he returned her stare. "This is a good place to hide from the world. This village, I mean. It's quiet. Private."

His head cocked to the side. "You think I'm hiding?"

"I think you have a look of a man who is trying to find something. Peace, maybe?"

"Peace will never be mine." His gaze shifted around her, and for just a moment he stiffened, but it was so fleeting she wasn't sure if she saw it. "And there isna a place in this wretched world I could hide from . . ." His voice trailed off and he lifted the glass to his lips again.

Whatever he had been about to say, he'd changed his mind. Laura left the whisky and took the money, his words unsettling her. As she turned back to the bar, she found Charon watching her. She walked to the register and put in the pound notes as Charon stood silently beside her.

"Who is he?" Charon whispered.

The feel of his warm breath washing over her neck as he leaned close made her sway toward him. Laura caught herself before she actually touched him and let Charon know just how much she wanted him. "He said his name is Ulrik."

"What's he doing here?"

"The same as anyone," she said, and faced Charon. "He came for a drink. He looks . . . haunted."

Charon closed the short distance between them. "What do you mean?"

"Look into his eyes," she said while struggling not to notice the heat radiating off Charon, or how his arms brushed against her. Their fingers connected, and Laura found it impossible to slow her breathing. "It looks as if he's seen everything, suffered every pain, and endured every agony. He appears to be a man who wants to hide, but . . ."

"But what?" he urged when she paused.

She shrugged and looked away. Charon was distracting. She couldn't get her thoughts in order, not when her blood had turned to lava and her heart pounded in her ears. "I don't know. I can't explain it."

"He has the look of a man who is searching for trouble."

Laura put her hand against Charon's chest to stop him when he would have gone to Ulrik. It was a mistake as soon as she did it.

Charon stiffened, his gaze jerking to hers. For just an instant, Laura could've sworn she saw desire in his dark depths.

"I don't think so. Let him have his drink. Let him have the entire bottle. He was looking for somewhere to rest, let him have his time."

Charon's dark eyes lowered to his chest, and Laura realized she was still touching him. She could feel the beat of his heart beneath her palm. But it wasn't his heartbeat that made her stomach flutter. It was the way his eyes watched her with such hunger that she forgot to breathe.

It had been two weeks since the night he returned with his torn shirt. Several times she caught him rubbing his chest as if it pained him.

Things had returned to normal. Except on the rare occasions she got too close to him. Or touched him.

Like now.

Even when she told herself to move on, there were times she didn't think she could. Times like this, when they stood close and he looked at her.

Times when they touched.

"All right," Charon finally said. "I'll leave him be."

With no other reason to keep touching him, Laura let her

hand slide from his chest. She cleared her throat and took a step back. "Are you ready for tomorrow and your meeting at Dreagan?"

One dark brow rose. "Aye. Because you'll be with me, remember?"

"What?" she asked, her mouth hanging open. "I thought we already talked about this."

"I made a decision. You kept talking."

"Charon, I . . . I'm not good in front of people like that. You can charm them. You don't need me. I've already told you this."

"But I do need you."

The words were whispered in that dark, seductive voice she'd heard him use on women before. It made her stomach clench with excitement.

And pleasure.

She was putty in his hands, her body on fire, waiting for him to touch her. Her nipples puckered and she had to grab hold of the bar to keep herself upright.

"You're coming," he whispered as he walked past her.

For several seconds, she couldn't move. Not because she had to go to Dreagan with him, but because his nearness always caused her heart to skip a beat.

When Laura turned around, it was to find Ulrik staring at her. He lifted his glass in a toast. She shook her head at him as her mobile phone vibrated in the pocket of her pants.

"Hello?" she answered it as she turned her back on the bar.

"Are you ready for our date?"

As soon as she heard Ben's voice, she shook her head. "Weren't you just here?"

"Aye. I'm waiting for you to agree to tomorrow night. Dinner with me. Sushi, perhaps?"

"Yes," she said with a laugh. "Tomorrow night sounds fine."

She felt bad for making him repeatedly ask her out, but he simply hadn't taken no for an answer. His persistence wore her down.

"Good," Ben said through the phone. "Be ready. I'll pick you up at eight."

She hung up and turned around to find Ulrik gone, the bottle of Dreagan whisky barely touched. Laura looked around the pub, but he was nowhere to be found.

It was a pity. He appeared as though he needed a friend. Yet there had been something dark inside him. Maybe that's what Charon had seen.

Thirty minutes later, Laura turned over the bar to the next bartender. She used to dread having to cover for them because it required her to interact with people, but she'd come to really enjoy it.

She made her way to the door that separated the stairs leading up to the second floor from the bar and slipped inside. The door closed behind her, shutting out the music of the pub as if a switch had been thrown.

For just a moment she paused, and couldn't help but think of Ulrik. He shouldn't take up so much of her thoughts. People came in and out of the pub all the time. So what was it about this man that made her dwell on him?

He was good looking if one liked the dark, moody, broody type that could either be a good guy or a bad guy. She suspected Ulrik was leaning toward the bad part.

Laura sighed and started up the stairs. Her heels clicked softly upon the wood, her hand sliding along the banister as it had done countless times.

When she reached the top and found Charon standing at the sliding glass door looking out at the forest, she knew something bothered him.

She glimpsed a half-empty bottle of Dreagan on the coffee table in front of the couch.

"Care for a glass?" Charon asked without turning around.

"Not particularly. What's bothering you?"

He shrugged, not looking at her. "I find it odd that after a year Dreagan finally decided to see us."

"We proved how well the pub is doing. Even in such a small village as Ferness."

Charon gave a soft snort. "What if it's more than that?"

"What do you mean?"

He turned toward her. As he did, the fingers he had stuck in the front pocket of his jeans moved to his chest and rubbed. Laura didn't think he even realized what he was doing, but it was a telling sign. One he did often of late.

"There are bad men out in this world, Laura."

"I know."

"You think you know," he said and took a drink of the whisky.

She perched on the arm of the couch. "Then tell me what it is I don't know."

He laughed, the sound holding no humor. "What would you say if I told you there were men trying to take over the world?"

"I'd tell you it's been happening since the beginning of time. How many kings killed and went to war just to take over more land? I could name ten right off the top of my head."

His lips thinned. "Aye, you're right."

He was going to let it go, but she wasn't. She knew there was something he was trying to tell her without actually telling her. Could this be what had been bothering him these last few weeks?

"Tell me," she urged. "You meant something else. Tell me what you mean."

"I can no'." The words were spoken softly, harshly.

Laura licked her lips and stood. "If you don't mean kings and leaders of nations, do you mean men closer to home? Say, as in Scotland?"

The tightening of his fingers on the crystal glass was all the answer she needed.

"You may not like to flaunt your power and presence around Ferness, but you have it, Charon. Use it to destroy whoever this is."

"Power," he repeated with a derisive snort. "Let's hope I can get to him before he comes here."

"Here?" At his wince, Laura knew he'd accidentally let the last part slip. "I don't want whoever this is here. Let me help."

She wasn't sure why she offered. She wasn't a fighter and only knew basic moves of self-defense, but Ferness was her home now, and she didn't want it destroyed.

Plus she wanted to help Charon any way she could.

His dark eyes hardened. "Nay. Doona dig more into this. You'll only get hurt."

Unease rippled through her at his words. It was obvious he knew much more than he was ever going to tell her. But there was no way she would allow him to get harmed. He was important to Ferness, important to so many people in the area.

And he was important to her.

She would do whatever it took to make sure he won against this unknown foe.

CHAPTER
SIX

Charon hid his smile as he drove along the road to Dreagan. He'd been in a morose mood when he first mentioned she should come with him, but the more he thought about it, the more sound a decision it was.

If he had to leave Ferness, his businesses would be in capable hands with Laura. All he'd worked for would be looked after. He didn't want to leave his home, but already some of them knew too much about him being a Warrior. He was just looking after his interests.

And if he wanted more time alone with her, well, that was an indulgence he allowed himself after the hell he'd gone through with Wallace.

Laura continued her argument to stay behind as soon as he arrived at her flat that morning. He simply ushered her to the car, stopped at the café to get them coffee and some breakfast, and started driving. Her reasons were long and varied. Before he could respond to one, she went on to the next.

So he sat and quietly listened.

It was just thirty minutes later she looked over at him and said, "You're going to make me go, aren't you?"

"Since we've been on the road for some time now, the answer is aye."

"I won't leave the car."

He glanced over to see her looking straight ahead, her fingers clenched around the paper coffee cup. "What are you afraid of? That you'll say something wrong?"

"Yes," she said, and briefly closed her eyes. "I don't want to mess this up for you."

"Laura, I say the wrong thing all the time. If we doona get the account, then that's Dreagan's loss. I'll continue to buy it myself and sell it to special clients."

He caught her swinging her head to him out of the corner of his eye. She had her hair loose about her shoulders this morning, the long, dark wavy strands lying tantalizingly over her shoulder to stop just short of touching her breast.

It was tempting him, tormenting him.

Exciting him.

"Getting Dreagan whisky has been important to you."

Charon shrugged and changed lanes as he dragged his thoughts away from her amazing breasts. "We've given them all we can. I want the best for my customers, but I willna beg for anything."

"I still think it's a mistake to bring me."

"You doona know your worth, do you?" he asked, and cast a quick glance at her. "Men melt in your wake."

She rolled her eyes. "As if. In the two years I've been here, I've had one man ask me out."

A sharp pain cut through Charon. He hadn't known anyone had asked her out, and the feeling wasn't a pleasant one. He wished her the best, but to know she was going out with someone felt as painful as the blade that had been pulled from his chest just weeks before.

"Someone asked you on a date?"

"Yes," she said softly, and looked at her hands. "Our first date is tonight."

Charon tightened his hands on the steering wheel. He should be happy Laura had found someone. It wasn't as if he could have her. Oh, he could, but he wouldn't do that to her or himself.

So why did jealousy sizzle through his veins at the thought of her smiles directed at another man? That she would eagerly walk into the arms of this man and welcome his kisses?

"We'll be back in plenty of time," Charon finally said.

They sat in silence for several minutes before he heard her soft exhale. He recognized it as a prelude to her troubled thoughts.

He might have deciphered her moods based on the music she chose, but there was so much about Laura he didn't know. He could have done a background check. It wasn't necessary though. Not when she wasn't a Druid.

Since she had no magic, she would mean nothing to Jason Wallace. It was the only thing that kept her safe. Her proximity to him, however, was a different matter entirely if Wallace ever turned his attention to Charon.

Another reason he might have to leave Ferness.

"Do you think it's wrong that I actually checked my date out online? I mean, I found Ben's credit score."

Charon couldn't stop the smile or the laughter that bubbled up. "Nay. You can no' be too careful. How long have you known this Ben?"

"Just a few months. He was persistent though."

Charon nodded. "Do I know him?"

"I doubt it. He lives in Inverness."

Charon wanted to ask the bastard's last name, but he managed to hold back the question. If Laura wasn't going to offer it, he wasn't going to ask for it. "What made you finally give in?"

"His perseverance," she said with a laugh. "I figure if a man wants to take me out to dinner that badly, he should get the chance."

"After you checked him out, of course," Charon said as he stole a look at her.

She nodded, her laughter growing. "Of course. What kind of woman would I be to just agree?"

How he loved her laughter. She gave it freely, honestly. There was nothing held back. The sound always managed to wring a grin from him, no matter what kind of mood he was in.

"You deserve happiness."

Her smile died as she placed her hand on his arm. "So do you."

"Some people are meant to search for happiness forever. Some are destined to never find it."

"You think you're one of those destined to never find it."

It wasn't a question, so he didn't feel the need to answer.

"That's sad," she whispered, and dropped her hand.

He hated how he missed her touch. She rarely got too near him. Perhaps, inwardly, she knew the monster he was and tried her best to stay clear.

But those few times they touched had been . . . heaven. Maybe that was just because Laura was a good person. Possibly it was because he sought something he could never have.

Not even the women he took to his bed helped him. And he'd stopped sleeping with them months ago. He still bought them dinner, still flirted, but he knew it was a waste of time to look in their direction.

If the Warriors at MacLeod Castle taught him anything, it was that if there was a spark of hope for his future, it was with a Druid.

Not only was there not one anywhere near him, but he wasn't sure he could trust one enough to get close. For all he knew, the Druid could come from Jason Wallace.

What a fucking mess my world has become.

"Are you sure we're going the right way?" Laura asked, breaking into his thoughts.

He nodded. "I'm following the directions. Though I've never visited Dreagan before, I'd heard it was notoriously difficult to find."

"Why? You'd think a distillery would want to be found to sell more product."

"Dreagan is no' like other companies. They like to keep to themselves. That could be part of the allure of why their scotch is so prized."

Charon slowed the car and turned off the dual carriage road onto a narrow road. There was room for only one car at a time, which wasn't uncommon in Scotland, but there weren't any pull-offs to allow a car to pass either.

"Well, I've seen a lot of the Highlands while I've been here, but this is a first," Laura said as she leaned forward to gaze out her passenger window.

"Aye," Charon agreed.

The road took them between two mountains that rose on either side of them like stone giants. Most roads were over mountains or on them, but not between them. The glen was narrow, the forest plentiful, which made it appear as if they were driving through a tunnel.

Charon drove slowly through the winding road. There wasn't much to see but trees and the rocky slopes of the mountains. It wasn't until he turned one tight corner that he caught something out of the corner of his eye.

When he looked, he found a man standing on the slope of the mountain, watching them. He was camouflaged well enough that a mortal would never see him. But then again, Charon was not mortal.

"Well, they know we're here."

"What?" Laura asked and turned her head to him. Her wealth of dark hair moved sensuously against her. Her brow puckered over her soft green eyes. "Why do you say that?"

"I saw a man."

"A man. So?" she said with a shrug.

It wasn't as if Charon could tell her it was an ancient tactic, one he'd employed on numerous occasions. "The man was hidden. He'll report what he's seen to whoever is in charge."

She rubbed her hands up and down her arms. "You did say they liked their privacy."

"Aye."

They remained silent the rest of the drive until one last curve and the trees opened up. Charon heard Laura's gasp, and even he had to admit he was taken aback by the sheer beauty.

Dreagan sprawled between mountains, the valley wide and expansive. On one side, white dots of sheep flecked the brilliant green pastures, and on the other, cattle grazed leisurely.

Farther back, Charon's Warrior sight allowed him to see a hint of another building, one he assumed was a residence by how they tried to hide it with the distillery buildings and gardens.

He parked the car and did a quick look around. There were people moving about doing their daily work, but it was the few men he saw posted about the land that told him Dreagan kept things secure.

But how secure against a Warrior?

He gave Laura a nod and they exited the car together. Charon looked over his shoulder in time to see a glimpse of a man leaving the forest, the same man he'd seen watching them.

A quick look at his watch showed they were ten minutes early. Charon would like to roam around on his own, but he doubted he'd be given that opportunity.

The tinkle of water could be heard, and he knew if he looked behind one of the buildings, he'd find a stream.

"Hello," said a woman as she came toward them.

Laura returned her smile. "Hello."

The woman stopped in front of Charon's Mercedes and clasped her hands before her. "You must be Charon Bruce."

Charon met the dark brown eyes of the woman, noting her long, straight dark brown-colored hair was pulled back in a ponytail. She wore dress slacks, a button-down shirt, and heels.

She looked the part of a businesswoman, but there was something about her which set off warning bells in Charon's head that was more than just her American accent.

"I'm Cassie Wilson. I'll bring you to the offices and give you a small tour before your appointment with Con."

She said all the right things, but Charon wasn't fooled. Her eyes were too direct, as if she were searching for something.

There was no hint of magic that Charon recognized surrounding Dreagan. That didn't mean there wasn't something going on. The privacy, the hidden men keeping guard? There was more to Dreagan than what was on the surface.

But what was it?

"Charon?" Laura asked.

He folded his arms over his chest and looked at Cassie. "Why was I brought here?"

Cassie's smile grew before she laughed. "Let's just say that Con and the others don't do things in a hurry. They like to take their time and investigate."

As much as Charon wanted to be a certified seller of Dreagan scotch, he wasn't sure he could take the chance. No matter how he had looked, nothing came up about Dreagan or who ran it besides Constantine.

And finding a photo of the bastard was impossible.

Charon found himself rubbing his chest. He dropped his hand, but glimpsed Laura's worried frown. After the last battle with Wallace, Charon was cautious of everyone.

"Investigate? What an odd choice of wording."

"Not really," Cassie answered. "It's what they did. Dreagan isn't the world's leading scotch distributor for nothing, Mr. Bruce."

"I'm no' interested in being investigated." What the hell would happen if they discovered his past identities and just how long he'd been in Ferness? That's not something Charon wanted to try to explain.

"You're wary of us." Cassie's smile was gone, but her dark eyes held an openness he hadn't seen before.

"One can never be too guarded."

Her gaze looked to the ground for just a moment before she swallowed. "Talk to Con, Mr. Bruce. He's . . . guarded . . . as well. I think the two of you might get along better than you think. Despite him employing an American," she finished with a laugh.

"I know several lasses from America. They're good women. I doona hold that against you."

Her eyes crinkled in the corners as she smiled brightly. "Good. Now, come. Let me show you Dreagan."

At Laura's questioning look, Charon merely shook his head. He couldn't tell her his worries. Not now.

Not ever.

As Laura moved to stand beside him, Charon had the overwhelming urge to take her hand and thread his fingers with hers. To keep from doing that, he put his hand on her lower back and felt the current that moved between them.

She stiffened for just an instant before her body relaxed. Had he helped ease her tension just by touching her? This reckless need, the uncontrollable hunger for Laura was driving him mad.

He should be thinking about the meeting or Wallace or why the *drough* blood affected him so, but all that filled his mind was Laura. Her sweet, clean smell, her smile, her kissable lips.

When they came to a doorway, Laura turned toward him and looked up at him as she walked through. There was no denying the desire he saw reflected in her pale green depths. It made his balls tighten.

He glanced down at her mouth to find her lips parted. He dragged his gaze back to her eyes and bit back a moan when his arm brushed her breast as they passed through the door together.

She turned away just before he gave in to the temptation and kissed her. Cassie was talking, but Charon heard none of it. He ground his teeth and made himself focus. Selling Dreagan whisky was his goal. He'd not mess it up because he couldn't keep his cock from standing at attention.

They followed Cassie around the area, looking at the distillery and meeting workers. Charon was impressed with how smoothly everything ran. But it was the beauty of the place that tugged at his heart.

It reminded him of the Scotland he remembered as a lad. Untamed. Wild.

Savage.

He longed to run through the mountains, to forget what he was and the world he now lived in. It made him yearn to take out his kilt and live on the land as he had done so many centuries ago.

To look up at the night sky, the stars winking good night as he fell asleep. To dive into the dark waters of a loch and bathe.

To walk for days and never encounter another soul.

"Few people understand why Dreagan is situated the way it is, or why we don't open ourselves to a constant flow of visitors. But I think you do," Cassie said softly from beside him.

Charon nodded. "Oh, aye. I do."

He knew much too well.

CHAPTER
SEVEN

The more Charon stayed at Dreagan, the more he knew there was something about the place that wasn't normal.

It looked normal. Its people appeared normal.

But there was much more to it.

Charon couldn't place his finger on what it was. There was no trace of magic that he could detect, yet at odd times he would feel something that seemed almost like magic.

It disappeared as quickly as it came.

Everywhere they went he spotted men watching, studying him. He'd know the kind of men they were anywhere from their stance and the way they held themselves.

They were warriors, fighters.

For who, was the question.

"I'll take you into the main building where Con's office is," Cassie said as she looked over her shoulder at him. "Con has done a lot of research on your pub, Mr. Bruce. He's impressed with what you've acquired in Ferness."

"It's more than just property," Charon said as he thought of his men. And Laura.

She really couldn't be included, but he wouldn't be standing at Dreagan today without her. Oh, he'd have eventually made his way in, but Laura had done it with finesse.

Cassie nodded as her gaze shifted to Laura. "Yes, he

knows of the dedication of Ms. Black. You're lucky to have such people surrounding you."

The slight stain of pink that tinged Laura's cheeks amused him. She was always so surprised when she was given praise. He didn't understand it, but he liked to see the pleased look in her eyes.

Charon ushered Laura in front of him as Cassie took them on a narrow path. Cassie and Laura walked beneath the wooden arch of flowers, and just as he was about to follow, his gaze was caught by three men.

They had their backs to him, walking away and at an angle, but they stopped him cold in his tracks. Or one man did.

There was something familiar about him, as if Charon should know him, but he couldn't place who it might be. He needed a closer look.

He took a step toward them when Laura touched his arm. His head snapped to her.

"Charon? What is it?"

"Who are those men?"

Cassie was instantly by his side. "Employees. Is there a problem?"

"Nay. One just looked familiar is all."

Cassie's brow was furrowed as she looked at the backs of the retreating men and then to Charon. "Shall I call them over?"

"Doona fash yourself," Charon said. "After taking so long to get this meeting, the last thing I should do is keep Con waiting."

With one last look at the place he had seen the men, Charon followed Cassie.

"I'm sorry," Laura whispered when they were making their way up the stairs to Con's office.

Charon shrugged off her words. "I doona know what it is about this place."

"I like it," she said as she leaned close and smiled. "It's peaceful."

"Aye. It is that."

Cassie turned the corner into a large room where four men stood. Charon noted how Laura stayed close to him. By the appreciative eye the blond man standing a little off by himself was giving her Charon wanted to punch him.

"I hope you enjoyed the tour. I'm Hal Wilson," said the tall man with black hair and moonlight blue eyes.

"Wilson," Laura said as she looked from Hal to Cassie.

Cassie smiled. "Yes, he's my husband."

Charon gave a nod to Hal. "Your wife is verra proud of Dreagan. I can hear it in every word as she spoke."

"That's good to hear," said the man next to Hal. He had light brown hair and pale brown eyes that watched Charon carefully. "I'm Guy. I'm sure you'll run into my wife, Elena, around here somewhere."

Charon held Guy's gaze until the man closest to Laura, a big brute of a man with short brown hair and gray eyes, spoke to her.

In an instant, Charon's gaze jerked to him.

As if knowing what he had done, the man simply grinned obnoxiously. "Nice to have you here, Charon. I'm Banan."

"And your wife?"

Banan laughed easily. "Aye. Jane is probably with Elena looking for one of the kittens that got out of the box this morning."

Still Charon didn't relax. He turned to the blond who watched him with a slight mocking smile and black eyes. Charon wasn't cowed.

He had been tortured with fists and magic alike. Had endured the agony of killing his own father in a fit of rage as he battled the god inside him.

There wasn't anything that could bend him.

The tension in the room escalated. Charon could sense Laura's growing unease as she shifted from foot to foot, causing her arm to brush his.

Heat seared through him, and he wanted to reach for her and haul her against him. It wasn't until the blond's gaze once more turned to Laura that Charon heard himself growl.

"I'm Laura Black," she hastily said, and sent him a quick

glance as she held out her hand to the blond. "I'm Charon's assistant."

Charon hands curled into fists when he watched the man take Laura's outstretched hand and shake it, his thumb gently rubbing across her skin.

"Nice to finally meet you, Miss Black. Your e-mails were most persistent that we give Mr. Bruce a chance to state why he should carry our brand."

Laura smiled nervously, her green gaze darting to him. "Charon and I are delighted to be here."

"Why are we here?" Charon asked before she could say anything else.

The blond lifted a brow. "I see my manners are lacking. I'm Constantine, but everyone calls me Con. As for why you're here, Mr. Bruce, I thought you knew the reason."

Charon narrowed his gaze on Con and took a step to the right, putting himself in front of Laura. "What I want to know is why all of a sudden am I here? Why now?"

"Remember I told you that you weren't the only one guarded, Mr. Bruce," Cassie reminded him.

Charon wished he had listened to Laura and left her in Ferness. Had he just stepped into a trap? Were those at Dreagan working for Wallace?

Damn, he was such a fool. He'd wanted Laura with him not just because she was good at talking with people and was a good candidate to take over his businesses, but also because he wanted to be with her.

His actions could very well have put her life in danger. The one thing he didn't want to do.

"Rest assured, Mr. Bruce, we're your friends," Con said, as if reading his mind.

Charon stared into the black eyes of Con, but could find no deceit, no matter how deep he looked. There was cockiness, confidence, and arrogance in spades, but no treachery. It helped that he felt not a trace of any Druid magic.

He pulled in a breath and nodded. "Call me Charon."

"Come," Con said, and turned on his heel to walk through a doorway behind him.

Hal, Cassie, Guy, and Banan all stayed behind. Charon hadn't asked what they did, but then again, he didn't need to. They, along with Con, had the same look about them as the other men Charon had seen around the property.

Con was prepared. But prepared for what?

After they were shown to their seats before the large wooden desk, Con poured three glasses of whisky and handed one to Laura and one to Charon.

"Why do you want to sell Dreagan whisky?" Con asked as he took his seat behind the desk.

Charon swirled the dark amber liquid in the glass and noted the dragons carved into the corners of the desk. "It's the best. My village may be small, but I like to give my people the best."

"And," Laura said with a glance at him, "the tourism plays a vital part in Ferness. It's close enough to Inverness and Pitlochry that people pass through to see the beauty of Ferness."

Con nodded and sipped the scotch, his gaze on Charon. "You own quite a bit of Ferness. Seems to have been in your family for . . . several generations."

"Aye." Charon stilled, Con's words alluding to a deeper meaning. Did Con know what he was? Had the *investigation* already gone that deep?

"I, too, own quite a bit of land that I inherited from . . . family."

Charon turned his head to look out the window to his left. The Highlands rose up around Dreagan at every turn. The sky, cloudless, was like a sea of blue that stretched endlessly across the horizon.

The way Con spoke of it, the slight hesitation told Charon Con not only knew he'd been alive for a long time, but that there might be something similar going on with him.

Warriors couldn't always recognize other Warriors, but in the centuries Charon had been around, no Warrior had mentioned anything about Con or anyone else at Dreagan.

"Inheriting land can be beneficial," Charon finally said.

"And sometimes difficult."

"Sometimes." He looked back at Con, wondering what he was alluding to and why. "You have men guarding your land."

"Just as you do."

Charon's nostrils flared in anger. "I see you've delved deep in your investigation of me."

"Perhaps," Con said with a blasé shrug. "Is that no' what men in our position do? We have others counting on us. We need to make the right choices."

Laura put her glass on Con's desk and stood. "I think that's my cue."

Charon sat forward, intending to rise with her until she held up her hand.

"No. It's time I stepped out so you two can talk properly instead of hiding meanings in your words because you don't want me to know."

Charon caught her arm as she turned away. He rose to his feet and looked into her green eyes. "Laura—"

"It's all right," she interrupted, and smiled softly.

Her skin felt warm in his hand, smooth. She smelled of cherry blossoms from her soap, and he wanted to lean nearer and breathe it in. "Stay close."

She pulled away, and he didn't stop her. It wasn't until she was out of the office, the door closed behind her, that he turned to Con. He was done beating around the bush.

"What do you know?" Charon demanded.

Con set down his now empty glass. "A lot, actually. But that is no' why you came. You came because you want to sell my scotch."

"I'm no' so sure anymore. I doona like being investigated."

Con made a sound at the back of his throat. "Charon, we're no' your enemy. And doona worry for Miss Black's safety. There are fewer places on this earth where she could be safer."

Charon instantly thought of MacLeod Castle. She'd be safe there. "Who are you? Really."

Con rubbed a hand over his chin. "A potential ally. A friend if you want it."

"Again, why?"

"I think the name Jason Wallace means something to you."

Charon squeezed the crystal so hard, the glass shattered in his hand. He put his palms on Con's desk and leaned toward him. "Is that why I'm here? Did Wallace pay you to trap me? Whatever he's paying you, I'll triple it as long as you allow Laura to leave."

"Nay, I'm no' working with Wallace," Con said calmly, and he got to his feet, seemingly unfazed by Charon's response. "My business is much more vast than most realize. I have my ear to the ground, so to speak, in various places. I know Wallace Mansion has been damaged. Again."

"No matter what you think you know, you doona know half of it. Stay away from Wallace. He'll infest everything you have until there's nothing left."

Con regarded him quietly for several long minutes. "Wallace isna the man his cousin was. Declan was out in the public eye showing off his wealth and power for all to see. But it's what he was doing behind the scenes that concerned me."

"What was that?" Charon would find out all he could from Con and then determine what to do about his knowledge of Jason Wallace.

"Lining other men's pockets. Declan might be dead, but doona make the mistake of underestimating Jason. Jason might no' have the good looks of his cousin, but he's smarter. You Warriors have done a fine job battling the *droughs,* but Jason Wallace is different."

Charon straightened, his hands clenched as he took in all of what Con said. The bastard knew he was a Warrior, and he'd known of the *droughs.* What else did they know?

He wanted to know how Con had discovered what he was, but more important was the information Con had on Wallace. Charon reined in his fury and focused on his nemesis as he walked to the window, where he shoved his hands in his pockets. "We already underestimated Jason. I'm going to make him pay though."

"Alone?"

"If need be."

"It'll be tricky."

"What do you know of it?" Charon asked. He kept his gaze out the window, but he was watching Con in the glass pane.

The head of Dreagan sighed heavily, his brow furrowed for a moment. "You've every reason to be mistrustful. In all the time we've been at Dreagan I've never invited a Warrior—or anyone, for that matter—into my home and told them what we are."

Charon waited, his mind racing with possibilities. Yet, he kept coming up empty of just what Con could be.

"I find even now I can no' actually say it. It's been a secret too closely guarded. All I'll tell you—today—is that you're no' the only immortal being around."

Charon placed his hands on the windowsill, his heart pounding in his chest. This he never expected. Some kind of Druid maybe, but another immortal?

"Why tell me now?" Charon asked.

"Because I doona think it can be put off any longer. Things are escalating. There may come a time when we can help each other."

Charon didn't hide his grin as he narrowed his gaze at Con's reflection and the distaste distorting his features. "That was difficult to say. I take it that you doona really think you'll ever need a Warrior's help?"

"We've been around since the beginning of time. We doona need anyone."

Charon faced Con and leaned against the window. Now, wasn't that interesting. "Really?"

Con sighed and drummed his fingers on the desk. "You know how difficult it is to keep a secret. You've kept yours a long time, but even now, some of your men know what you are. We've kept our secret for thousands of millennia."

There was so much Charon wanted to ask, but he knew

by the set of Con's jaw that nothing more would be said
about it today. If Con was offering to be his ally, then he'd be
a fool to turn it down.

"Do I get to sell your whisky or no'?"

Con's smile was slow as it filled his face. "Aye, Charon, I
think you're just the type of man we want selling our brand."

CHAPTER EIGHT

University of Edinburgh

Aiden couldn't believe how much Britt discovered in the time she had been studying the blood. Though he wished things had moved along quicker, he wasn't going to complain about it as long as the information kept coming.

He finished sending off the latest e-mail to everyone at the castle, explaining that Britt was trying to isolate the property in the Warrior blood to determine why it reacted so violently to the *drough* blood.

Although Britt had no idea the blood was Warrior and *drough,* or why it was so important to him. She asked often enough, but so far, Aiden had been able to keep her in the dark.

"I've never seen blood do this to other blood before," Britt said, her face pressed against the microscope lenses.

Again and again, she had tested the *drough* blood on the Warrior blood. Each time the results were the same. The red and white blood cells instantly began to die off.

Aiden rose from his seat in the lab and walked to look out the window. It had been raining for two days, and didn't look to be letting up anytime soon.

"Tell me, Aiden, please," Britt urged.

For two weeks Aiden had spent most of every day with

her in the lab. He sat silently staring at her, dreaming about her while she worked. They had shared numerous meals, but all eaten quickly while she looked at her notes or talked about the blood.

All the while he listened, he waited for the times she would look up at him and snare him with her eyes. Those brief moments were enough to last him until the next time.

The more he was around her, the more he wanted her. He'd made sure to "accidentally" touch her as often as he could. Britt always had a ready smile for him, but she had been so involved with her work that he hadn't been able to decipher if she was as attracted to him as he was her.

Perhaps it was time to find out.

"Let me take you to dinner tonight," Aiden said as he turned to her.

She blinked, her blue eyes holding a hint of surprise. She tucked a pencil into her hair, it joining the three others she had stuffed in her loose bun. "Dinner? You want to take me to dinner instead of telling me about the blood?"

"Aye." Aiden sighed and spun a pencil on the table. "Britt, I keep the information from you to protect you."

"And to protect your family in case what I find ever gets out in the world."

"Aye."

She tucked a loose strand of hair behind her ears. "Do you have that hard a time trusting people?"

"If you knew all I had been through, you'd understand."

"Then tell me."

Aiden bit back a laugh. "I admit, it would be easier if I could."

"But you won't," she finished.

He shrugged. "There are people out there who would kill you just for helping me. It's why we do this in secret, why I ask you no' to tell anyone what you're working on."

"Tell me one thing, then. Is one of those blood samples yours?"

"And if it was?"

She smiled as she slid off the stool and set aside the samples she'd been looking at. "I have a class I can't miss again."

Aiden watched as she grabbed her stuff and started for the door. She suddenly stopped and turned to look at him over her shoulder.

"Pick me up at seven."

He grinned and rocked back on his heels, feeling a bit of happiness for the first time in weeks.

Laura sat in the kitchen area having tea with Cassie when she heard Charon's voice. Her heart kicked up a notch when she turned and spotted him on the top landing smiling with Con.

"I think things went well," Cassie said.

Laura nodded. "I knew they would. Charon can charm anyone when he sets his mind to it."

"I hope this means we'll get to see more of you and Charon around Dreagan."

Laura's head swiveled back to Cassie. "But I thought Dreagan was more private than that."

"There are a few clients we invite on a regular basis."

Why did Laura feel there was so much going on around her without her truly understanding it? She'd felt it from the moment they drove onto Dreagan land, and the sensation grew the longer she was here.

"I know Charon likes it here."

Cassie beamed as she stood and motioned for Laura to do the same. "Come. I'll take you to him."

As they walked to the stairs, Cassie leaned close and said, "Charon is a handsome man. Men like him don't stay single for long."

Laura missed a step and nearly fell on her face. She glanced at Cassie and shook her head. "Charon is my employer."

"Then why do you look at him the way you do?"

She was saved from having to answer when they reached

the stairs and started up them with Charon watching. As always, Laura was caught off guard by his dark eyes and the way he held her gaze.

It was easy to forget everything, including her past in England, when she was drowning in his eyes. It was easy to forget she was just his employee and not the woman he desired.

It was easy to forget that he would never be hers.

"Thank you for your tenacity, Miss Black," Con said, breaking into her thoughts and shattering the haze that had taken her. "Charon will now be selling Dreagan whisky."

Laura smiled, but it was directed at Charon. She alone knew how much this had meant to him. "Congratulations. I told you it would all work out."

The boyish grin Charon wore made her stomach flutter. He was pleased, and if she wasn't mistaken, the look that passed between him and Con was full of a deeper meaning that alluded to the conversation they'd had before she left them.

With a handshake and farewells, Charon was soon walking toward her. When he reached her, Laura found his hand upon her lower back as he walked with her down the stairs.

His touch was light, barely grazing her clothes, but she felt it all the way to her bones. She slowed enough that his hand came in full contact with her. It was such a small pleasure, but she would take anything she could.

She was torturing herself. Yet in these few moments, she could pretend Charon was hers. There would come a day when she knew she'd have to face the fact that he'd fallen in love with someone else. Until then, however, she had her fantasies that got her through each day.

There was so much she wanted to ask Charon about his visit with Con, but she would have to wait until they departed the mansion. Just when she thought she'd get the chance, Cassie and Hal offered to walk them out.

"They want to make sure we doona snoop," Charon whispered as she passed him while he held the door open.

Laura coughed to hide her laugh, but she couldn't stop

the grin. Charon's dark eyes twinkled with merriment as he spoke to Hal.

By the time they reached the car, Laura had already promised to call Cassie in the next few weeks to set up a time to visit. She was so dazed at having made that promise without grasping that's where Cassie had been heading her that she didn't realize Charon was opening her door for her until he reached for the handle.

He was always a gentleman, but he had never opened her car door for her before. She looked up and was ensnared by his eyes.

"Laura!" Cassie yelled.

Out of the corner of her eye, Laura saw something small and furry rush by her feet, and then she spotted something huge coming at her.

In an instant, she was hauled against the car, Charon's body pressed against hers. Laura inhaled deeply, letting the spicy sandalwood scent of Charon fill her senses.

Her hands automatically took hold of his shoulders, and the feel of the thick sinew beneath her palms caused her heart to race.

But it was nothing compared to the amazing feel of the entire hard length of him against her.

It was the loud, deep bark that brought her eyes open. Laura spotted a harlequin-colored Great Dane skid to a halt and collide with Charon.

The dog went down on his front paws and ducked his great head beneath the car with his butt in the air and tail wagging. A moment later, the dog stood with a small solid white kitten held loosely in its mouth.

"Duke," Cassie admonished as she rushed to them. "I'm so sorry. Duke doesn't understand he isn't the momma to the kittens. He won't let them out of his sight."

"Are you all right?" Charon asked softly near Laura's ear.

"I'm not the one who almost got taken out by a Great Dane. Duke ran into you." Though she had barely felt the collision.

Charon's face was inches from hers. He was so close she

could see the black ring around his deep brown eyes. Her breasts were crushed against him, causing her blood to sear her veins.

If she were the take-charge kind of girl, Laura would close the space between them and kiss him as she'd been yearning to do. Instead, she stood there, hoping, praying he'd be the one to kiss her.

Charon knew he needed to step away from Laura, but he couldn't. His body was ablaze. For her.

Her large pale green eyes watched him carefully, hiding her emotions perfectly so he had no idea what she was thinking. Was she appalled that he was so near her? Did she enjoy it?

Damn, but Charon hated not knowing. Even that couldn't put the distance between them. Laura's luscious curves called to him, begged him to learn more of her.

He'd been careful never to get too near her. Now he knew why. Somehow, someway his body had instinctively known its reaction to her. But now that he'd had that amazing curvaceous figure against him, he wanted more. Needed more.

Charon didn't know how long they stood there looking at each other. He was desperately trying to get his body under control when all he wanted to do was lean down and take her full lips in a fiery kiss.

It was the crunch of rocks as Hal drew near that managed to bring Charon to his senses. He took a step back and looked away before he screwed up everything by kissing Laura.

"Is Laura all right?" Hal asked, concern marking his face.

Before Charon could form an answer, Laura said, "Yes, yes. I'm fine."

"Duke is a good lad, just doesna know his own size," Hal said with a laugh as they watched Duke allow Cassie to take the kitten.

Charon forced a smile when Duke came trotting back to him. More words were spoken, but he didn't hear any of them as he absently rubbed the Great Dane. He concentrated on his breathing in an effort to stop himself from hauling Laura against him again.

God, what was wrong with him?

No woman in six hundred years had affected him so. Why did it have to be Laura? Why couldn't it be a Druid, so at least Charon had the hope of something more?

Charon waited for Laura to get in the car before he closed her door and walked to his side. He slid behind the wheel, wondering how he was going to sit alone with her for the next few hours and not touch her.

They had just driven away from Dreagan when Laura asked, "Did you get everything you wanted?"

It took Charon a moment to realize she was referring to the whisky and not her. He scratched his jaw and nodded. He'd come away with much more than he expected. And a lot to think over. "Aye. Con seems like a reasonable man."

"I shouldn't have gone in the office with you. I didn't realize there would be things to discuss I didn't need to hear."

"Neither did I." That had come as quite a shock to Charon, and he couldn't wait to tell Phelan about it. "You did nothing wrong. I asked you to come, and if I had no' wanted you in the meeting with Con, I would've asked you to stay back."

"I know," she said, and fiddled with her purse strap. "The entire time we were there, it was like there was an undercurrent of something going on everyone knew but me."

Charon didn't answer, because he didn't know what to say.

"Does this have to do with our conversation yesterday? The one where you were telling me someone was trying to do something bad?"

He briefly squeezed his eyes closed and wished like hell he had kept his mouth shut. Laura shouldn't know that little bit, but he'd needed to talk about it. And then she was there. How could he resist?

"You know I'll keep your secrets," she said in a low voice.

Charon glanced at her. "Aye, I know. If I didna trust you, you wouldna be working for me."

"Then why don't you tell me what's going on? I might be able to help."

"If only you could. It's better if you know nothing."

She crossed her arms over her chest and looked out her window. "I hear the whispers around Ferness about you."

"People talk." He didn't care what others said, but he didn't want Laura to know the monster that he was.

There was only one fortunate thing about the entire mess that night a year ago, and that was that Laura had gone to Inverness to get some legal papers from his attorney.

Charon could only imagine her expression had she seen him shift into his Warrior form.

Laura made a sound in the back of her throat. "You're a powerful man in the community, but even you can't stop people from talking. Nor could you make all the damage disappear. Something attacked the village. People were killed. And then you left."

Charon turned to see her reflection in her window. She had her head averted, which kept him from looking into her green eyes and telling her everything she wanted to know.

"Will you tell me what really happened? Not the story that there was a freak storm, but the truth?"

"I can no'."

"I didn't figure you would."

The entire drive back to Ferness was made in silence from that point on. Laura wouldn't even look at him. Charon could practically see the distance between them growing, and he did nothing to stop it.

If he were smart, he'd keep that distance between them by keeping as far away from her as he was able. She was asking too many questions. As intelligent as she was, she might very well put it all together.

The thought of not seeing her daily left him sick to his stomach. It'd be easier if he could get her to leave. But she loved Ferness as if she'd grown up in the sleepy little town.

Charon might be a monster, but he wasn't completely heartless. He wouldn't make her leave.

By the time he pulled up in front of her flat, he already

had a plan in place. "Good luck with your date," he said as she opened the car door.

Even that couldn't get her to look at him. She hesitated for just a moment before she murmured a thanks and got out of the car.

Charon waited until she was inside her flat before he pulled away. Hating himself more every minute.

The only thing that kept him on course was knowing it would save Laura's life in the end.

CHAPTER NINE

Laura knew it wasn't Ben's fault. No one could compete
with someone like Charon. And even though she was
angry with Charon, she still couldn't stop thinking of him.

Not a good thing when she was on a date for the first time
in years.

"I thought you liked sushi."

She jerked her head to Ben, his voice dragging her away
from her thoughts again as they walked down the streets of
Ferness. "I do. I'm so sorry, Ben. It's just been crazy at work
lately. We only today learned we'll be a seller of Dreagan
whisky, and there are a million things I need to do."

He shrugged, but she saw how irritated he was by the
way he held his mouth. "Doona worry about it."

"No, I feel terrible. You deserved better than this."

"Aye, I did."

At first she thought he was kidding, but when there was
no smile, she knew he meant every word. It was on the tip of
her tongue to ask him to allow her to make it up to him, but
she suddenly realized she didn't want to be around Ben anymore.

The entire date was spent listening to him go on about
himself as he stuffed sushi in his mouth. Not once did he ask
her about her family or her past. She should have been grateful since she didn't like to tell people why she left her family.

What kind of guy isn't interested in his own date?

Laura breathed a silent sigh of relief when her flat came into view. She couldn't wait to get rid of Ben and forget about the entire, painful night.

She thought to say goodnight next to his car, but he continued walking to her door. Laura glanced around to find the streets deserted.

Ferness was small, and it was after midnight, but usually there were people around. At least the pub was down the street a ways and she could go there if need be.

Odd that she never felt so uneasy around Ben before. It was something she should have picked up on. Laura discreetly dug out her keys in her purse and kept them in her hand.

There was a feeling lodged between her shoulders that she hadn't been able to get rid of all evening. It took her a moment to recognize it as the apprehension she'd felt her entire life while living under her mother's roof.

Only now, after being away from her parents and sister, did she understand what that feeling was that had always plagued her.

And now it was back again. Not a good sign.

"Thank you for dinner," she said when they reached her door.

Ben smiled, his hazel eyes holding none of the charm she was used to seeing. "I thought we might have a nightcap."

"All right," she said, thinking fast. "I don't have any liquor, but the pub is just up the street."

"I wanted some alone time with you."

Laura's heart began that slow, sickening beat as fear filled her. She'd thought—hoped—to never feel that kind of fear again.

"Ben, it's been a really long day, and I'm tired. Can we do this another night?"

He took a step toward her, crowding her against the door as she stepped back. "Is this what you do, Laura? Do you string guys along for weeks before finally giving in to dinner, and instead of paying attention to your date, your mind is elsewhere? You flirt and promise things only to fall through on them."

"I didn't promise you anything."

Ben's voice had become low and dangerous, which caused Laura's blood to turn to ice in her veins. She prayed someone was around, that anyone would suddenly come out onto the sidewalk so she could ask for help.

"I think you owe me, Laura."

"I don't owe you anything."

A scream lodged in her throat as he grabbed her arms and started to drag her to his car. Laura fought for all she was worth. She'd taken self-defense classes after striking out on her own, but no one had bothered to tell her that she would have a difficult time remembering anything through the terror that seized her.

She scratched his face, and kicked out with her foot, hoping to connect with something.

"Help!" she screamed, only to have her head jerked around when his meaty fist slammed into her cheek.

"Get in the bloody car," Ben growled as he continued to drag her to his car.

Charon was in the woods, leaning against a tree when he felt *mie* magic. The panic mixed in the magic had him rushing toward it.

It was instinctive. As a Warrior, he could sense the magic of Druids. A *mie*'s magic was soft and gentle, and a *drough*'s magic felt vile and oppressive.

There was no doubt it was a *mie* he felt, and the Druid was in danger. In his village. Charon might not live at MacLeod Castle, but he fully supported the Warriors who fought to keep the few remaining Druids safe.

He was surprised to find the feel of the magic came from Ferness. But more surprising was that as quickly as the magic had washed over him, it disappeared.

Charon came to a stop in the alley between two buildings and tried to pick up the Druid again, but whoever it was, was long gone.

"Damn," he muttered.

He was turning away when his enhanced hearing heard a scream and then a struggle. Charon whirled around and raced toward the voice, a voice he recognized all too well.

Laura.

With his speed, he was out of the alley and racing toward Laura's flat a heartbeat later. He could see some man with his hands on her while she fought him off like a wild animal.

Charon heard the god inside him roar with rage. He growled, agreeing with Ranmond. And in an instant, something barreled into him from the side, sending Charon crashing into another alley.

He rolled and came to his feet, ready to battle whoever dared to get between him and helping Laura.

"Enough," Phelan said with a growl.

Charon started to move past him only to have Phelan grab his arm.

"You can no' go to her looking like this."

"Like what?" Charon demanded.

Phelan lifted Charon's hand to show him the copper skin and claws. It was then Charon felt the fangs in his mouth. He had shifted without even knowing.

"Laura needs help," he argued.

"No' anymore."

Charon peered around the corner to see the man still had a hold of Laura, but Brian from the pub was suddenly running toward her.

He huffed and leaned against the building wall as Laura got free and rushed into her flat. The man, who Charon assumed was her date, fled away in his car.

"I think I'll go for a run," Phelan said, and chased after the car.

Charon knew Phelan would discover who the man was and why he'd attacked Laura. It took a moment, but Charon was able to get his god back under control.

That in itself shook him. It had been centuries since he

struggled with his god. He was in control, and had been since the days of Deirdre and Cairn Toul Mountain.

But the thought of Laura in trouble had sent all those centuries of restraint flying on the wind like a feather. It was because of Laura that he had gone to the forest.

Charon drew in a steadying breath and walked out of the alley. He frowned when he saw the door to her flat was barely hanging on its hinges, which told him she had tried to get away and the bastard hadn't let her.

He stood in the doorway, the sound of her scream echoing in his head. Charon stepped over the threshold to find Laura standing in the middle of the tiny kitchen, staring at nothing.

"Laura," he called as he approached so he wouldn't spook her.

Yet she didn't appear to hear him.

Charon came to stand in front of her. She blinked and lifted her head, her eyes coming to focus on him.

"Charon."

"Aye," he said, trying to mask the fury that welled inside him as he saw the bruise forming on her jaw. "He hit you."

"I think I need to do better on my background checks," she muttered.

She was in shock, and by the way she looked around her flat, Charon knew she didn't want to be there. And he didn't want her alone. The weasel might come back.

"You doona need to stay here," he said, and wrapped an arm around her shoulders.

It wasn't until she laid her head on him and her shoulders began to shake that he lifted her in his arms and strode from the flat. Whatever distance he'd wanted put between them no longer mattered.

She'd been hurt. She needed him, and he wasn't about to let her down. If there was one thing he could do, it was protect her.

"You'll be safe with me," he murmured.

He took long strides crossing the street. Charon didn't go

in through the pub, instead went around the building to gain entrance at the back.

In no time he was inside. He took the stairs up to his private quarters and walked into the bedroom. Yet, he couldn't make himself release Laura.

He sank onto the bed with her still in his arms. She clung to him, though she had stopped trembling. "I need to get you something for your face."

"He said I teased him."

"He's a liar. Forget him."

She raised her head so her eyes met his. "He was adamant about me going with him. Desperate even. I never wanted to be manhandled like that again."

Again? Charon wished now he had dug into her past. "He willna touch you ever again. That I can promise."

A ghost of a smile played on her lips. "I don't think I'm meant to find anyone."

"Because of one date with a deranged man? Doona base your facts on that."

"I base my facts on my life. If you knew my family, you'd understand."

It was the first time she had spoken of her past, and he didn't want to let the opportunity slide. Plus it would keep her mind from the attack.

Though he had no such problems. As soon as Phelan returned to let him know where Ben was, Charon planned on paying him a little visit.

"Tell me about your family."

"They're . . . I don't talk to them."

"Why?"

"It's better that way. Tell me your secret now."

He smoothed her hair back from her face, careful not to touch her bruise. It felt so good to touch her and have her in his arms. His secret wouldn't be shared with her. Ever. "Did Ben say why he wanted you to go with him?"

"No."

Laura began to shake again, and Charon silently cursed

himself for bringing the bastard up. He set her on the bed and rose to pour some scotch.

On his way back, he grabbed a shirt from his closet and took them both to her.

"Drink this now. All of it," he instructed. "Then go change into this. You're sleeping here tonight."

When she stared at him, he nudged her hand holding the glass until it was at her lips. Once she had drained it, Charon took the glass and watched her go into the bathroom.

It took everything he had not to follow and pull her back into his arms. But after the night she'd had, it would be the last thing she wanted.

"Charon."

He looked to find Laura standing in the bathroom doorway in her torn dress. She walked to him, rose up on her tiptoes, and placed her lips on his.

Fire rushed through his veins as his body roared to life. He'd dreamed of kissing her, yearned to take her lips.

His arms locked around her, refusing to let her go. For a moment, he simply savored the feel of her body and mouth. Then he tilted his head and slipped his tongue past her lips.

He deepened the kiss, the taste of her more erotic and intoxicating than he could ever have dreamed. The place in him that had been empty for so long began to diminish as she tangled her tongue with his and sank her hands into his hair.

Flames of desire, potent and exciting, coursed through him. They licked at his skin, urging him to taste more of her, touch more of her.

With his hands splayed on her back, he made himself pull back from the intensity of their kiss. It was the last thing he wanted, but he couldn't take advantage of her after the night she'd had.

It was the hardest thing he did, but Charon slowly, reluctantly ended their kiss. When he looked down at Laura, her eyes were filled with desire and longing that rocked him to his very core.

How could he have ever thought to push her away?

CHAPTER TEN

Jason Wallace stood alone under the night sky on the back porch of the hunting lodge. Every hour he spent at the lodge told him it was one of the best investments he'd made since inheriting Declan's money.

"Any word?"

He smiled as Aisley's voice reached him. She was another of his cousins, one who had very powerful magic. Aisley didn't yet understand her true role in his plot, but she would. Very soon.

"No' yet," he answered. "I suspect verra soon to be hearing from Ben."

Aisley's heels clicked on the stone patio as she walked to a potted plant and leaned down to smell the roses. "And you think that taking someone close to Charon will hurt him far more than just killing him?"

"Aye. He willna be expecting it. The Warriors think they're so smart, hiding in MacLeod Castle. Deirdre was able to penetrate the castle. Even Declan was able to, but nothing ever came of it. I decided to approach things another way."

Aisley straightened before she sank onto a nearby bench and leaned back on her hands. "You're taking a big chance that this woman means anything to Charon other than an employee."

Jason briefly smiled as he turned to his cousin, the pull of the stitches in his cheek reminding him of his deformity, his lack of a healer, and the fact that for some reason his magic couldn't heal him. He'd have to take precautions from now on.

"Ah, but I do know, cousin. You forget I was watching these Warriors for months before they knew anything of me. I know more about them than they expect."

"In other words, they'll underestimate you."

"Precisely. Once I have the woman, I'll use her to get Charon out of hiding."

"He should be easy. After all, he isn't at MacLeod Castle."

Jason narrowed his gaze at Aisley. She was the one who had dared to try to leave him. Once. He'd taken care to ensure that would never happen again, but he also knew she didn't always agree with him.

"Why the sudden interest in my thoughts, cousin?"

She shrugged nonchalantly and looked at a passing lightning bug. "Mindy was running her mouth again. I had hoped I'd seen the last of the whiny bitch, but I wasn't that lucky."

"You're going to have to learn to like Mindy. She's a part of this team."

Aisley looked down at the bloodred heels she wore and rotated her ankle. "I'll tolerate her because I don't have a choice."

"You doona have a choice about a great many things, Aisley. Doona forget that."

"Never," she said, and stood. "You don't let me."

If there had been any heat, any sarcasm to her words, he would have punished her right then. But she was just stating a fact, so he let her walk away.

Jason turned back to the stars. He could barely contain the excitement running through him. A smirk tugged at his lips as he imagined Charon's face when he learned his precious Laura was gone.

Charon might not have taken Laura to his bed, but Jason had seen the way Charon looked at her in the surveillance pictures.

The Warrior who thought he could live among humans was about to get the surprise of his life. Jason could hardly wait for Charon's arrival.

He could almost picture the copper Warrior demanding the release of Laura. There was no doubt Charon would offer a trade: himself for Laura.

It was a trade Jason was more than willing to make.

Charon was the first he would attack in such a way, but the others wouldn't be the same. No, Jason had devised a unique approach to hitting each Warrior where it hurt the most.

The plan had unfolded in his mind hundreds of times. The Warriors wouldn't see any of this coming until it was too late. There would be nothing they—or the magic of their Druids—could do about it either.

The buzz of his phone sent a spike of anticipation through him. "Aye?"

"We have a problem," Ben's voice said through the phone.

"Tell me you have the woman."

"She got away."

Jason fisted a hand to control his rising temper. "Explain."

"She fought me. Someone heard the commotion and came to help her. I ran off before they could call the police."

"Did Charon witness any of it?"

"I doubt it," Ben answered. "He'd have charged me if he had. I heard no roar of a Warrior and saw nothing."

Jason opened his eyes. "Damn. Where are you now?"

"I had to stop for some petrol, so I took the chance to call you. Do you want me to go back for her?"

"Nay. They'll be expecting you." Suddenly Jason laughed as a new plan took flight. "But they willna be expecting what I do next."

"What do you want me to do?"

"Where are you?"

"Outside Inverness."

"Good. Stay there. You'll hear from me soon."

Jason ended the call and turned to the open doors that led

into the study. He shoved the mobile into his pocket and strode into the house.

Phelan flexed his hand as his claws lengthened from his fingers while his enhanced hearing picked up the entire phone conversation. It would take just one slash to sever the head from Ben's body.

He wasn't surprised to learn Ben was connected to Jason Wallace. It was becoming impossible to decipher who was with Wallace and who wasn't.

Phelan edged closer to Ben in the shadows of the petrol station. The lights were blinding and left little hiding places, but Phelan didn't need to get that close with his hearing. It also helped that Ben didn't care if anyone heard his conversation.

Phelan was blindsided to learn Jason had been watching Charon and the others for months. With the way he moved around constantly, Phelan was sure he hadn't been followed.

But he hadn't been looking for it, so it was a possibility.

"Bloody hell," he murmured when the call ended.

Phelan wanted to stay with Ben and see what was next, but by Jason's words, Phelan couldn't chance it. For whatever reason, Jason was focused on Charon now, and it was up to Phelan to make sure his friend made it out of this cluster fuck alive.

With one last look at Ben, Phelan turned and started back to Charon.

Charon sat in the dark, watching Laura sleep. He'd taken the chair beside the bed since he couldn't climb in with her, nor could he go into the next room because of his worry.

She had taken a long time in the shower. So long, Charon almost went in after her. When she finally came out, she immediately climbed into his bed, where she had been ever since.

For hours, he had been going over everything she told him about Ben and then the attack. Something wasn't adding up. From what Laura had told him, Ben was a stand-up guy with a good job. Why turn into a lunatic so suddenly?

Charon ran a hand down his face. He leaned up and braced his elbows on his knees and looked at Laura. She was on her stomach, one arm tucked beneath the pillow and one long, lean leg out of the covers.

She wore the faded denim button-down he'd tossed her, and the hem was hiked up to where her leg met her buttocks. His hands itched to smooth up her thigh and cup her arse.

But he wanted to do so much more than that.

He smoothed a lock of hair away from her face and saw the bruise. Once more, rage consumed him. He never understood why some men felt the need to hit women, but Ben would pay for what he'd done.

Charon was also going to make sure Laura could defend herself from now on. She'd done a good job, but with some training, she could have set Ben on his ass with one or two good punches.

It was the sound of someone on the deck outside that had Charon on his feet, releasing his god, and in the living room in the space of a breath.

As soon as he saw Phelan, he tamped down his god and motioned his friend inside. Charon had been prepared for bad news, but by the look on Phelan's face, it was worse than he expected.

And then the full impact hit him.

"Wallace."

Phelan gave a nod as he shut the sliding glass door behind him.

"Shite. How did this happen?"

Phelan leaned a shoulder against the wall and folded his arms over his chest. "He's had you followed for months. He has photos of you and Laura, and God only knows who else."

"How could I no' have known?"

Phelan shrugged. "We can no' do anything about that now. I did, however, take a look around the village. The guards you have set up are still patrolling, but I did find one of Wallace's men who had a spot on the roof opposite this building."

"Then I need to have a word with him," Charon said, and started for the stairs.

"There's no need."

Phelan's words halted him. Charon whirled around and glared at his friend. "I need to hit someone. You wouldna let me go after Ben, and now you take care of the weasel who is watching me and Laura."

Phelan gave him a crooked grin. "You were no' the only one in need of a battle, though the man watching you was no' much of anything. He passed out when he saw what I was. I woke him up and learned he had been hired to watch you. That's all he knew. He didna even know his employer, just sent the photos to an e-mail address."

"And you believed him?"

"I saw the proof. No' to mention, the man was scared shitless. He pissed himself. Twice. He was telling the truth."

Charon began to pace the length of his home. Laura's life had been put in danger because of him. He'd feared this, which was one of many reasons he had never shown her any interest.

But what had he done to make Wallace take notice of Laura? He didn't want to even think about what Wallace would have done to her just to get his attention.

"I knew something was no' right about the entire situation with Ben and then the attack. Now it's all coming together." He stopped and looked at Phelan. "Tell me you didna kill Ben?"

"Nay, but I left him alone. There's more, Charon."

"Fuck," he ground out, and raked a hand through his hair as his mind went through possibilities. "Let me guess. Jason is pissed that his plot to kidnap Laura didna work?"

"Aye. He has something else planned. Jason didna say what it was, only that Ben needs to be ready."

Charon blew out a harsh breath. "They're coming here."

"That's my thought as well. With your men, and both of us, we can hold them off."

Charon was shaking his head before Phelan finished talking.

"Why the hell no'?" Phelan demanded.

"Last year when Deirdre attacked, I lost men. People learned what I was. The secret I had been keeping from them was exposed."

"And?" Phelan asked wearily. "What's your point? The cat's out of the bag, brother."

"This . . . war . . . is between Wallace and us. It's bad enough Druids have been brought in on this, but I willna sacrifice more innocents."

"You mean Laura."

"Innocents, but especially Laura."

"Then what do you plan?"

"I need you to take Laura to the MacLeods. She isna a Druid, but Jason has targeted her, so they'll give her sanctuary."

Phelan gave a quick shake of his head. "Bad plan. Call Fallon and have him use his power to teleport and take Laura. That'll leave me here to help you."

Charon caught Phelan's blue-gray gaze. "Jason wants me. Doona put your life in danger. It'll be there soon enough. Besides, the MacLeods will need you with the others. The more Warriors there to fight, the better. Just take Laura."

"No," Laura said from behind him.

He turned to see her standing in the doorway with steely determination in her pale green eyes.

"No," she said again. "No one tells me what to do anymore."

CHAPTER
ELEVEN

Laura had woken to the sound of male voices. For several minutes she was content to simply listen to the cadence of Charon's voice, the sexy timbre and how it put her at ease knowing he was near. Until she heard her name.

Then she began to pay attention.

The mention of Druids, Jason Wallace, and the MacLeods was of interest. Something big was going on, and somehow it involved her. She could hardly wrap her head around the idea of Druids, let alone hearing Charon and the other man speak of them as if they were a part of their everyday lives.

But when Charon asked the man to take her away, Laura could no longer sit back and listen.

"Laura," Charon began.

She held up a hand to stop him. "No. I left England because my family kept running my life. I made a promise to myself then that I wouldn't let it happen again. Ever."

"You doona understand," the man said.

Charon sighed and motioned to his friend. "Laura, this is Phelan."

"Nice to meet you," she said, and turned her gaze back to Charon. "Are you listening to me? The only one making decisions about my life is me. When I left England, I left that part of my life behind."

"Maybe if she knew what was going on, she might change her mind," Phelan said.

Laura gave a nod of thanks in Phelan's direction. "A capital idea. Charon?"

Charon lifted his deep brown eyes to her, and she saw the indecision and worry that filled them.

"I recognize you're concerned for me, and I appreciate that," she said. "What Ben did was . . . well, it was unconscionable. However, that doesn't give you the right to decide my life."

"It does if I'm trying to save it."

"Tell me what's going on. Talk of Druids and teleportation. What the hell, Charon? You're beginning to freak me out a little."

When he didn't answer, Phelan rolled his eyes and pushed away from the wall. He walked to the table and poured whisky into a glass.

"Druids are real," Phelan said.

Laura frowned. "Yes, I'm sure they were. Once."

"Nay, as in now," Phelan insisted.

Charon sank onto the couch. "He's right. They're real. We know several."

"You mean like the fanatics they show on the news sometimes, dancing naked during some old Celtic holiday?"

"Nay," Charon said softly. "These are real Druids, Laura. They have magic, good magic. They're called *mies*."

She stared at him for several beats, unsure what to think. The fact that he believed every word was evident in his body language and his tone.

Then something struck her. "If there are good Druids, are you telling me there are evil ones?"

"Aye. They're called *droughs*," Phelan said.

Charon rubbed his hands slowly together, his brow furrowed deeply as he stared at the floor. "They give their blood and their souls to Satan, and in exchange they use black magic. They're evil to the core. It was one of those who was behind your attack tonight."

"Ben?" she asked.

Phelan gave a snort as he turned away.

"Nay," Charon answered, and lifted his gaze to her. "Jason Wallace."

Laura put a hand to her forehead as her mind began to spin. If it were anyone else but Charon, she would think it was all a jest. But she could see by the penetrating way his eyes held hers that it was far from a jest. "You both believe this?"

Phelan was standing in front of her so fast, she hadn't seen him move. "Aye, we believe it because we live it every damn day."

"Phelan," Charon said sharply, a low growl coming from him.

Laura lifted her chin and stood her ground until Phelan turned away. The anger in his blue-gray depths frightened her much more than the truth she saw there.

"There are Druids," she repeated, testing the words out on her tongue. She moved to the couch and sank down beside Charon. "If what you said earlier is true, then I'm just a pawn to Jason?"

"A pawn to get to me," Charon confirmed. "I—"

"We," Phelan corrected.

Charon flattened his lips as he glared at Phelan. "Fine. We riled Jason a few weeks ago."

"His mansion was nearly destroyed," Laura said, remembering hearing something about it on the news. Then the impact of his words hit her. She gaped at him. "You did that?"

Phelan smiled proudly but Charon couldn't meet her gaze.

"You better believe we did," Phelan said. "We'd have done more, but Ch—"

"Enough," Charon interrupted. He raked a hand through his hair, a muscle jumping in his jaw. "She doesna need to know all of it."

Laura watched Charon rub his chest again. She began to piece everything together then. She knew she didn't have all the pieces, but it wasn't hard to fit them together. "That's the night I couldn't get ahold of you. You came back the next day with your shirt torn and bloodied. Were you injured?"

Charon refused to answer her, so she looked to Phelan.

Phelan gave a small nod, a frown troubling his brow. "You're rubbing your chest, Charon."

Instantly Charon's hand dropped.

"Does it still hurt?" Phelan pressed.

Charon was on his feet, his back to them both as he walked around the couch. "Drop it."

"Nay," Phelan bit out. "I willna. You said you were fine."

"I'm alive."

Laura watched the exchange intently. Charon didn't want her to know what had happened that night two weeks ago, but it appeared he didn't want Phelan to know the full extent of it either.

"Dammit, Charon!" Phelan exploded. "Sonya needs to know her healing magic didna take care of all of it. And the MacLeods need to know as well. Every Warrior needs to know."

"What's a warrior?" Laura asked.

"Nothing," Charon said the same time Phelan turned his head to her and said, "Us."

Laura looked down at her bare feet, watching her toes painted a bright coral dig into the rug. It was tearing her up to see Charon so out of his depth.

He'd been injured. That explained the shirt, him rubbing his chest, and why he'd taken off to the forest whenever he could.

The injury couldn't have been that bad. Could it? They had mentioned Druids and someone named Sonya with healing magic. Maybe the wound had been as bad as she feared.

Just what had she found herself in the middle of?

Laura touched Charon's shirt, which she still wore. He'd kept his secrets from her because it was a different world. A world of magic, with Druids apparently.

And warriors.

Charon was definitely a warrior. She also knew him to be

honorable and decent. If he had attacked Jason Wallace, it was for good reason.

There was only one thing Laura could do, and that was trust Charon. She had put her trust in him the moment he served her ale that day two years ago. Why should she stop now?

She lifted her gaze to him. It made her bristle to have anyone—even the man she'd yearned for—tell her what to do. But she was a liability.

Ben had tried to kidnap her to get to Charon. The why of it didn't matter. What mattered was that she remove herself from whatever game was being played so Charon could do whatever it was he needed to do.

"If I have to leave, Charon, then I will. But on my own terms."

His shoulders dropped at her words, and it was then she realized how desperately he wanted her to go. The sting of it was softened only because she was beginning to suspect the danger surrounding Charon was great.

"You can never return," Charon said as he faced her. "Change your name, your hair color . . . change everything. You have to begin a new life, one that doesna include Ferness or me."

It felt as if someone reached into her chest, clamped a hand around her heart, and squeezed. She'd made a home, a life in the village. After all she'd been through with her family, she finally had a place and she wasn't prepared to give it up. "Ferness is my home."

"Wallace is coming. He'll come for me again and again. And he'll hurt those closest to me."

"If he's as powerful as you think, then he'll find me wherever I go."

Charon glanced at the floor. "No' if you go to the Mac-Leods."

She slapped her hands on the couch in frustration. "Who are these MacLeods?"

"People who can protect you," Phelan said. "The Druids

there shield the castle with magic so no one can see it. Their magic is extremely powerful."

Laura looked at Charon, but once more he wouldn't meet her gaze. She didn't want to leave him, because she knew if she did, she'd never see him again. He'd erase himself from her life, from Ferness.

The sorrow that came sucked her under until she couldn't get her bearings. "How long will I need to stay at the MacLeods?"

"Until this is over," Charon answered. "I doona know how long that'll be. We've been battling this evil for what seems like eternity."

She glanced at Phelan to see him watching Charon intently. "Will you come to the MacLeods?" she asked Charon.

When he didn't answer, she rose and walked to him. She stood in front of him until his gaze locked with hers. Growing up in England, she had been meek and subservient to her mother and sister while her father pretended everything was all right.

She did whatever they wanted, whenever they wanted. Until one day she snapped. Laura left her family behind and began to live for the first time. But it hadn't been until she met Charon that she realized what she really wanted. Him.

Now he was sending her away. To protect her, yes, but it would mean never seeing him again.

"For so many years I was afraid to take what I wanted. I'm not going to stand aside now," she whispered before she rose up and kissed him.

For a heartbeat he simply stood there, his lips unmoving against hers. Then, as if a dam broke, his arms clasped her to him as he roughly turned and pushed her against the wall to cover her body with his.

He seized, he captured.

He conquered.

Laura's fingers delved into the cool strands of his dark hair. One jeans-clad leg wedged between hers, the rough denim rubbing against her bare thigh.

He kissed her with abandon. Wildly, recklessly. Madly. His tongue touched every part of her mouth as if he were learning her, exploring her.

All she could do was hold on to him as he deepened the kiss, urging her to let go. So she did. His hands held her even when her legs gave out from the sheer amount of passion coursing through her.

Dimly, she heard the glass door open and close and knew Phelan had left them alone.

She clung to Charon as his kisses made a path down her neck and into the vee of her shirt. Her breasts swelled, eager for his touch.

"Laura," he murmured, his warm breath fanning her skin.

Her name had never sounded so beautiful as it did coming from his lips. He spoke it like a prayer, whispered and reverent.

And then he was kissing her again.

She clawed at his shirt until she found skin. He broke the kiss long enough to yank the shirt over his head, and then he claimed her lips again.

Laura ran her hands up his chest, learning every valley and ripple of steely muscle beneath his warm skin. How many times had she seen him without his shirt and longed to touch him?

Her lungs seized when his hand touched her bare thigh and slowly, leisurely moved upward. He squeezed her butt and ground his hips against her. Instinctively, she rocked her hips, his hard arousal causing her own passion to quicken.

His hand moved to her hip, where he rested it for the barest of moments, fingering the lace of her panties, before he continued his upward journey to her waist and stopping just short of her breasts.

Laura moaned with need, silently urging him to cup her breast. She needed him to touch her like she needed the air to breathe.

His thumb grazed the underside of her breasts, causing her nipples to harden. Laura wrapped a leg around his, anything to bring him closer and quench the burgeoning need that was rapidly overtaking her.

And then, finally, he cupped her breast.

Laura sighed into his mouth, but that sigh quickly turned into a moan as he ran his thumb over her nipple.

He pressed his hard cock against her, urging her higher. Laura sank her nails into his shoulder when he rolled her nipple between his fingers.

She was panting with need. Every fiber of her being centered on Charon and his touch.

Suddenly, he gripped the edge of her shirt and ripped it open. The sound of buttons hitting the wood floor and bouncing away was drowned out by his low moan.

"My God, you're beautiful," he murmured.

Laura didn't shy away from him as Charon gazed at her breasts. She'd always thought them too big, but with the way he was looking at her, she suddenly enjoyed them.

She tucked a finger in the waistband of his jeans and heard his quick intake of air as that same finger grazed the head of his cock.

In quick succession, she unbuttoned his jeans and lowered his zipper. He wore nothing beneath, which made her smile, because, somehow, she wasn't surprised.

Charon grinned as he bent and lifted her in his arms before striding into his bedroom.

CHAPTER
TWELVE

Charon's body burned. And it was all because of Laura. Her kisses, her touch sent him careening over the edge, an edge he'd been afraid of.

But now . . . now he didn't care. It was all about her. Touching her, learning her.

Loving her.

It didn't matter that she now knew part of his secret. Laura was mixed up in the mess, so it was only fair she knew why. Yet, there was nothing that could convince Charon to tell her what he was.

Her pale green eyes were filled with passion and need. She gazed at him as if he were the only thing she wanted. It was how he wanted to keep it.

Nothing—and no one—would ever make him tell her he was a Warrior. He would do anything and everything it took to keep that information from her.

He gently laid her on the bed before he straightened to kick off his shoes and hurry out of his jeans. His hands itched to feel more of her silky skin and know the weight of her breasts once more.

She had been a temptation he resisted, but now he didn't know why. All those wasted months he could have been enjoying her body and her amazing lips.

Charon put one knee on the bed, his body demanding he take her now. But he wanted to go slow, to savor every second.

He knew Phelan would guard the building, but in the back of his mind, he comprehended that he couldn't dally as he yearned. Yet there was no way he could walk away from what Laura offered. Not when he craved her as he did.

"Charon," she whispered, and rose up on her knees as if she knew his indecision. "Leave tomorrow for the rising of the sun. Let us have now."

He moaned when her hand came to rest on his chest and slowly caressed downward until her long, slim fingers closed around his cock.

She gave a slight squeeze, sending his already inflamed blood to boiling. Charon wrapped one arm around her while his other hand cupped her breast.

Her head dropped back and the ends of her hair teased his thigh. He wanted all that glorious hair draped around him like a curtain as she leaned over him, riding him hard.

His cock jumped at the mere thought of it.

Charon claimed her mouth again. He couldn't get enough of her and her soft moans as he teased her nipple. He wanted more.

He wanted all of her.

Laura moved her hand up and down the hard, thick length of Charon's arousal. She loved the feel of his rod in her hands, loved the sounds he made in the back of his throat as she continued to stroke him.

But he was laying an assault on her senses with his kisses and fondling her breasts. His hands were everywhere. Touching, caressing. Learning.

Then his mouth moved down her throat once more. A soft cry fell from her lips as his lips closed over a turgid peak. He ran his tongue back and forth over her nipple, sending desire shooting straight to her sex.

Laura rocked her hips, seeking anything to ease the need within her. It tightened with each caress, each kiss . . . each lick.

She gasped when he cupped her sex, the heel of his hand putting pressure against her clitoris.

Charon shifted his mouth to her other breast, craving more of her. His fingers parted her curls to feel the dampness between her legs, and he groaned in response.

He pushed a finger inside her, her cry of pleasure made his god preen. Slowly, he moved his finger in and out of her, wringing more sounds of satisfaction.

It was just what he needed to ease the yearning inside him. Every sound that fell from her lips made him burn hotter. He wanted to lay her back, spread her legs, and bury himself within her tight folds.

Somehow he held back because he wanted to give Laura more than that. He wanted . . . He didn't know what he wanted anymore. His mind was too full of the beautiful woman in his arms, his body too full of desire to think of anything but Laura.

Seductive, irresistible, all too alluring.

Laura.

Her hand on his cock was driving him wild. If she didn't halt, he was going to spill.

He leaned forward, which sent her tumbling onto her back. For a moment, he simply gazed at her. The dark strands of her hair were spread around her, disheveled and wild.

It was her lips, swollen from his kisses and parted that made his balls tighten. But her eyes, those beautiful pale green eyes beckoned him to sample more of her.

Charon leaned over her with hands on either side of her head. He lightly kissed her before moving down her body, stopping to nip each of her breasts for a second. Then he continued over her stomach to her hips, and then to the glorious triangle of black curls between her legs.

He shifted his shoulders beneath her legs and parted her folds.

Laura fisted the covers in her hands as Charon's tongue touched her. She arched her back, the pleasure almost too intense to handle.

Then he found her clitoris, swirling his tongue around the tiny nub until she shook with the ecstasy filling her. He held her hips steady, refusing to allow her to move.

He licked, laved, stroked.

Her body was not her own. He commanded her, and she was helpless to do anything but follow, giving him everything and more.

The desire tightened until she thought she would burst from it. She was on the edge of an orgasm—so close it was within reach. Laura craved the release, but the more she moved toward it, the more Charon pushed her higher.

Charon opened his eyes to see Laura tossing her head side to side, her body tight as a bow. He knew he could give her the release she sought with one lick, but not yet.

He gave one final kiss to the inside of her thigh before he reached up and grasped her breasts. He squeezed her nipples, wringing a cry from her.

His attention focused on her lovely breasts gave her a slight reprieve. He lifted himself up and over her, his gaze on her sex spread beneath him, open and inviting. Her hips moved, seeking him.

His cock jumped in response, and suddenly Charon couldn't hold back anymore. He guided his aching arousal to her core, and then thrust.

Charon buried himself to the hilt in one smooth push. She was tighter than he imagined, and so incredibly hot. He held still, holding back the tide of his own climax, but Laura had other ideas.

She began to move beneath him, her hands at his waist urging him to join her. He met her gaze and couldn't deny her. With a hand braced beside her head, he shifted his hips.

Laura couldn't look away from Charon's dark gaze. He opened himself to her, allowed her to see into his soul for a heartbeat, but in that moment she knew he was a man she couldn't walk away from.

Ever.

Her legs wrapped around his waist, her ankles locked at

his buttocks as his tempo increased. Her already primed body began to tremble with this new pleasure.

With her breaths coming in great gasps, she meet him thrust for thrust. Body to body, heart to heart they gave in to their desires.

The longing within her was filled, her need met by a man who was much more than he admitted. The world ceased to exist. There was only the two of them, locked in a dance as old as time.

Each time Charon plunged within her, he went deeper, harder, faster. Her skin was drawn tightly over her bones as the pleasure coalesced into a fiery ball within her.

The orgasm hit her like a tidal wave. She was swept away and over into an abyss of pleasure so intense, so amazing she lost herself in it.

Just when she thought it might end, Charon continued to move and prolong her bliss until she screamed his name, the second climax taking her before the first was finished.

Laura held on to him, refusing to let go for fear that she might not come back to herself. The muscles beneath her hands moved and bunched as he continued to thrust.

He pumped mercilessly within her, until he plunged deep and gave a shout as he climaxed.

She didn't know how long they lay there before she felt him pull out of her, and then tuck her against his body. She didn't want to think of what was coming, but reality was quickly crashing down around them. Whatever time they had, she would take it and cherish it always.

A smile formed when Charon's arms tightened around her. It made her feel special, something she hadn't ever experienced before. But then again, just being with Charon had always made her feel like she truly belonged.

She knew he was awake by the way his fingers played along her skin, as if he couldn't stop touching her. Laura squeezed his arms and saw the room begin to lighten from the coming dawn.

"There's more to the story, isn't there," she whispered. She didn't want to bring it up, but she had to know.

Charon's fingers paused before he said, "Aye."

"It's a part you don't want to tell me, why?"

"Because of what you'll think of me."

His honesty brought tears to her eyes. "I know what I think of you already. That won't change."

"I doona wish to test your theory."

She sighed when he kissed her neck. "Our time is at an end, isn't it?"

"Unfortunately."

"It wasn't long enough."

"I fear an eternity wouldna be long enough for me to explore your body."

Laura sat up and faced him. His words gave her the courage she needed to tackle what was coming. "I'll go to the MacLeods, but I expect to see you there. Promise me you'll be there, and I'll go."

The wicked grin he gave her sent chills along her body. "I'll be there once I'm finished with Jason Wallace."

"No," she said with a frown. "I don't want you going after him by yourself. He isn't alone. He'll have people with him. I'll go to the MacLeods, just keep Phelan here with you."

"Laura—" he began.

She gave a shake of her head, refusing to give in. "That's the only way I'll go to the MacLeods."

He blew out a loud breath as he came up on his elbow. He stared at her before he nodded. "All right. Get dressed. We'll gather a few things from your flat while I contact Fallon."

It was good enough for her. She jumped from the bed and hurried into the bathroom where she had discarded her clothes when she took her shower. She glanced over her shoulder to see Charon getting dressed as well.

Laura finished putting on her bra and panties and grabbed another shirt from Charon's closet when Phelan was suddenly standing in the doorway.

"We need to move. Now!" Phelan shouted as he tossed a bag at her.

Charon didn't hesitate to find his boots and quickly put them on.

Laura opened the bag to find jeans, hiking boots, and a shirt from her flat. She dressed in record time with her heart thumping wildly in her chest.

"Did you call Fallon?" Charon asked Phelan as he grabbed her hand and dragged her out of the bedroom.

She fought to keep her balance as fear began to course through her. "What's going on?"

Phelan gave a vicious shake of his head. "The damn mobile phones willna work. I tried the phone in the office and pub, but the lines have been cut. I wanted to get you and Laura on the road before I tried to find another phone."

Laura collided with Charon as he came to an abrupt halt. Charon's face was filled with fury. She'd never seen him so angry, and she almost felt sorry for anyone who would dare to challenge such a man.

"We willna be going on the road," Charon said as he went still as death.

"What?" Laura and Phelan asked in unison.

Charon glanced out the opened sliding glass door and then to Laura. "We're going into the woods. No one knows this forest like I do. There's a place we can hide until the others arrive."

"Charon," Phelan said, his voice low with uncertainty.

"If we get on the road, I guarantee Wallace will have something waiting for us," Charon said. "He expects that I'll take Laura to the MacLeods."

She watched the two men stare at each other for several long tense minutes.

"Fuck," Phelan ground out as he turned away. After a moment he faced them again. His face was set in grim lines. "I'll get the others as quick as I can. Just make sure you doona let Wallace find you."

"He willna," Charon promised.

Laura then found Charon staring at her. She tried to smile, but the growing apprehension wouldn't let her.

"Do you trust me?" he asked.

"Implicitly."

With a nod to Phelan, Charon once more dragged her

after him. They ran down to the second floor, and then out of the building and down the stairs.

Just before they reached the woods, Laura glanced back, but Phelan was already gone. An ominous feeling overtook her, one that said very bad things were coming.

CHAPTER
THIRTEEN

Charon kept his pace slow. He knew it would be easier to pick Laura up and use the speed his god gave him to get them to safety, but then that would open up questions he didn't want to answer.

But was her life worth those questions?

"Shite," he said as he came to a halt.

Laura was already gasping from running over the rough, ragged terrain, and they hadn't gone quite a mile yet.

"What is it?" she asked, leaning over with her hands on her knees.

Charon looked back the way they had come. He could already feel the sickening, cloying feel of *drough* magic. It turned his stomach.

The forest was vast, but was it big enough to escape Jason Wallace? Charon looked at Laura. She was an innocent, targeted because of her association with him.

What a fool he'd been to waste those precious few hours making love to her instead of getting her safely to MacLeod Castle. That lost time could well seal her death.

"He wants me," Charon said. "If you run while I lead them away, you might have a chance."

She slowly straightened, her forehead creased in a frown. "You're leaving me?"

"To save your life." He hated the accusation in her voice,

but perhaps that's because he didn't want to leave her. He wanted to stand beside her, to feel her body next to his.

"I'll be safer with you."

Charon raked a hand through his hair as his frustration mounted. "I'm powerless against a Druid, Laura. Once he finds me, it's over. If you're near, your life could well be forfeit."

"We have a head start."

Charon wasn't sure how quickly Phelan could get ahold of the MacLeods. Would it be in time to save Laura? He was certain it wouldn't be in time to save him.

After so many centuries, his death had finally arrived. He had to die, but Laura didn't. And she wouldn't. He'd make sure of that.

"I've fought Jason and his Druids before. I know what to expect. You said you trusted me. I'm asking you to trust me now."

She swallowed and put her hands on her hips as she looked away. "What do you want me to do?"

He grabbed her shoulders to force her to look at him. "The cabin is another three miles. Continue southeast on this same heading. You'll find it."

"And if I don't?"

"You will," he said reassuringly. "I'll keep them heading in the opposite direction. Wait for Phelan at the cabin. If Phelan doesna show, only go with Ian Kerr."

"What of the MacLeods you speak of?"

"Ian will be with them. He and his woman, Dani."

"Charon—" she began.

He gave her a hard, quick kiss and turned her in the direction she needed to go. After a second, he gave her a little push. "Now, hurry!"

She stumbled forward, and then took off at a brisk run. Charon watched her for a beat before he turned the other way. He quickly removed any evidence of him and Laura, and then set about making sure he left a trail anyone could follow.

* * *

Phelan wanted nothing more than to walk up behind Jason Wallace as he got out of his BMW and snap his neck. But getting close enough with all the *droughs* surrounding Wallace was the problem.

Phelan growled, his god instantly rising to his call. He looked down at his hand to see his skin turn gold. He clicked his long claws together, itching to sink them into the flesh of a *drough*.

How he despised them. It was always *droughs* who continued to think they could take over the world. Based on the idea that they were better than anyone else.

Phelan stayed in the shadows, his eyes glued to Wallace. The man was a prick, and would soon follow Declan and Deirdre into death.

There was a niggle of worry in Phelan's mind though. Jason had proved to be smarter than either Declan or Deirdre. The question was, was he smart enough to best the Warriors?

Phelan waited until Jason and several *droughs* went into Charon's pub before he glanced at a nearby rooftop to see one of Charon's men watching him for the signal.

Phelan gave a nod, and the man ducked from view. Thanks to Charon's careful planning, the town knew what to do in case of such an event. Phelan just hoped everything went according to plan.

He'd have liked to wait and see where the other *droughs* with Jason were going as they fanned out in the village, but Phelan kept his gaze on the big brute of a Warrior with Jason.

There was little time to waste, so Phelan crept away and entered through the back door of the bakery. The old woman lifted her head from stirring the batter and gave him a swift nod before going back to her baking.

Phelan reached for the phone on the wall and quickly dialed Fallon MacLeod's number. Fortunately, Fallon answered on the second ring.

"We have a problem," Phelan said as he kept watch through the small window of the kitchen door that led out into the main store.

"Phelan?"

"Aye. Wallace is in Ferness. He had a man try to kidnap one of Charon's employees, a woman. The kidnapping failed, so Wallace showed up here. They were going to use Laura to get to Charon."

There was a mumbled curse through the phone before Fallon asked, "Where are Charon and the woman now?"

"Wallace somehow cut off the mobile phones. Phelan took Laura out into the woods to try to stay hidden until you and the others arrived."

There was a sound as if someone covered the phone, and then Phelan heard Fallon bellow for Quinn and Lucan.

"I've no' been to Ferness so I can no' jump there," Fallon said when he got back on the phone. "But Ian has been to the village. Where are you?"

"At the bakery. Be warned, Wallace and the *droughs* are all over town."

There was some talking Phelan heard through the phone, and he picked up Ian's voice. Then suddenly, Ian was on the phone.

"Phelan, can you get to the roof of the inn?"

"Aye," Phelan answered.

"Good. Meet us there. Now."

Phelan hung up the phone and hurried out of the bakery. The inn was across the street and four buildings down. He was halfway there when he spotted Ian atop the roof before he disappeared.

In the next instant, there were nine people surrounding him.

"Fuck me," Phelan muttered as he stumbled backwards when he collided with Ian.

Phelan looked around at the Warriors—Fallon and Lucan MacLeod, Hayden, Ian, Ramsey, Logan, and the only female Warrior, Larena, who was also Fallon's wife.

Next Phelan took note of the Druids who had also come—Gwynn and Isla, Logan and Hayden's wives respectively.

Phelan barely glanced at Isla. He hadn't forgiven her yet

for following Deirdre's orders and tricking him when he was
just a small lad to go with her. He'd been locked in Deirdre's
mountain until he reached manhood, and then she unbound
his god.

"We doona have much time," Phelan said.

Ian glanced around. "Where in the woods is Charon?"

"There's a cabin he uses. It's deep in the forest, and verra
difficult to find."

"Have you been there?" Ramsey asked.

Phelan gritted his teeth. "Nay. That was the one place
Charon wanted absolute privacy. I never tried to find it."

"Holy hell," Quinn said.

Isla let out a deep breath. "We can't sit around. We need
to get in the woods and find the cottage."

"What we need is Broc," Fallon said before he disappeared.

Phelan was thankful for Fallon's teleportation abilities.
Broc—who was able to find anyone, anywhere—would help
make up lost time in discovering where the cabin was.

In a matter of seconds, Fallon returned with Broc.

Phelan glanced down the alley to the street. "I'll make
sure no one sees you."

They lined up behind him as Phelan pointed to the pub.
"The quickest way into the forest is behind the pub."

"I've found him," Broc whispered as he stood with his
eyes closed. "Charon is alone."

Hayden frowned and turned his gaze to Phelan. "I
thought you said there was a woman with him."

Phelan stopped himself from rolling his eyes. "Charon
probably sent her to the cabin while he led Jason in the opposite direction."

"Aye," Broc said. "Jason and six *droughs* are in the woods.
But . . ."

"But what?" Phelan ground out when Broc's voice faded
away.

Broc's black eyes opened to stare at him. "Wallace isna
heading toward Charon. He's following another trail."

"Laura," Phelan whispered.

Ian clasped Phelan's shoulder. "Get us in the woods."

Phelan was all too happy to use the power of his god. It was a trick that had come in handy more times than he cared to admit.

The ability to alter someone's perception of reality was easy enough to do, especially when all he had to do was hide the fact that he and the others were crossing the street.

He gave a nod to let everyone know it was time to get moving. They all crossed without any mishap, Phelan walking right behind a *drough* in the process.

Just when he was about to take the *drough* out, Ramsey caught his eye before Phelan could kill the Druid. Phelan knew they couldn't risk being discovered, but if one less *drough* was out in the world, the better.

Once they were all safely in the woods, Phelan released his power. Now it was time to find Charon and Laura. And hopefully end Jason Wallace.

Charon knew the instant Jason decided to track Laura instead of him. Fear snaked down Charon's spine as he used his unnatural speed to race through the forest toward Laura.

His legs pumped faster than ever before, while the question of why Wallace wanted Laura so desperately rolled through his mind.

Charon jumped down a cliff, landing on bent legs, before he leaped over a wide stream. He was close to the cabin, and the feel of *drough* magic was so thick, he was gaging with it.

When the cabin came into view, he almost sighed with relief since Jason wasn't there. Yet.

Charon busted through the door of the cabin in time to see Laura whirl around. She flew into his arms, and he held her tightly, squeezing his eyes closed at the feel of her.

"I didn't think you'd get here," she said as she pulled away.

Charon pulled out of her arms to shut and bar the door even though he knew it wouldn't keep Jason out. Then he slowly turned to face Laura. "It didna work. My plan. Jason followed you, no' me."

"Me?" she asked, confusion marring her face. "Why?"

"I suspect he wants to make me suffer. What better way than to do it to someone I care about."

She leaned against a wall, dazed with the knowledge he shared. "What do we do?"

"We wait and hope Phelan has gotten ahold of the Mac-Leods."

"And if he hasn't?"

"Phelan willna let us down."

She sighed loudly. "How long do you think it'll take?"

Charon opened his mouth to answer when he felt the *drough* magic closing in. They were out of time.

Which meant he had only one option. But he would do anything to keep her safe.

He walked to Laura and pulled her against him as he took her mouth in a sensual kiss that convey his need, his longing for her.

"I'm sorry," he said. "I'm sorry I waited so long to kiss you. I'm sorry you're in this mess. But mostly I'm sorry for what you're about to see."

He turned and walked to the door. He placed his hand on the doorknob when she called his name.

"What are you doing?" she whispered.

Charon looked over his shoulder at her and forced a smile. "I'm saving you. When I go out there, they'll be distracted. Leave through the hidden door beneath your feet. Run. Doona stop, Laura, and doona look back. Phelan and the others will find you."

"Charon, wait."

"Be ready," he warned. "As soon as I go out, you have to run."

He waited until she moved aside the rug and found the handle to the hidden door. Charon had built the cabin on the side of the mountain for any kind of emergency.

Now all he had to do was keep Jason focused on him, and pray Phelan found Laura.

With one last look at Laura, Charon opened the door.

CHAPTER
FOURTEEN

Laura's hand wrapped around the handle, but she couldn't pull up the hidden access in the floor, because her gaze was locked on the place Charon had been.

The look he had given her before he walked from the cabin left her cold, hollow. Empty. There had been sadness and resignation in his dark eyes, a misery that yanked at her heart.

Charon, the man she'd wanted for years, had finally been hers for a few splendid hours. He hadn't told her how he was involved in a world of magic, but she knew him well enough to know he was worried.

That in itself gave her pause. Charon had never shown fear for anyone or anything. Whoever this Jason Wallace was had Charon troubled. Laura knew she needed to run away, but she couldn't make herself leave Charon.

She released the handle and straightened. The cabin had numerous windows to gaze at the beauty of the forest, which gave her a good view of Charon and the people who had surrounded him.

These were the Druids he'd been running from? The ones who had followed her instead of him?

Evil Druids.

Laura fisted her hands at her sides in an effort to keep them from shaking. Magic wasn't supposed to be real. People weren't supposed to use magic, but there was no doubt looking at the people who appeared, they were definitely evil.

She wanted to help Charon. He was one man against many. Yet how could she? What few self-defense moves she had picked up hadn't helped her with Ben. That left her little option in how to get both her and Charon away.

A glance around the cabin showed no weapons of any kind. She had never fired a gun, but for Charon she was willing to give it a try. If only he had one in the cabin.

"Bloody hell," she said, wishing he could have been there to hear her cuss.

Her attention was snagged when a man with blond hair and five vicious gashes across his face stepped out of the group. He held his hands in his pockets of his dress pants, a knowing smirk on his hawkish face while his frigid blue eyes looked Charon up and down with revulsion.

"You've foiled my plans, mate," the man said.

Charon shrugged. "You can see how much I'm torn up about that, Wallace. I think the scars on your face improve your appearance somewhat."

So this is Jason Wallace. God, how Laura wished she could see Charon's face. His voice was filled with sarcasm. And anger. His stillness told her of the rage he barely contained.

A muscle in Jason's jaw jumped as he glared at Charon. "You know you doona stand a chance against us."

"Care to find out?" Charon said and held out his arms.

Laura took in the sight of Charon with his shirt straining against his thick muscles, a sheen of sweat covering him. With the sun alighting upon him through the tree limbs, it looked as if he were offering himself to some ancient god.

Her thoughts halted while she watched, transfixed, as Charon's tanned skin changed to a beautiful copper right before her eyes. She took a step back in alarm when long, gleaming copper claws extended from his fingers.

But it was the deep, resonating growl coming from him that made her heart skip a beat.

This was what he hadn't wanted her to see. This was

what the villagers had been whispering about for months. This was his secret he hadn't wanted to share.

Laura hurried back a few steps, knowing she should run, but she couldn't. What Charon had become scared her more than she could put into words, but he had never harmed her.

He had protected her, watched over her. And made love to her.

"Oh, God," she mumbled, her stomach knotted with disbelief.

Druids and whatever it was Charon had turned into. Phelan had said he and Charon were warriors. Could this be what he meant?

Her thoughts were torn away from what Charon looked like and what he could possibly be by the tension growing around them. It pulsed angrily, steadily expanding until her skin all but buzzed with it.

Laura gasped and covered her mouth with her hand when Charon turned his head and she saw the large, thick, dark copper horns that protruded from his temples to wrap around his forehead and come to points that nearly touched.

He was a beautifully terrifying spectacle to behold. The muscles she had spent hours caressing were rigid, straining as he flexed his claws as if he couldn't wait to sink them into Jason.

And then all Hell broke loose.

Jason raised a hand and suddenly Charon was jerked backwards. He crashed through the cabin wall as if it were paper.

Laura dived to the side and covered her head with her arms as debris slammed into her. She expected to look up and find Charon dead, but he jumped to his feet as if nothing had happened.

His shirt was shredded, and through it she witnessed the deep gouges acquired when he went through the window and wood begin to heal.

Laura was glad she no longer stood, because she was sure her legs would have given out.

"You doona stand a chance against my magic, Charon,"

Jason said, laughter in his voice. "How many times must I show you that?"

"Until I'm dead."

Laura squeezed her eyes closed, tears gathering, when she heard Charon's response.

"You came for me," he continued. "Get on with it."

Jason chuckled, the others joining him. "Ah, but it's no' any fun if I doona have something to make you suffer. That's what the woman was for."

Charon's lips peeled back, and Laura caught a glimpse of what she thought were fangs.

"Good luck finding her. She's out of your reach."

Laura wanted to stand and see Jason's face, because given his lack of a witty response, she imagined he was furious.

"I'll find her," Jason promised menacingly. "I'll find her and torture her. She may no' be a Druid, but she'll bleed just the same."

She jerked when Charon threw back his head and roared. The sound left her ears ringing it was so loud and fierce. She knew she had to keep quiet, but she wanted to call out to him when Charon's legs bent and his gaze focused on something, probably Jason.

One moment Charon was standing there, and the next he was gone. She scrambled up, and caught sight of him using his claws to sever one of the men in half.

Laura barely registered that fact when a man with skin the color of light green leaped atop Charon. The newcomer had the same long claws and fangs, but no horns. He and Charon seemed to be matched with strength and speed by how viciously they attacked each other.

The others, who Laura assumed were Druids, began to laugh and jeer at the fight. She took a step toward one of the non-broken windows when Charon's arm was stopped mid-swing by some unknown force.

"Magic," Laura whispered.

Charon was held in place, his roars drowning out everything else. Then his opponent sank both sets of claws into Charon's abdomen.

"No!" Laura screamed.

Her shout was lost to the whoops and hollers of the others. Laura scanned each of the Druids and saw a woman with black hair standing apart. She didn't clap at the spectacle, but she didn't stop it either.

Maybe if Laura could get to her, she could make the woman help. That thought was quickly banished as Charon's attacker yanked out his claws and began to slash Charon's chest over and over.

Blood poured down his front to stain the ground. Laura gagged, knowing she was watching Charon die before her eyes. She hated feeling so helpless, so . . . useless.

She began to shake—not from fear, but from fury. That emotion escalated, intensified . . . expanded. She took hold of that anger, welcomed it when Jason came to stand in front of Charon.

Her breaths were ragged and her head began to pound. It was her skin, and the feeling as if something was moving inside her that made her fist her shaking hands before she began to scratch her skin. Laura looked down at her hands, not understanding what was happening.

Charon's bellow of pain brought her head forward and she spotted Jason holding his arm over Charon as his blood dripped into Charon's injuries.

"No," she said as she watched.

Her body began to vibrate from whatever was inside her. She didn't want to fight it. She wanted it out, loosened upon Jason and the others. The need within her was too great, too powerful to ignore.

"No," she said louder when she saw Charon grit his teeth in pain.

Whatever was inside her flowed easily, fiercely through every part of her until she felt as if she were glowing from it. From a great distance, she swore she heard the low beat of drums . . . and chanting.

But none of that mattered. Freeing Charon did.

Charon writhed with agony, his face mottled with pain.

It was the last straw.

"No!" she screamed, and threw out her arms.

Light flew from her hands, blinding her. Elation swept through her at the amazing sensations that took her. The release of whatever had been pent up inside her was astonishing, surprising.

Glorious.

When she blinked open her eyes she discovered the cabin obliterated and everyone sprawled on the ground. Unmoving.

Laura looked down at her hands and felt the same pulsing begin again, stronger this time. She lowered her arms and started toward Charon when Jason groaned.

Charon was on his back, the copper skin, horns, and claws no longer visible. He was the man she had always known, but his chest wasn't moving with breath.

It seemed impossible that the man who had always been there for her was dead. Laura's knees threatened to buckle as tears clouded her eyes. He'd faced Wallace so she could get away.

He'd planned to keep Wallace occupied and sacrifice himself. For her.

Laura didn't understand what happened to her in the cabin, but she did know she was the one who wrecked the cabin and killed Charon.

The tears wouldn't stop, and the anger that had driven that odd feeling inside her was gone. Once more she was the scared little girl who spent her life hiding from the world. She reached out a hand to touch Charon when Jason's arm moved.

Laura whirled around and ran. She had to get as far from the cabin as she could. Charon was gone, but Jason wasn't. And Jason had promised he would make her suffer.

All Laura could hope for was that Phelan found her like Charon had said.

She crashed through the forest, not caring how much noise she made while she put distance between her and the Druids.

* * *

Jason sat up and touched his aching forehead. When he looked at his fingers he found blood. "I'm tired of fucking bleeding," he declared as he climbed to his feet.

He looked around, unable to believe what his eyes saw. It looked as though a bomb had gone off inside the cabin. Nothing was left.

"Jason," Mindy said as she reached for him from her position on the ground.

He helped her to her feet and looked at Charon. At least one Warrior was dead.

"What the hell happened?" Jason demanded.

Dale flung boards off himself as his pale green skin faded away. "It was a *mie*. Charon had a Druid with him."

"The girl? Laura?" Mindy asked with a snort.

Dale shrugged. "I doona know."

"Find this *mie*," Jason ordered. "Whoever she is, she's in these woods. I want her brought to me."

Dale hesitated, and Jason lifted a hand to send a blast of magic at him, only to have nothing. Jason lowered his arm, pretending as if he'd changed his mind.

He had no magic all of a sudden, but the others couldn't know that.

"Why do you wait, Dale?" Mindy demanded.

Dale meet Jason's gaze. "I can no' feel the *mie*'s magic anymore."

Jason didn't like what he was hearing. Could this Druid's magic be able to disrupt other Druids' magic and Warriors' powers?

The idea left him reeling, but it was something he needed to consider. Unless the *mie* had some spell that halted others' magic for a time.

Jason began to turn when he saw Dale move away boards from the cabin to reveal Aisley. He had suspected for a while that Dale had some kind of attachment to Aisley, and this proved it.

Dale helped Aisley to her feet, but Jason realized then that not all his Druids were moving.

"See who's dead and who's alive," he demanded.

A few minutes later, and the count of dead had reached four. "Find this *mie*," he commanded. "Now!"

The remaining Druids, along with Dale, fanned out into the forest.

Jason held out his hand to Mindy. "Shall we go find us a Druid?"

"I do so want a new toy," she said with a grin.

CHAPTER
FIFTEEN

Aiden rubbed his eyes and fought to stay awake. The dinner he and Britt had planned fell through the moment she got immersed in her work.

She hadn't told him why she was so excited, only that one of her tests had shown a breakthrough.

So, instead of dinner and small talk, they had takeout and the radio. Aiden had never been away from MacLeod Castle for so long.

Though he expected to feel free from being away for such an extended time, he found he missed it. All of it. Not just his parents and the others, but the castle and the magic.

He missed the dinners where everyone was talking at once, the laughter, and even the arguments.

He missed movie night and the playful fights on who would get to choose the movie.

He missed the crash of the waves against the cliffs, wind that could sweep him off his feet at the top of the towers, and swimming in the swift-moving currents of the sea.

His parents had envisioned a time when the threat of evil was gone and the shield protecting the castle could come down. Aiden long ago realized their words had been nothing more than a dream.

There would always be evil, maybe not to the extent of Deirdre, Declan, and now Jason, but evil would always exist.

The shield could never come down from the castle. For too long, there had been no MacLeod Castle. It couldn't suddenly appear.

Not to mention, it was Isla's shield that kept the Druids immortal. Aiden couldn't imagine how his father would react if his mother died. Love bonded Quinn and Marcail, but that bond was linked to their souls as well.

"Shit," Britt said as she threw down her pencil.

Aiden jerked at her outburst. "What is it?"

"What is it?" she repeated testily. "I can't find what makes this different."

He glanced at the slide beneath the microscope. "Which blood are you looking at?"

She released a loud sigh and reached back to rub her neck. "Sample B. Everything I put into the blood, which would eradicate a normal sample, doesn't faze it. Nothing. I thought I had found something, but I was wrong."

"Is that what you've been working on?"

"No," she said, and leaned her head from side to side to stretch it. "I thought I found what made this blood so different. I was trying to isolate it."

"You couldna do it?" he guessed.

She cut him a look. "Of course I did it. It just didn't work."

Aiden scratched his chin, the sound of his fingers scraping against a day's growth of whiskers loud once Britt shut off the radio.

"What's next?" he asked.

"Maybe if I really knew what I was looking at," she began.

Aiden shook his head. "No' going to happen."

"I know," she said wearily. "I just thought I'd try again."

"Let's get you home. You've been at this for hours."

The fact she didn't protest told Aiden just how exhausted she was. She continued to work with such dedication even though she didn't know the real reason. Not many people would have done that.

He gathered up the blood samples while she put away

everything else. Aiden slipped the strap of his messenger bag over his head and waited for Britt by the door.

"Has any other strange person, besides me, approached you recently?" he asked as he removed the pencils she'd stuck in her hair at the base of her ponytail.

Britt flicked off the lights, her steps slow. She grasped the door handle and closed and locked it behind them as they walked out. "I have tons of strange people approach me on a daily basis, Aiden. I'm at a university. Raging male hormones and all that."

"Besides that," Aiden said with a wink.

They were side by side, walking down the stairs, when he glanced up and spotted his father waiting below. Quinn lifted his head and looked at them in that moment.

"Wow. He looks like you," Britt said.

Aiden hadn't expected to see his father, so was unprepared for a response.

"Aiden," Quinn said as he pushed away from the wall.

Britt continued down the stairs at a faster pace, ahead of Aiden. She stopped in front of Quinn and held out her hand. "I'm Britt. Are you Aiden's brother? You have the same eyes."

Aiden hurried to Britt. It was then he saw the worry in his father's dark green eyes.

"Hello," Quinn said, and took her hand. "I'm Quinn. It's nice to meet you. How's your work coming?"

"Slow," she said with a sigh.

Aiden cleared his throat and faced Britt. "Do you mind giving us a moment?"

"Of course. I'm heading home anyway."

"Wait for me to walk you out."

She smiled, her blue eyes crinkling at the corners. "You really think someone would hurt me for looking at the blood."

"Aye," Quinn answered. "We willna be long, Britt. Please wait for Aiden."

She looked from one to the other, and then gave a nod. "All right. I'll be right outside."

Aiden waited until the door closed behind Britt before he faced his dad. "What is it? Is it Mom?"

"Nay," Quinn said. "Wallace has been watching Charon for months. He tried to kidnap a woman who works for Charon."

"A Druid?"

"She isna a Druid."

Aiden frowned and crossed his arms over his chest. "Then why does he want her?"

"To make Charon suffer. Apparently Charon cares for this woman."

"Oh, shite," Aiden said as realization dawned.

"It gets worse."

Aiden was tired of it always being worse. He braced himself for any possibility then. "You said Wallace tried to kidnap this woman. That means he failed."

"He did, but he went after Charon and Laura himself. Wallace jammed mobile phone communications and had the phones disabled in Charon's building."

"Did he . . . did Wallace kill Charon?" Aiden liked Charon, even though the Warrior didn't spend much time at the castle. Charon had always been there when they needed him.

"I've no' heard yet," Quinn said, and rubbed the back of his neck. "Phelan was in Ferness. He's the one who called the castle while Charon and Laura went into the forest."

Aiden digested that bit of news, not liking how it unsettled him. But he also knew his father hadn't come to tell him just that. "You think since Wallace was watching Charon that he has someone watching the castle?"

"I'm nigh certain of it, son," Quinn said, and hooked a thumb in the front pocket of his jeans. "I've done a search around the university, and I doona detect any Druids."

"Wallace would be smart and hire others, no' Druids."

Quinn nodded. "That was your mother's guess as well. I know you wanted to come here by yourself—"

"It's all right," Aiden interrupted him. "I understand. I'm your only son. You worry."

"You have magic of your own. Be prepared to use it, especially for Britt."

"You think they'd harm her?"

"Without a doubt."

Aiden looked at her through the glass doors as she stood staring at the night sky. "I willna let that happen. Keep me posted. I'm going to walk Britt to her car."

"I've sent Galen to her flat to have a look around. He'll take watch tonight."

Aiden gave a nod to his father. "Thanks."

"You like her," Quinn said, a half smile on his lips.

Aiden rolled his eyes. "That talk is for another time." Quinn's laughter followed him out of the building to Britt. "Sorry about that."

"Is everything okay? Quinn seemed a tad upset."

Aiden was trying to figure out a response when she started walking.

"Let me guess," she said with a meaningful look. "I can't know."

"Unfortunately, aye. Trust me, you doona want to know."

"Maybe I do," she argued. "It might help me with my understanding the different blood you've given me."

Aiden wanted to tell her, and perhaps he should. Her life was in danger from simply walking with him. He looked around, peering deep into shadows and stepping in front of her anytime someone drew near.

"You're freaking me out, Aiden," she whispered. "What the hell is going on?"

"I wasna kidding when I said your life was in danger."

"Yeah," she replied sarcastically. "I get that. I think you owe me more than the standard 'you doona need to know' bit."

He found himself fighting a smile as he glanced at her. "There are things in this world you wouldna believe."

"Try me. I have an open mind."

"Magic."

She rolled her eyes as they halted beside her car. "Magic? That's all you've got?"

"Magic is in this land. It's in the verra air we breathe, in the water we drink. It's in the soil even. If you've magic, you can feel it all around you."

"Are you telling me you have magic?" she asked carefully.

Aiden looked into her blue eyes and knew he was taking a huge chance. But he wanted to tell her, wanted her to know the real him. "Aye."

"So, one of the blood samples has . . . magic in it?"

"It does."

She leaned back against her car and made a sound at the back of her throat. "Well. That's not something I expected to hear. But not every sample has magic in it?"

Aiden gave a single nod of his head.

"Are you making this up just to shut me up?"

He looked at the lamppost behind him, then glanced back at Britt to make sure she was watching. It took just a small thought to shatter the lightbulb.

"Oh, hell," Britt said as she ducked.

Aiden hoped that satisfied her curiosity for the night, since he knew his father was watching and wouldn't approve.

"You weren't kidding."

"Nay, I was no'," Aiden said as he opened her car door for her. "Be safe tonight, Britt."

He began to turn away when her hand touched his arm. Aiden looked back at her.

"Thank you," she said.

"Doona trust any new people you might meet. There are those out to harm me and my family. You helping me could verra well put you on that list, too."

"All right. Until tomorrow."

Aiden walked into the shadows, but stopped to watch her drive away. Even if Britt gave him all the answers he wanted tomorrow, he still couldn't leave her.

Not just because he liked her, but because he knew Jason Wallace would find her. If Wallace was now harming those the Warriors and Druids cared about, then it was imperative Britt be safe.

How he was going to do that, he didn't know. Aiden was sure she wouldn't enjoy being shut away in a castle. But how else to keep her away from Wallace?

CHAPTER
SIXTEEN

CHAPTER SIXTEEN

Ramsey skidded to a halt beside Broc as they took in the destruction of what used to be a cabin. "Shite."

"Charon!" Phelan yelled as he rushed past them.

The group hurried to Phelan, who knelt beside an unmoving Charon.

"Let me," Isla said, and crouched on the other side of Charon.

Ramsey may not have healing magic, but his magic was potent, and he would eagerly lend it to the other Druids if they needed him.

By the look of blood coating Charon, he had fought Wallace. It just hadn't been enough. Why couldn't Charon have waited for them? There hadn't been a need to sacrifice himself, not when he was a necessity for the battle to come.

Because Ramsey knew there would be a battle. And it would be one that could very well end them all.

Fallon squeezed his eyes shut a second before he asked, "Isla, is he—?"

Before Isla could answer, Phelan gave Charon a hard shake, his jaw clenched. "Wake up, damn you."

It was odd to see Phelan so emotional. Ramsey knew he and Charon had formed a friendship, but since Phelan was a wanderer, no one realized just how deep that friendship went until that moment.

Ramsey looked at Hayden, each of them understanding the pain cutting through Phelan. They had felt such an ache with the loss of Duncan. Their anguish was nothing compared to Ian's, however, since he hadn't just lost a friend in Duncan, he'd lost his twin.

They had all sacrificed so much. Ramsey never wanted to lose another Warrior. After surviving the unbinding of their gods, the horrors of Deirdre's mountain, and then gaining control over their gods, the bonds binding the Warriors were strong.

And when one of those bonds was severed . . .

Ramsey's thought ceased when Charon's eyes suddenly opened.

"Laura," he whispered before he sat up.

Charon looked around, not understanding why his cabin was in shreds all around him. He barely took notice of his friends as he gained his feet and called for Laura again.

"What the hell happened?" Fallon asked.

Charon didn't want to take the precious few moments to tell him. "Jason Wallace."

"Phelan told us that much," Ian said.

Charon went to body after body on the ground, but none of them was Laura. Panic began to set in. "Laura!"

"She's no' here," Phelan said as he moved debris. "She's gone."

"I told her to leave. I told her to run." Charon looked in the direction she would have gone. He had to find her before Wallace did.

Jason's threats, his taunts of hurting Laura sent his blood to boiling.

"Charon!" Ramsey shouted near him.

He spun around to find the others staring at him. Charon's gaze ran over each of them, noting the concern and worry clouding their eyes.

"I have to find Laura. Jason is after her. He wants to hurt her."

Broc immediately closed his eyes. Charon waited tensely for Broc to find her, but minutes went by with nothing.

Finally, Broc opened his eyes, his lips pressed tight. "I can no' find her. There's something blocking my power."

"We need to know what happened," Larena said calmly.

Gwynn gave a solemn nod and smoothed back her hair behind her ears. "To find Laura, Charon. Please."

He blew out a harsh breath. "I tried to lead them away from her, but somehow Jason knew she was at the cabin. As soon as I discovered that, I came here. When I built the cabin, I built a trapdoor in the floor that led out to a ladder down the mountain. It's hidden. I told her to use it and run. I promised I'd find her."

"That explains why Laura isna here," Phelan said. "It doesna explain why there are dead *droughs* and your cabin is in splinters."

Charon looked down at his chest and slowly ran his hand where Wallace had poured his *drough* blood into his wounds. "I came out to distract Jason so Laura could get away. I knew she'd see me, and I knew I didna stand a chance with the *droughs*."

"But you wanted to give her a chance," Isla whispered.

Charon nodded, silently searching for any hint of *drough* magic so he could find out which way Jason and his group went. But there was nothing.

"Jason admitted he wanted to torture Laura to make me suffer. He plans that for all of us. It isna enough to kill us. He wants us to suffer."

Lucan kicked a board at his feet and mumbled, "Shite."

"Why did Wallace no' kill you?" Logan asked.

Charon gave a slight shake of his head. "That's just it, Logan. He did, or he was. That big brute of a Warrior, Dale, and I fought. Jason didna allow that for long before he used his magic and pinned me as Dale sliced me open. Then Jason cut himself to use his blood to kill me."

He could still feel the agony of the *drough* blood touching his wounds. It had been like a nightmare, the pain unending. The sheer agony of it growing until only one thought remained—*Laura*.

"I don't understand," Gwynn said. "Shouldn't you be dead?"

Charon snorted. "And my cabin should still be standing."

"You doona remember anything?" Ian asked.

He started to say no when he paused. "There was an explosion of some sort. Then . . . nothing."

"Jason didna have a need to blow up the cabin," Lucan said.

Fallon nodded grimly. "Who would?"

Logan bent to place his hand on the ground. "Despite the magic Jason used here, as well as the dead *droughs,* I feel no magic present. No' even from Gwynn or Isla."

"And I can no' seem to use my power," Broc added.

Charon had heard enough. "I have to find Laura before Jason does. She shouldna be a part of this war. She's no' a Druid. He only wants to hurt her to get to me. I willna allow that to happen."

"Let's find her," Phelan said as he moved to stand behind him.

Fallon looked at one of the dead *droughs.* "I need to get Isla and Gwynn back to the castle, and then contact Quinn immediately so he can get Aiden out of Edinburgh. Since I've been trying to jump back to the castle for a few minutes now, I think whatever happened is affecting all of our powers."

"And my magic," Isla said.

Gwynn glanced at Logan. "Mine as well."

"I need to get the girls away from this area in order to use my power," Fallon said. "At least I hope it's the area. Who knows what that explosion really did."

"Or who did it," Phelan said. "If Wallace had that kind of power, he'd have used it before."

Ramsey looked around before meeting Charon's gaze. "Was the explosion aimed at you or Wallace?"

"Why do you ask that?" Charon demanded.

Ramsey pointed to the cabin. "It came from within the cabin."

"The only thing in that cabin was Laura before she climbed through the trapdoor. I wouldna have left her inside if there was anything that could've harmed her."

"Nay, you wouldna have," Phelan said.

Logan cut his hand through the air. "We can figure out what was inside the cabin later, after we're able to use our power and the Druids can use their magic."

"Aye. Everyone needs to be at the castle," Charon agreed. "Get anyone who might be acquainted with any of you safe. Jason will strike at anyone to draw us out."

Ramsey said, "I'm staying to help search for Laura."

"Me as well," Broc said. "Whatever is preventing my power willna last forever."

Lucan grinned. "Count me in."

Ian met Charon's gaze in an unspoken agreement.

"The rest of us will set up patrols at the castle," Logan stated.

Fallon glanced at Larena. "That's after we get Galen, Quinn, and Aiden back to the castle."

With a nod to Fallon, Charon started off in the direction Laura should have gone. It didn't take long to find the broken twigs and bent stalks of plants from someone who had fallen upon them.

"It's Laura," Phelan said from a short way ahead.

Charon went to Phelan and spotted the print of Laura's hiking boot. "Aye. She did get away. She shouldna be that far ahead of us."

"Nay, but others are following her as well," Ramsey said as he knelt beside another print.

Lucan examined the track. "It's big and deep. I'm guessing they sent Dale after her."

"No' just Dale," Ian said. "I've found at least six different tracks. I think they're all hunting her."

Charon was grateful the others were with him. He still didn't understand why he wasn't dead. He'd felt his organs begin to shut down from the *drough* blood. Yet, somehow he'd been healed in a mere moment.

How when Phelan's blood hadn't been able to heal him

from the previous attack? There was a different kind of magic at work, one they had never experienced before.

They followed Laura's tracks as long as they could until the trail disappeared. They were about a mile from the cabin, and Broc's power still didn't work.

The Warrior wasn't at all happy, and neither was Charon. If Broc could use his power, they could find Laura in a matter of minutes and get her away from Jason.

It felt almost as if something were standing in their way, preventing him from finding Laura.

And for once Charon didn't think it was Wallace.

The stitch in Laura's side brought her to a halt. She struggled to breathe past the pain, all the while her mind was urging her to run.

She grabbed her side and bent over, gulping in air to try to calm her racing heart as she rested. The sun was nearly above her, but it was difficult to see with all the trees and cloud cover, so she had no idea which way she was going.

But she had to keep moving. That was her only choice as she waited for Phelan to find her. Somehow.

The image of Charon lying on the ground flashed in her mind. Laura couldn't believe he was dead. She should've listened to him instead of fighting him when he wanted to send her away.

He might still be alive if she hadn't let her pride get in her way. So what if he had been repeating the actions of her family, he had been doing it to save her life, not trying to run it.

How could she have been so stupid, so foolish? Her actions had cost a good man his life.

Or was he a man? Charon appeared to be a man, but whatever he had turned into was certainly more than just a man. He'd moved with supernatural speed, and he'd been able to heal.

That gave her pause. She had seen his wounds heal. There might be a chance he wasn't dead. But then she remembered the explosion, the way she had somehow obliterated everything.

No, she was alone now while some psycho with magic chased her. Even if she knew how to blow something up again, she wouldn't chance it since she could harm innocents in the process.

The stitch eased enough that Laura began to run again. She wasn't moving as quick as before, but she was moving. She kept as quiet as she could, though it sounded to her like her breathing could be heard all over Scotland.

She was sure that at any moment Jason Wallace and his group would jump out at her, but somehow they didn't. Laura didn't question her fortune, just kept running.

When she came to a stream, she rested again and drank deeply. Her stomach growled with hunger. She hadn't eaten anything since the awful date with Ben.

Had that really happened only the night before? It seemed years ago. Perhaps because her life had changed so much in the hours afterward.

The shade from the oaks and pine cast shadows over the water, the sound of the gurgling stream easing some of her weariness.

It was so beautiful in the forest, so peaceful and wild that it almost felt as if she were in another world. Is that why Charon always sought the solace of the woods?

She took another drink of water, and once more started running. No matter how she tried, she couldn't stop thinking of Charon.

Maybe she should have stayed and seen to him. She could have hidden so Jason and the others couldn't find her. If only she'd been brave enough to stand her ground instead of hurrying away.

Each time she began to think about the explosion and the feeling that had coursed through her body, she immediately turned her thoughts to something else.

Laura wasn't ready to think about what she had done or how. It was too scary for her mind to comprehend all of it. She wanted to deny she caused the blast, but she knew the blame lay squarely on her shoulders.

Instead, she kept jogging over hills and through valleys.

Occasionally she'd stop by a stream to drink and rest, but hour after hour, she kept moving.

"Dang it," she muttered when she tripped over a root and raised her hands to stop her face from slamming into the ground when she pitched forward.

Laura tried to make herself get up and keep moving, but her body was exhausted. She managed to sit up, then lean back against the trunk of a pine.

The light filtering through the thick canopy of limbs dimmed the sunlight. The summer sun wouldn't officially set until around midnight, but it was well into evening. Sounds she hadn't heard in the forest before grew louder. If she hadn't been so tired, she might have been frightened.

As it was, she couldn't keep her eyes open. That didn't stop the same swell of emotion to begin within her again. It was the same feeling, the same swirling of something bright and powerful that happened at the cabin.

Her skin felt stretched, her body pulled in a thousand different directions. Laura slammed her palms onto the ground and focused on keeping herself calm and breathing evenly so as not to blow anything up and alert Jason to where she was.

Every time the bright swirling mass felt as if it were going to shatter her, she pushed it through her palms and out of her body.

She was just drifting off to sleep when she heard the steady beat of distant drums.

And the beautiful chanting that seemed to call, to beckon.

"Laura . . ."

CHAPTER
SEVENTEEN

"Nay," Aiden repeated for the fourth time. "We're close. Give Britt a few more days."

Quinn slammed his hand onto his thigh as he sat at the tiny table in the even smaller hotel room. "Did you hear nothing your uncle said?"

Aiden looked at Fallon and nodded. "I heard every word. I also saw what the *drough* blood Jason is using does to you Warriors. I'd rather risk my life to learn the answers than see any of you suffer as Charon and Malcolm did this last time."

Before Sonya's healing magic had been able to work. That along with the other Warriors using their blood. But this last time with Jason Wallace, something had changed.

It had shaken Aiden to his core. He'd taken for granted his father's immortality and ability to heal. He'd also taken for granted the magic of the Druids. He couldn't do that anymore.

"Aiden," Fallon began.

But Aiden held up a hand to stop him as he turned and looked at his father. "I've kept Britt separated from every-one. I've also made her promise no' to tell a soul what she's working on."

"Do you actually think she'll keep that promise?" Quinn asked.

"I do."

Quinn growled as he scrunched up his face. "You're confusing lust with truth."

"I need you to trust me on this."

"Do you know what would happen to me and your mother if we lost you? It'd destroy us."

Aiden stared into the same dark green eyes as his own and said, "And how do you think I'd feel if I lost you? This war we're fighting has already taken casualties. Jason Wallace willna stop, and he's upped the game. We need to do the same."

"I hate to agree with the lad, but I do," Galen said from the door, where he lounged against the wall.

Aiden hadn't even heard him come into the hotel room. Still, he wasn't sure his argument would win against his father and uncle. And even though Galen wasn't technically blood, he'd grown up calling every Warrior in the castle uncle, and every Druid aunt.

Family was family, and Aiden was happy to have Galen's support.

"Damn," Fallon said as he turned away to sit on the end of the bed. "Quinn, your son has a valid argument. Arran told me how close we were to losing Charon. And Larena . . ."

Aiden swallowed past the lump in his throat as he thought of Fallon's wife. Larena had died, but somehow—through the magic or Warrior blood given to her—she miraculously came back to them.

"I doona want you to go through that," Fallon continued after clearing his throat. "I doona want any of us to go through that."

Galen glanced out the window of their hotel, which just happened to be across from Britt's flat. He grabbed an empty chair and moved it near the door before he sank onto it. "We can no longer count on the magic of the Druids or our own blood to save each other if we're hit with *drough* blood. We need to have another plan."

Aiden watched his father as he stood with his hands braced on the small table, his head hanging down. For long, tense moments Quinn stood quietly as the rest of them watched.

Finally, Quinn lifted his head and straightened. He caught Aiden's gaze and said, "All right. You've all made your points, but if we're going to do this, we do this the right way."

"Which is?" Fallon asked.

"We stay close to Aiden and Britt at all times. Wallace has shown he can strike when least expected. I refuse to return to Marcail and tell her we've lost our son."

"Agreed," Galen said. "I've already spoken to Reaghan, and she thinks we have to keep an eye on Britt even if we leave tonight."

Aiden was relieved in his father's decision, but he knew things had gotten more complicated for them all.

"Britt needs to know everything." Aiden didn't break when three pairs of eyes pinned him.

"Why?" was all Quinn asked.

Aiden moved to sit in the chair opposite Galen. "She's been asking since I first began working with her. The more she knows, the more she might be able to tell us. Not to mention, it would help her work more efficiently and faster."

"It would also help if we had some *drough* blood," Fallon stated.

Galen smirked. "Shall I go pay Wallace a visit to see if he'll give us a pint?"

They all shared a laugh, but it quickly died.

"I know this is a difficult situation," Aiden said. "No one but Druids and Warriors are supposed to know about us, but Jason has begun to use mortals. We doona have any other choice but to do the same. This is their war, too, even if they doona know it."

Quinn folded his arms over his chest as he straightened. "Aye, but we're the only ones losing people."

"Whatever happened today, Wallace lost four *droughs*," Fallon said. "Druids are no' easy to find anymore. He willna be able to replace them quickly."

Galen leaned forward and put his forearms on his knees. "How is Charon holding up?"

"No' well," Fallon said with a long sigh. "He's focused on finding Laura, but he's rattled about Jason using her."

Quinn dropped his arms and leaned back against the wall. "That's twice in a matter of weeks Charon's had *drough* blood inside him. I recall all too clearly what that felt like."

"It's hell," Galen stated.

Fallon's lips flattened. "And the *drough* blood Jason is using does more damage to us than anything before. I can no' imagine what Charon went through either time."

"Or how it affected him," Aiden said. The three Warriors looked at him, causing Arran to shrug. "No' a single one of you asked how he or Malcolm were doing."

Quinn's forehead creased in a deep frown. "We did, Aiden. Both men said they were doing fine."

"And I'll bet any amount of magic that both are lying. How much blood was Charon given by the other Warriors in his wounds? Phelan, whose blood is able to heal any type of injury, wouldna even work to revive Charon. There is something more going on than just more pain."

"Oh, fuck," Galen murmured.

Fallon stood and gave Aiden a quick hug. "Work fast, lad. Wallace's attention is on Laura and Charon. Doona give him a reason to come here. No' yet, at least."

"Be safe," Aiden told his uncle before Fallon teleported out of the room.

Quinn pushed away from the wall and strode to the door. "I think it's time I did another check around Britt's flat."

Aiden waited until his father was gone before he sank onto the bed and dropped his head into his hands.

"You're doing the right thing," Galen said. "It's hard, I know, but staying here is the right call, lad."

"Is it? I've put Britt's life in danger. I'm keeping you and my father away from your wives."

There was a creak as Galen shifted in the chair. "Aiden, when will you learn that as Warriors, we do whatever is needed to keep the ones we love safe? Reaghan understands this, as does your mother."

Aiden lifted his head and looked at Galen.

"Besides, you needed this. Just as you need Britt. Doona think we have no' noticed how you look at her. Take my advice, lad, and doona let happiness slip through your fingers."

Aiden looked out the window to Britt's flat and saw her shadow walk past her window. All he could think about was her. Her smile, her amazing blue eyes, and that wealth of golden hair.

"Nay. I willna let it slip through my fingers."

Laura smiled and wrapped her arms around Charon. His hands were on her body, touching her as only he could. His weight shifted atop her as the blunt head of his arousal sought entry into her body.

She had waited for him for so long, but finally he was hers to caress, to hold.

His body rocked over hers, the long length of his cock sliding deep within her. She moaned, her hands tightening on his back.

He whispered her name, soft and seductively. She opened her eyes and his dark gaze caught hers as he thrust again and again inside her.

The climax was close. Each stroke from Charon sent her hurtling toward release until it . . .

Laura gasped as she jerked awake. She scanned the forest, thankful that the sun had risen again. Her body still hummed from the delicious, erotic dream she'd been having.

But it was just a dream. As much as she wanted it to be real, Charon wasn't with her.

"Oh, Charon," she whispered as she slumped back against the tree.

Another sound to her left got her attention, and she knew whatever it was had woken her out of her good dream for a reason. For several heartbeats she waited, listening, but didn't see or hear anything else.

Something brushed against the back of her hand, and she looked down to see flowers had sprung up between her fingers and all around her palms that were still flat on the ground.

Laura jumped to her feet as she stared at the two patches of wildflowers that hadn't been there when she stopped the night before.

She glanced at her hands. "What the bloody hell is going on?"

The sound of a twig breaking had her swinging her head in that direction. The sound came from the same path she'd traveled yesterday.

She wanted to think it might be Phelan, but Phelan wouldn't be sneaking around. He would be looking for her, possibly calling her name.

Unless he knew she was being tracked by Jason and the others.

"Bugger it," she whispered.

Did she stay and see who it was? Did she chance being found by Wallace? Or did she run again?

Fear won out.

Laura moved as silently and quickly as she could through the woods. Sunlight broke through the branches of the trees, leaving many shady spots where someone could hide.

She was passing just such a spot when someone stepped in front of her.

"Ow," she said as she barreled into them.

Huge hands wrapped around her arms and she found herself staring up at the face of the man who had battled Charon. The same man whose skin had been a pale green. Her mouth gaped open, and she struggled to get away but he held her easily.

There was no excitement in his gaze at capturing her, only cold acceptance of how things were. Which made Laura's stomach plummet to her feet.

Because where this brute was, Jason wasn't far behind.

"Well, well, well," Jason Wallace said as he stepped out

from behind the man holding her. "Did you snare something, Dale?"

Laura struggled again to get loose, but Dale's hold didn't relent. He kept a firm grip on her, not too tight to hurt her, but not loose enough that she could break free.

"Did Charon tell you that you were a Druid?"

Jason's question stilled her. Laura looked into his chilly blue eyes. What had he just said? Surely he was wrong. "What are you talking about?"

"You're a Druid, Laura. Charon knew all along, but he used his power to tamp down your magic."

She frowned, not believing a word he was saying. "You're lying."

"Do you deny that you were the one who blew up the cabin?"

"I don't have magic," she repeated, hoping it was true, because she couldn't add that to her growing list of problems. And neither denying nor admitting to blowing up the cabin was her best bet.

Jason laughed. "Oh, but you do. You doona seemed shocked at hearing about Druids. I'm guessing because Charon told you about us, right?"

She refused to answer, which only made Jason smile. Laura wanted to slap that smirk off his face. He'd hurt Charon—twice—hunted her, and did only God knew what else.

"I see I'm correct about him telling you of Druids," Jason said with a grin. "Did he tell you what he is? Did he tell you he's a Warrior with a primeval god inside him? Did he tell you he was evil?"

Laura numbly moved her head side to side.

"Ah, then I suppose he didna bother to tell you he's the bad guy in all of this? I had Ben find you, dear Laura, to save you from Charon."

She wanted to scream for him to stop, to claw out his eyes. But mostly she wanted Charon to come for her.

"Ben wasn't there to help me. He hurt me," she said, and showed him the bruise on her cheek.

Jason shrugged and rolled up the sleeves of his dress shirt. "Ben, unfortunately, got passionate in his zeal to get you away from Charon. But regardless. You are a Druid."

"I'd know if I was a Druid." She didn't want to listen to him. His words were like poison infecting her brain.

Or were they?

"You've heard the chanting and drums, have you no'?" Jason asked.

Laura squeezed her eyes closed.

"That's the ancients calling to you, Laura. Let them in. Let them show you what your magic can do."

"You're evil," she said as her eyes flew open. "You wanted to kill me. I heard what you told Charon."

Jason scratched his chin. "When you're dealing with evil, a person will say anything to get a rise out of them. Charon and the other Warriors from MacLeod Castle are a bane upon this earth. They're immortal creatures, but they can be killed. By *drough* blood."

"*Droughs* are evil. They use black magic," Laura repeated Charon's words.

Jason tsked softly. "Sweet Laura, I see Charon has told you wrong once more. It's the *mies* who are evil. They are the ones who use black magic. The *droughs* are the good ones in this war we've been fighting for centuries. I'm no' the first to fight the Warriors, but I'll be the last. I'll be the one who kills them once and for all."

Laura looked at Dale, who watched her with no emotion on his face. His bald head and dark goatee gave him a sinister look.

"You have a Warrior working with you," she pointed out.

"I do," Jason said. "He wants to undo what has been done to him, so he's helping me."

She shook her head, feeling . . . peculiar. It was almost as if someone were in her mind, pushing this way and that.

Laura gave her head another shake and fought to hold on to thoughts of Charon, of all the good he had done for Ferness and the people. How could she believe what Jason said when Charon was willing to sacrifice himself for her? Nothing evil would do that.

"Evil never looks like we expect," Jason said, as if reading her mind. "They are beautiful, gorgeous creatures who worm their way into our lives and trick us. You've been tricked, Laura. Let me show you the way," Jason said as he held out his hand for her.

CHAPTER EIGHTEEN

Near Inverness

Malcolm stood on the shore of Loch Ness and watched the tourist boats leave the dock, the announcer's voice blaring over the speakers while the water amplified the sound.

But Malcolm didn't need the aid of the water to hear the voice. He was able to do that all on his own, thanks to the god inside him.

He squatted and dipped his fingers in the cool water. Loch Ness had always been dark. The stories of some creature living in the depths had been around long before Malcolm ever entered this world.

"Are they true, though?" he murmured.

The stories his nurse had told him of Druids and Warriors were meant to frighten him and keep him on the path of good. But they had been truth.

Well, partly. His old nurse hadn't known the entire truth. Yet all stories originated somewhere. It left him wondering if there was a Nessie, and if she felt as out of place as he did.

Malcolm slowly released a deep breath as his mobile phone rang. He knew without looking that it was Larena who called.

His cousin liked to check up on him. He didn't have the heart to ask her to stop. Every time he spoke to her, she begged him to return to MacLeod Castle and once more be a part of the family of Warriors and Druids there.

Larena didn't understand that he couldn't. Just being within those ancient stone walls made him feel as if his skin were ripping at the seams.

It wasn't the potent magic of the Druids. It wasn't the Warriors and their power.

It was what he had done while in service to Deirdre.

The man he'd been, the one who had sacrificed his very lands to protect Larena, was gone. He was a distant memory, and one that faded every day.

Malcolm looked down at his hand. It would take the briefest of thoughts to have his claws shoot from his fingers. The deep burgundy his god favored hid the stain of blood, but Malcolm knew it was there.

He had killed Duncan. Deirdre had commanded it, and Malcolm hadn't hesitated. He'd expected Duncan's twin, Ian, to exact his revenge. It was his due.

But Ian had forgiven Malcolm.

Malcolm ran his hand through his hair as he straightened. Forgiveness. He didn't deserve it, hadn't sought it out, but those at the castle had given it to him freely.

How did he tell them it didn't matter? He felt nothing anymore. Not remorse, happiness. Not even hope.

His phone rang again. Malcolm answered the mobile with a tired, "Hello?"

"Thank God you answered," Larena's voice said through the phone. "I've news on Jason."

Malcolm stood gazing at the loch as Larena filled him in on Laura and Charon. There was an odd note to her voice, but he attributed it to Wallace.

When she finished he said, "What do you want me to do?"

There was a pause before she said, "I don't want you to do anything. I wanted to let you know what Jason was up to. He's likely to target all of us."

"No doubt he'll try."

"Malcolm, where are you?"

He looked over the rippling waters of the loch. "Does it matter?"

"I worry about you."

"I ken, Larena, but you need to stop. I've given my word that I'll help in taking down Wallace."

"But you don't want to be with us in the meantime."

He hated the sadness he heard in her voice. He was staying away to keep what he had become from her. If Larena realized he was dead inside, she'd make it her mission to fix him. And there was no way to repair him.

"It's better this way," he said. "Trust me."

"I do. You know that. I just . . . I miss you, Malcolm. I need you here."

Her words tugged at his heart, and the old Malcolm would have immediately gone to her. "Keep me posted on Wallace. I'm no' far from Ferness. I'm here if Charon needs any help."

For several minutes they sat in silence. Malcolm knew there was more Larena wanted to say, and she was struggling to find the right words.

"Arran and Ronnie finished the sketch of the necklace as it was described in the ledger from the dig site," Larena said.

Malcolm wondered how long it would take Arran and his woman to get the sketch right. Within that necklace lay the spell to bind the gods inside all Warriors forever.

"It doesn't match the one from the Web site Gwynn found talking about Druids," Larena said into the silence.

"That's too bad."

Fallon and the others were searching desperately for the necklace, but Malcolm wasn't sure they would use the spell even if they found it. How could they battle evil such as Jason Wallace as humans?

"Any leads?" Malcolm asked the expected words.

"Gwynn scanned the drawing into the computer yesterday, but so far nothing has come up in her search."

Malcolm watched another tourist boat pass. "I doona believe you'll find it. Whoever transferred the spell into the necklace, and then hid it, knew how important it was. It might have stayed buried for thousands of years in that chamber, but I wager whoever took it also knew what it was."

"So you don't think we'll find it?"

"Nay," he answered. "I think it's something being kept safely guarded. Ronnie's ability to find magical objects might bring you to it. Have you asked her?"

"She's tried. So far nothing."

Malcolm knew how important it was for Larena to have children. It's all she had ever talked about. She and Fallon had held off having children because of the battle with evil they waged.

"We'll find the spell, Larena. You and Fallon will have the children you want."

She sniffed through the phone. "I'm not so sure anymore. I can't even bring up the idea of babies to Fallon since . . ."

Her voice trailed away, but Malcolm knew all too well she was referring to the night she died. He hadn't been at the castle, but one look at Fallon's face when they met at Wallace Mansion to attack had told Malcolm everything.

"I still remember the first time you saw Fallon," he said. It had been at Edinburgh Castle four hundred years earlier, when Larena was hiding the fact she was a Warrior.

Larena laughed softly. "He hadn't wanted to talk to me."

"You just had to get his attention. I didna agree with you sneaking into his chamber to do it, however."

"Ah, but it worked."

Malcolm turned his back to Loch Ness, "I knew Fallon loved you before he did. All I had to do was look at him as he watched you. It was there on his face. Even then, he would've done anything for you."

"I know," Larena replied softly. "I want you to have that same happiness."

"Keep me informed of what's going on with Charon," he said, and ended the call before Larena could say more.

She meant well, but he didn't want to hear how she wanted him to find someone and fall in love. Love. How could he care for someone when he had nothing inside him?

He was empty, his soul drained of everything good that he'd been.

What kind of woman would want someone like him?

The break of the new day only drove Charon harder. He had the unshakable feeling Jason had already found Laura.

During the brief darkness of their summer nights, Broc had taken to the skies and searched for Laura, to no avail. Charon wasn't the only one who was disappointed. Broc wasn't handling it well that his power had failed them.

Broc folded his giant indigo wings and crossed his arms over his bare chest. "There's something going on here."

Charon's gaze searched the thick woods around them. "Aye. I know Laura had to stop and rest. We should've caught up with her by now."

"Should have," Ramsey said.

Phelan gave a short whistle that had the others rushing to his side. "Look," Phelan said to Charon as he pointed to the ground.

"That's Laura's boot print," Lucan said.

Charon's stomach tightened with dread. "With several others all around it. They found her." Just as he'd feared.

The realization slammed into him like a truck. He had known it, but the truth staring him in the face made him ill.

"Wait," Ramsey said. "I've found more of Laura's tracks, and she's alone."

Charon rushed to see what Ramsey found. Elation erupted through him as they began to follow her tracks. For the next forty minutes, they pursued her trail, lost it, and found it again numerous times.

He wanted out call out to Laura, but since they didn't know if Jason and the *droughs* were still around, Charon couldn't chance it.

"We'll find her," Phelan said from beside him.

Charon nodded, unease beginning to creep up on him again.

He was the first to see the tree with the flowers blooming in bright vibrant colors at its base. Laura's trail led right to the tree, but the flowers were out of place in the deep shadows.

Ramsey knelt on one knee and peered close at the flowers. "Magic did this. *Mie* magic," he said, and turned his head to Charon.

"Laura has no magic," Charon said.

Lucan leaned a hand upon the pine as he looked at the flowers. "Are you sure?"

"I'd know. I looked for it often enough," he grumbled.

"Someone blew up your cabin," Phelan said.

Broc's wings shifted, his lips pulled back in a scowl. "Someone is also preventing us from using our power. I doona like it."

Charon ran a hand down his face. "I've known Laura for two years. No' once did I ever feel magic from her. She's no' a Druid."

"Oh, shite," Lucan said, and backed up a few steps. "Laura had visitors."

Phelan gaze lifted to Charon filled with regret. "Lots of visitors. And by the looks of it, Laura left with them willingly."

Charon couldn't believe it. Wouldn't believe it. Laura knew how dangerous Jason was. He had told her. Why would she go with him?

There was a gust as Broc jumped into the air and his wings caught the wind. He maneuvered through the limbs until he soared above the trees, his body skimming the top branches.

It was a huge chance he took taking flight in the middle of the day when a mortal might see him. Charon stilled, waiting, hoping that Broc found Laura.

Suddenly Broc dived between trees and swooped to land in front of Charon. His face was set in hard lines as he shoved his blond hair out of his eyes. "I found her."

Charon released the breath he hadn't known he was holding, a smile forming. He'd be happy once she was back in his arms.

"She's with Jason."

The smile died instantly. Charon swallowed, his mind racing with possibilities as he met Broc's gaze. He knew the depravity that Jason could do. Charon wouldn't leave Laura to suffer that alone.

He'd known there was a chance he'd have to fight Wallace again to get Laura free. And he was prepared for that.

Charon walked around Broc to head in the direction the Warrior had flown. He hadn't taken two steps before Phelan blocked his way.

"Where are you going?" Phelan demanded.

"To get Laura."

A half smile pulled at one side of Phelan's lips. "Good. I'm coming with you."

"We all are," Ramsey said.

Charon turned to look at Ramsey, Lucan, Ian, and Broc. "Nay. You four have wives. Go home to them. Protect them. Who knows when Jason will strike next."

"You can no' do this alone," Lucan said.

"We willna let you," Ian added.

Charon cursed and began to pace.

"You know it's a trap," Phelan stated as he held up a hand and let his claws elongate one finger at a time. "Jason expects you to come for Laura, and when you do, he'll kill you."

Charon halted and leaned his head back to look at the sky through the thick branches above. "Aye. I know."

"And you would walk into such a trap?" Lucan asked.

Charon lowered his head and glanced at Phelan. Only he knew the depth of Charon's feelings for Laura, or as much as Phelan could guess.

"Laura is my responsibility. I vowed to keep her safe. I promised her Jason wouldna harm her."

Phelan leered, the need for blood shining in his blue-gray eyes. "Then we get Laura back."

CHAPTER NINETEEN

Aisley followed behind Laura Black. She was surprised the *mie* had believed the lies Jason told her, but then again, Jason could be very convincing when he wanted to be. She had firsthand knowledge of that.

But Aisley also had a sneaking suspicious Jason used magic when Laura didn't immediately believe him. Jason was predictable when it came to using his magic.

"What is it?" Mindy asked mockingly as she waited for Aisley to catch up with her.

Aisley didn't so much as glance at her hated nemesis. Mindy thought she was a rare beauty, but the thick coating of makeup and the bright red nails and lipstick did nothing to help her pallid complexion.

"Try a new shade of lipstick. That one makes you look like a damned vampire," Aisley said.

Mindy gave a gasp of fury and sank her nails into Aisley's arm. "How dare you talk to me that way. Do you know what I mean to Jason?"

"Oh, I know," she replied, fighting the urge to gather magic in her palm and slam it into Mindy for touching her.

Mindy pushed her nails farther into her skin, but Aisley refused to show any emotion. If she did, Mindy would win, and that couldn't happen.

"What's that supposed to mean?" Mindy demanded.

Aisley shrugged her other shoulder. "Let it mean whatever you want it to mean, I really don't give a shit."

"Keep it up," Mindy said with a malevolent smile as she leaned close. "I see the way Jason looks at you. You're a liability. You've only stayed around this long because you're family."

"I've seen what Jason does to family, Mindy, and that's not why he keeps me around."

Mindy's black eyes narrowed. She pulled Aisley to a halt and leaned in close. "Explain yourself."

"Ask Jason. I'm sure he'd enjoy telling you how he killed my family."

"Then why not kill you?"

Because I was foolish enough—and desperate enough—to believe him. "I've no doubt he's getting to that very soon. But not before I take you out."

Mindy shoved her away hard and stormed off. Aisley bit back a smile when Mindy rushed to Jason and began telling him of their conversation.

But what little joy their exchange provided her evaporated when she saw Laura turn and look at her. There was something in the *mie*'s soft green eyes that caused a niggle of apprehension.

Was it the hope that was slowly dying? Or perhaps the knowledge that the truth wasn't easy to discern.

Aisley thought back to the last time she'd clung to hope. It was such a distant memory that it took some time to find it, but when she did, she could hardly recall the girl she'd been.

That girl had been full of life and laughter. The world had been so bright and shiny, and Aisley had known she'd find all her dreams out in that big, beautiful world.

Two months later, everything had changed.

Pain shot through her heart as she recalled those awful times better left buried. And what she had done to her family. Not to mention what her supposed friends had done to her.

Aisley paused beside a tree and leaned her hand upon the

rough bark of the elm. She shut her eyes, hoping to push away the memories. The floodgates had opened, and with them, the dreams she'd once had.

Had she really ever been so naïve, so innocent? Had she really believed she could conquer the world? Had she dared to think after pulling herself out of the gutter that fate would be kind?

Instead, she'd fallen into Hell itself.

She opened her eyes to find she stood near the edge of a cliff. Far below were the jagged rocks rising up from the earth and surrounded by more trees.

Above her, Aisley heard the cry of an osprey, the sound clear and loud. As if it called to her. The wind brushed by her face, its touch feather-light, like a kiss.

She moved around the tree until the ball of one foot hung over the cliff. With one jump, she could end the nightmare that was her life.

No more would Jason be able to hurt her or threaten her. She would no longer have to feel the evil flowing inside or crave the power her black magic gave.

Her soul was destined for Hell anyway. No one would care that she took her own life.

"Aisley."

Dale's deep voice was soft, his tone careful as he whispered her name. She should have known he would be watching.

"What are you doing, lass?"

"Contemplating jumping," she answered.

He moved to stand beside her. "I can jump and live. You can no'."

"That's the point."

There was a beat of silence before he murmured, "Death is no' the answer."

"I made my choices, Dale. I know what awaits me in death. I've seen Satan."

"Did you enjoy him so much, you want to hasten to get to him?"

She jerked her head to him and frowned. "No."

"Then doona jump."

"And do what? Continue with this life of hell?"

Dale glanced away as he rubbed a palm over his bald head. "I'm here. I can help you."

"Why?"

"You really doona know, do you?"

Aisley looked away, uncomfortable with the way Dale was looking at her, as if she were a prize just out of reach. "You'd be wise to consider who I am."

"I know who you are. It's why I willna allow you to fall to your death."

She drew in a shaky breath. It had been a long time since someone showed concern for her. She hadn't realized how much she missed that connection until Dale had given it to her.

"I won't jump. Today," she said, and turned away from the cliff.

It didn't take long for her and Dale to catch back up with the others. Jason was moving slowly through the forest, as if he wanted Charon and the other Warriors to catch them.

Aisley once more found Laura's green gaze on her, and she wondered how long someone like Laura would last once Jason got his hooks in her.

Laura saw the woman with the black hair and dark eyes rejoin the group. She was tall and solemn. But it was obvious by the way Jason watched her that she was important. Laura just didn't know how.

"You'd do well not to let him find you staring."

Laura jerked in surprise to find the woman standing beside her. Her eyes were a pale brown, direct and penetrating. Her mane of glossy black hair was pulled back in a high ponytail to hang past her shoulders. The woman wore her jeans, formfitting black shirt, and boots as a model would—to perfection.

"Why?" Laura asked.

The woman cut her gaze to Jason before she looked back

at her. "I'm Aisley. I'm also cousin to Jason, so when I tell you to watch yourself, you might want to heed my words. I've seen his viciousness firsthand."

"Why help me?"

Aisley gave a little snort. "Damned if I know."

"Who is the woman beside Jason?"

"Ah. That's Mindy, his lover. She's a bitch, so be prepared for her cruelty."

Laura stepped over a fallen tree. "Is what Jason told me the truth? Are *droughs* really the good Druids?"

Aisley paused too long before she replied in a choked whisper, "Yes."

Laura thought back to how Charon had gone to confront Jason so she could get away. He hadn't caged her, hadn't kidnapped her. Yet Jason had tried to kidnap her, and she imagined that if she tried to leave now, he wouldn't let her.

Who was the villain?

Charon had secrets, secrets he went to great lengths to conceal, but was she any worse by keeping her past and what her family had done to her a secret?

Was that enough to condemn Charon as a villain?

Two years with the man, and she'd given him her absolute trust. She'd given him her body. Not once had she ever doubted him. Why, then, did she now?

No matter how much she wanted to doubt Jason's words, for some reason, she couldn't. Every time she tried, her mind told her he was right and Charon had lied.

Laura had so little information she wasn't sure who to trust. Druids and Warriors. Magic and power. How was it they were in her world and she'd never known about them?

More importantly, how was she a Druid and hadn't known about it?

Her controlling family popped into her head, and Laura inwardly grimaced. If they could see her now, they would say she should have let them run her life and she wouldn't be in such a predicament.

Laura was tired of not knowing what to do. She thought

she'd gotten past that when she left her family behind. Now, she found herself in a much more dire situation.

The way the people surrounded her, caging her without chains, made her begin to shake from the memories of her youth.

"Where are we going?"

Aisley kept her gaze straight ahead. "Somewhere Charon will never be able to find you."

If Laura believed all Jason told her, then she would feel better knowing Charon couldn't find her. But all she felt was an overwhelming sense of dread.

For the next fifty yards, she fought against all Jason had told her, and something snapped in her mind. Like a rubber band holding something back, everything became clear.

"I can't," she whispered as she came to a halt.

Aisley stopped and looked at her, a frown marring her forehead. "Can't what?"

"Go with Jason. He did something to my mind, I know it. Whether Charon lied or Jason lied, I need to find out the truth on my own. I don't want to go with Jason."

"It's too late." Aisley glanced to where Jason led them through the trees. When she looked back, there was defeat in her brown eyes. "He'll never let you go."

Her whispered words only propelled Laura to get free that much quicker. She thought of what was inside her, magic or something else, and felt it flow through her veins thick and hot as lava.

It gave her strength and helped to calm her nerves even as they began walking again. She had only one shot to get free, and she needed to make sure it was a good one.

Laura let her magic build and build until her body hummed from it. No one seemed the wiser until the big brute who had fought Charon whispered Aisley's name.

Aisley looked over her shoulder and moved her gaze to Laura. "You'll never make it."

"I'll stay if you can honestly tell me Jason is the good guy here. Tell me he isn't the monster Charon said he is."

Aisley hesitated a second too long, and that's all it took for Laura to make her decision.

She let instinct guide her as she halted and let her magic rise up within her. It swirled around her, in her, through her. The sensation was heady and amazing.

The sheer power of it left her reeling and searching for more. It felt good to be in control, to be the one others might fear.

Because she was tired of people messing with her. It began with her mother locking her in her bedroom, her father refusing to see what was happening, and her sister ruling every second of her life. Then Jason had dared to fiddle with her mind, using his magic to get what he wanted.

No more would she be a stepping-stone. No longer would she be bullied and pushed around.

Her magic—yes, it was magic!—saturated every pore, permeated every particle of her being. The sound of distant drums reached her once more. The chants were softer, the words difficult to make out.

Then, in her mind, she heard a thousand voices scream, *"Now, Laura!"*

She let loose her magic. It was uncontrolled, violent. It was ten times the force that had destroyed Charon's cabin. And it felt glorious!

Her eyes closed before the white light blinded her, but it was the potency of the magic itself that sent her flying backwards.

Laura landed hard on her side, her head slamming into the root of a tree. Through it all, she kept her mind on her magic, on punishing Jason and getting free. She heard a woman scream and men cursing.

Then . . . nothing.

Laura drew in a ragged, broken breath and opened her eyes. Her head pounded, her heart raced. All along her skin, magic sizzled, waiting for her to use it again.

She climbed to her feet and smiled when she surveyed everyone laid out on the ground. When she spotted Jason, she walked to him. She could kill him. It would take just one thought and her magic could do it, but she wasn't a killer.

"Come after me again, and I will kill you," she promised his unconscious form before she turned and ran.

Charon felt the wave of magic that blasted through the forest with the force of a cannon. It made no sound as it sailed through the woods, but he knew instantly who it belonged to. "Laura."

"How the hell is she a Druid?" Phelan asked.

Charon had no idea, but he planned on finding out.

"This way!" Broc shouted as he ran through the trees.

They others easily caught him as six of them moved as silently as ghosts and as quick as the wind. All the while, Charon's heart pounded in his chest as he raced toward Laura. He couldn't wait to hold her in his arms again.

And God help Wallace if he'd laid a hand on her.

This time Charon would tell her everything from beginning to end. After he made love to her again. He should have told her what he was and how the Warriors came to be when she asked.

Maybe then she wouldn't have willingly gone with Jason.

Their story was a secret only Druids and Warriors knew, but it had also been a reason to keep her from seeing him as the beast he was.

How had he not known she was a Druid? Was she so powerful a Druid that she could hide her magic from him? At the moment he didn't care. He just wanted to know she was all right.

Charon jumped across a stream and couldn't help but wonder what Jason had said to convince Laura to go with him. Two years, Charon had known her and never lied. Why hadn't she waited for him as he asked?

As much as that question bothered him, it was her answer he was afraid to hear.

CHAPTER
TWENTY

Laura ran as if the Devil himself were after her. She didn't slow when she slipped and slid down a hill, or when the rain started.

She didn't care that her legs ached and the stitch in her side demanded she stop. All she wanted was to get to Ferness so she could pack a few belongings and get the hell away from Charon and Jason and everyone.

Who was telling the truth? And who was lying?

There was something dark, something evil about Jason that made her run. He'd used magic on her. She didn't know how she knew, only that she did.

Until she could get her mind straightened out, she was better on her own.

Laura ducked beneath a low-hanging limb as she spotted a building through the trees. She didn't want to think of Charon, but she couldn't help it. He was gone, and with him any chance that she might find out the truth.

She could look for Phelan, but why would he tell her anything if Charon hadn't? Trusting anyone now was going to be impossible.

With her clothes soaked and clinging to her, Laura slowed to a walk as she reached the edge of the forest. She had somehow managed to come out of the trees behind the pub.

She strode by Charon's Mercedes, running her fingers along the sleek car as she thought about the last time they were together, before hurrying through a nearby alley. It didn't do her any good to think of Charon. He was gone and unable to help her.

Laura peeked around the corner of the building to see if anyone was about. When no one came in sight, she dashed across the street. She had leaned on Charon too much. She saw that now, now that it was too late and no longer mattered.

She wiped at a tear. Why did he have to die? Why couldn't her magic have killed Jason instead of Charon?

Laura's heart thudded in her chest when she spotted the door to her flat still hung precariously on its hinges. The memory of Ben trying to pull her into the car was one she knew she'd have the rest of her life. Yet it faded in comparison to Charon striding through the door and lifting her in his arms before taking her to safety.

He hadn't wanted anything other than to keep her safe. He'd been gentle, his touch soft, as if he were afraid she might shatter into a million pieces.

And through it all, she felt his rage at what had been done to her.

Laura touched her cheek where the bruise was. Ben hitting her was nothing to what she had endured over the last few hours. Even then she didn't want to think about magic.

It was inside her, flowing through her veins just as her blood did. It pulsed bright as the sun just beneath her skin. Laura had no idea what to do with it, nor did she know how to use it.

Where had her magic been when she'd fought helplessly against her sister and mother? Where had that magic been when Ben had tried to kidnap her?

Was it something that would come and go, or was the magic something she could count on from now on? And did she even want to know?

"Charon, I wish you were here."

Any time she had a question, he always gave her a truthful answer, even if it hadn't been what she wanted to hear.

Had he known she had magic? Was that why he had hired her?

She exhaled and shoved the thought of magic and Charon from her mind as she pushed the door open a crack and stepped inside. Laura turned to her bedroom and stopped in her tracks when she saw her sister standing in front of her.

"Lacy."

Her sister smiled tightly and took a step toward her. "Hello, little sister."

"How did you find me?" Laura demanded.

There was only one reason Lacy tracked her down, and Laura knew it had nothing to do with sibling love and everything to do with controlling her again.

Lacy laughed, the sound too loud in the quiet of the flat. "We've always known where you were, silly goose. We'd have liked you closer to home, but I made things work."

"What are you talking about?" Why was Lacy suddenly there? After two years, why show up now?

There had never been any love lost between the sisters. Lacy was their mother's first child, born when she had been just seventeen and unmarried. Laura hadn't come along until ten years later, after their mother married.

Lacy hadn't been cruel exactly, just controlling like their mother. Or at least that's how Laura had always seen her. Now, however, Laura was seeing her with new eyes, and she didn't like what she saw.

"How did you do it?" Lacy asked, and took another step to her. "How did you get your magic back?"

The room tilted around Laura so that she reached out and grabbed the back of the sofa to keep herself upright. *Magic.* How did everyone know but her? "You knew?"

Lacy rolled her eyes. "Well, of course, we knew. We come from a long line of Druids. But our magic was running out. There was hardly any left to even make a plant grow. Then you were born."

"You knew," Laura repeated, her mind still trying to wrap around the notion that her family had kept what she was from her.

"My perfect, beautiful little sister didn't just get the great hair and body, you also got an incredible dose of magic. Mom and I could never figure out how," Lacy said nonchalantly, a sly tilt on her lips as she fingered a dish towel. "It infuriated both of us. It was quite by accident when I stumbled across a way to syphon your magic."

Laura thought she was going to be sick. Her stomach roiled viciously. "You took my magic?"

"Oh, that first taste of your potent magic was . . . addictive," Lacy said with a laugh. She grabbed an apple from the basket on the kitchen counter and tossed it up in the air before catching it. "Once Mom and I had a taste, we couldn't stop taking it from you. And you never knew."

"Why are you here now? Was my magic not enough? Do you want my life now?" Laura glared at her sister, anger and hate threatening to swallow her.

Not even when she had been locked in her bedroom had she felt such impotent rage. She had thought she escaped her family, when in truth they had simply let her leave. How infuriating after it had taken her unbelievable amounts of courage to make her break from them.

"You always were so dramatic. If you'd only grown a backbone, we might have let you have some of your magic."

Laura curled her hands into fists. "Let me?" she repeated, fury causing her voice to shake. "You might have *let* me have my own magic. How very generous of you. And here I always thought you such a bitch."

"Ohhh," Lacy said, and threw up her hands in mock fear, her eyebrows raised and her eyes wide. "Did I strike a nerve?"

"Leave. Leave now. I don't want to ever see or hear from you again."

Lacy looked at the apple and gently ran her finger over it. "I'm not leaving until you give me back my magic."

"It's my magic!" Laura's chest heaved from the violence she felt, which caused her heart to pound like a drum.

"Wrong response."

Laura didn't have time to duck as the apple came flying at her head.

* * *

"I found her!" Broc yelled. "Laura is in Ferness."

Charon didn't care how Broc had all of a sudden been able to use his magic. He raced toward Ferness, his sole thought to get to Laura and have her safe.

Even if she didn't go with him, he just wanted her protected. Charon wasn't looking forward to explaining why he hadn't told her about himself. But there were answers he wanted as well. Like how the hell was she a Druid?

Worry began to niggle at him when he couldn't feel any Druid magic. If Laura was in Ferness, shouldn't he feel her?

Charon didn't slow when they reached Ferness. Broc pointed to her flat, and Charon busted through the broken door to find Laura sprawled on the floor, unmoving.

"Laura," he called, and rushed to her.

Phelan knelt on the other side of Laura. "Where is she injured?"

Charon did a quick look. "I can find nothing."

"Then get her, and let's get out of here," Lucan said.

Ramsey stood at the door and looked over his shoulder at them. "I agree. I feel *drough* magic. Jason is most likely on his way."

"Mobiles still doona work," Lucan said with a growl.

Charon lifted Laura in his arms. "I'll run all the way to MacLeod Castle if I have to."

"You willna have to," said a voice behind them.

Charon turned around to see Malcolm standing in Laura's kitchen.

Malcolm gave them a brief nod. "I'll find what's causing the mobile phones no' to work. It'll take but a moment. Then get the hell out of here with the woman."

"Thank you," Charon said.

Malcolm paused on his way out the door, but didn't say anything.

"He's getting worse," Ramsey said softly.

Broc sighed. "He carries too much guilt."

"That's no' guilt," Charon said. He carried enough of it

that he knew what it looked like. What was wrong with Malcolm was much worse.

Phelan stood. "Nay, it isna guilt. There's nothing left inside him."

"That's shite," Lucan said, his face scrunched in a frown. "If he didna feel anything, he wouldna be here."

"He came because Larena told him what was going on," Charon said. "Malcolm always helps when Larena asks."

Their conversation ended abruptly when lightning exploded through the village. Lucan immediately reached for his mobile. A second later, he was exchanging words with Fallon.

Charon looked out Laura's window, searching for Malcolm when Fallon appeared. He wasn't given a chance to say anything as they were all transported back to MacLeod Castle.

He held on to Laura tightly and looked around the great hall. As Charon scanned the faces in the crowd, he realized Quinn, Aiden, and Galen weren't present.

"Malcolm said to leave him," Larena stated into the silence. "He wants to watch Jason and the others."

Fallon turned away, a string of curses falling from his lips.

"I've prepared a room," Sonya said as she came up beside Charon. "Bring Laura so I can heal her."

Charon walked behind Sonya up the stairs to the second floor. Then they turned right and proceeded down the corridor until they stopped at a door on the left.

Sonya waited as Charon slowly lowered Laura to the bed. He straightened but couldn't leave. She had been alone in the forest for an entire day and night. Alone. Until Jason found her.

He looked up when Sonya touched his arm. "I didna find any wounds. The bruise on her cheek is from when they tried to kidnap her."

"I'll see to her. Rest, if you can," Sonya said.

Charon rubbed his eyes with his thumb and forefinger. He was weary to his bones, but it was Laura he worried over. What had Wallace said to her? More important, how had she gotten away from him?

What was most disturbing was that he couldn't feel any magic from Laura. It was like it had never been there.

A strong hand clamped on his shoulder, and he turned his head to find Phelan. His friend nodded and stood beside him. "She's strong. Laura will be fine."

"Yes, she will," Sonya said. "I've healed the bruise, and it appears as if someone knocked her out by the bump on her head."

Charon leaned a shoulder against the stone wall of the narrow chamber. "Who would have done that and no' taken her?"

"Good question. Let her rest, and then we'll ask," Phelan said.

Charon let Phelan nudge him from the room. He walked silently down the corridor and stairs to stop in the great hall. Everyone wanted answers, answers he didn't have.

"Thank you for helping Laura," he said to the room at large.

Ramsey wrapped an arm around his wife, Tara, and said, "We did it for you."

"Jason isna done with me," Charon said instead of responding to Ramsey's statement. "He'll be looking to hurt each of us in ways we willna expect."

"I told them," Fallon said, his face lined with worry.

Marcail cleared her throat and tugged on one of the many small braids atop the crown of her head. "Aiden is being extra careful. My son knows what's at stake, and it's why he wants to stay and learn what he can of the blood. Quinn and Galen are keeping watch over Aiden and Britt, who is helping him."

"Blood?" Charon asked with a frown.

Phelan lowered himself onto a bench at the long table. "Aye. After the battle at Wallace's mansion and my blood didna heal you, it was mentioned that Wallace might have done something to the *drough* blood to make it a stronger weapon against us."

"Aye," Camdyn said as he gently moved his infant daughter out of his arms and into those of his wife, Saffron. "If it can be determined what makes the *drough* blood react to ours, then we can have something to counter it when Wallace uses the X90s."

Charon found his hand lifting to rub his chest, but stopped himself before he could touch the wound. "That's a good plan."

"What is it?" Logan asked when Charon paused.

"When Wallace used the *drough* blood on me yesterday, I was healed in an instant by the blast of magic that destroyed my cabin."

Hayden grunted. "I'd like to know who is capable of that."

Charon glanced down at his hand. "I felt *mie* magic right before I was knocked unconscious. The only other person near us was Laura."

"I didna feel magic from her when you arrived," Arran said.

Charon frowned in worry. "Neither did I for two years, but I did today. That's the crux of the problem."

CHAPTER
TWENTY-ONE

"What do you mean she's gone?" Jason demanded.

Malcolm recognized the Warrior with Jason from his vantage point atop a building in Ferness. Dale merely shrugged, which sent Jason into a rage.

"She can no' be gone!"

The leggy dark-haired woman with Jason picked at her fingernails and said, "She's gone. Move on to the next plan."

The next instant, Jason was in her face. "Aisley, I doona need your comments."

Malcolm narrowed his eyes on Aisley as she dared to return Jason's glare. The *drough* had gumption, but whether it was from lack of knowledge to what Jason could do, or indifference, Malcolm didn't know.

"Why you let your cousin talk to you like that, I doona know," replied another woman. Her skin was so pale, it looked sickly, and her bright red lipstick and nails did nothing to help.

So, Aisley was his cousin. Interesting.

Jason's voice lowered into a whisper as he bent his head toward Aisley. Malcolm might be several blocks away, but his enhanced hearing allowed him to pick up the slightest of murmurs.

"Are you testing me?"

Aisley's bored look didn't change, but Malcolm saw a subtle stiffening of her body. "I wouldn't dream of it. Cousin."

"See that you doona." With one final glare, Jason turned away and opened the door of a white BMW. "I'll get Laura soon enough. Time to regroup."

Malcolm flicked his thumb over one of his maroon claws as Jason and his entourage departed Ferness. He hadn't planned on coming here, but after Larena's call, he found himself heading north.

He stood, the sound of someone approaching putting him on guard. Malcolm turned to watch a tall, barrel-chested man walk out onto the roof of the building.

His gaze scanned the area until he spotted Malcolm. The man cleared his throat. "I saw you with Charon a bit ago. I need to know if everything is all right with the lass and all."

Malcolm frowned until he realized the man was referring to Laura. "I've no' heard. Charon took her somewhere she'll be safe."

"Good, good," the man said and shifted from one foot to the other.

"Are you one of the men Charon spoke about who helps guard this village?"

The man nodded. "Aye. I'm Brian. Phelan told us to keep watch, but we've no' gotten further instructions."

"Charon will return soon. Until then, continue to stay on guard. If Jason Wallace or any of the group that was with him returns, call Charon immediately."

Malcolm walked past the man to the stairs, since he couldn't jump off the building without raising suspicions. He wasn't sure how much Charon's men knew.

"Are you staying?" Brian asked.

Malcolm stopped and looked at the distant mountains. Thick mist obscured the peaks, promising miles of solitude, lochs of crystal-clear water, and plenty of glens to get lost in.

"Nay," Malcolm finally answered. "My job is done."

* * *

Laura came awake in an instant. Her eyes flew open the same time she sat up. She quickly examined the narrow room to discover she was alone. In a bed.

She had no memory of getting there. However, she remembered all too clearly Lacy's visit.

The door creaked open, and Laura lifted her eyes to Charon who filled the doorway. Her heart stopped in her chest to see him standing there, hale and hearty. Her lips parted, words locked in her throat.

How could he be alive? Then she remembered seeing his wounds heal. Had he never been dead? Had she mourned for nothing?

His dark brown hair was parted to the side and looked as though he had run his fingers through it multiple times. He sported a deep shadow of whiskers on his cheek and jaw, but it was the worry in his beautiful dark eyes that caused her stomach to clench in dread.

"I thought you were dead," she whispered when she finally found her voice. It was still such a shock to see him standing there.

Charon let out a long exhale and softly closed the door. He leaned against it, his hands shoved in the front pockets of his faded jeans. "How much did you see?"

"I saw . . ." She swallowed when her voice gave out. "I saw you change."

"I dreaded as much. You doona need to fear me, Laura. I'd never harm you."

"Where am I?" she asked, not yet ready to talk about what had happened.

Charon dropped his chin to his chest. "MacLeod Castle. It's the only place I know of that Wallace can no' get to easily and hurt you."

She assumed as much by the stone walls and floors. Laura gathered the blanket in her fingers. "Are you a Warrior?"

"Aye," he answered without hesitation. "I'm immortal with special powers from the primeval god inside me. I suppose Wallace told you that."

Laura nodded and looked at Charon through her lashes. "He told me *droughs* were good."

"Of course he would." Charon's voice was flat, emotionless. As were his eyes when he lifted them to her. "Is that how he got you to go with him?"

"How did you know?"

"We're excellent trackers."

Laura couldn't hold his gaze. So he had come for her. Why had she doubted him? "Yes, that's how I went with him. One minute I was scared, and the next, I felt as if I were safe. I suspect he used magic on me."

"I'm sure he did."

"You tell me *droughs* are evil, he tells me it's the *mies* who are evil. I don't know what to believe. It's all so confusing." She swallowed and looked at him. "I'm scared, Charon."

For several long minutes he said nothing. Finally he replied, "There is a group of people downstairs who've risked their lives for centuries to protect you and every person in the world. The Druids are *mies*. Their magic is pure and powerful, and they have helped take down two evil *droughs*—Deirdre and Declan. They'll aid us in taking down Jason as well.

"The Warriors have gone through Hell and back again. We've lost brethren and friends, but we keep fighting because if we doona, the evil would win."

He paused, a muscle in his jaw jumping. "The MacLeods have opened their home to you. Everyone here would put their lives on the line to protect you. If you doona believe the people in this castle are no' evil, then do everyone a favor and leave."

Laura felt as if she'd been kicked in the stomach. She gasped, struggling for a hold in this ever-changing world she was now in. "If you didn't want me here, then why did you bring me?"

"A question I've been asking myself. For all I know, you're working with Wallace now, and you're here to betray me."

"I'm not."

He laughed wryly. "They all say that, but we've seen how a *drough* can use magic to get in someone's mind. I have to know for sure, Laura."

She tucked her hair behind her ears and looked at her hands. No longer could she feel the magic inside her, and no matter how much she called to it, it didn't answer. "You told me of the Druids, and I was hesitant to believe you. Yet I did because you've never lied to me. I have magic. Or rather, I did."

"What does that mean?" Charon asked as he stared intently at her.

Laura wasn't quite ready to tell him everything yet. "Why didn't you tell me what you were?"

"The obvious reason is because you were no' a Druid, or at least I didna think you were."

"But you told me of the Druids."

"I had no choice," Charon said between clenched teeth and lowered his gaze to the floor. "I didna want to tell you that much, but Wallace was determined to have you, and you wouldna listen to reason. I was prepared to do anything to ensure you were kept out of his clutches."

The old hurts returned with a vengeance, and even though she knew Charon hadn't had anything to do with her family controlling her, she couldn't stop the emotions filling her. "So, just because you said so, I'm supposed to do it."

His gaze snapped to hers. "You're damned right. I was trying to save your life."

"I swore when I left my family that no one would ever tell me what to do again!" she yelled, hating how her rage was taking her, confusing past hurts with current concerns, especially after Lacy's visit.

"People tell you what to do every bloody day, Laura!"

She dug her fingers into her palms as her body began to shake from her rage. "Is this where you make love to me again to convince me to do what you want?"

In the blink of an eye, he had her on her back, her arms

over her head and his face inches from hers. "You think I brought you to my bed so you'd do my will?"

His voice was too soft, too mellow. It belied the fire that burned in his deep brown gaze. "You told me to do something, and when I didn't do it, you tried another approach."

"Do you think so little of yourself? What I did was find another plan." His voice was low, deadly, as he pushed away from her and stood. His body stood still as stone. "Besides, you're the one who kissed me. I didna call for Fallon and have him take you, kicking and screaming, to MacLeod Castle. I risked everything to keep you safe."

His words drew her up short.

"You don't understand—"

"You're damned right I doona," he interrupted. "Because you willna tell me. Keep your secrets. God knows I've kept mine."

She closed her eyes against the pain his words caused, pain because she knew how stupid she had been in not leaving Ferness when he told her to. When she thought he'd died, she blamed herself, knowing it was her pride in not leaving when he asked.

And now she would argue with him again.

Laura wanted Charon to tell her all she wanted to know about Druids and Warriors, and she'd foolishly tried to use anger to get him to do it.

The truth was, she knew the evil was Jason. He had used magic to control her, lied to her, and kidnapped her. Charon and Phelan had done nothing but try to protect her.

Someone who hadn't endured her youth wouldn't understand why she didn't want to be told what to do. How could she explain to someone that there wasn't an aspect of her life that her family hadn't controlled?

Twice she had dared to rebel, and twice she had been punished. Her father was always gone on business, but neither of her parents had ever laid a hand on her. No, her mother had other ways of exacting punishment.

Charon rose and walked to the door, but stopped with his

hand on the knob. "The others will want to talk to you. Reaghan is a Druid who can tell if a person is lying by looking
in their eyes. Dani can search your mind to see if there's a
spell controlling you."

"By all means, send them up," Laura said as she pushed
off the covers and swung her legs over the bed. Clean clothes
had been set out on a chair, and she was anxious to get out of
her dirty ones. "The sooner everyone understands the only
one controlling me is me, the sooner I can leave."

"You are no' a prisoner here. It's one of Fallon's rules. No
one is held against their will."

"First bit of good news I've heard today."

Laura hurt. Not from any wound, but from her heart. The
night Charon made love to her had been special. There was
a connection, or at least she'd thought there was.

She wished she could stop lashing out at him because of
what happened to her. It was as if her world were in a raging
storm and she couldn't see land in sight.

Just when she thought she might get on course, something
else occurred to send her back out into the storm. At least
now Jason's magic was easing its hold on her and she knew
who was evil and who wasn't.

She was overjoyed in seeing Charon alive. She wanted to
throw her arms around him and hold him close.

"Where is your magic?"

Laura slid off the high bed, the stones beneath her bare
feet cool as she stood. "I don't have it."

"It was you who used magic at the cabin."

It wasn't a question. Laura couldn't look at him because it
hurt too much. There was too much between them now, and
no matter how much her body—and her heart—might want
him, they could never be together now.

"I saw you and Dale fighting. I saw you winning. Until
something kept you from moving. I know now it was magic,
but all I knew then was that you couldn't defend yourself.
Then I saw Jason pour his blood in you. I heard . . . I heard
you bellow. The next thing I knew, I had something inside

me, almost like a presence. It built the longer they held you, until it exploded from my hands."

"Your magic saved me. *Drough* blood is poisonous to Warriors. I was dying."

Laura swallowed as tears threatened. She hadn't been wrong. He had been dying. It was that emotion that had fueled her magic.

But what had caused her to be able to use it after all those years without even knowing she had it? Could it have been the fact Charon was hurting?

Or was it something else entirely?

CHAPTER
TWENTY-TWO

Britt looked at Aiden MacLeod over the rim of her wine-glass as she let the deep red liquid slide down her throat. Aiden's green eyes were warm and smiling as they stared at her.

Yet, several times during their dinner she had seen him glancing around the restaurant, his gaze intent and probing. He wasn't ignoring her. Not once did he fail to respond to something she said or asked.

Aiden nodded to the waiter who removed their plates. Then Aiden turned those amazing eyes to her. He smiled, his wide, full lips snagging her attention.

He had a mouth she'd dreamed of kissing since the moment she looked up from the microscope to see him standing in the lab. It wasn't just his mouth either. It was all of him.

She came across many good-looking Scots during her time in Edinburgh, but there was something about Aiden the others lacked. He had confidence, but it was some unnamable thing that gave him an edge other men would never have.

"You've been different since Quinn showed up," she said as she set aside her wine.

"I doona know what you mean," Aiden answered, and ran a hand casually through his wavy, light brown hair.

Britt leaned forward and moved aside a lock of his hair that had fallen onto his forehead. She itched to run her own fingers through the strands that fell haphazardly around his face and brushed the rim of his jaw.

He caught her hand, his eyes darkening as he captured her gaze and held it while he placed a kiss atop her knuckles.

Britt's heart raced from the feel of his lips on her skin. They had shared many dinners and lunches before this, but always while working. This night was different, special.

If she let it, she knew something could develop between them. And how she wanted it to. Even with his secrets, she wanted him.

"You know exactly what I mean," Britt said, and reluctantly pulled her hand away. "You look so much like Quinn. I know he's related to you. Why won't you tell me how?"

Aiden shrugged and leaned back as the dessert was placed on the table. "Because it doesna matter."

"Doesn't matter, huh?" she asked, and reached for the fork. She slid the utensil into the cheesecake and placed it in her mouth as she considered the man across from her. "You tell me you have magic, prove it to me even, and yet tell me it doesn't matter who Quinn is."

"Britt, please," he whispered, his face closed off.

"What is it about you that's so different from everyone else? You dress the same, but that's where the similarities end. Some of the words you use are from another century. The way you stand and watch people. It's as if you're waiting for something to attack."

He looked down at the plate of mousse. "I'm just a man."

"A man with magic and secrets. It makes you different, but without it, you'd still stand out in a crowd. I've seen the way people clear a path around you, almost as if they sense something that marks you as someone they need to stay away from."

"You doona stay away from me."

"Because I don't want to. I'm not sure I could even if I tried. Who are you really, Aiden MacLeod?"

Aiden's green eyes lifted and caught hers. "You wouldna believe me if I told you."

"Try me."

"How close are you to discovering the differences in the blood?"

She shrugged and took another bite. "I feel as if there's a key piece missing."

"There is. What if I can get it to you?"

Though she wanted to know about Aiden, she had realized weeks ago that to learn who he truly was, she had to find out the differences in the blood. "If I had that, then I think two, three days at the most."

"It might take me a few days to get it, but once I do, we need the information as soon as possible."

All night they had talked of mundane things like the city and her childhood. Not once had the conversation turned to her research on the blood or why he needed it. As soon as they had begun to speak of it, Aiden's attitude shifted.

Gone was the smile and relaxed man who had sat across from her in the crowded restaurant. He was tense, his voice low and urgent, sending off warning bells in her head.

"What's happened?" she asked quietly as she let her eyes wander slowly around the restaurant.

"My enemy is closing in. He's also begun to target those close to us. I fear you may be next, Britt. Already he's tried to kidnap someone in an effort to hurt one of my friends."

"Who is this asshole anyway?"

Aiden gave her a wicked grin of approval. "Jason Wallace."

She recited that name to memory. "I'll be on guard. I'm not without skills, you know. I lived in San Francisco, London, and Berlin. I can take care of myself."

"He has magic."

That deflated her somewhat, but she didn't let it show. "Will he leave me alone once you're gone with your information?"

Aiden's head moved side to side. "I doona believe he will."

"So what? You stay with me the rest of my life for protection?" It had been said as a joke, but after the words passed her lips, the idea of him being there appealed to her entirely too much.

Britt looked away and put her napkin on the table as silence stretched between them. So he might not feel the same. It wouldn't be the first time. It seemed she was into guys who didn't feel the same or vice versa.

For once she'd thought she might have gotten it right with Aiden.

Finally he said, "If I thought that would work, aye, I would. It willna be enough. Until Wallace is gone, I'd like you to come with me."

"And where is that?" She drank more wine to calm her nerves and the excitement his offer brought, but nothing seemed to help. The thought of going with Aiden wasn't what frightened her, it was how much she wanted to go that did.

She had missed countless classes and deadlines for papers while helping him, but she didn't care. For so long, she had strived for degrees and doctorates, anything to fill her life with some kind of meaning.

One cause, one man had changed her way of thinking in the blink of an eye. She'd found that meaning with Aiden, but she didn't want to tell him that, since she was unsure how he would take it.

"Aiden? Where would I be going?" she asked again.

He sat forward and placed his forearms on the table. "A castle."

There was more to it. That she knew instantly by the way his eyes watched her. "That sounds nice. I've toured a few castles while here, but I've never stayed in one."

"I doona believe you know how serious this all is."

"I do. You've made it clear from the beginning how dangerous this was."

"But you didna believe me," he said, daring her to lie.

Britt speared another piece of cheesecake. "No, I didn't believe you until I studied the samples you gave me. This might not make sense to you, but the idea of studying something so unbelievable is too good to pass up."

"Even if it costs you your life?"

She hid a smile as his eyes darkened while he watched her slowly put the fork in her mouth and wrap her lips around it. Then, slowly pull the utensil out. She swallowed the dessert, her blood heating with his gaze.

Maybe he wasn't as immune to her as he would have her believe.

"Didn't you tell me you'd keep me safe?"

He cleared his throat and looked away. "Aye. I did. I am," he hastily corrected.

So he was drawn to her. Britt wondered why Aiden hadn't made a move on her. She'd begun to think he wasn't interested, but that had been blown out of the water.

What held him back? And did she want to wait on him?

The answer to that was a definite "hell no." She wanted Aiden. Even when she knew she should be running the other way and putting as much distance between them as she could because of the danger surrounding him, she couldn't.

She was drawn to him, pulled toward him regardless of the consequences.

Britt smiled and sat back. His gaze lowered to her lips before dropping to her breasts. It was the first time she'd worn the deep purple dress she bought a year ago, and she was so glad she had.

"You deserved a night out on the town after all your hard work," Aiden said.

"We need to get back though."

He nodded and pulled out his wallet. After tossing down several pound notes, he stood. "Wallace's attention is on my friend, but I doona know how long that'll be the case."

"Then home it is."

Britt enjoyed how he pulled out her chair and offered her his arm as they left the restaurant. She preened inwardly when she observed how women watched Aiden with lust in their eyes.

He was a fine cut of a man in his slacks, shirt, and jacket.

Added with his long hair, the confident way he walked, and his sly smile, he was irresistible.

He didn't notice he was being watched, which made her want him even more. As soon as they stepped out of the restaurant and onto the sidewalk, Britt turned and kissed him.

For a full second, Aiden stood there, his body soaking in the feel of Britt's soft curves against him. Then he wrapped his arms around her and pulled her closer.

He groaned at the sweet taste of her. Many nights he'd dreamed of kissing her, and now that she was in his arms, he feared he might never let her go.

Aiden's cock swelled when he heard her soft moan. He deepened the kiss, wanting more, needing more.

Someone bumped into Aiden from behind. He tore his mouth from Britt's and turned to give a piece of his mind to whoever had dared to interrupt them. But one look at the hulky, bald man with the goatee, and all Aiden could think about was getting Britt away.

"You're wanted," the man said.

Aiden pushed Britt behind him as he let his magic fill him. "No' going to happen. Tell Wallace to go bugger himself."

The man smiled. "So you know who I am."

"I know a Warrior when I see one."

"You would with your father and uncles being Warriors. Let's no' make a scene, lad. You and the girl need to come with me now."

Galen stepped out of the shadows behind the man and leaned against the side of the building. "Ah, Dale. You think you'd learn you're serving the wrong side."

Dale shifted so he could look at Galen as well as Aiden. "One Warrior willna stop us. I'm no' alone."

"Neither are we," Aiden said and smiled coldly.

In an instant, Dale called up his god, his skin turning a pale green. He swiped at Galen with his claws the same time Aiden caught movement across the street.

He turned to shield Britt as his father barreled into Dale and sent them tumbling down an alley.

"Get her away!" Galen shouted.

Aiden glanced at Britt to see her eyes wide and her face pale. "If we run, Wallace will catch us."

"Then we stay." Her voice was unsteady and she trembled in his arms, but she didn't faint or run away screaming.

He nodded. "No matter what, stay with me. If you can no', find Galen or Quinn."

Aiden didn't wait for her agreement as they slid into the alley to find his father fighting Dale. Quinn's skin had turned the black of his god, and it was hard to keep track of him in the shadows.

Dale's growls of rage brought a smile to Aiden's lips. Galen was standing nearby watching. Suddenly he swung around.

"*Droughs*," he said between clenched teeth, his fangs showing when he pulled back his lips in a growl. His skin turned the green of his god, and he bent his legs, his claws out and ready. "Wallace comes."

Aiden pushed Britt down so that she squatted against the wall. Then shrugged off his blazer and stood beside Galen and called up his magic.

"Your father is going to skin me alive if anything happens to you. You know Quinn wouldna want you here," Galen said.

Aiden knew it all too well, but everyone needed to understand he was a man, not a child. And it was time he let them see it.

Two *droughs* turned the corner into the alley. Aiden sent a blast of magic at one. Galen used his speed to reach the other and kill him before any magic could be used against him.

As soon as Aiden's opponent went down, Galen sliced the neck of the *drough* with his claws.

That was just the first wave. Aiden knew Wallace wouldn't give up that easily.

CHAPTER
TWENTY-THREE

Charon stalked down to the great hall with Laura's words ringing in his head, but came to an abrupt halt when he saw everyone looking at him. The inhabitants of MacLeod Castle were scattered throughout the hall, some at the long table, some in chairs around the hearth.

"How is Laura?" Ronnie asked.

Charon didn't look at Arran's woman. Instead he pinned his gaze on Fallon. "Laura is no' to be questioned until I'm done with her."

"You think Wallace is using her?" Fallon asked, his brow furrowed in worry.

"I doona know what to think," Charon admitted. He needed some time to collect his thoughts before he told the others too much. "I know it was her who used the magic, but she has none now. Unless she knows how to conceal it."

Reaghan said, "If she can hide her magic, that would make her a very powerful Druid indeed."

"Has any Druid ever been able to do that?" Camdyn asked.

Isla turned her bright blue eyes to Camdyn. "I've never known one who could. Not even Deirdre managed that, though I don't know if it's because she didn't want to hide it or couldn't."

"How did Laura escape Wallace?" Phelan asked into the silence.

Charon scrubbed a hand down his face. "He said *droughs* were the good Druids and that Warriors were evil. I told Laura of the Druids, but nothing more. So she doesna know what to believe. It was Jason's story, along with some of his magic that convinced her to go with him. But she didna tell me how she got away."

"Why are you no' still questioning her, then?" Lucan asked.

Charon glanced at his hands. He still felt her smooth skin against him, still remembered what it was like to thrust into her tight body and make her scream with pleasure.

There was more to Laura than what met the eye. He needed to earn her trust if he was going to learn anything. After working so closely with her, he'd thought he knew Laura. Apparently her secrets were as great as his own.

"I had to clear my head."

"The night Laura was almost taken. I felt *mie* magic. It was brief, but I felt it," Phelan said.

Charon looked at his friend. "I, as well. I've known Laura for years. I'd know if she was a Druid."

"Would you?" Tara asked as she sat on the arm of Ramsey's chair.

"I worked with her every day," Charon said, holding back the anger, not at Tara, but because Tara was voicing doubts that he had already asked himself. "I'd know."

Ramsey laid his hand atop Tara's arm. "It's true, love. Charon would've picked up on it."

"Then how is it one minute she has magic and the next she doesn't?" Cara asked.

Charon didn't have an answer for Lucan's wife. "She admitted to having magic, but she said it's gone again."

Ian gave a snort. "That doesna make sense."

"It does," Tara said defensively. "I could never count on my magic. Maybe hers is the same."

Marcail walked to him. "Tara has a point. You said yourself you couldn't always feel Tara's magic, Ramsey."

"Aye," Charon murmured. If he could only get Laura to trust him again, she might tell him everything.

"I can help you."

Charon looked at Marcail and the hand she hovered over his arm. Her gift was the ability to take away emotions, but in doing so she made herself ill.

"Nay. No' only would Quinn take my head for making you sick, but it wouldna help." He needed to work through all the emotions—as difficult as they were to piece together. All because it involved Laura.

Marcail rolled her turquoise eyes. "Quinn would understand that I did it for a friend. Besides, I think it would help. You've too much in that head of yours. You want to believe Laura isn't working with Jason, but you can't be sure."

"I can clear that up with just a few minutes with Laura," Reaghan said.

Charon didn't turn away the glass of whisky placed in his hand by Hayden. He drained it in one swallow. It was filled again immediately.

The Dreagan whisky slid smoothly down his throat and spread warmth as it landed in his stomach. It dulled the ache that had gripped his chest like iron manacles since the moment he knew Jason had Laura.

But the unanswered questions, and the tormented look in Laura's pale green eyes kept him on edge. It wasn't just the anguish he read on her face, it was a bone-deep betrayal that distressed her. Who, exactly, had betrayed her?

He wanted to hand Laura over to the Druids so his mind wouldn't be jumbled anymore. Let them sort out the answers in just a few brief moments. But before Laura was his lover, she had been his friend. She deserved more. Especially from him.

"Magic was used in her flat," Ramsey said. "I noticed it when we found Laura unconscious, but I assumed she'd been the one to use it. Perhaps it was no' her."

Lucan crossed his arms over his chest. "You might be right, Ramsey."

"Sonya said she had a bump on her head. Maybe she was

knocked out, and that's when she lost her magic," Dani suggested.

Charon squeezed his eyes tightly shut as he recalled Laura's words during their conversation. When he opened them, he looked at the amber liquid in his glass. "Laura said it was seeing Wallace pour his *drough* blood in me that caused her magic to rise. There was something in her voice, something that said she hadna known what it was."

"Until Wallace told her," Broc said with a growl.

Charon drained his glass again and set it down on the table with a thud. "If only we had gotten to her first."

"What's done is done," Larena said. "We deal with what we have."

Fallon looked at Charon. "Larena is right. I'll honor your request to question Laura on your own. Until such time as it begins to put everyone else in danger."

"Agreed," Charon said.

He started to turn away when Isla called for him to wait as she rushed into the kitchen. A moment later, she returned with a tray of food.

"I'm sure she's hungry," Isla said.

Charon took the tray. "Thank you."

"Trust your heart. It won't lead you astray."

He remembered Isla's words as he walked the stairs back to Laura's chamber. Charon would rather have taken Laura back to his house, but that option was lost to him now. Thanks to Wallace.

Charon paused outside Laura's door and swallowed as he shoved thoughts of Jason Wallace aside. He shifted the tray and raised his hand to knock when he heard the shower.

He opened the door before quietly walking inside. Steam billowed from the tiny bathroom and the half-closed door. Charon set the tray down on the bed and closed the door, where he stood waiting for her while doing his damnedest not to stalk into the bathroom and join her in the shower.

After finally giving in to his desire for her, Charon found it difficult to deny his cravings. Laura was like a drug. He'd had a taste—and needed more.

A few minutes later, the water shut off. Charon thought remaining where he was would make it easier on him.

It only made it worse.

He imagined the water coating her body, a drop hanging on the edge of a nipple, waiting for him to capture it in his mouth. His eyes slid shut when all the blood rushed to his cock as he remembered lovely rose-tipped breasts.

With a groan, he clenched his teeth. He heard her moving around and could picture Laura drying off, the towel moving over her silky skin just as his hands had a day before.

His eyes snapped open when she walked out of the bathroom in tight leggings and a shirt and halted as she caught sight of him. He met her gaze before he nodded to the bed. "I brought you food."

She said not a word as she combed out her wet hair and hurried to the tray.

"Jason told you his story of the Druids and Warriors, but let me tell you mine," Charon said.

When she looked at him, silently waiting, he figured that was as close to a yes as he was going to get.

He inhaled deeply and began. "In the history books, it describes the Celts as tribes who were always at war with each other. They're described as savages, wild as the land they inhabited.

"But that wasna the case. Aye, the Celts were savage fighters. They held off the Romans for years. Their ability to use the land as an advantage over the Romans is one reason Hadrian's Wall was built. Rome never conquered Scotland or her people, but they wouldna give up."

Charon leaned back against the door, thinking to an earlier time in history when the clans had ruled as his gaze shifted to the window. "The Druids had roamed the land for generations. They were the teachers, the healers, and sometimes even the judges. Clan leaders turned to the *mies* for guidance and advice on everything from where to hunt to when to go to battle."

He found Laura intently listening while she continued to devour the food on the tray.

"The Druids, like anyone else in this world, have a good side and an evil side. The good are the *mies*. They use the pure magic given to them by nature. They can make plants grow, heal, speak to the trees, and many other amazing abilities.

"The *droughs,* on the other hand, are evil. They perform a ceremony where they give their blood and soul to the Devil in order to use black magic. You can tell the evil Druids by the cuts on their wrists from the ceremony, as well as the Demon's Kiss."

He paused as he tried to find the words to describe it. "A Demon's Kiss is a silver vial worn around a *drough*'s neck. It holds the first drops of their blood after becoming *drough,* and it can be used to heal them.

"When it appeared the Romans might actually conquer the Celts, they turned to the *mies* for advice, but the Druids didna have an answer for them. Having nowhere else to go, the leaders went to the *droughs.*"

"What did they do?" she asked softly.

Charon crossed an ankle over the other. "The *droughs* called up primeval gods long locked away in Hell. The strongest, bravest warriors of each family stepped forward to take the gods into their bodies. The men became Warriors. They had inhuman strength and speed along with enhanced senses. More than that, the Roman army didna stand a chance against them."

"Rome left then?"

"Aye. But the Warriors answered the gods' call for blood. With no more Romans to kill, they slaughtered whoever crossed their path. The *droughs* tried to pull the gods out of the men and back into Hell, but the gods had a firm hold of the men."

Her pale green eyes watched him raptly. It took everything he had not to go to her and pull her into his arms, to promise her that he would set everything aright. He wanted—nay, *needed*—to have her in his arms again.

That need was as strong as his god's call for death. It startled Charon, how deeply he felt for Laura.

He popped the knuckles in his left hand. "The *droughs* are strong with their black magic, but nothing they did could move the gods back to their prison. The *droughs* might be stronger individually, but when a group of *mies* combine their magic, the force of it is incredible. The *droughs* knew this, so they turned to the *mies* for help.

"It was the first time in ages the *mies* and *droughs* combined their magic, but even that was no' enough to send the gods to Hell. All they were able to do was bind the gods inside the men. The gods, however, moved through each bloodline, going to the strongest warrior each time, waiting, hoping for the day they would be released."

Laura swallowed the last bit of her food. "And the men the gods first inhabited? What became of them?"

"They returned to the life they led before."

"Were you one of the first?"

He gave a quick shake of his head. "Nay."

"Who unbound your god?"

Charon pushed away from the door and sighed. "Her name was Deirdre. She was a *drough* who lived for a thousand years by killing every Druid she came across and taking their magic. She found a scroll with the spell to unbind the gods. Over seven hundred years ago, she attacked this *verra* castle and killed every living thing inside it to get to the MacLeod brothers."

Laura looked away. She didn't want to believe Charon, but the emotion that filled his words left her little choice. His tone made it even more convincing because she didn't think Charon knew how emotional he sounded.

An odd twinge unsettled her as she listened to his tale. When his voice shook slightly as he spoke of Deirdre, anger had pervaded her.

This was the story he hadn't wanted to share before. Now, he was telling her all of it. Despite the fact that retelling it seemed to pain him. And she hated to see him hurting.

"What happened to the MacLeods?" she asked as she got to her feet and looked out the window. She couldn't look into Charon's dark gaze anymore and see the misery and doubt.

"Deirdre's magic was the ability to communicate with stone. Cairn Toul Mountain was her fortress. Inside that mountain was where she lived and practiced her black magic. She brought Fallon, Lucan, and Quinn to the mountain and unbound their god. As brothers equally strong in battle, they shared a god. They were lucky enough to escape Deirdre after their god was unbound to return here."

Laura watched the sea roll endlessly from her window. The birds flew along the currents hunting for food, but she never heard them. She was too focused on the sinfully gorgeous man behind her and his tale she wasn't sure she wanted to know anymore.

"Deirdre didna stop with the MacLeods," Charon continued. "Ramsey was the next to be taken. So many more men were captured and their gods unbound."

Her hands gripped the windowsill as her heart pounded in her chest. He had yet to speak of himself. What had happened to him? Was it as dreadful as she feared, as the slight tremor in his voice bespoke? "And you?"

"I was taken. Six hundred and twenty-some odd years ago."

She swallowed hard. No wonder Charon always had the answers. He'd been around for six centuries. He'd seen everything.

"Does it bother you that I'm so . . . old?"

Laura looked at his reflection in the glass and found his gaze locked with hers. She slowly turned to him. "No. A lot about you is beginning to make sense now. Will you tell me more?"

"Are you sure you want to know?"

She shrugged one shoulder. "No. But I think I need to know."

"You do need to know. Even if I hadna felt your magic, I'd be telling you this now. Wallace put you in the middle of our war. It's a place I never wanted you to be."

"Sometimes it doesn't matter what we want. Fate does whatever she wants."

There was a long stretch of silence before Charon began talking again. "The screams from Druids and men alike from Cairn Toul still fill my head when I sleep. The pain of every muscle shredding, every bone breaking in multiple places as my god was released is indescribable."

Laura's heart missed a beat as she watched fury and despair fill his dark brown eyes. She wanted to go to him, to touch him as he relived his time with Deirdre. He didn't need to go into detail. She knew the pain he suffered by watching how his body had gone utterly still, every muscle locked.

"The real agony was battling my god for control. Deirdre kept all of us in dungeons deep beneath the earth. We were tortured with magic, brought to the brink of death, and healed by our gods dozens of times a day for months and years, all to break us to her will. Yet, there were a few who were able to stand against Deirdre, who gained control of our gods instead of them controlling us."

Laura wanted to ask him to stop, but his eyes shone with such stark desolation that she couldn't get the words past her lips.

"I make no excuses for what I am. I'm a monster, Laura, a beast who dares to walk among mortals. I didna ask to become this, but I will fight against evil until my dying breath."

His sun-kissed skin disappeared, copper taking its place. Claws a dark copper sprang from his fingers. The horns she'd glimpsed before were startling—and exquisite—with their penetrating copper color and the way they curved around the front of his forehead. She caught a glimpse of fangs, but it was his eyes that held her spellbound.

Copper colored his eyes from corner to corner, bleeding out any white. It was eerie and beautiful to look upon. She could practically feel the coiled violence beneath his muscles, waiting to let loose, but he kept a tight leash on it.

She'd seen how quick and agile he moved when fighting Dale. Before her stood a warrior in the truest sense of the word, a master at battle with the power of a god.

"I'm a Warrior. Ranmond, the god of war, is inside me. He gives me immortality, speed, enhanced senses. And the power to disintegrate anything."

CHAPTER
TWENTY-FOUR

Aiden yelled at Galen and sent a blast of magic against a *drough* going after the Warrior. Aiden stood in front of Britt, protecting her while she huddled against the building. His magic was nothing compared to that of the *droughs* attacking, but he wasn't going to give up. Only death would bring him to his knees.

"Aiden!" he heard his father shout behind him.

Galen dived to the ground to miss a blast of magic from a *drough*. He came up on Aiden's right and said, "Get Britt out of here."

"Nay." The Warriors were impossibly fast, but they weren't immune to magic. His father and Galen needed him. "We leave together."

Galen growled and beheaded a *drough* before the Druid could use her magic.

Aiden couldn't believe his eyes when Galen jerked and fell to his knees as black magic held him painfully in its grip. Aiden quickly spotted the *drough* responsible and sent several blasts of magic at her.

Her red lips twisted in a sneer right before she turned her magic on him. Aiden deflected her first shot as he saw Galen climb to his feet out of the corner of his eyes. Before Aiden could blink, he was hit a second time by the female the instant two other sets of magic slammed into him.

Aiden bit back his bellow of pain. It took every ounce of strength and his growing fury to keep himself upright as his body spasmed, but at least Galen was back on his feet. Aiden could feel his magic slipping away, being drained by the *droughs* and their too-powerful black magic.

Then he thought of Britt, of his father and Galen, and Aiden pushed aside the agony to focus on his magic pulsing within. He would give them all the time they needed to get free.

Aiden pivoted at the last minute as another blast came at him, and his gaze snagged on a tall woman who stood off to the side, watching. He couldn't see her face in the shadows, but he knew she was *drough*. Aiden had no idea why she wasn't fighting alongside the others. If she joined them, he didn't stand a chance.

But she didn't.

It was a reprieve, and he wasn't going to complain.

Aiden kept himself upright by gripping the side of the building while Galen used his speed to rush the *drough* with the bright red lips. Galen was almost upon her when Dale intercepted him. But not before Galen sliced the *drough* down her arm.

The *drough* cried out, and Dale lifted her in his arms and sped away before Galen could finish her off. The other *droughs* were quick to follow, leaving the alley quiet and still once more.

"We need to get you and Britt out of here," Quinn said as he walked up.

Aiden's chest heaved from the exertion of battle, and his body was a ball of aches. Yet, he'd never felt more alive than at that moment. His father's shirt was gone but his wounds were healing, and he had a satisfied grin upon his face.

"You wanted *drough* blood?" Galen asked as he held up his hand, blood dripping from his claws.

Aiden laughed, and then gripped his side, where the magic had pummeled him, as the throbbing reminded him how close he'd come to death.

That smile faded when he remembered Brit and all she

had witnessed. Aiden turned to find her eyes wide, staring at all three of them in a combination of shock and alarm.

God only knew what she thought of him now, but Aiden would deal with that later. First, he had to get her out of the alley before the *droughs* returned.

"Britt, this is my father," Aiden said, and pointed to Quinn. He then jerked his chin to Galen. "And this is Galen. I can explain everything."

Britt stood and visibly swallowed. "If I'm to sample the blood on Galen's . . . claws . . . I need to do it immediately."

Aiden would give her credit. She didn't melt into a puddle of screams as Galen and Quinn stood in their Warrior forms next to him. It was just another reason Aiden found her irresistible.

"Wallace knows what we've been doing," Quinn said, his voice hard with anger. "We can no' chance returning to the lab now."

Aiden shook his head. "We can no' give up on this. We have to finish."

"I've got equipment at my flat," Britt said.

Galen's nostrils flared as he exhaled. "No' safe enough. Wallace will have that watched as well."

"The hospital," Britt offered, her hands shaking as she clasped them in front of her. "I can get in there to do some testing."

Aiden stared at Britt in amazement. She might be traumatized by all she'd witnessed, but she pulled herself together to help him. "We need to get moving, then."

"We doona have time to walk. We need to use speed. Warrior speed," Quinn said with a wink to Britt. He then held out his hand. "Shall we, lass?"

Aiden let out a sigh when Britt took his father's hand and Quinn lifted her in his arms, then ran toward the hospital. Aiden pulled his hand away from his side and looked at the blood coating it

"Oh, shite," Galen grumbled. "You should've told your father."

Aiden grinned through the pain. Battle was exhilarating,

but not when loved ones' lives were on the line, or when black magic rendered him almost useless. "Britt can give us answers. I can no'."

"Nay, you imbecile, you're just his son. Quinn would give his own life for yours."

"I know." Aiden leaned his shoulder against the brick of the building and let his eyes close for a second. It was becoming more and more difficult to keep on his feet. "But I'm no' the one who defeats the evil. It's you, my father, and the other Warriors."

Galen let loose a low growl of frustration. "Come. They'll be waiting on us. You'll have that seen to when we get there."

With Galen's speed, he got them there just as Britt was using a keypad to open the door into the hospital. Aiden leaned against the wall for support, the blood seeping between his fingers now.

Britt winked at him when the door gave a loud beep and opened. He tried to smile, but the world was going black at the edges of his vision.

"Aiden!" Britt yelled.

He wanted to tell her it would be all right, but the darkness already claimed him.

Britt's hands shook while she took samples of the blood on Galen's dark green claws as she worried about Aiden. She kept glancing at him, hating how still he lay on the table as his father—father!—cleaned his wound.

"Why didn't he tell us he was hurt?" she asked.

Quinn tossed aside another towel soaked with blood. "Because he's as stubborn as his mother."

"Nay," Galen said. "He's like his father."

Quinn turned green eyes to Galen that were filled with worry. "He's my only son. I can no' lose him."

"Then call Fallon. He can have Sonya here before your next breath."

Britt listened to them, questions rushing through her mind. Druids, magic. What else was there? It terrified her, but she had come to know Aiden, and her findings on the blood were career changing.

Or they had been. Now she understood why Aiden hadn't wanted to tell her anything. She wouldn't have believed him, for one. But seeing for herself tended to alter everything.

Once she had several samples of blood from Galen, he wiped off his claws. The next time she looked, they—along with his fangs, green skin, and freaky eyes—were gone.

"You doona have to be afraid of me," Galen said gently. "I willna hurt you."

She nodded jerkily. "Aiden trusts you. So I trust you."

"He likes you," Quinn told her. "Aiden, I mean."

Britt glanced at Aiden. "I like him."

"I willna let him die," Quinn stated into the quiet.

Quinn's promise gave Britt the courage to turn to the microscope. After all she'd witnessed that night, she believed him.

She ran several quick tests on the *drough* blood while Quinn was on the phone with someone named Fallon.

"About time," Quinn said suddenly.

Britt looked up to see another man in the room. He had deep brown hair, and eyes a shade darker than Aiden's. What really snagged her attention was the gold torc around his neck so similar to the one Quinn wore.

"This is my brother, Fallon," Quinn told her. "And this is Sonya."

Britt was so confused by Fallon's having gotten into the room without her hearing him that she hadn't even seen the redhead. She gave a nod to both people, more questions than ever filling her mind.

"Sonya is a Druid with healing magic," Galen told her.

Britt forgot about the tests she was running and watched as Sonya walked to the table were Aiden lay. The Druid winced and lifted her gaze to Quinn when she saw the wound.

"It's bad, Quinn. The magic he took was meant to kill. I'm not sure how he survived."

"He's a MacLeod," Quinn said, his eyes never leaving Aiden.

"I'll do what I can," Sonya said.

Next, Sonya lifted her hands, palms down, over Aiden's body. She closed her eyes and whispered words Britt didn't understand.

Britt couldn't look away, and a few moments later when the blood from Aiden's wound began to slow to a trickle, she was glad she hadn't. During those few minutes, magic had been used. She couldn't feel it, couldn't see it, but there was no other explanation.

The waiting became unbearable as she silently urged Aiden to open his eyes and look at her, to give her that charming smile that always made her stomach flutter. The longer he went without moving, the more anxious she became.

She needed something to do to occupy her mind. So, Britt turned back to the microscope.

In between running her tests, Britt would glance over at Aiden. Quinn stood by his son, his gaze never leaving Aiden's face. Galen and Fallon were like sentries on either side of the door while Sonya continued to use her healing magic.

Magic. Britt had never considered it could really exist before she met Aiden. He'd shown her himself, but the real proof came from the battle she'd witnessed. Was it magic that kept Quinn looking as young as Aiden?

Britt forgot about magic when she put a drop of the *drough* blood into sample C and the sample began to die instantly.

"It's a good thing he didn't take that hit directly," Sonya said, breaking in to Britt's thoughts.

Britt lifted her head from the microscope and glimpsed Quinn running a hand down his face in a gesture so similar to Aiden's.

"He shouldna have been here," Quinn said.

Fallon blew out a harsh breath. "Where would you want him? Hiding with the other Druids? He's a Highlander,

Quinn. You can expect no less of him than what you yourself would do."

"You didna tell Marcail, did you?" Quinn asked as he
looked from Fallon to Sonya.

Sonya shook her head of short red curls. "No, but I will
when I return. You'll face her wrath later."

"I know."

Fallon's dark green gaze turned to her then. "Thank you
for helping us, Britt. We'll keep you safe from Wallace, that
I vow."

Then he laid a hand upon Sonya and they disappeared.

"What the hell was that?" Britt asked, too shocked to
move.

Quinn licked his lips before he sank onto a stool beside
Aiden. "You saw us tonight, Britt. You saw my skin change,
the claws and fangs."

"And the eyes," she added.

Galen nodded. "And the eyes. We're called Warriors. We
have primeval gods inside us that grant us immortality."

"Aiden is my son." Quinn took a deep breath and slowly
released it. "My wife, Marcail, is a Druid, which makes
Aiden a Druid as well."

Britt frowned. "But not a Warrior?"

"No' as long as Quinn is alive," Galen answered.

"How is this possible?"

For the next fifteen minutes, she listened to the story of
Rome and the Warriors' creation. She learned of *mies* and
droughs, and MacLeod Castle. She found out it was a shield
of magic surrounding the castle that allowed Aiden to grow
up, and then stop aging while he was within the shield.

"So he'll age if he's not in the shield," Britt said.

Quinn nodded. "His mother and I have been verra protective of him. It was his idea to find out why the *drough*
blood reacted the way it does to Warriors, and why another
Warrior's blood can combat the *drough* blood."

Britt pulled out the slide of blood she had been testing.
"This is Warrior blood, then? One touch of the *drough*
blood, and it destroyed the red and white blood cells."

"Aye, that's my blood," Quinn answered.

Britt set aside the slide and motioned for Galen. He went to her without question, and didn't so much as flinch when she pricked his finger. Several drops of his blood landed to mix with Quinn's.

She then hurried to put the slide under the microscope. "Oh, shit," she mumbled.

Britt looked up from the microscope at Galen and Quinn. "Now that I know what's really going on, I know what I need to do."

"We can no' stay here," Galen said. "It'll be only a matter of time before Wallace finds us."

A ghost of a grin showed on Quinn's face as he grabbed his phone. "I've got an idea."

CHAPTER TWENTY-FIVE

Charon watched Laura carefully as he paused in his telling of the story. He had waited for her to turn from him, or tell him to stop. But she just returned his look.

"How long were you in Deirdre's dungeons?"

"Too damn long," he said, and turned his head to the side. "Time no longer seemed to matter as I had to fight every second of every day from letting Ranmond take over. Hearing him demand blood and death in my head constantly. It would've been so easy to give in."

He expected her to be repulsed by his words. When she met his gaze, he continued. "Deirdre liked to use the threat of harming a Warrior's family to get him to align with her. When I refused, she tortured me until I forgot the man I was. I let Ranmond take over for just a moment, but it was during that small space in time that she put my father in the dungeon with me."

"Oh, God," Laura murmured.

Charon sighed, but even after so many centuries, the pain of what he had done was still with him. "When I once more got control from Ranmond, I opened my eyes to discover I had killed my father. Deirdre threatened to toss in other members of my family if I didna spy for her."

"Did you?"

"Aye. The thought of killing another member of my family, whether they were my immediate family or, years later, extended family, I couldna imagine it. So, I spied on Quinn, Ian, Duncan, and Arran for her. But I didna tell her everything."

"You would've been strong enough not to kill anyone she put with you."

"Was I?" he asked softly. "I'm no' so sure. I have control of Ranmond now, but the *droughs* always seem to know what to do so that I lose that control."

"You're here with the MacLeods now. They've forgiven you."

Charon shrugged. "Perhaps. I have no' forgiven myself though."

"Is that why you didn't tell me who you really were?"

"I kept all of this from you no' because you're a woman, but because I didna believe you a Druid."

"Others in Ferness know what you are."

He wished it otherwise, but the situation had been out of his control. "Aye. When Deirdre sent her wyrran, I had no choice but to defend the village."

"Where is Deirdre now?"

"Dead. As is Declan Wallace, the man responsible for bringing Deidre forward in time."

Laura tucked her feet beneath her. "If Deirdre was such a powerful *drough*, how was she defeated?"

"She underestimated us. Declan did the same, but we assumed Jason would be like Declan. He's no'. Jason has a different strategy altogether."

"Can Jason be defeated?"

Charon wanted to say yes, but he didn't want to lie to Laura. She deserved the truth. "We'll keep fighting him until he is dead."

"What happens to me now?"

He'd spent too much time locked in a dungeon to ever want to place anyone he cared about in such a situation. But he wasn't convinced Laura wasn't working with Jason.

"Tell me what happened to your magic," he urged.

Laura was on her feet in one smooth motion. The tight

leggings hugged her trim legs, and the shirt she wore hung just to her hips, giving him a glimpse of her firm ass.

"For two years I worked for you, and you never told me what you were."

"What good would it have done?"

She began to pace. "I want to believe you. Too much has happened. I can't wrap my head around any of it."

Charon followed her with his eyes. She was agitated, but it had to do with more than just discovering the truth. It also had to do with her magic, he was sure of it.

"I told you my story. Tell me yours."

"Not yet. I need . . ." She trailed off as she came to a halt in front of him. "I need a mobile."

"Nay."

"Please, Charon. Just let me have a mobile."

He grabbed her shoulders and gave her a shake. "There is an infant here! These people have saved my life, they've befriended me. I willna put them in jeopardy."

It was a mistake to touch her. He knew it the instant his hands made contact with her. Instantly his body roared to life, demanding, yearning to have another taste of her.

Ranmond shouted inside him, urging him to pull Laura against him and claim her lips. Claim her body. It would be so easy, so simple to mold her curves to his body.

To caress her warm skin.

To kiss her soft lips.

To sink into her tight, wet body.

His gaze focused on her mouth. Such sweet cries of pleasure had fallen from those amazing lips. He wanted to hear them again. Nay. He *needed* to hear them again.

For so long, he had kept himself apart from everyone, but Laura hadn't let him. She'd brought him into her world, whether he wanted it or not.

Then he had made love to her. It shouldn't have felt so damn good. He had been upset she wasn't a Druid, now he wished she weren't.

Somehow their bodies leaned toward each other. Charon

saw the erratic beat of the pulse at her throat. He could take her. With one kiss, she would melt against him.

But she wouldn't be the only one affected. The overwhelming, irresistible longing told Charon he was already in too deep with her. If he guessed wrong and she was helping Jason, he put everyone's lives in danger.

Charon made the mistake of looking into her pale green eyes. He lost himself in her gaze. He was falling, sinking into a vast ocean of green as deep and clear as the forests.

He gripped her shoulders firmly while he summoned the strength to push her away. Then he saw the desire, stark and blatant, in Laura's eyes.

Inwardly cursing himself for ten kinds of fool, Charon found his arms pulling her to him instead of pushing her away. His balls tightened when her hands came to rest on his waist.

It could all be an act, a tactic for her to worm her way farther into his psyche. Yet it didn't matter when she was so near. He wanted her, craved her like no other before. His hands itched to peel the clothes from her body.

And his cock ached to be buried inside her.

Her lips parted, inviting him to taste her. Her breathing grew harsh, rapid as she pushed her breasts against him.

With a growl, Charon spun them so she had her back against the wall and he was pressed against her. Her breath hitched and her fingers dug into his waist, letting him know her need was as great as his.

She rocked her hips against him, making his cock jump. No longer could he hold back. He had to have her, all of her.

Charon captured her mouth in a rough kiss. He laid claim, took, seized—and she gave it all to him with a soft moan.

Her hands clawed at his shirt until her palm touched skin. He had no qualms about ripping the shirt down the middle and tugging it off her. He deepened the kiss and reached between them to cup her breast. Charon growled as the weight settled in his palm. God, he loved her breasts.

Need, strong and powerful, rushed through him, but

Charon was determined to ignore it. He stroked a thumb over her nipple and smiled at her gasp of pleasure. His hand slid down her side and into the waist of her leggings. It took one jerk to slip the material down her hips, along with her panties.

Charon caressed her ass and trim legs. Then he palmed her sex, putting pressure with the heel of his hand against her clitoris.

She tore her mouth from his and whimpered as she clung to his shoulders. He wanted her screaming, yearned to hear his name upon her lips as he brought her to orgasm.

He slid his finger into her curls and found her wet. She bucked against his hand, and it nearly shredded his control.

Charon held on by a thin thread as he pushed a finger inside her. She moaned, her eyes closed while her hips rocked against him.

Laura's body was no longer her own. It belonged to Charon. He knew where to touch her, how to touch her to make her burn. She was on fire, scorched with the intensity of her need.

And he continued to take her higher.

Each stroke of his finger inside her, slow and sure, made her tremble, made her shiver in anticipation of what was to come.

He was a master at kissing, touching . . . teasing. The pleasure was too much to take when he swirled his thumb around her swollen clitoris.

Then a second finger was added to the first as he increased the tempo of his hand. She cried out from the desire turning her blood to molten heat.

Charon took her mouth in another fiery kiss. He couldn't help himself. He had to have her, all of her. Her legs buckled, and he wrapped an arm around her to keep her up.

If he could stop time, he would linger in this moment, in the beautiful woman in his arms.

He pumped his fingers deeper all the while her nails sank into his shoulders. Charon didn't feel the gouges, though.

All his attention was on her moist heat, the walls of her sex clamping down on his fingers.

Even when her body began to tighten, he didn't relent. He continued to stroke her, arouse her.

His breath quickened when she screamed her release. But even then he didn't stop. He took her clitoris between two fingers and gave it a soft tug.

She screamed again, this time his name falling from her lips as she peaked. Charon rested his forehead against hers while he fought not to yank his jeans down and slide into her.

The need to be inside her was crushing. He knew if he gave in, he'd find peace. The same peace that had been his for a short time after he made love to her.

Laura's head moved to his shoulder. With a soft curse, Charon lifted her in his arms and laid her on the bed. When he went to pull away, her arms constricted around him.

"Don't go," she whispered.

Charon had never been able to refuse Laura anything. Even with his doubts about her, he couldn't stop wanting her. It frightened him, the depth of his longing.

"Charon, please," she begged.

He looked into her moss green eyes and kicked off his shoes. She lifted the covers so he could crawl in beside her. The bed was tiny, which allowed little room for one person, much less two. But he enjoyed having her in his arms, her back against his chest.

"I'm not working for—or with—Jason," she said into the silence.

"He has magic you couldna comprehend, Laura. He's gotten into people's heads before without them even knowing it."

"You said the Druids here could tell if he'd used magic on me, or if I was colluding with him."

"Aye."

"Then why not let them? You'd have your answers and be able to trust me."

Charon looked at the painting on the wall of the sun setting over the Highlands. "I might have my answers, but will you? You say I could trust you then, yet I know you wouldna trust me."

"Let's find out."

"I betrayed those below before. I willna do it again. I'm protecting them as much as you by keeping you separated."

"Yet you brought me here," she whispered.

He swallowed and ran his thumb over her arm while he held her. "Aye. I wanted you safe from Wallace. I couldna bear it if he harmed you in any way."

"But you worry now if I'm worth protecting."

"I know you are," he said more harshly than he intended. Charon let out a breath. "Tell me what happened to your magic."

"My family. They syphoned my magic."

He waited for her to continue, but when she didn't, he asked, "What do you mean?"

"I left my family because they controlled me. I don't mean rules or curfews. I mean they told me who I could talk to, what I could eat, where I could go. At all times they dictated my life."

Charon was speechless. As stubborn as Laura was, he couldn't imagine anyone trying to rule her. Now he understood why she had balked when he told her what to do. "Why did they do it?"

"I never knew. My mother didn't do it to my older sister. My father was always away on business, so it was just my mother, Lacy, and me. I had no friends, except for the ones Mother told me I could have. I found out later those supposed friends spied on me for her. They told her when I went against her wishes."

"And you were punished," he guessed.

She nodded. "I tried to run. Both times I was locked in my room for two weeks with only bread and water. I wasn't allowed electricity or to bathe."

He wished he could see her face. Charon heard the pain in her words, but he knew her eyes would hold so much more. As furious as he was at her family, it just might send him over the edge to look into Laura's eyes. "How did you get away?"

"I waited until my father came home. He took me to lunch, and I told him I had to leave. He'd always known I was unhappy, but he didn't believe me when I told him what had been done. The lunch was interrupted by a business call, and while he was taking it, I left. I got on a train and never looked back. I'd been preparing for that day for years, so when the opportunity came, I had enough money to get me wherever I wanted to go."

Now he understood why she'd looked so lost when she walked into his pub.

"I spent several years in England until I feared they would find me."

"That's when you came to Ferness?"

"Yes. That's when I met you."

CHAPTER
TWENTY-SIX

Britt stood with her eyes closed as Fallon teleported them
from one place to another in quick succession. Her stomach
turned and pitched each time Fallon used his power.

Power. Immortal Warriors. Druids.

Her life had taken a drastic spin, and as frightened as she
was, there was also a steady build of excitement. She was a
risk taker, always had been. Why else would she have traveled Europe alone or gotten her degrees in universities others would never dream of looking at?

She kept her hands locked with Aiden's, who still lay unconscious, and Quinn's. How many more times would Fallon
jump them? Britt wasn't sure she could keep down the wonderful dinner she and Aiden had shared earlier.

"Britt," Quinn whispered.

She turned her head to him. "Yes?"

"You can look now."

The smile in his voice calmed her racing heart enough so
that she opened her eyes. And found herself standing in a
fully outfitted lab. "Where are we?"

"Outside of London in a facility owned by a friend," Fallon said. "I doona know how long you'll be safe."

Britt kicked off her heels and walked to the microscope.
"Give me three hours."

"Three hours," Fallon said with a nod. Then he looked to Quinn. "Do you want me to take Aiden back to the castle."

"Nay," Aiden said hoarsely.

Britt rushed to him as he sat up. "You stupid fool of a man. Don't you ever get injured like that again. Do you understand me? You scared the hell out of all of us."

His wicked grin made her stomach flip. "It wasna that bad."

"Actually, son, it was," Quinn said solemnly.

Britt watched Aiden's beautiful green eyes flicker with concern. "Are you really all right?" she asked.

He squeezed her hand. "Aye. Where are we?"

"One of Saffron's businesses she bought over the last year," Galen said as he walked into the room. "I sense no Druids yet."

Fallon nodded and looked to Quinn. "I'll return in three hours. Hopefully by then Charon will have some answers from Laura."

Britt turned back to Aiden when Fallon teleported away. Aiden's skin was still pale, but the wound was gone, as if it had never been.

"Here," Quinn said, and tossed a clean shirt at Aiden, who caught it easily. "Thought you might want that."

Britt moved from the table where they had laid him so Aiden could stand. She began to turn away when he stopped her with a hand on her arm.

"Britt," he whispered, and drew her close. "I didna want you a part of this."

"I became a part of it the moment I agreed to study the blood samples."

"You didna really know before. Now you do."

"I'm not running away, am I?" she asked him, narrowing her eyes. "And don't think this gets you out of another dinner. You owe me."

She couldn't keep the grin from her face as she teased him, but there was no smile on Aiden's lips.

"You should run. Far away from me."

Britt leaned forward and rose up on her toes so that they were nose to nose. "No. What you're looking for, what you brought to me, is important. I saw that firsthand tonight. You asked for my help, you can't change your mind now."

"Stubborn woman," he growled, but his lips had begun to pull up at the corners.

"I like her," Galen said with a chuckle.

Britt ran her hands over Aiden's chest, stopping just short of touching the ripped and bloodied section of his shirt. "I don't understand your world, but I want to."

"Do you like danger that much?" he asked with a frown.

"No. I like you that much."

Aiden hadn't been prepared for such a response. If his father and Galen weren't in the room with them, he'd have Britt underneath him in less than a heartbeat.

Instead, he covered her hands with his. "I doona know how long this war will rage, or if I'll come out of it alive."

"There are always wars. So what that this one has magic and immortals."

He cupped her face and looked deep into her blue eyes. "You're a verra special woman."

"And don't ever forget it," she said, and gave him a quick kiss before she walked to the microscope.

Aiden knew he wore a goofy grin, but he didn't care. Britt wanted to stay with him. How had he gotten so lucky?

"Well done," Quinn whispered as he moved to stand beside him.

He shrugged. "I didna do anything."

"You're a MacLeod, son," Quinn said with a wink. "That's all it took."

Aiden pulled off his ruined shirt and walked to the sink to wipe the dried blood off when the mobile phones started to go off.

Galen was the first to answer his, and Quinn second. Aiden's gaze locked with his father as dread filled him. By the furious look on Galen's face, and the desolation on his father's, Aiden braced himself.

"What is it?" he asked when Quinn ended the call.

Quinn sighed. "Jason wasna happy that we escaped him. He retaliated."

"By giving the people of Edinburgh a fucking epidemic," Galen ground out as he paced the room.

"Epidemic?" Britt repeated. "How is that possible? The authorities would check this out immediately. There's no way he can get away with this."

Galen snorted. "Oh, but he will. I've no doubt Jason has spent the last few months buying members of parliament as well as the authorities. If he's anything like his cousin, he's blackmailing the ones who didna join him. But it's no' just that. This is a medical crisis. No one will know it was done with magic."

"How do you know it was done with magic?" she asked.

"It began in the area we fought." Quinn raked a hand through his hair. "I didna expect him to take this battle to innocents."

Galen leaned his hands on a table and blew out a breath. "We should have."

Suddenly Aiden's mobile rang. He pulled it out and saw the number was blocked. After a glance at his father, he put the call on speaker.

"Aye?"

"Well, Aiden, that was a nice escape," said a male voice. "Needless to say, I'm no' happy. And when I'm no' happy, people get hurt."

Aiden clenched his jaw as blind fury filled him. "Wallace. Too bad I didna see you tonight."

Jason's disembodied evil laugh came through the phone. "You doona stand a chance against me. None of you do. You keep trying to save the innocents and those who mean the most to you, but that's what's going to win me this war."

"We've taken down two *droughs* before you. We'll bring you down as well," Quinn said.

"Ah, Quinn. I knew you wouldna be far from your lad. How much do you think it's going to hurt when he's dead after you kept him immortal for four centuries?"

Quinn and Aiden exchanged a look. "Never going to happen."

"Doona be so sure," Jason said with a knowing laugh. "Tell me, how is Laura doing? Is Charon trying to convince her who he is?"

Aiden shook his head at both Quinn and Galen. He didn't want to give Jason any information. Whether Laura was working with Jason or not, the less Jason knew, the better.

"You tell us?" Aiden said. "We're worried about her. What have you done with her? She's an innocent."

"As are the people suffering in Edinburgh!" Jason yelled. "Those 'innocents,' as you call them, are writhing in agony. You can stop it. All you need to do is give yourself and the sweet little blond that's been by your side these last few weeks to me. Tonight."

Aiden knew in his heart they could win against Jason, but could he live with himself if he sacrificed all those innocents? But he couldn't turn Britt over to Jason either.

"You can have me," Aiden said.

Quinn roared over his words and knocked the phone from his hands. "Never!"

"Dad," Aiden whispered urgently as Jason's laughter drifted through the phone. He hurriedly put the call on mute. "Listen to me. It's the right thing to do. Britt is needed. I'm no'."

"You're my son!"

Aiden took a deep, steadying breath. "I can no' live with myself if all those people die."

"Wallace will never agree," Galen said.

A muscle worked in Quinn's jaw as he stared at Aiden. "Wallace will torture you, and though you've heard us talk about being tortured by magic, you've never experienced it."

"I'm a Highlander, a MacLeod. I'll get through it."

"Holy hell," Quinn said as he turned away.

Aiden looked to Britt. She was shaking her head, her beautiful eyes pleading with him. He took the phone off mute to hear Jason still chuckling.

"Where do I meet you?" Aiden asked.

Jason tsked. "Did you no' hear my instructions? I said you *and* Britt. No' one without the other. Both."

"You can have me."

"Oh, I'll have you, Aiden." Jason's voice had gone cold with anger and malice. "I'm going to make you suffer unbearable pain. And all the while, your father is going to be helplessly watching."

Aiden couldn't look at his father. He knew Jason meant every word, but Aiden couldn't just stand by and do nothing.

"Two people are already dead, Aiden," Jason said, his voice calmer. "Those deaths are on your head. How many more will stack up before you and Britt come to me?"

Galen's phone vibrated. He glanced at it, then looked up at Aiden and sliced his hand back and forth across his throat for him to shut off the phone.

Aiden immediately ended the call. "What is it?" he asked.

"Isla, Larena, Sonya, and Reaghan are in Edinburgh, trying to combat the epidemic." Galen swallowed, his blue eyes troubled. "If that bastard so much as touches a hair on Reaghan's head, I'll have his balls for dinner."

Aiden pocketed his phone. "This could all be a trap. Wallace would know we wouldna stand by and do nothing. He knows Druids will go to Edinburgh."

"Fuck," Galen said as he hurried to dial his phone. "Fallon, get here now!"

In the next moment Fallon was standing beside Galen. "What is it?"

"Get the girls out of Edinburgh. It's a trap."

Fallon put his hand on Galen's shoulder, and in a blink they were both gone.

"Well," Britt said as she used a dropper to get a sample of blood. "I hate to point out the fact that Jason stayed on the phone with you for a bit, Aiden. The trap could extend to here, since he was so adamant about getting us."

Quinn snorted. "You say it so calmly, lass."

"Just pointing out a fact. That doesn't mean I'm not scared," she added before she bent to look in the microscope.

Aiden turned his head to his father, and he was sure the grim expression Quinn wore was the same one on his face. It seemed Jason was at least a step ahead of them at every turn.

"He doesna know where Laura is," Aiden said suddenly. "He was hoping we'd admit to it."

"That could mean she isna in league with him," Quinn added.

Aiden wasn't sure of anything anymore, but it was a gamble they had to take. Jason changed the game each time they played. It was time they took control.

He took out his phone and dialed Charon.

CHAPTER
TWENTY-SEVEN

Lacy Black walked down the street of the small village she had stopped for petrol and food. Magic hummed through her veins once more.

She hadn't realized how much she had gotten used to it until Laura managed to snap the syphoning spell in two. Leaving Lacy with no magic.

It was fortunate for Lacy and her mother that they used their magic to discover where Laura had gone months before. Luckily for them, Laura was still in Ferness.

Lacy held up her hand as magic raced along her skin, making the ends of her fingers buzz with the strength of it. Even with Laura's magic split between Lacy and her mother, the sheer amount of it was staggering.

What would it feel like to have all Laura's magic? Lacy smiled as she thought of everything she could do with her sister's potent magic.

"Oh, the fun I could have," Lacy said to herself.

She was just a block away from her car when something invisible shoved her into a narrow alley. Lacy called up her magic, and though she could feel it inside her, she couldn't use it.

With her mouth opened to scream, she found herself behind the building before she could blink. She dropped her purse and held up her hands in front of her as her magic answered her call.

Before she could launch the first blast into the unseen assailants, the air began to swirl around her. Particles the color of ash encircled her until she had to shut her eyes to protect herself.

She didn't dare to open her eyes until the wind had died down. And when she did, she let loose the scream from before.

The tall ash-colored monsters with their long, stringy white hair closed in on her quickly. Her scream was cut short when the first one sank its fangs into her arm.

Soon, the rest were on her. The pain from their bites was unimaginable, but it was nothing to the feel of her blood and magic being drained from her.

The magic she had worked so hard to keep for herself—the magic she would have killed for—was no match against the monsters on her.

There were so many they blocked out the sky. It became impossible to keep her eyes open. She knew she was dying. A single tear fell from her eye as she realized no amount of magic could have prepared her for the vicious beasts that were killing her.

The buzz of magic faded from her fingertips just before the last drop of blood left her body.

Charon rested his chin atop Laura's head as she snuggled next to him. He was still rocked with the knowledge that her mother and sister had ruled her life and syphoned her magic.

"What does your family have to do with magic? Are they Druids?" he asked.

"Yes." She bit her lip. "I didn't know they had magic until today. I . . . I can't really explain what happened when I watched you dying in the forest. I was so angry and felt so bloody helpless. And then suddenly there was something inside me, some power I had never felt before. It consumed me."

Charon didn't move or utter a word as he silently begged her to continue.

"It was magic. I know that now," she continued. "It built inside me until it exploded from my hands. When I opened my eyes, the cabin was demolished and everyone was on the ground. I went to you, but you weren't breathing. And then Jason moved."

"You ran," Charon whispered.

She nodded and turned in his arms so they were face-to-face. "I ran for hours or days. I don't know. I just knew I had to get away from him."

Charon smoothed back a strand of her dark hair from her face. "What happened?"

"I ran until I couldn't move. I slept, I guess." Her eyes took on a faraway look. "I heard drums and chanting, and I thought I heard voices. It was all around me."

"Your magic."

She blinked and focused on him again. "When I woke, I knew I wasn't alone. Jason was there, and I was surrounded. I already told you how he used magic to convince me what he said was the truth."

"Aye."

"I feel so damned violated," she ground out. "His magic didna last long, though. I was able to use mine to knock everyone unconscious. I was lucky enough to make it to Ferness. When I walked into my flat, Lacy was there. She told me she and Mum had been the ones taking my magic. Before I could deduce what she was about, she threw an apple at my head. Then I woke up here. Without my magic."

Charon wanted to ignore his phone when it rang, interrupting his conversation, but he knew he couldn't.

He rolled away from Laura and got to his feet. He frowned when he withdrew his mobile from his pocket and saw Aiden's name on the screen. "Aiden?" he answered.

"Charon, I need your help."

He was instantly on alert, his gaze locked on Laura, who still sat on the bed. "What is it?"

"I doona think Laura is working with Jason. He just called, asking about her. His questions make me think he has no clue where she is, but he wants her."

"That's no' going to happen."

"I thought you'd say as much." Aiden paused. "Jason will call off the epidemic upon Edinburgh if Britt and I give ourselves up."

Charon ran a hand down his face. "That means he knows you're on to something. You can no' stop."

"I know. Yet, I can no' allow innocent people to die in our war."

"Damn," Charon muttered, and sank into a chair. He braced his elbows on his knees and squeezed his eyes shut. "What else did he say?"

"He's angry. He thinks he's one step ahead of us, and he is. He always has been."

Charon opened his eyes to see Laura staring at him. She was part of his war now, a Druid. Jason would be coming for her, but Charon would be waiting. "We have another option."

"What?"

"I doona want to say yet in case it doesna pan out. Give me a couple of hours."

Aiden sighed. "Is there any way Laura can help?"

"Nay. Maybe. I doona know," Charon replied. He wanted to trust Laura, but he couldn't put his friends in jeopardy. At least not more than they already were.

"Hurry, Charon. I've already got two deaths on my conscience. I'd rather no' have more."

Charon ended the call and returned his phone to his jeans pocket. "I have to leave."

"To go where?" Laura asked with a frown.

He didn't want to lie to her, so he didn't answer.

"I see," she said. "I told you of my magic. I told you why I didn't have it before. I've nothing in which to harm any of you. Why won't you believe me?"

Charon frowned, hating the situation. "I want to, but there is so much at stake that I can no' chance it."

"Because you think I'm working with Jason," she said flatly.

"I believe what you've told me. I just need some time."

"Meanwhile, you want me to stay here?"

Charon stood and put his back to her. Jason was a thorn in their side. The fact Laura had gone with him only added to the irritation. He was glad she hadn't fought them, because he knew all too well what Wallace would have done.

Yet, it rubbed him raw that she had gone with Jason. Magic or not.

It's that she began to wonder if you told her the truth.

Charon hated when his conscience was right. Wallace had put doubts in her head, and Charon hadn't told her everything when he had the chance.

"You can't get past that I went with Jason. What was I supposed to have done?" she asked angrily.

He heard the bed creak and knew she had risen to her feet. Still he didn't face her. He refused to see the pain and frustration in her beautiful green eyes anymore.

"They outnumbered me, Charon," she said. "I was alone and scared. I was trying to figure out what happened at the cabin as well as why I all of a sudden had magic. What choice did I have?"

"You could've fought him. You have the magic to do it." He knew as soon as the words left his mouth that wasn't what he would have wanted for her.

She laughed wryly. "I don't know the first thing about magic. I don't even know how I used it the two times I did."

"I know."

"Then why are you so angry with me? You know I did the right thing."

Charon fisted his hands at his sides to keep from turning and pulling her in his arms. "You believed him, Laura. After I told you what a monster he was, after I fought him to make sure you were kept safe. You believed him."

"You didn't tell me the entire truth."

Charon whirled around to face her. "I didna know you were a Druid! If I had, you'd have known everything without me having to tell you."

She raised a dark brow and crossed her arms over her chest. "I've worked for you for two years. We were friends. I trusted you. Yet at the slightest mistake, you turn your back on me."

"I'm no' turning my back on you."

"The hell you aren't," she ground out. Laura dropped her arms and took a deep breath. "You won't admit you did wrong."

"Because I didna. We have a code. No one who isna a Druid or a Warrior is to know about our world. It's to keep everyone safe."

She rolled her eyes. "And the fact Jason tried to kidnap me to get to you, and you knew he was coming after us, didn't warrant me knowing the entire truth?"

"You wouldna have believed me."

"I guess we'll never know, will we? You didn't trust me enough to find out."

Charon had had enough. He sliced his hand through the air. "Enough! We can debate this later. Right now I've got to save my friends."

"And what am I to do?"

"Will you stay here? Until I return. I willna be gone long."

She cocked her head to the side, her wealth of dark hair falling seductively over her shoulder. "You want me to stay here? In a place where you don't trust me to go outside of this room because I might be working with Jason?"

"Aye." He clenched his jaw when she gave a snort of annoyance. "I can no' take you with me, Laura. Inside this castle you'll be safe. I need to know you're safe from Wallace."

An expression of genuine disbelief crossed her face. "Why?"

Before Charon could stop himself, he pulled her into his arms, his lips descending on hers. To his surprise, she didn't turn away. Instead, she opened for his kiss.

He groaned when her hands slid up his chest and wrapped around his neck. Charon knew kissing her was wrong, especially when he wasn't sure of her loyalties.

But when it came to Laura, he was powerless to deny his

body what it craved. He knew there was a chance she wouldn't stay at the castle when he left. The only way to ensure she did was by locking her in the dungeon, which he refused to do.

Knowing this might be the last time he held her, Charon deepened the kiss. She tasted of seduction, pure unadulterated female at her finest.

His blood burned with need, and his cock ached, it was so hard for her. It would be easy to give in to his desire and lay her back on the bed. But his friends needed him.

Charon reluctantly ended the kiss. He bit back a groan when he saw Laura's kiss-swollen lips. Her moss green eyes were dazed as she stared up at him.

"I wish there was more time," he whispered, and rested his forehead against hers. "Please stay here. If for no other reason than I asked you to."

He didn't expect her to reply, and when the silence stretched between them, Charon knew it was time to leave. He dropped his arms from around her and took a step back.

She met his gaze, but he was unable to read her emotions. With a nod, Charon turned on his heel and walked out of the chamber. With every step away from her, a little piece of him died.

By the time he reached the great hall, the spot in his chest where the knife coated with *drough* blood had entered him ached so that he couldn't stop rubbing it.

He paused when he saw the chaos around him. Druids were running in all different directions while the few Warriors still at the castle were looking at a map of Edinburgh.

Charon knew they were looking at every possible way of getting to the infected area of the city without Jason knowing. He walked past them until he found Ronnie standing alone as she stuffed a backpack full of supplies.

"Ronnie," he called as he walked up.

She lifted her head of wheat-colored hair. "Any news about Laura's loyalty?"

"No' yet. I have to leave for a wee bit."

"Leave?" she asked, her forehead furrowed.

He nodded. "It's to help us."

"I know. I'm just surprised you'd go alone."

Charon glanced around him and shrugged. "Everyone is busy, and it's better if I go alone on this anyway. I'll be back."

"And Laura?" Ronnie asked before he could walk away.

"Leave her."

Ronnie zipped the backpack and flattened her lips. "You know she might try to run away."

"She might."

"I see," Ronnie said after a moment. "Godspeed, Charon."

He forced a smile. "Stay safe, Druid."

Charon walked to the kitchen where the keys to the vehicles were kept. Since his was still in Ferness, he had no choice but to take one of those at the castle.

He grabbed the keys to the quickest car they had, a Porsche 911 GT2 RS, and hurried out the door. Charon grinned as he spotted the fastest production Porsche ever made in the bailey.

Once he slid into the seats of the red sports car and started the car, he eyed the open gates at the gatehouse. He put the car in first, gripped the red and black steering wheel, and gunned it. The engine gave a loud, feral roar before the car raced out of the bailey.

Laura hid in the shadows of the second-floor balcony and watched Charon talking to a woman in the great hall. The woman wasn't happy with whatever Charon said, and then a moment later he walked out of the castle.

For several minutes, Laura simply stood and watched the activity of the hall. There was something major going on by the way everyone hurried about. Was it Jason?

Charon had said he needed to save his friends. With the Warriors being immortal and having powers, and the Druids using magic, she wasn't sure why they would need help. Then she recalled Jason.

He was as evil as they came. Just thinking of his voice

and the way he smiled sent a shiver of dread running through her. He had used his magic so effortlessly on her.

She felt as violated as she had when Ben tried to kidnap her. Jason had to be stopped. There was no denying that. Ignoring him wouldn't make him go away.

Laura glanced back at the hallway that would take her to the room Charon had put her in. She couldn't simply wait for Charon to return. Not when she knew she could help in this fight by getting her magic back.

She waited until the hall was all but clear before she quickly sneaked down the stairs. Laura hurried to the doorway she'd seen Charon get the keys from.

The few people in the hall didn't even notice her as she ducked through the door and found herself in a kitchen. She spotted the hooks where several sets of keys were kept.

Laura paused as she went to grab a set. She'd never stolen anything in her life, but it wasn't as if she had a choice. She could get her magic back and help Charon. Maybe then he would see she was on his side.

She grabbed the first set of keys nearest the door. Just as she was about to retrace her footsteps, she heard someone approaching. Laura glanced and saw a door leading outside.

With just seconds to spare, she rushed out the door, closing it quietly behind her. She found herself in a small garden area outside. To her left was the sea, and to her right was the bailey.

Laura ran into the bailey, punching the unlock button on the key fob to find out which vehicle she was stealing. Elation filled her when she slid into the black Range Rover and started the engine.

She drove off, looking in the rearview mirror to see if anyone saw her. When no one came running outside to stop her once she was through the gate, she gunned the vehicle.

Time was of the essence.

CHAPTER TWENTY-EIGHT

Jason stood in the corridor of the hospital and watched with glee as more and more people were brought in with the disease he had created.

Not even the sight of a little boy covered in the oozing blisters gave him pause. If the MacLeods wanted to play, he was up for it.

They would be the ones losing sleep at night over the countless deaths they could have saved had they simply given in to his demands.

"We should've done this sooner," Mindy said as she walked up beside him, holding her recently stitched arm.

She couldn't contain her excitement at what they were doing, and it set his blood pounding with need. It had been that way since the first time he saw her, ten months earlier. She understood him as no one else did. And she understood what he was after.

Aisley walked slowly down the hall, her hands shoved in the back pockets of her jeans. She reached them and rammed her shoulder into Mindy. "Try not to look so pleased with yourself."

"And why shouldn't I?" Mindy retorted angrily.

Aisley glanced at Jason before she said, "You can't take credit for this. This was Jason's handiwork."

"I'm not taking credit." Mindy then turned to him. "Jason, baby, you know I'm not taking credit."

He wrapped an arm around Mindy and brought her against his side. "Of course no', darling. However, Aisley does have a point. These are our people dying."

"They'd die anyway," she said with a shrug. "So what if it's a few years early. Besides, the population needs to be thinned out. The weak have no place with us."

Jason raised his gaze to Aisley. His cousin's hatred of Mindy grew by the day, as did Mindy's for Aisley. There would come a time he didn't want to keep them from the showdown that had been brewing since he brought Mindy to the mansion.

He wasn't sure who would win, though. Mindy was powerful, but she was reckless. She often used her magic without thinking things through, which caused her to lose.

Aisley was much better in battle, but he still wasn't convinced her heart truly lay with his goals. She did everything he asked without fail. Yet, he couldn't help but think that she had doubts.

"Do you no' share Mindy's view, cousin?" Jason asked, his tone soft and deceptively light.

Aisley held his stare. "Killing adults is one thing. Killing a child or a baby is another."

Mindy began to laugh, and Jason watched as Aisley's face flushed red with anger.

"Why do you care about babies?" Mindy asked.

Jason didn't stop Aisley when she grabbed his lover and shoved her up against the wall. He smirked when Mindy gave a scream of outrage.

"Don't speak of what you don't know," Aisley said through clenched teeth as she got in Mindy's face. "If you do, not even Jason will be able to protect you from me."

"Now, now," Jason said as he gently pulled Aisley from Mindy.

It took a minute, but eventually Aisley released her. She

turned to Jason and poked her finger in his shoulder. "Control your bitch."

He watched her walk away with long, angry strides, her high-heeled boots clopping loudly, until she disappeared around a corner.

"I can't believe you let her talk to me like that," Mindy whined.

"There are things about Aisley's past you doona know, darling, but if I were you, I'd heed her warning."

She frowned up at him. "You wouldn't protect me?"

"You're a Druid. Protect yourself."

"But," she said, and then paused. "I'm your lover."

Jason resumed his stance against the wall. "What do you think that affords you?"

"Besides your attention? It should also afford me your protection."

He raised a brow at her petulant tone. "If I wanted to protect a woman, my lover wouldna be a Druid. You share my bed, Mindy, because you're powerful. You earned the spot in my bed. You'll earn everything else as well."

Just as he expected, Mindy stomped away, her exit much less dramatic than Aisley's. But then again, his cousin always had a way with flair.

Jason forgot about Aisley and Mindy as two more people came rushing into the hospital with symptoms of the contagion.

"A prelude to things to come," he said with a smile as he watched a man collapse on the floor.

Charon reached Dreagan property faster than he expected. Even with it raining. Then again, that's what happened when he drove like a madman.

He didn't slow as he pulled onto the one road in and out of Dreagan. The only time his foot came off the gas pedal was when he pressed on the brake to stop the car.

Charon opened his door and stepped out in the rain to find Guy standing before him.

"That was quite an entrance. Do you often practice sliding your vehicles to a halt on gravel?" Guy asked with a cocky grin.

"I doona have time for games. I need to speak to Con."

Guy's grin slipped as he motioned Charon to follow him. Charon slammed the Porsche's door closed and jogged to catch up with Guy.

He expected to be taken to the front entrance as he was before, but instead Charon found himself entering the conservatory.

Charon whistled at the sheer size of the room and all the plants held within. He shook his head, sending droplets of water over everything near him.

"You brought the storm," Guy said as he, too, shook off the rain. "Follow me."

Charon was taken through the conservatory and into the front parlor before they started up the stairs. He paused beside the doorway when Guy gave a single knock before opening Con's office door.

Constantine got to his feet when he spotted Charon. "I didna expect you back quite so soon."

"A lot has happened since I was here."

Con took his seat as he motioned for Charon to sit.

Guy poured three glasses of whisky before handing one to Charon. "Does this have to do with the epidemic in Edinburgh?"

Charon tilted back his glass and downed the whisky in one swallow. He normally savored the rich flavor, but all the way to Dreagan, he'd gone over and over in his head his conversation with Laura.

He knew without a doubt she had left MacLeod Castle. That bothered him, but not so much as wondering if she was with Jason or not.

"Charon?" Con urged.

"It is," Charon answered, pulling his attention to the matter at hand. "I doona know how you know what I am. I'll tell you anything you want to know as long as you can help us."

Constantine leaned back in his chair and regarded Charon

silently for several minutes. "I know all there is to know of Warriors."

Charon shook his head, somehow not at all surprised by Con's response. "Why did you no' tell me that before?"

"You were no' ready to hear it," Guy said as he leaned a shoulder against the wall, his glass of whisky in his hand.

Charon ran a hand through his hair. "Jason Wallace started the epidemic because he learned we had someone studying how *drough* blood affects us as well as why other Warrior blood counters it."

"A good plan," Con said.

Charon shrugged. "It wasna my idea. I think this last battle with Jason where I was injured and nothing helped is what spurred this. Wallace has done something to the *drough* blood he's using. It's more powerful. It was thought that perhaps it was time we did some experimenting of our own."

"What have you learned?"

"Nothing. I know we have someone in Edinburgh——"

"Aiden MacLeod," Guy said. "His father, Quinn, and another Warrior, Galen, is also there."

Charon leaned his head back to look at the ceiling as he realized just how long Con's reach was. "Will you tell me how you know all of this?"

"You didna think you were the only magical creature, did you?" Guy asked with a smile. "Arrogant arse."

Con cleared his throat and cut Guy a look. "The truth is, Charon, there's a lot about Dreagan you doona know. Yet. We've made it our business to keep informed of Druids and Warriors."

Charon lifted his head and met Con's dark gaze. "Is there anything that's happened that you doona know?"

"What happened at Ferness?"

"Jason Wallace. Again." Charon pinched the bridge of his nose with his thumb and forefinger. "He was after Laura. He wanted to kidnap her to make me suffer. Wallace didna count on Laura fighting back, or for someone to interfere."

Guy slammed his crystal glass down on Con's desk. "Wallace went after Laura?"

Charon gave a single nod of his head. "I decided to keep watch over her after that. But I didna get her to MacLeod Castle in time. Wallace arrived with his *droughs*."

"Does he have Laura?" Con asked slowly as he sat forward and braced his forearms on the desk.

"Nay. We took to the forest, but they found her. I went out to fight them so she could get away." He trailed off as he remembered the feel of her magic.

It had been so . . . beautiful and pure. The force of it made his soul shudder and beg for more at the same time. No magic had ever felt so perfect.

Guy took the seat next to Charon. "She didna run, did she?"

Charon shook his head. "She stayed. And watched them slowly kill me. I didna know it was her magic that shot from the cabin. One touch of her magic, and it was like the *drough* blood inside me didn't exist anymore."

"Damn," Con murmured. "I didna realize she was a Druid, and one obviously powerful."

"I'd worked with her for two years and never knew she was a Druid. She says she didna know either, that it was her mother and sister who syphoned her magic from her."

Con's lips twisted in anger. "It's been done before, so it's plausible if you're doubting her."

"Deirdre and Declan have both used others to get inside MacLeod Castle and hurt them. I have to be cautious."

Guy nodded. "But you believe her, do you no'?"

"Aye. Is it because I want to, or because I can tell she speaks the truth?"

"Use the Druids at the castle to find out," Con said.

"It may come to that."

Guy poured them all more whisky. "Finish the story. We need to know what happened in Ferness."

"She ran after the explosion of the cabin," Charon said as he swirled the amber liquid in the glass. "Wallace found her before I did, and since I didna know she was a Druid, I hadna told her everything. Jason told her lies and used magic, and she believed everything he told her."

Guy rubbed the side of his thumbnail against the upholstery of the arm of his chair. "You can no' fault her for that."

"Too many times MacLeod Castle has been besieged by spies. I didna want to be blamed for another."

Con nodded. "So what happened?"

"Laura's sister was at Ferness waiting for her," Charon continued. "She took back Laura's magic. We got Laura to MacLeod Castle, but we doona know if she's working with Jason or no'. Before I could find out, Aiden called to say Jason had given an ultimatum. He'd stop the plague in Edinburgh if Aiden and Britt turned themselves in to him."

"They can no'," Guy said.

Charon shrugged one shoulder. "I know. Which is why I'm here. You offered to be allies. I'm asking for your help now."

Con scooted back his chair and stood. "First, you need to know what we are. We can no' just go barreling into a fight like you can. For the most part, you Warriors are able to stay hidden. Though we are powerful in human form, to tap the full potential of our magic, we need to be in our true form."

"And that would be?" Charon asked.

Con jerked his chin to Guy, who flipped open his phone and pressed a few keys. Charon waited for something to happen, but nothing did.

"You'll get a better view from here," Con said, and motioned Charon to the window.

Charon walked around the desk and looked out over the rolling hills. Thousands of sheep and cattle were scattered as far as the eye could see.

He was taking in the beauty when something moved in the low-lying rain clouds. Charon lifted his gaze to see the massive form of a dragon with scales the color of emeralds.

CHAPTER
TWENTY-NINE

Britt put her hands at her waist and arched her back as she stretched. Her dress was ruined, and her feet cold from kicking off her heels and walking barefoot on the floor. How she wished she had some jeans and a shirt. And socks.

All of it would be better to run in, she mused. She adjusted herself on the stool while thinking over what she had just discovered.

"Everything all right?" Aiden asked.

She turned her head to him, surprised to find him so close when she hadn't heard him approach. "Yes."

"I hear a bit of hesitation in your voice," he said with a lopsided smile. "Why no' take a break? I know you're weary."

Britt shook her head. "It's only been a few hours. I'll be all right."

"Liar."

She laughed, her eyes fastening on his lips. Lips that had kissed her with such hunger and passion that she was still reeling from it.

"Britt," Aiden murmured in his deep, husky voice thick with a brogue that made her stomach feel as if butterflies had taken flight inside. "Doona look at me like that."

She blinked and forced her gaze up to his beautiful green eyes. The desire she saw darkening their depths caused her breathing to ratchet up another notch. "Then don't be so damned tempting."

"Ah, lass." His fingers threaded into her hair while his thumb caressed her bottom lip. "You're the tempting one."

Britt knew if she didn't stop them, they were likely to start kissing again. With so much at stake—not to mention his father in the room—it wasn't a prudent idea.

She licked her lips and turned her head away, missing his touch instantly. There was no denying she was more than a little freaked at all she had seen and experienced that night, but none of it diminished the incredible, crushing desire being near Aiden caused.

"I've found something," she said.

Aiden's stance shifted as he leaned against the table. "Tell me."

She glanced to find the desire gone from his eyes, replaced with an intensity that made him who he was. Appealing, daring, and fierce. "I've found an enzyme."

"Shite," Aiden said as he turned to his father and Galen. "Both of you might want to see this."

As soon as Galen and Quinn reached her, Britt told them what she had just explained to Aiden.

"I'm no' a scholar," Galen said. "I understand that you've found something important, but how does that relate to us?"

Britt looked at each of them before her gaze came to rest on Aiden. "It means, I've found a way to combat the *drough* blood when it reaches a Warrior's bloodstream."

"How?" Quinn asked.

If Britt thought there would be a celebration for her discovery, she'd been dead wrong. She pulled the sample from the microscope and held it in front of her. "It's the unique nature of the enzyme that causes the *drough* blood to essentially begin attacking a Warrior by reaching all the organs through the blood."

"Unfortunately, most of us know that part," Galen said with a frown.

Britt could only imagine how painful it must feel after

witnessing it through a microscope. She cleared her throat and continued. "Let me show you."

She placed another slide beneath the microscope and moved so they could peer into the machine. "This is a sample of your blood, Quinn."

Once the three of them had seen it, Britt then put a sample of *drough* blood under the microscope for them to see. When they had looked their fill, she got a fresh slide and put a drop of Quinn's blood on it before adding a drop of *drough* blood. Britt hastily put it under the machine and stepped back.

Aiden was the first to look. His face was ashen as he stepped aside and motioned for his father to look.

Quinn was silent for a long time before he straightened. "Holy hell," he murmured.

"This explains a lot," Galen said as he looked through the microscope.

Britt nodded. "What you're seeing is how the *drough* blood consumes Quinn's blood. Now, let me add Galen's sample."

Aiden watched as Britt moved with efficient speed, taking the slide out of the microscope and adding in more blood before replacing the slide.

"Here, you'll be able to see what more Warrior blood does to the attacking *drough* blood," she said, and stepped back to give them room.

Aiden motioned for his father to look first. Quinn's brow was furrowed when he stepped away to allow Galen a chance to view it, and then it was Aiden's turn.

He watched, mesmerized, as the attacking *drough* blood was stopped in its tracks. "I doona understand," he said as he lifted his head. "Why couldna the blood already within the Warrior no' stop the *drough* blood?"

"I suspect because it doesn't have time with the *drough* blood attacking it," Britt said. "New, fresh Warrior blood is too much for the *drough* blood. Each Warrior has a god inside him giving him immortality and powers, so it's no wonder the blood helps other Warriors."

Galen was the first to speak into the silence. "Can we isolate it, or can we create something to counteract the *drough* blood?"

"That's what I'm working on," Britt said.

"The X90s bullets they use are filled with *drough* blood," Quinn said. "We doona stand a chance against them. Is there any way to have something to counter them before we get hit?"

Aiden watched Britt's lips compress as she began to think. He could practically see the wheels turning in her head.

"Possibly," she said. "I'll need more time, though."

Aiden jerked when he heard an explosion somewhere in the building. "We need to leave. Now!"

Quinn and Galen instantly shifted into their Warrior forms as Aiden began destroying Britt's samples.

"What are you doing?" she demanded.

Aiden pushed her hands away when she tried to stop him. "It's Jason. I can get you more samples, Britt. We can no' leave anything for Wallace to find."

That seemed to spur her into action. With her help, it took no time for them to remove all evidence of her work.

"Wallace is here," Galen said as he ran back into the room.

Aiden knew their time had run out. There was nowhere left for them to run, and by the way Quinn squeezed his mobile phone at his ear, he couldn't get a hold of Fallon.

Quinn lowered the mobile and turned to Galen. "Get my son and Britt out of here."

"I'm no' leaving you," Aiden said, furious that his father would sacrifice himself.

Quinn smiled sadly. "You and Britt are the future. Together, the two of you can find a way to beat Wallace and any *drough* who dares to take his place."

"I need you. We all need you," Aiden argued.

"It's the only way."

Galen stepped between them. "Nay. I'll stay behind and

create a diversion. I'm no' the one with a child, Quinn. Take your son and Britt, and get the hell out of here."

"Stop it!" Britt yelled. "We can all leave if we quit arguing about it."

Aiden raised a brow in question at both his father and Galen. When they nodded, Aiden grabbed Britt's hand and pulled her out the door with him.

He could hear Wallace getting closer. The maze of corridors in the building kept them a ways ahead of Jason and his gang. But would it be enough?

"Dragons," Charon whispered, hardly able to believe his eyes as he tracked the green dragon meandering lazily in the clouds.

"Dragon Kings, to be exact," Constantine said. "We ruled this realm long before man ever appeared. Imagine dragons of every shape, size, and color in the skies, on land, and in the water."

Charon watched the green dragon spread its wings and catch a current that took it back into the clouds. He turned to Con and Guy then. "And when man came?"

"We Kings were able to shift from dragon to human and back again to help keep the peace between dragons and humans," Guy explained.

"As with all things, it didna last," Con said softly.

Charon knew there was more to the story, but he wasn't going to find out that day. "So all of you are Dragon Kings?"

Guy nodded. "I'm King of the Reds. Hal, who you saw out there, is King of the Greens. Con is the King of Kings."

"And here I thought you were just some CEO," Charon said with a grin. "Did you rule all dragons?"

Con leaned a hip against his desk. "I was King of the Golds, as well as being leader to all Kings."

"How does no one know what you are?"

"That's a long story," Con said, and set down his whisky. "Suffice it to say, we've been verra careful. We've never interfered in the world before, but I've been watching your war with the *droughs*. You and the other Warriors, along with their Druids, have made a good stand against evil. However, Jason Wallace is proving to be a more dangerous enemy than I ever expected."

"Can you help? Will you help?" Charon asked.

Con smiled. "I wouldna have allowed you to know what we are, or told you I knew you to be a Warrior if I didna plan to offer our aid."

Guy rubbed his hands together. "It's been so many millennia since I've had a good fight. I'm eager for this."

"Your secret will be revealed. You do understand that, right?" Charon asked.

Con straightened and clamped a hand on his shoulder. "How long have you Warriors thought you were the only ones left to battle evil?"

"Hundreds of years."

"It was my decision to keep my Kings from helping any of you. Our dragons are gone, Charon, and with it, a part of our souls. We've lived a certain way for eons, but as it's recently been pointed out to me, times have changed. It's time we Dragon Kings changed with it."

Charon wanted their help, and he knew he needed their help. Still, the idea of the world discovering the Dragon Kings made him wonder how it would all turn out.

The sound of a dragon's roar was louder than the thunder. So much about Dreagan made sense now, and he was loath to shatter what the Kings had built there.

"I'm no' sure it's worth it," he said. "Any of you daring to be seen as a dragon will turn attention here."

"It's already happened," Guy said. "In London, actually. We . . . well, let's just say there was an incident that couldna be avoided. Two Kings had no choice but to shift to beat our enemy. No one has heard about that."

Charon raked a hand through his hair and paced the office. He knew all about risk. He had risked his village discovering what he was for four hundred years.

Even now that they knew he wasn't just a man, the illusion he had created was his armor. What the Dragon Kings had built was so much more.

He stopped and blew out a harsh breath. "If you help, I want to make sure the only people who might see any of you will be Druids and Warriors. The Dragon Kings need to be kept from the world."

"I like him," Guy said with a broad smile to Con.

Con laughed. "As do I. I agree with you, Charon. Battles, though, have their own way of happening without any help from the players."

The door to Con's office was thrown open as a man with dark hair and aqua eyes stood in the doorway. "The selmyr have struck again, Con."

Charon's blood turned to ice as he recalled Arran's run-in with the ancient creatures who fed off magic. His first thought was of Laura, until he realized her magic was gone again.

"Where?" Charon demanded as he took a step toward the man.

Con's forehead furrowed as he asked, "You know of these creatures?"

"Aye. Another Warrior was nearly killed by them when his woman accidentally released them. I thought you knew everything."

Con's lips pressed into a tight line before he said, "We can no' be everywhere."

"I need to know where the selmyr are at," Charon said, his tone brooking no argument.

"Follow me and I'll tell you," Con said as he walked from his office.

CHAPTER THIRTY

Laura pulled off the road and parked the SUV. She stared down the street to her parents' house. Pots overflowed with a bright array of flowers, just as she remembered.

But what she didn't remember was the red paint peeling from the door. Her mother had been fastidious about keeping everything in perfect condition.

She inhaled, both hands on the wheel, and wondered what the hell she was going to say to her mother and sister. They had her magic. There was no way for her to get it back from them. She knew nothing of magic.

Laura recalled the drums and chanting she'd heard while she was in the forest for the brief respite when she'd had her magic. The chanting had comforted her and offered her solace in a world that seemed to have gone crazy.

Her magic—as well as the chanting—was gone, and yet the world was crazier than ever.

Laura leaned her head back against the seat and briefly squeezed her eyes shut. "What have I gotten myself into?"

Though it wasn't really her fault. She was angry at Charon for not telling her everything and for not believing her, but she didn't blame him. She'd probably doubt her as well if she were in his shoes.

She wished he was with her, his strong arms around her as he whispered words of comfort. Charon was always so ready and able to face whatever came his way. Now she knew part of it was because he was a Warrior and immortal.

But another part she knew was something that was simply Charon, something that was in his DNA long before he had his god unbound. It's what made the god chose him, what made Charon the only man who could ever affect her the way he did.

"Damn you, Charon," she said. "I knew it'd be a disaster to care about you."

Before she changed her mind, she opened the door and got out of the Range Rover. Her legs were unsteady as she slowly walked to the red front door.

She paused before her shaking hand could knock on the door. A gust of what she thought was wind whipped by her, blowing her hair in her eyes. She clawed at the strands and caught sight of what appeared to be something pale gray swirling around her before it vanished.

A shiver of foreboding crawled down Laura's spine. "Mother," she called out as she pounded on the door, her nerves forgotten as worry set in. "Lacy!"

There was a scream from the back of the house. Laura jumped a hedge and raced to the wooden gate. Her fingers slipped on the latch in her hurry, but before she could get it open, someone grabbed her from behind.

"Laura, nay," Charon whispered tightly.

She stilled, terrified screams reverberating around her. Laura focused on his face to keep the chaos she felt swirling around her at bay. "Charon."

"Aye."

"My parents."

"I know, lass, but we have to leave."

She heard the urgency in his voice, but her legs wouldn't move. Laura tried to say Charon's name again as something slammed into her. She jerked, her entire body feeling as if a current of electricity went through her.

"Shit," Charon said and lifted her in his arms. "Her magic is returning. We have to get her out of here now."

Laura wanted to know who he was talking to, but her

eyes were riveted on the gate. Something was on the other side. Something she innately knew was there to do her harm.

"Go. I'll hold them off," a male voice said.

Charon started running, and Laura wound her arms around his neck. She felt her magic humming through her veins once more, and it was amazing.

She didn't know how she had managed to get it back, but it was hers once more. And she wouldn't give it up again.

Charon unceremoniously dumped her in the backseat of another SUV. She scooted to her side and turned her head to ask him what was going on when she saw the tall, gangly monster with ash-colored skin bust through her parents' gate with one swing of its fist.

"Bloody hell," she murmured.

Charon slammed his door shut. "Can we leave him?" he asked the driver.

Guy smiled in the rearview mirror, his pale brown eyes ringed in black crinkling at the corners. "I feel sorry for anyone wanting to tangle with Con. Rhys is with him, too, so he'll be fine."

The SUV sped off with a peel of tires as it started to rain. Laura turned in the seat to look through the back window as Con and the ash-skinned creature circled each other while several other similar beings began to close around them.

"What are those things?" Laura asked.

They turned a corner so sharply, she careened into the door. With her parents' house out of view, she turned and faced forward, her heart hammering in her chest.

"They're called selmyr," Charon said, his eyes looking dead ahead. "They're ancient monsters who hunt and feed off other magical beings."

Laura put her hand atop his. "My parents? I heard screams."

His gaze dropped to her hand before he looked at her. His long dark hair was in disarray, and his eyes were filled with sorrow. "They came for your mother. They felt your magic in her, Laura."

"Why didn't you try to save her?"

"There was nothing to save," Guy said from the front. "The selmyr move on the wind. If you feel them, it's already too late."

She braced a hand against her forehead. "I came to make them return my magic."

"Her death did it," Charon said. "The selmyr took your sister as well."

Laura nodded numbly and lifted her head. She felt sorrow in losing her mother and sister, but it wasn't the anguish she should feel toward her family. "And my father?"

"The selmyr doona bother anyone without magic. Your father will be fine unless he gets in the way," Guy said.

Charon moved his arm so that he took her hand in one of his. She wanted to cry for the loss of her mother and sister, but couldn't do it.

"How did you find me?" she asked.

Charon's thumb moved in small circles on the back of her hand. "Lacy was found about forty miles away."

"By who?" she asked.

Charon and Guy shared a look in the rearview mirror. Finally Charon said, "By one of Con's men."

"We guessed the selmyr might look for the closest magical being," Guy added. "Which brought us here."

Laura looked at Charon's large hand against hers. "You saved me again. If you hadn't of been there . . ." She trailed off, unable to finish.

"Nay." He put a finger beneath her chin to lift her head. "Doona cry over your mother and sister. They got what they deserved after what they did to you. And your father . . . he deserves the same for standing by and allowing them to treat you that way."

She tried to nod but was ensnared by his dark chocolate gaze. His hand slid sensuously along her throat to the back of her neck. His fingers were firm but soft as they sank into her hair.

Laura had never been able to deny the attraction she felt

for Charon. With him as close as he was, and looking at her with such heat and longing, she couldn't have pulled away had her life depended upon it.

Each beat of her heart caused her blood to heat and desire to pool within her. All too easily she remembered how it felt to be in his arms, how he had touched her, kissed her.

Loved her.

Charon's head dipped to hers, his long eyelashes lowering as his eyes slid closed. Laura's did the same a second before his lips touched hers.

And passion consumed them.

Her hands were on his chest, feeling every hard muscle beneath her palm as if it were the first time. She could feel his body straining to get closer to her. Laura unbuckled her seat belt as Guy took a turn in the road, throwing her on top of Charon.

Charon's hands cupped both sides of her face as he searched her eyes. "Are you hurt?"

"No."

"Good," he murmured before he claimed her mouth again.

Laura groaned softly when he slid down the seat so she was lying on top of him. His hands gripped her butt and squeezed as he deepened the kiss.

"Um . . . you might want to put your seat belt on," Guy said.

She lifted her head and looked at Charon right as the SUV hit a huge hole, jostling Laura several inches into the air. In less than a heartbeat, Charon had her sitting up and her seat belt buckled before she knew what he was doing.

"Where are we?" Charon asked.

Guy chuckled. "Dreagan land. We're just taking a bit of a shortcut."

"Shortcut?" Laura repeated as sheep scattered away from the SUV.

"We needed reinforcements."

Laura looked at Charon for clarification, and all she got as a response was a shrug.

Guy cleared his throat then and caught Laura's gaze in

the rearview mirror. "I know you've seen a lot over the past few days, lass, but it looks like you'll get to see a wee bit more."

She frowned, gripping the handle above her as the SUV bounced them around over the rough terrain. Laura opened her mouth to ask what Guy was talking about when she looked through the windshield at a dark shape in the sky that was drawing closer.

"I'll explain it all," Charon said as he took her hand.

Her breath locked in her lungs when she realized it was a dragon she saw in the sky. She followed its flight through the moonroof, and then turned to watch it out the back window.

"That was a dragon," she said, and looked at Charon.

He grinned as he met her gaze. "Aye, it was."

"Dragons are real?" she whispered. "I thought the legends were only stories."

Guy said, "We're much more than legend."

Laura realized then she was sitting in a vehicle with a dragon. Before she could even begin to wrap her head around that, Guy let out a warning shout.

Suddenly Charon had his arms wrapped around her, and in the next second something slammed into the SUV, sending it skidding sideways before it began to roll down the hill.

CHAPTER THIRTY-ONE

Aiden knew he gripped Britt's hand too tight, but he wasn't going to chance losing her. His shoulder slammed into a corner when he glanced behind him and spotted Jason Wallace.

"Go!" Quinn bellowed from behind Aiden.

There was a loud crash ahead of them, and they turned a series of corners to find Galen had kicked in a door. Just as Britt started to go into the room, Galen grabbed her and pointed to the stairs ahead, his finger over his lips.

Aiden pushed Britt ahead of him. He'd never envied his father's abilities as a Warrior. Until then. If he were a Warrior, he would have been able to use his speed to get Britt away from Wallace.

But Aiden was just a mortal. He had magic, but it was nothing compared to being a Warrior.

Britt's foot caught on a step, causing her to pitch forward. He wrapped an arm around her waist to steady her. She gave him a nod to let him know she was all right before she continued upward.

The steps were steep, and Britt was fast losing steam. Before Aiden could help her, Galen lifted her in his arms.

"Time to go," Galen whispered with a grin.

Aiden was happy to see Galen use his speed to get Britt to safety. Then, to Aiden's surprise, his father hefted him over his shoulder and did the same.

Though he didn't particularly care to be saved in front of Britt, he knew their lives were more important than his ego. In just moments, Quinn deposited him on the roof.

"What now?" Britt asked as she walked to Aiden.

He took her hand in his, noting how cool her skin was. Aiden looked around him, noticing that they were far from Edinburgh.

"Now we wait for Fallon," Quinn said.

The words had barely left his mouth when Fallon appeared beside them.

Galen moved away from his position at the door, which led to the roof, and glared at Fallon. "About bloody time."

Fallon didn't say anything as he waited for them to get in a circle. Once each of them had laid a hand on the other, Fallon would teleport them away to safety.

Except nothing happened.

"Uncle Fallon?" Aiden said.

A muscle in Fallon's jaw jumped. He dropped his hands from Quinn and Britt and took a step back. In an instant he was gone, and then returned.

"Holy hell," Quinn mumbled.

Fallon let out a harsh breath. "The bastard has done something. I can no' take any of you away from here. At least no' with my power."

Aiden released Britt and walked to the edge. He spotted a ladder leading down the side of the building. "This way then," he called out.

"And then where?" Quinn asked when he reached him.

Aiden looked at his father. "We keep moving. I'm no' going to stay here and watch you or Galen sacrifice yourselves. Nor am I going to allow Wallace to get his hands on Britt."

Quinn glanced at Fallon before he lifted Britt in his arms. "Hold on, lass," Quinn said before he jumped over the side to land softly on the ground.

When Aiden looked at Galen, Galen was smiling.

"Your turn," Galen said.

Aiden rolled his eyes and hurried to get on the ladder. "No' on your life."

Fallon and Galen were with Quinn and Britt by the time Aiden reached them.

"Our only choice is to get far away," Galen was saying.

Aiden nodded in agreement. "We have no other option but to keep moving."

"And Britt's research?" Quinn asked. "That's important to us all."

Fallon rubbed the back of his neck. "We need Phelan. He can use his power to distort reality."

"Will that work?" Aiden asked.

Quinn shrugged, smiling wryly. "We doona have another choice. Phelan is our best chance right now."

"That's if you can find him," Galen said.

Fallon flipped open his phone and pressed a number. "If Phelan doesna answer his phone, Charon will know how to get ahold of him."

"It's been over three hours," Aiden said. "We should've heard from Charon by now."

The way Fallon wouldn't look at him told Aiden he hadn't heard from Charon either.

A moment later, Fallon hung up his phone. He compressed his lips in a tight line as he stared off into the night. "We're forty minutes outside of Glasgow. Keep heading west toward Oban."

"The old cottage of mine," Galen said with a grin. "It's all but run down and hidden on a farmer's land. I'll get them there."

Fallon nodded and teleported away.

"We need a car," Quinn said.

Aiden turned his head to get Britt, only to find her gone. "Britt!"

"Here," she called from down the street.

He spotted a car door open and then saw Britt's shapely leg sticking out. A second later, and the car roared to life. Britt sat up, a smile on her face as she motioned for them through the windshield.

"I'm liking her more and more," Galen said as he jogged to the car.

Quinn slapped Aiden on the back. "She's certainly handling things well."

"Aye," Aiden mumbled, his grin growing by the moment at how she had calmly broken into a car and hot-wired it.

Britt moved to the passenger seat as Galen climbed behind the wheel. Aiden and Quinn jumped into the back, the doors slamming closed as Galen drove away.

"I'm looking forward to hearing how you know how to hot-wire a car," Aiden said to Britt.

She looked over her shoulder and winked at him. "I wasn't always a doctor, you know. I was quite the bad girl in my little town in California."

Aiden looked through the back window when they merged in traffic, but there was still no sign of Wallace.

"How long will it take him to know where we've gone?" Aiden asked.

Galen gunned the car and changed lanes, then turned the corner. "He knows Fallon can no' teleport us away, so we're limited to where we can go."

"He'll suspect we took a car," Britt said. "At least I would. It's the only viable option for a group who needs to get far away."

"Maybe too viable," Quinn murmured. "Maybe we stay in Glasgow."

Aiden was shaking his head before his father finished. "We can no' chance it. Wallace's magic is too great. He'd find us. And quickly."

"I agree," Galen said. "We keep moving. We willna have long once we're at the cabin, but perhaps it'll be enough time for Britt to get some work done."

"And for my brother to find a way to teleport us," Quinn added.

Even with miles lengthening between them and Wallace, the knot of dread in Aiden's gut didn't lessen.

Phelan walked out of the dance club, the loud music cut off with the closing of the door. Yet, the steady beat of the bass could still be heard outside.

He walked to his Ducati motorbike parked next to the curb and sighed. Why hadn't he heard from Charon? Or anyone? He'd tried taking his mind off things, but not even the two beautiful women vying for his attention had helped.

Instead of going home with one of them to ease his body, he'd walked away from both. Not something he did.

Phelan raked a hand through his hair and glanced at the sky. The moon was hidden behind thick clouds. More rain was on the way.

He pulled out his mobile to check for messages and saw he had a missed call from Fallon. There was no message, so Phelan quickly dialed his number.

"Fallon," he said when the line connected.

"Where the fuck have you been?" Fallon demanded.

Phelan's brows rose. Fallon rarely lost his cool. He was a natural born leader, meant to be laird of the MacLeods. When Deirdre destroyed the clan, that legacy ended. But Fallon had found his way by leading the Warriors.

There was a rush of air sounding through the phone as Fallon sighed. "We need you, Phelan."

"Is it Charon?" he asked, his worry intensifying.

"Partly. We've no' heard from him, and Laura is gone."

Phelan rubbed the back of his neck. "Is that why you called?"

"Nay. I'll fill you in on that later. Right now, we've a more immediate need of you. How far are you from Oban?"

He swung a leg over the seat of his motorbike and reached for his helmet. "Doona worry about that. Just tell me where you need me and when. I'll be there."

"There's a farmer northeast of Oban. On his land toward the back is a run-down cottage that Galen used centuries ago. He, Quinn, Aiden, and Britt are on their way there now."

"Why didna you just jump them there?"

"Wallace."

That's all Phelan needed to hear. "I'm on my way."

He pocketed the phone and secured his helmet before he started the bike. A moment later and he gunned the Ducati, tires squealing on the pavement as he raced out of town.

* * *

Charon stared out the window of Dreagan Mansion while Laura lay unmoving on the bed. He could still hear the crunch of metal as the Range Rover went rolling down the hill.

He'd tried his best to take the brunt of the impact, but by the time the vehicle came to rest upside down, Laura had a fractured leg, two broken ribs, and glass embedded along one side of her face.

The crash had been caused by the selmyr, but the dragons quickly drove them off. Charon hadn't wanted to move Laura and cause her more pain. He had reached for his phone to call Phelan so he could use his blood to heal her, but Con had extended a hand through the busted window and covered the phone.

"She needs to be healed," Charon had said through clenched teeth.

Con merely moved his hand from the mobile phone to Laura. The magic that filled the area was stronger than anything Charon had ever felt before, but it was completely different from Druid magic.

It was . . . dynamic, omnipotent. Supreme.

Before his eyes, each bit of glass fell from Laura's skin to drop with a soft *ping* upon the cracked moonroof. Soon, even the cuts were healed. It was a few minutes more before Con removed his hand and looked at him.

"You can move her now. She's healed."

A white G-class Mercedes SUV pulled up then. Charon gathered Laura in his arms and kicked the Range Rover's door off its hinges. In no time they had all piled into the Mercedes and were on their way to the mansion while several dragons still flew above them.

"We'll patrol the sky and grounds," Con had promised.

Even now, an hour later, Charon couldn't stop watching the dragons. Con had vowed Laura would eventually wake, but it wasn't until Charon checked her broken bones himself to make sure they were healed that he believed Con.

He braced his hands on either side of the window as fat

drops of rain began to hit the glass. The three hours he'd asked Aiden to give him had long ago come and gone.

Charon's mobile had been broken in the accident, but Guy had brought a new one by thirty minutes earlier. The fact no one was answering at MacLeod Castle, he couldn't reach Phelan, and Aiden's phone went straight to voice mail didn't bode well.

The door opened and Banan walked into the room. He glanced at the bed before he came to stand beside Charon.

"Any news?" Charon asked.

"We have no' found Aiden. Fallon and most of the Warriors are in Edinburgh, trying to contain what Wallace has done."

"And the Druids?" There was no way the Warriors would leave their women unguarded. Charon knew that for fact.

Banan stuffed his hands in his front pockets. "There are a handful in Edinburgh. The others . . . they seem to have disappeared."

Charon jerked his head to Banan. "What? That's impossible. The castle is the safest place for them."

"Is it?" he asked. "How many times did Deirdre and Declan send in spies? How many times did Deirdre attack it?"

Charon pushed off the wall and faced the Dragon King. "The Warriors won those battles."

"But no' you."

He clenched his jaw, hating that the bastard was right. "I wasn't part of all of those battles, nay."

"The castle is empty, Charon."

There was no way Charon could believe Banan, yet the King had no reason to lie. There was something more going on, and he feared it could very well destroy all of them.

"I can no' stay while my friends fight this evil. I came here for help."

"Of which Con has said we would give," Banan said softly. He sighed heavily. "The selmyr have complicated things. We can stand against them."

Charon rubbed his hand over his jaw. "How? I thought

they fed on magical creatures, and you are the biggest magical creature there is."

Banan chuckled. "Aye we are, but we're also the most powerful. The selmyr are dangerous. They were trapped before, we just need to do that again. Until that time, we're battling two different enemies at the same time."

"Can we win?"

"Aye."

He frowned when he heard the slight hesitation in Banan's voice. "But you are no' happy about others knowing your existence."

"We've lived in secret for hundreds of thousands of years. What do you think?"

Charon started to answer when he glanced at the bed and found Laura's beautiful moss green eyes opened and looking at him.

CHAPTER
THIRTY-TWO

Laura smiled and Charon forgot all about Banan as he walked past him.

"How are you feeling?" Charon asked as he sat on the edge of the bed.

She paused as if taking stock of her body. "Rested. What happened?"

"The selmyr hit the Range Rover, and there was a bit of an accident." He heard the sound of the door closing, which signaled that Banan had left.

She looked away, her hands fiddling with the edge of the blanket. "How badly was I injured?"

"No' bad. Just a few bumps."

"Liar," she said softly, and met his gaze.

He could never look into her green depths without drowning, and now was no different. "You're healed now. That's all that matters."

"Who healed me?"

"Con."

Her eyes widened. "He can heal?"

"Apparently. And quickly, as well."

"I must have been bad off."

"It's over now," he said and entwined his fingers with hers.

The fingers of her other hand lightly caressed his forehead. "Then tell me why you're frowning. What has you so worried?"

She knew him well, possibly much too well. "Everyone is gone from the castle."

"I don't understand."

"Neither do I. It's the one place the Warriors and Druids always stayed when they had a choice. It was the one place they knew they were the strongest."

Her arm lowered to the bed, and she used it to help push herself into a sitting position. "Have you spoken to Phelan?"

"Nay." Charon rose from the bed and paced. "Aiden is waiting on me as well. I've tried to call them both. Neither answers."

"Call again," she urged, and motioned to the phone.

Charon looked at the mobile phone resting on the bedside table. He reached for it and dialed Aiden's number. Just as before, it went straight to voice mail.

He hung up and dialed Phelan's number. Charon let out a sigh of relief when Phelan answered on the second ring.

"Phelan," he said.

"Where the bleeding hell have you been?" Phelan yelled. "I couldna get ahold of you."

Charon sank onto the bed and leaned forward, his head resting in his hand as he braced his elbow on his leg. "My phone was crushed, and then when I got a new one, I couldna reach you."

"What's going on?" Phelan demanded.

Charon closed his eyes when Laura's hands rubbed his back as she sat up. "So much. The selmyr attacked again. They got Laura's sister and mother."

"So Laura has her magic back?"

Charon glanced at Laura. "Aye. We got her away safely, though."

"We?" Phelan repeated, his voice holding a note of concern over the phone.

"I'm at Dreagan."

There was a long pause before Phelan let out a string of

curses. "If they helped you with the selmyr, that means they know of us."

"Aye."

"And the Druids?"

Charon smiled into the phone. "Aye."

"What are you no' telling me?" Phelan asked in a deadly calm voice.

Charon looked out the window in time to see an amber dragon fly near the mansion. "They're dragons, Phelan."

"No' possible," he said immediately. "There's no way they could have kept that a secret from us."

"They did. For a verra, verra long time, too. Trust me. I've seen them in action. The selmyr doona like them, and I think they're the only things that can stand against the selmyr."

Phelan sighed loudly into the phone. "I'm glad you and Laura are all right. I was getting worried."

"Join us here."

"I can no'. Fallon sent me to Oban to meet up with Galen, Quinn, Aiden, and Britt."

Charon stood, his hand clenched at his side. "So Wallace didna get Aiden and Britt?"

"No' yet. I'm checking the perimeter around the cottage where the group is to hole up, and Quinn told me Wallace did something to prevent Fallon from jumping them away."

Charon didn't like what he was hearing. Their one advantage was the powers they were able to use as Warriors. The Druids already had an influence in that they could stop a Warrior. If Wallace took away their power, the Warriors were no better than the mortals walking around.

"Fallon could teleport himself away, but no' the others," Phelan said. "Fallon plans on coming here in a bit and trying again. He thinks the farther away from Wallace, the better their chances."

"What do you think?"

Phelan chuckled. "I think I'm itching for a fight. Wallace has done enough. Now, thanks to Aiden, we have Britt, who is making headway with discovering what it is about *drough* blood that hurts us so much. When Galen told her how you reacted, she said she wanted a sample of your blood."

Charon didn't like being reminded that he had nearly died. Twice. The second time he had only been healed by Laura's magic. And that had been purely by accident, since she hadn't known what she was doing.

"Why is no one at MacLeod Castle?"

"That's the first I heard about it," Phelan said softly. "We're scattered, Charon. We're more powerful as a group, and Wallace knows it."

Charon put his hand on the window as lightning forked in the darkening sky, showing him several more dragons flying through the clouds. "Then we group once more."

"How? Especially with what's happening in Edinburgh?"

"We'll have to make a choice. Wallace knows we'll help innocents. He's counting on it."

Phelan snorted. "He's now the one underestimating us."

"Exactly. Talk to those at the cottage. I'm going to call Fallon."

Charon disconnected the call and immediately tried Fallon, but couldn't get him on the line. He tried Larena's, Lucan's, Hayden's, and even Broc's phones before he tossed his mobile on the table.

"They aren't answering?" Laura asked.

Charon faced her and shrugged. "Phelan knows only a little more than I do about their whereabouts. I've got a bad feeling."

"Then go to them."

"In Edinburgh? No' a good place to bring the dragons."

She tossed aside the covers and walked into the bathroom. "Give me a few minutes to take a shower. By the way, clothes would be nice. Don't think I can wear this oversized shirt while I'm battling Jason."

When he didn't reply, she turned at the door and looked at him. After losing her mother and sister, how could he tell her he still wasn't completely sure of her loyalty?

The Warriors and Druids needed to be unified, because Charon had a feeling if they lost this battle with Wallace, it was over for good.

"I went to my parents' home to get my magic back," she said.

Gone was her smile. She looked sad and weary, and Charon wasn't sure if it was because he didn't believe her still or because she lost her family. Or both.

"How were you going to do that?"

She shook her head with a half smile as she looked at the floor. "I kept asking myself that as I drove to them. I had no magic, and I knew they could hurt me with their own, but I had to try." Her gaze lifted to his. "I had to try for you. I knew the only way for you to believe I was on your side was to get my magic back and use it against Jason."

Charon crossed the room in four strides. He rested his hands on her shoulders, ever amazed at the remarkable woman that she was. There were tricks Declan and Deirdre had used to get into a Druid's mind to control them.

There was no need for Laura to know about that. Once he got her back with the other Druids, he would ask Dani to look into Laura's mind and see if Wallace had bespelled her.

"You could've been killed," he said.

She lifted one shoulder in a shrug. "You didn't leave me much of a choice. My life hasn't exactly been a good one, but I found a home in Ferness. You gave me that, Charon. You gave me a job and even though you might not realize it, you helped give meaning to my life."

"Is that why you fell so easily into my bed?" he teased, unaccustomed to such praise from anyone.

She didn't smile in return. Instead, she rose up on her tiptoes and wrapped her arms around him, her face breaths from his. "No, you fool of a man. I fell into your bed because I've wanted to be there since the first moment I laid eyes on you."

He moaned at the touch of her lips on his. Charon tried to hold back his desire and let her take the lead in the kiss, but his need was too great.

With a slight turn of his body, he had her pinned against the bathroom door. He slanted his mouth over hers and showed her just how much he yearned for her in his arms.

Her soft, pliant body only made his blood scorch through his veins. They had no time for pleasures of the flesh, but he couldn't release her, couldn't think of anything but the Druid in his arms.

"Charon!" called a voice outside the bedroom door before there was a knock.

Charon grudgingly ended the kiss. "I don't think as long as we're around the Dragon Kings that I'm going to be able to do more than kiss you."

"It doesn't appear that way, does it?" she asked with a laugh.

The pounding on the door started again. Charon released Laura and waited until she shut the door to the bathroom before he opened the bedroom door.

He frowned when he saw Guy standing with his face set in grim lines. "What is it?"

"The selmyr. They've surrounded us. We willna be leaving to help your friends anytime soon."

"I have to leave," Charon stated. Anger surged within him, and Ranmond was quick to urge him to battle. Charon promptly tamped down his god, but not before his skin flashed copper.

One of Guy's dark brows rose in question. "Is your god difficult to control?"

"I thought you knew all there was to know of Warriors."

"We've watched you," Guy admitted. "We know some seemed to give in to their gods."

Charon looked at his hands and allowed his claws to extend. "When Ranmond was first released, he drowned out my own thoughts. His need for blood and death was overwhelming. As god of war, that's all he thought about, all he longed for. It would've been easy to give in to his demands."

"Why did you no'?"

When he looked to find Guy's eyes reflected genuine curiosity, Charon tamped down his god until his claws disappeared and said, "Deirdre put my father in the dungeon with me. Ranmond was in control then. I killed my own father. It was that realization after I had calmed down that helped me get the upper hand on my god. Every day is a battle to stay in control."

"Even now?"

"Even now. Especially now," Charon admitted, and glanced at the bathroom, where Laura was taking a shower.

Guy flattened his lips. "We might be able to distract the selmyr for you to leave, but it willna take them long to know what happened. They'll come for you. You'll never make it to your friends."

There was no way Charon was going to accept that. There had to be some way he could get himself and the dragons to his friends.

Suddenly he smiled and began to chuckle. "We willna be leaving Dreagan, Guy. We're going to bring Wallace here."

CHAPTER
THIRTY-THREE

Aiden blew out a harsh breath and looked at the midnight drenched land. He felt a little of the pressure taken off his shoulders since they had arrived at the cottage. But that would last only until Wallace found them.

He peered around the door of the cottage to find Britt's head leaning against the back of the chair, her eyes closed. Her beautiful purple dress was torn and dirty, her glorious mane of blond hair was in disarray, but it didn't stop the need clawing inside him to kiss her again.

His hands fisted at his sides, eager to feel her skin beneath his palms and learn every inch of her.

He could wake her. They were alone for the moment since his father, Galen, and Phelan were outside, patrolling the area. Yet Aiden knew how exhausted she was. It wouldn't be fair to wake her, especially when he didn't know the next time they would be able to rest.

"I've always heard it's not nice to stare," Britt said, and smiled, her eyes still closed.

Aiden's gaze dropped to the swell of her breasts and the ample view the deep plunge of her dress afforded him.

When he finally raised his gaze to Britt's face, her eyes were open and trained on him. She wordlessly held out her hand.

Every fiber of his being shouted for him to go to her. Just

one taste, one touch. That's all he needed to sustain him for a few more hours.

Aiden closed the short distance between them and placed his hand in hers. The corners of Britt's lovely mouth lifted softly. She tugged him down until he squatted beside the rickety chair.

"This is the first time we've been alone since dinner," she whispered.

His balls tightened at the husky, desire-filled sound of her voice. "Aye."

"Then kiss me instead of wasting this time," she said, and leaned toward him.

Aiden didn't need to be told twice. He covered her mouth with his. The brush of her lips, the sweet taste of her kiss broke through the carefully constructed wall he'd erected around himself so long ago.

He wasn't able to hold back the swell of longing that claimed him. And he didn't want to.

It felt good to let go. More so when Britt's hands delved into his hair and a soft moan sounded in her throat.

Aiden had never truly understood—or appreciated—the love shared between his parents and their private smiles and whispered words. Until that moment with Britt in his arms.

It all became perfectly, crystal clear.

He ended the kiss and stood. His head was filled with thoughts of Britt while his body burned for her. Yet, he had dragged her into a dangerous world she had no place in.

And he had no right to want her there.

"Aiden?" she whispered, her brow furrowed.

He turned his back to her. If he looked at her, if he saw the desire burning in her blue eyes, he wouldn't be able to stay in control.

That control hung by a thin thread as it was. Knowing she was so close quickly had that thread unraveling. It was only the thought of her death that kept him from giving in to his body's need.

"There's no place for you in my world," he said into the silence.

The chair creaked as she rose. Aiden prayed that she would storm out. Her anger would keep her away from him. It was his last resort, since he knew he was too weak to keep his distance. The more he was with her, the more times he kissed her, only strengthened his yearning to keep her by his side.

He was shoved in the shoulder, spinning him around. Britt's face was set in hard lines as she jabbed a finger in his chest.

"I've never met a more controlling, confident, maddening man in all my life. How dare you make decisions about my life. That's for me to do. And only me."

Her eyes blazed with anger, and it only made Aiden's blood burn hotter.

"This is the twenty-first century, and you need to remember that," Britt continued. "I'm not some weak female who needs you to come to my rescue. I'm perfectly capable of saving myself."

Aiden barely heard what she said. His gaze was trained on her mouth while he battled the urge to drag her against him.

"So, I'm making the decisions for me. And I choose you, Aiden MacLeod. Get used to it."

The words scarcely penetrated his brain before she rose up on her tiptoes and placed her lips on his. The kiss was frantic as their mutual need fueled the other to new heights.

Aiden backed her against the wall. There he kissed her as if it were their last night together. He poured every ounce of need, of the urgent, insistent yearning into the kiss.

Britt had to touch him, had to feel his warm skin. She tore at his shirt until she heard buttons hitting the wooden floor.

The deep, resonant moan that filled the room when she placed her hands on his chest made her heart skip a beat. How she had longed to caress him, to run her hands over his finely sculpted chest she'd glimpsed only in his tight shirts.

Her head tilted to the side when his mouth trailed down her neck, his tongue and lips doing wonderful, wicked things to her flesh.

Her fingers clung to his thick shoulders when he tugged down the strap of her dress. It fell against her arm while his fingers caressed softly, seductively along her skin as he followed the edge of the dress until he came to her breast.

"Lovely," he whispered near her ear.

Chills raced along her skin as she silently begged him to take more. She was offering all of herself, if only he would take it.

He kissed down her chest, following the same path of his fingers until he came to her décolletage. There he paused before he cupped one of her breasts.

Britt sucked in a breath, her heart pounding uncontrollably. No one had ever made her shudder so wantonly with just a few kisses, but Aiden wasn't like any other man in the world.

A gasp tore from her mouth when his thumb moved over her nipple, causing her breasts to swell and her nipples to harden painfully.

"Aiden," she whispered, her knees threatening to buckle.

He kneeled before her, his hands gripping her hips as he lifted his face to her. His smile, so gorgeous, so irresistible made her blood race.

She bit her lip when his hands smoothed down the outside of her legs until they reached the hem of her dress. Then he dipped his hands beneath her dress. His eyes burned with desire as his hands slid up along her skin, dragging her dress with them up over her hips to her waist.

Desire centered low in Britt's belly. She craved his touch as her body craved oxygen. And she feared she would never get enough of him.

"So damn beautiful," Aiden murmured before he placed a kiss next to her navel.

Britt's head dropped back against the wall and her eyes slid shut. His hands were everywhere, touching her, learning her as she longed to do to him.

Her sucked in a breath when his thumbs hooked her panties. Slowly he pulled the lace down until the garment puddled at her feet.

She shook from the need tightening within her, and Aiden hadn't truly touched her yet. He very gently lifted each of her feet until the panties were completely removed.

And then his hands were on her legs again. His touch was firm but smooth as he skimmed his hands from her ankles to her thighs.

He gave her little warning before he lifted one of her legs and draped it over his shoulder. His touch was soft as he ran his fingers through her curls.

Britt placed her hands flat on the wall in an effort to keep herself upright while her heart hammered in her chest. She groaned when he skimmed her clitoris, the little nub aching for more.

Aiden moaned when he felt how wet Britt was. He plunged a finger inside her, stroking her tight core as her soft cries filled the cottage.

He added a second finger, her fingers digging into his shoulders. His cock jumped when he grazed her clit and heard her cry out.

There was no more waiting. He had to have her, had to claim her. Medieval thinking or not, that was the truth of it.

Aiden removed his fingers from her the same time he shrugged her leg off his shoulder. And in one fluid motion, he stood.

There were no words. Just frantic fumbling of their fingers on his pants and kisses frenzied by the need burning within them.

When his pants were finally unbuttoned and unzipped, Britt stopped him in his tracks with her hand upon his length. He stood stock-still while her hand ran up and down his arousal.

Then it became too much. He grabbed her hips and lifted her. Instantly her legs locked around his waist.

Britt felt the head of Aiden's cock against her flesh a second before his hips thrust forward. She gasped as the hard, hot length of him slid inside her.

For several moments they stood as they were. He pulled

out of her until only the head of his arousal remained. Then he thrust inside her again.

She clung to him, their gazes clashed as their bodies began to move. In and out he pumped, her body tightening with each stroke of his rod.

The urgency, the need driving them pushed them. The sound of their bodies meeting and their harsh breaths filled the room.

Britt's legs constricted when he began to pound ruthlessly into her until, a heartbeat later, her climax claimed her. Her mouth opened to scream her release when Aiden kissed her to keep her silent.

Not even that could diminish the bliss that was her orgasm. She was floating on a cloud of pleasure so amazing she knew she would never come down.

Aiden never stopped thrusting. He prolonged her climax until his own claimed him. It was fierce as it ripped through him, his seed spilling inside her.

He buried his face in her neck, his body slick with sweat. Aiden wanted to do nothing more than find a bed and make love to her again and again. But reality crashed upon them with the sounds of approaching feet.

Aiden lifted his head to find Britt smiling at him. She ran a hand down his face to smooth away his hair before she kissed him.

"I don't regret this. I've never been happier, and if you ruin it by telling me it was a mistake, I won't be responsible for what I do to you."

He grinned and gave her a quick kiss. "I was going to say I wish we were alone with a bed so I could take you to it."

"Oh, now, that sounds wonderful," she said wistfully.

Aiden pulled out of her and released her legs. There was so much he needed to say to her, but before he could, the door opened.

He shifted so that he was between whoever had just come in and Britt. She hastily lowered her dress while he buttoned his pants.

With a wink, she walked around him and began talking

to Galen. Aiden reached to button his shirt when he noticed all but one of the buttons was gone. He spotted several on the floor around him.

He inhaled and just as he was about to turn around, he spotted the silver lace panties on the floor. Aiden bent and put them in his pocket as he stood.

Only to find his father standing behind and to the side of Galen, watching him.

"Anything?" Aiden asked.

Quinn's gaze raked across the area. "It's quiet. Too quiet. Wallace should've found us by now."

"Let's give ourselves some credit," Britt said. "Besides, I'm in no hurry for him to show up."

"Nay," Fallon said as he suddenly appeared in the room beside them. "But he's coming. Let's try to get you all out of here."

They all quickly stepped forward except for Aiden. "What about Phelan?"

"He has other business," Galen said cryptically.

Which Aiden knew meant Charon. Whatever was going on there, Phelan wouldn't leave Charon to go it alone.

Aiden took his place between Britt and Galen. Fallon put his hands on Galen's and Quinn's shoulders to take them out of there, but nothing happened. Just as before.

"Fuck!" Fallon shouted, and spun away.

Footsteps running toward the cottage filled the silence that followed. A second later and Phelan flung open the front door.

"I just spoke with Charon. He has a plan."

CHAPTER
THIRTY-FOUR

Charon watched Con as he stared out the windows of his office. Charon had laid out his plan for Constantine, and now all that remained was Con's approval.

Of course, Con didn't know that Charon had already told the plan to Phelan.

"You want to have the battle here," Con said.

It wasn't a question. More of a statement, but it was the humor in his tone that caught Charon off guard. "You offered your help. My concern was keeping the identities of you and your Kings a secret."

"And you think having the battle here will do that?"

Charon glanced at both Guy and Banan, who stood off to the side. Neither King so much as batted an eye. Charon then glanced over at Hal, the green dragon he'd seen earlier, and another King by the name of Laith.

The solidarity of the men reminded him of the Warriors at MacLeod Castle. Further proof that Charon had no one but himself to count on.

Phelan was the closest thing he had to a friend, but Charon didn't know if Phelan would allow himself to be called friend. Not to mention that Phelan was notoriously difficult to get ahold of if he didn't want to be found.

"You know these glens and mountains," Charon said.

"Wallace knows nothing of you, and we can use that as an advantage. A surprise attack he'll never see coming."

Con clasped his hands behind his back. "There's no doubt you're a good battle strategist. I think it's one of the reasons your god chose you."

Charon looked at the floor. He didn't know what Con was getting at, but he didn't like—nor want—to talk of his past. "If you say so."

"I say so." Con chuckled then. "You're immortal, Charon, but you've lived only six hundred years. I've lived for thousands of millennia. I've seen countless battles and wars. I've even watched you fight as a Warrior. I know what I'm talking about."

"Then the problem is?"

"Cheeky bastard," Guy mumbled with a grin.

Charon scratched his cheek with only his middle finger, causing Guy to have to cough to cover up his laughter. Banan, Hal, and Laith all ducked their heads to hide their smiles.

Con turned to face Charon. "You seem verra confident that Wallace can be beaten. Have you forgotten the outbreak in Edinburgh? Five more people have died, including a little boy."

The cocky grin Charon had worn a moment before dropped as anger took its place. He was careful to keep his god tamped down, because while he wasn't afraid of the Kings, he needed their help.

"While you and the other Kings have whiled away your years in luxury and privacy, the Warriors have defended the entire fucking planet from evil. I have no' forgotten a damned thing. We've lost friends, innocents, and our families because none of you did a thing about Deirdre."

"She wasna a priority."

The fury Charon kept tightly controlled erupted. Fangs filled his mouth the same instant his claws elongated from his fingers. He didn't need to look down to know his skin had turned copper.

"Wasna a priority?" Charon repeated in a low, dangerous voice. "Do you know the havoc she wrought? Can you even comprehend what she did to us and the other Druids? Or were you too wrapped up in no' having your precious dragons to order around?"

Con leaned forward, his hands resting on his desk as his lip curled in anger.

"Struck a nerve, did I?" Charon taunted.

Con tucked his chin, and Charon bent his legs ready to fight when the door was thrown open and Laura rushed in to stand before him.

Her hands were braced against his chest, and even though Charon had his lips peeled back as he growled, it didn't seem to faze her.

"Enough," she said. When neither he nor Con relented, she tried again. This time she yelled. "Enough!"

Hal crossed his arms over his chest. "Brave woman."

Charon straightened, but he didn't tamp down his god. He had come to the Kings for help, but it looked as if he had ruined that.

Perhaps Phelan had been correct when he said neither he nor Charon were meant to be a part of anything.

"Look at me," Laura coaxed Charon.

He wasn't ready to give any ground to Con, but Laura wasn't giving up.

"Charon, look at me," she demanded in a louder tone.

He blew out a harsh breath and lowered his gaze to her. "You shouldna be here."

"And where should I be while you and our new friends are about to fight? Luckily for you, Cassie happened to be walking by and heard the exchange. She came to get me."

Hal rolled his eyes and shifted from one foot to another. "Happened to be walking by, my arse," he mumbled.

Laura could feel the fury rolling off Charon in waves. He stood against five Dragon Kings without so much as a tremor. His copper skin glistened in the lightning flashes, and he was careful to keep his claws away from her.

She let her hand trail down his chest before she turned

and faced Con. "Charon is right. You stood by while thousands died. Did I hear wrong, or were you able to shift from dragon to human so you could protect the humans?"

"Humans doona need protecting. It's the rest of the world that needs protecting from them," Con said with his teeth clenched. He pushed away from his desk and glared at Charon.

Laura sighed. She had hoped by coming into the office, she might help defuse the situation, but she'd been wrong. She faced Charon, knowing she had one more chance with him.

"It's bloody difficult to admit we need them and they don't need us, but you wouldn't have come here if you didn't think they could help."

Charon's eyes lowered to her. She looked into the copper eyes, waiting for his decision. To her amazement, she watched the copper bleed away to reveal the deep chocolate color of his eyes she knew so well.

He took her hand in his, the claws and copper skin gone, before he said, "You're right. We do need them."

Laura had seen Charon calmly break apart fights in the pub, effortlessly broker deals with liquor distributors, and methodically woo women. She'd even seen him bravely stand up against Jason Wallace.

And through it all, she had known the loyal, steadfast, honorable man that he was. He made her heart pound and her blood heat. He made her believe in herself, but more importantly, she believed in him.

"Whatever happens, I'll stand beside you," she told him. "I don't know how to work my magic, but I'll use what I can."

His lips lifted in a half smile that sent her stomach fluttering. "Thank you. Go back to the room, I'll return shortly."

Laura started to walk away when she paused, and then turned back to Charon. She rose up and gave him a quick hard kiss on the lips before she glanced at Con over her shoulder. Then she walked out of the office and softly closed the door behind her.

"What a woman," Laith said with a whistle.

Charon looked at the door after Laura left. "You've no idea."

He wanted to follow her back to the room and make slow, sweet love to her for days. Instead, he had to smooth over his loss of temper to the one person who could turn the tide of the war.

With his mind full of ways to try to talk Con into helping, Charon turned back to the King of Kings to find Con standing in front of him with a glass of whisky held out.

Charon took it and drained the glass in one swallow. "A twenty-five-year single malt."

"You know your whisky," Con said.

He shrugged. "I had no right to say those things to you."

"Actually, you had every right," Con said as he leaned his hips back against the desk. "It's something I've told myself for centuries. But it's also a balance we must keep."

Banan moved a chair so that he could sit down. "The simple truth is that we can no' interfere with every war that crops up, no matter how much we might want to."

"It was a heated debate about whether we should take Deirdre out," Hal said.

Laith walked over to the sideboard and grabbed the decanter of whisky and four more glasses. He handed Hal, Banan, and Guy each a glass before refilling Charon's. "In the end, we saw the MacLeods escape. We were counting on them taking a stand."

"And if they had no'?" Charon asked.

Con shrugged. "We probably would've taken Deirdre out ourselves, but then what would've happened to all the Warriors? The next question would've been, do we kill all of you as well?"

Charon swirled the liquid in his glass. "It's easy for me to say what you should've done, but I think I understand now."

"Each of you suffered, but look where you are now," Guy said.

Charon snorted. "Fighting yet another *drough*. This one

is stronger than Deirdre and Declan combined. How is that possible? Deirdre was alive for a thousand years and stole magic from countless Druids. How can Jason Wallace, who has been *drough* for just a year, be so powerful?"

"A verra good question," Banan said. "One I've been asking myself."

Con set down his glass and braced his hands on either side of him on the desk. "You are no' afraid of us, are you?"

"Nay. You could kill me with barely a thought, I know, but I survived having my god unbound, killing my own father, unimaginable torture for decades at Deirdre's hand, and controlling my god. I've been in battles with *droughs*, wyrran, Warriors, and humans. Twice now I've died by *drough* blood, and twice I was somehow brought back. There isna much I'm afraid of, but you are no' one of them."

Con's smile was huge as he looked at Charon. "Good. Now, tell me your plan on how to get Wallace here."

"That's the easy part. He's following Aiden and Britt. Britt is apparently some genius who studies blood. She's found something, and Wallace doesna want her to share it with the rest of us."

"Or learn more," Hal added.

Charon nodded. "Precisely. He's done a spell so that Fallon can no' teleport them somewhere else. Right now they're north of Oban, hiding in one of Galen's old cottages he used."

"Wallace might have prevented Fallon from helping, but I doubt Wallace factored in something a tad larger getting Aiden and Britt out," Guy said with a sly grin.

All five smiled at Guy's meaning.

"We willna have a lot of time to get them," Con said.

Charon finished off his whisky. "I think we need to bring Fallon here first."

"Get everyone no' a King out of Dreagan. Except your mates," Con amended before Hal could speak up. "Close off the road, and wake the rest of the Kings. We're going to need them."

"The rest?" Charon asked.

Banan winked. "Did we no' tell you how many of us there are?"

"Nay."

"Another time, perhaps," Guy said with a wide smile.

"What about the distillery? Will you shut it down?" Charon asked.

Con shook his head. "Some will run the distillery as needed while others fight. We survived years without the aid of humans. We can again. Now, I think it's time you called Fallon."

Charon drew out his phone and quickly dialed Fallon, who answered in the middle of the first ring.

"Charon? What's this plan Phelan is talking about?"

Charon smiled into the phone. "It'll be quicker if I show you instead of telling you."

"You told Phelan."

He hadn't told Phelan all of it, just that he wanted to bring everyone to one location where the selmyr were. "Please," Charon said.

The sound of a sigh could be heard through the phone. "Where are you?"

"Dreagan."

There was a long pause before Fallon asked, "Did you say Dreagan?"

"I did. I need you here immediately."

"I've no' been there. You know that. I can no' jump somewhere I've no' been."

But Charon had already thought of that. "Let me talk to Galen. I'll describe it to him. He'll envision it, and then you can jump here."

"It's worth a try, I suppose," Fallon said.

A moment later, Galen was on the phone. Charon described the parking lot of Dreagan to exact proportions as he and the five Dragon Kings walked out of the house to await them.

"Galen? Did it work?" Charon asked.

By the time he got the last word out, Fallon was standing in front of him. The leader of the Warriors did a quick glance around before he looked at Charon, and then each of the men on either side of him.

"Welcome to Dreagan, Fallon MacLeod," Con said as he stepped forward. "I'm Constantine. King of the Dragon Kings."

Fallon's gaze jerked to Charon, who gave a nod of his head and pointed upward. They all looked up as a huge amber dragon soared over them.

"Shite," Fallon mumbled in awe.

Charon couldn't stop his grin. "They're going to help us. We're going to get rid of Jason Wallace once and for all."

Fallon lowered his gaze to look at Con before he shifted his eyes to Charon. "And what of the outbreak of whatever it is Wallace caused in Edinburgh? I need Warriors there to protect the Druids who are trying to use their magic to stop what Wallace has done."

"I hate to admit it, but Jason Wallace is verra intelligent," Constantine said. "He wanted your men and Druids divided. Divided, your attention is split, thereby you willna see his true intentions."

Charon pointed to the amber dragon they had been watching. "The dragons are our only chance."

"I can no' watch innocents die!" Fallon shouted.

"And Aiden?" Charon asked. "What will you tell Quinn or Marcail? That their son's life mattered less than everyone else's."

Fallon's skin turned the black of his god as he took the step separating him and Charon and got in his face. "You know that isna true."

The deep threat in his voice didn't deter Charon. "The only way to stop Wallace from getting to Aiden and Britt is to lure him here. We kill him, then his magic is gone. Whatever he's done in Edinburgh will stop."

"So you think." Fallon whirled around, but didn't tamp down his god. He paced a few steps away before he faced

Charon again. "You didna want to be a part of us. You chose to live in Ferness instead of MacLeod Castle. Yet, you're asking me to trust you now."

"You didna have a problem trusting me before when you needed another Warrior." Charon didn't hide the fury bubbling inside him. He had expected this from Fallon, but that didn't mean it didn't hurt.

Fallon peeled back his lips to show his fangs as he sneered. "And how many times did you watch us battle evil while you did nothing?"

"How many times did you lift a bottle instead of helping your brothers?" Charon taunted.

Fallon launched himself at Charon, but suddenly Banan and Hal were between them. Charon wanted to shove Hal away from him. Instead, he took a step back.

"Our chance is now, Fallon. Make a decision," Charon stated.

Constantine released an exaggerated breath. "He's right, Fallon, and you know it. There's nothing you can do about the outbreak. You can save your nephew and an innocent woman who just might be the answer to the Warriors' problem with *drough* blood."

Fallon instantly tamped down his god and ran a hand through his hair. When he looked at Charon, there was remorse in his green eyes. "I never liked having to choose who lived and who died. Let's get to the details of your plan before Wallace, the bastard, reaches Aiden."

CHAPTER
THIRTY-FIVE

Aisley sat in the front seat of the Jaguar as Dale drove. She was careful to keep her face passive since Jason and Mindy were in the backseat.

Even now, Aisley could feel Jason's eyes on her. The five raised gnashes along his left cheek emphasized his eyes even more, making him look more sinister—if that was possible. He was always watching her, as if he knew the dark, desperate thoughts she had in the early hours before dawn.

He should know that they were just thoughts. She would never—*could* never—leave him. He had ensured that.

"Why do they continue to run?" Mindy asked in her whiny voice that grated on Aisley's nerves.

Jason chuckled. "Ah, but you would run, too, love. It's human nature."

"They're Warriors."

Aisley rolled her eyes and gripped the door to keep from telling Mindy just what a stupid ninny she was.

"They may have a god inside them, but they're human," Jason replied in a voice used for very small children or the mentally impaired.

It made Aisley grin. When Dale glanced at her while battling his own smile, she couldn't stop the laugh that bubbled up. Aisley quickly covered it with a cough.

They had been driving for a few hours, and she was ready

to get out of the car. Being in such a confined space with Mindy was giving her hives. Several times, they had pulled over so Jason could go off by himself and do some spell.

The fact that he didn't want anyone to see him caused suspicion to well up within Aisley. Not that it did her any good. She may hate Jason with a passion, but it did nothing to ease her position.

She was well and truly fucked.

"We're close," Jason said, triumph clear in his voice. "Verra close."

Aisley rested her hands palm down on her legs. How many more times would she go into battle with Jason and live? She had been wounded already, and if it hadn't been for Dale, she was sure she'd be dead.

In some ways, she welcomed death. It would get her away from Jason. Yet, her soul was promised to Satan. As awful as her life was on earth, she was sure it wouldn't get any better once she was in Hell. Or would it?

It made her wonder if that was why Deirdre prolonged her life by killing other Druids. The power Aisley had wanted and needed when Jason found her had been too alluring to turn away.

At the time, she hadn't thought her life could get any worse. Living on the streets, starving, with the thought of selling her body just to have food ever-present in her mind.

Then Jason found her. He'd given her food and shelter. He had somehow known of the meager magic she possessed and promised her the world.

Fool that she was, she believed him. Hook, line, and sinker.

There was no doubt she deserved what was coming to her. She could have turned away during the ceremony and refused to become *drough*. Jason would have killed her on the spot, but that would have been preferable to what she was now.

"Stop," Jason told Dale.

Aisley withdrew from her musings when Dale pulled the

car off the road next to a large farm. She looked at Dale, only to see him shrug.

Jason slapped the back of Aisley's seat. "They're here. Somewhere on this land, Aiden and Britt are here. They've no' moved in some time."

"They think they're safe," Dale said as he peered out the window. "Shall I have a look around?"

"No' yet. We'll wait on the others to catch up to us."

Aisley saw the lights in the distance. "Surely Aiden wouldn't have gone to the house."

"Oh, no," Jason said as he opened the car door and stepped out. "They're attempting to hide."

Mindy scooted along the seat and got out beside Jason. "Don't forget they have two Warriors with them."

"Who doona stand a chance against me," Jason said, and put an arm around her. "You should know that."

"I do. Just want you to be cautious, lover."

Aisley rolled her eyes again. The two of them made her physically sick.

Suddenly, Dale's large hand came to rest atop hers. "I've got a bad feeling," he whispered.

"Me, too," she agreed while nodding her head. "They kept on the run. Why stay in the same place now?"

"It's a trap."

Aisley flattened her lips as her gaze roamed the rows of wheat in front of the headlights of the car. "Yes. A trap."

By the time Charon and the Kings finished explaining the plan to Fallon, it was late into the night. Fallon didn't have all the answers about the Dragon Kings, but for now he would leave it alone.

Charon had no doubt Fallon would be back after the battle.

After the battle. He hoped there was a time after the battle. Both Con and Fallon liked his plan, the question was—would it succeed?

"You can no' see Laura worrying so," Guy said as he caught up with Charon on the stairs.

Charon paused, a hand on the banister and one foot on the step above. "I know."

"We've all agreed it's a good plan. It'll succeed."

"You've no' battled Druids."

Guy shrugged nonchalantly and grinned. "You've never battled dragons."

"You said the humans were able to kill dragons."

Guy's smile disappeared instantly. "Dragons aye, but no' Dragon Kings. All dragons have magic, but they could be killed."

"And you can no'?"

"There is much you doona know. Suffice it to say, a *drough*'s magic willna kill us."

"It can halt us in our tracks, though."

Guy shrugged one shoulder. "I agree it willna be an easy battle. Whatever you did or said to get Con's attention, I'm glad of it. With us on your side, the scales have now tipped in your direction."

"Which scares the hell out of me," Charon confessed as he looked away. "We thought things were done. After killing both Deirdre and Declan, it should've been over."

"It's never over."

Guy's tone, harsh and low, brought Charon's gaze back to him. There was something in Guy's eyes that let him know as powerful as the Kings were, they weren't without enemies.

"You'll get periods of peace," Guy continued. "But remember, it's never over. Enjoy those times of peace and prepare for the next periods of hell."

"What are you fighting?"

Guy glanced down at the stairs. "One of our own. People who want to expose us as shifters. And others of us fight the unending march of time."

"How old are you?"

"We've been here since the beginning of time. The exact number I couldna give you, because I lost track. We all have."

And Charon thought his life had been long. There were

times he hadn't believed he could get through another day. How did the Kings do it?

"Go to your woman," Guy said as he walked past him and clasped him on the shoulder.

His woman. Charon wanted to think of Laura that way, but could he? Did he dare? He'd made love to her. He'd kissed her repeatedly.

There was no doubt he couldn't keep his hands from her. The fact she was a Druid should have made things easier. But it didn't.

He ought to let her go. He should get her far away from Scotland so she would never be touched by the same type of evil that seemed to breed here.

Yet, he couldn't.

Charon took the stairs three at a time until he reached the landing and strode down the hallway to the room given to Laura.

He placed his hand on the doorknob, but hesitated instead of turning it. Music drifted to him through the door. With his enhanced senses, he heard Rihanna's voice singing a fast melody.

So as not to startle Laura, Charon slowly turned the knob and opened the door. Only to find her sleeping in the overstuffed chair next to a table laid out with food.

He smiled as he closed the door softly behind him before he took the glass of wine dangling from her fingers. Charon had been dreaming of making love to her, but there was no way he was going to wake her after all she'd been through.

Charon set the half-empty wineglass on the table and walked into the bathroom to strip off his clothes. He could use a long hot shower, especially when he knew what was coming.

Wallace wouldn't attack that night, and neither would the selmyr, thanks to the dragons. So they had a slight reprieve. And he intended to make the most of it.

Laura came awake to the sound of the shower mixed in with the music from her iPhone. She stretched and yawned as she glanced at the table to find everything just as she had left it while trying to stay awake.

She turned and looked out the window to see the sky was beginning to lighten, but this far north in the summer, that could be deceiving. A quick check on her phone told her it was just after two in the morning.

Laura rose from the chair and smiled when she saw the steam rolling out of the bathroom. Charon had pushed the door to, but hadn't closed it.

While he finished with his shower, Laura filled two glasses of red wine and snagged a cube of cheese to pop into her mouth.

Next, she removed her jeans, shirt, bra, and panties. She folded them neatly in a pile to set atop the dresser before she grabbed Charon's discarded button-down.

She lifted it to her nose and inhaled the scent that was all his—sandalwood. When she heard the water cut off, she hastily slid her arms into the sleeves of the shirt and buttoned two of the buttons below her breasts. Leaving just enough of a gap to show cleavage.

Laura looked at herself in the mirror hanging on the back of the door and smiled. She couldn't have imagined being so bold a week ago, but then she hadn't tasted Charon's kisses or known the exquisite pleasure being in his arms could give her.

It wasn't her magic that gave her the courage to be so daring. It was the all-consuming, overwhelming desire for Charon that did it.

He had turned her into the woman she had only dreamed she could be.

She'd always known she would do a lot for Charon, but she hadn't realized to what extremes she would go to until recently. Instead of frightening her, it felt amazing. Freeing.

Laura leaned back against the wall next to the window and watched as Charon came out of the bathroom with nothing but a towel wrapped precariously low around his hips.

Droplets of water dripped from the ends of his long, dark

hair to his shoulders, where the beads traveled either down his back or over the muscled planes of his chest.

God, he was a gorgeous man. She didn't understand why he wanted her, but it was enough that he did.

He stopped short when he glanced at the chair she had been in and found it empty. In the next instant, his gaze swiveled to her. The dark chocolate depths of his eyes heated as they landed on her.

"How did it go?" she asked.

With a wicked twinkle in his eye, he reached for a glass of wine. "Thanks to your interference, perfectly."

"You're not angry with me for barging in?"

"I'm glad you did. I needed to calm down. You helped with that."

Laura crossed an ankle over the other and hid a smile when she saw Charon's gaze lower to her legs. "Is everything in place?"

"Aye. Fallon is probably still here talking to Con, but I wanted to see you."

"See me?" she asked coyly.

Charon lifted the glass to his lips and drank deeply of the burgundy wine. "Oh, aye."

"So do you believe I'm not working with Jason?"

His forehead creased as he set aside his wine. "Laura, please understand I—"

"I do," she interrupted him. "I understand everything. I just want to be sure that you trust me."

"Aye," he said softly.

She wasn't sure if he meant it or not. In time, she would prove her loyalty to him. For now, he said he trusted her. That was enough.

"Good," she said and pushed off the wall to walk to him. "I think we've wasted enough of our time talking."

CHAPTER
THIRTY-SIX

Laura put her hand against his chest and gave him a push. She knew she allowed her to do it, just as he allowed himself to fall back into the chair she had occupied a few moments earlier.

"Is there something you want with me?" Charon asked with one side of his mouth lifted in a devilish grin.

"Me? Not at all." She moved to stand between his legs. "I just figured with all the kisses you've given me, you might be in some . . . need."

"Need?" he repeated, choking on the word. "You could say that, lass."

She ran her fingers through his wet hair. "I wouldn't be doing my duty as your personal assistant if I didn't help you out."

"I do pay you rather handsomely to take care of all my needs."

"Exactly," she said, and let her hand trail down the side of his face to the hard line of his jaw.

He snagged her hand in one of his and brought it to his mouth. There, he spread her fingers and placed a kiss on her palm. "What need are you going to take care of tonight?"

"The one that burns you. The one I can see when you look at me."

"Is it that obvious?" he asked, still holding on to her hand.

She nodded. "To me it is, but then I'm looking for it."

"Are you?"

The lighthearted mood had somehow altered, grown more serious. Laura knew that sometime very soon, she would have to face the feelings churning within her. She feared they went far deeper than she knew.

Loving Charon, however, was a risky move. One she wasn't sure she was brave enough to chance.

"Laura," he whispered. His dark gaze was intense as it held hers.

She pulled her hand from his and reached down to pull open his towel. The sight of him full aroused and hard made her blood burn through her veins.

"You're the most handsome man I've ever seen," she confessed before she straddled his legs.

Charon's hands were instantly on her bare legs. He moved them up her thighs, shoving the hem of his shirt higher as he did. "If you want to talk beauty, I'm looking at it."

Her breath hitched when his thumbs grazed the curls of her sex. To feel the wonderful heat of him so close was driving her mad. The seductive lust, the soul-wrenching yearning she had to once more be in his arms was too inviting to ignore.

For two years, she'd been content to work beside him, to be the one he turned to when he needed something in his business. She never expected to call him friend, yet it had happened.

Lover was one name she certainly never dared to even dream.

With one yank of his hands, Charon jerked her shirt open, sending the two buttons flying across the room before he pulled her down. Her chest was heaving as she watched him gaze so lovingly at her breasts.

And then he cupped them in his hands.

Laura's eyes slid closed and her head dropped back. Her breasts swelled, aching for more. She rocked her hips forward as Charon's thumbs teased her nipples into hard little points.

Desire filled her, encircled her.

Claimed her.

And when his hot mouth closed over a turgid peak, Laura cried out from the sheer pleasure of it. With one hand on her back, he licked and laved her nipple with his tongue.

Laura's body was no longer her own. It was Charon's to do with as he pleased. She arched her back to thrust out her breast as she wrapped her arms around his head.

He moved from one breast to the other, wringing more cries from her until she was a shuddering mass of need.

Charon grabbed her hips and pulled her against the long, hard length of him. She gasped at the contact along her sensitive flesh, but when she tried to reach for him, he quickly grabbed her hands.

"Nay. I'd spill the instant you touched me," he whispered in her ear before he sucked her lobe in his mouth.

Laura continued to rock against his arousal until his fingers dug into her hips to halt her. She whimpered, needing the contact against him.

Charon smiled when her sigh of pleasure filled the room as he sank a finger into her hot, wet channel. He'd never been so close to a climax before, and he wasn't even inside her yet.

The feel of her magic only sent his already heated body into a frenzy. He hungered for her, longed for her with a force that frightened him.

But that's what Laura did to him. She touched parts of him he no longer thought existed, parts he was sure had died after he killed his father.

It was Charon's turn to moan when Laura's hands slid sensuously over his chest and shoulders down to his stomach. The back of her hand grazed the head of his cock. His balls tightened and his blood quickened.

That's all it took. One touch, one look from Laura and he was putty in her hands.

He watched the pleasure fill her face and her lips part on a sigh as he moved his fingers in and out of her. His cock jumped, eager to fill her.

Charon loved watching the way her body moved against his. Slowly, sensuously. Wantonly. With her back arched and her breasts begging for attention while her hips met his hand each time he thrust his fingers inside her.

His breathing became ragged, his blood pounding in his ears as her cries grew louder. Her hands were braced behind her on his legs. Charon bent and took a nipple in his mouth as he swirled his fingers around her clitoris.

He groaned in excitement when her nails raked down his back. Charon wanted to hear her scream his name again, needed to see her body flushed with pleasure. Pleasure he had given her.

Laura began to rock faster against his hand. Suddenly, her body clamped down on his fingers as she climaxed. He continued to thrust his fingers to prolong her pleasure until she went limp in his arms.

Charon's body shook, he wanted her so desperately. He stood and carried her to the bed. As he laid her down, her eyes opened to look at him.

In her beautiful moss green depths, he saw something stark and profound, something that a year ago would have sent him running from the room. He didn't know if he was ready for it, but he couldn't run. Not from Laura.

He lifted one of her legs and guided his cock to her entrance. She was slick with her own arousal, and it only fired his blood even more.

Charon wanted to go slowly, but she had already sent him well past his control. With one thrust, he seated himself inside her. She sucked in a startled breath, and then moaned.

He was beyond thoughts, beyond words. All he could center on was Laura. Charon began to pump his hips, plunging into her hard and deep.

His tempo increased when she matched his thrusts. He released her leg and leaned his hands on either side of her head. Her hands caressed his sides before sliding up to encircle his neck.

Their bodies were slick with sweat, their moans filling the room. Charon couldn't hold back the tide of his desire.

He ruthlessly, relentlessly pounded into her. She locked eyes with him, and then wrapped her legs around his waist. He sank farther into her, the angle taking him even deeper.

Her eyes widened a second before her body jerked and she screamed his name. The feel of her body clamping around him sent Charon over the edge.

He gave one final plunge and buried himself inside her as the climax swept through him, over him.

It took him, seized him.

Held him.

Just as Laura's loving arms did as she pulled him down atop her. They lay in each other's arms, their limbs entwined and their bodies joined.

Charon had never been more content or happy.

And he knew Wallace would try to destroy that happiness. Just as Charon knew if Laura weren't in his life, there would be no reason for him to exist.

The sound of rain hitting the windows filled the silence of the room. How many hours did Charon have before he went out to battle? How many minutes did he have to cherish the woman in his arms?

"Why do I feel like this is the end?" Laura whispered.

Charon lifted his head to look at her. He gently wiped away the hair stuck to her cheek and smiled. "I've only just begun making love to you. We've several hours until dawn. I plan to love you until you can no' walk."

There was no answering smile from her. "I want nothing more than to stay just as we are."

"You doona think we'll win?"

"I've not had the experience you have with fighting such evil. I'm frightened. For myself, yes, but more so for you. I saw what Jason did to you. I saw you die."

Charon rose from the bed and grabbed the wineglasses. He handed one to Laura once she sat up. "That's no' my first time being nearly killed with *drough* blood, and I can no' say for sure if it'll be my last. Aiden and Britt may have the answer. Regardless, as much as I'd like to hide away from it all, I can no'. I'm a Warrior. It's my duty to fight Wallace."

There was no condemnation or anger in Laura's green eyes as she stared at him. "I know. It's one of the reasons I've always been attracted to you."

"Always?" he teased before he drained his glass.

She finally smiled. "Always."

"Why did you no' say something?"

Laura lifted the glass to her lips and drank before she said, "I was waiting on you to notice me."

"Ah, so it's my fault."

"Of course," she said with a wink.

Charon closed his eyes as Laura's magic filled the room suddenly. "Shite, your magic feels wonderful."

"You felt that?" she asked.

He opened his eyes and nodded. "What did you do?"

"I just wanted to make sure my magic was still there, so I called to it."

"You've no idea what that does to me."

She set aside her wineglass on the bedside table and looked at him with a sly smile. "Why don't you show me?"

He didn't have to be told twice. Charon grabbed her ankle and pulled her toward him. As soon as she was flat on her back, he covered her body with his.

A groan tore from him when her hand slid between them and wrapped around his cock.

"My turn," she whispered before she shoved him onto his back.

CHAPTER THIRTY-SEVEN

Malcolm stared at the sky as he lay upon his back in the grass. He'd done just as he wanted—gotten lost in the glens.

There was much of the Highlands left almost as he remembered it four centuries earlier. He could thank his countrymen for that, at least.

The baaing of sheep reached him on the wind. It was distant, barely discernible except for his enhanced hearing. He could smell rain in the air as well.

Malcolm shifted his gaze and turned his head to the right. Dark, ominous clouds were headed straight for him. He inhaled sharply and felt the lightning currents run through his veins beneath his skin.

Ian had hidden out in the caves for months, seeing no one. Malcolm could do the same. It would be for the best, he was sure.

Though he quite liked many of the modern conveniences he'd discovered after being thrown forward in time, they didn't outweigh what he sorely missed from the past.

He couldn't stop the thought of what life might have been like had he not gone to MacLeod Castle to warn Larena and then gotten attacked by Deirdre's Warriors. He'd have become laird of his clan, married, and hopefully had many children.

Longing, pure and true, hurtled into him. It was so fierce he couldn't turn away from it. He should have known it would happen had he dared to think of the past and what could have been.

From the time he was old enough to understand he'd be laird, he'd dreamed of the title. His father had trained him from the moment of his birth to be the kind, strong, fair laird he was expected to be.

And Malcolm had wanted it as he'd never wanted anything before.

He let his fingers trace over the scars on the right side of his face. Only once had he dared to look in a mirror. The five gnashes had slit open his cheek, part of his forehead, over his eye, and diagonally over his nose and mouth.

It was a horrible sight. Malcolm could barely stand to look at himself. It was difficult to ignore the gasps from women and children, and the pity from men when they caught sight of him.

Malcolm opened his eyes to watch the clouds drift rapidly overhead. The wind had picked up. The storm coming would be a bad one.

He sat up with a curse when he thought of Charon and Laura. Malcolm knew they had made it to the castle, but he also knew that wouldn't stop Jason.

"Sod it all," he growled as he jumped to his feet.

He wanted to forget all of them, but he couldn't. Larena would never let him. And even though reception for his mobile was spotty where he was, he knew in his gut she was trying to call.

Now wasn't the time to lose himself in the mountains. But soon, soon he would walk away from Larena and the rest of them forever.

Malcolm turned to the left and began running toward the nearest town. He'd learn what he could without going to MacLeod Castle. Then he would sit back and wait to see if he was needed.

* * *

Aiden stood outside the cottage. The few hours of darkness in the summer nights were gone, leaving the area swamped in light.

"Where is Britt?" Quinn asked as he came to stand beside Aiden after his patrol around the cottage.

Aiden glanced behind him. "Sleeping, but now that I see the structure, I'm no' sure it's safe that she's inside."

"It's shelter," Quinn said with a grin. "And more rain is coming."

"Aye." Aiden had felt it hours ago. The storm would be a bad one, too. "I guess you've no' heard from Fallon or Charon?"

Quinn's lips flattened as he gave a shake of his head. "Nay, and my patience is wearing thin. Your mother and the other Druids have made no progress in halting Wallace's magic in Edinburgh."

"More have died." Aiden didn't have to be told. It was a truth that Wallace had shoved down their throats."

"They have. None of the magic of our Druids has any effect at all."

"Combined, the magic of the *mies* is supposed to be more powerful than a *drough*'s."

"Supposed to be." Quinn crossed his arms over his chest and looked out at the rolling land and the sheep that grazed on land not farmed.

Aiden didn't like the worry that lined his father's face. Many times he'd seen the Warriors get out of tight spots, but he was concerned about what awaited him.

The Warriors might have gods inside them, but Jason Wallace had the upper hand. Someone was going to die in the next few hours. Of that, Aiden was sure.

It couldn't be Britt. Not just because he had feelings for her—feelings he suspected went a lot deeper than lust—but also because she was crucial to the Warriors' having something to combat Wallace.

"You know how important Britt is," Aiden said as he turned his head to look at his father.

Quinn raised a brow. "Important to you?"

"Important to the Warriors." He swallowed, then admitted, "And important to me. Verra important to me."

"Do you love her?"

Aiden hooked his thumbs in the front pocket of his jeans and considered his father's words. "I think I began to fall in love with her the first moment I saw her."

They were silent for several moments before Quinn dropped his arms and said, "You want me to keep her safe over you."

"Without a doubt."

"You're my son," Quinn said, his voice hoarse with emotion.

Aiden faced his father and grinned. "You'd ask the same of Fallon or Lucan in regards to Mum."

Quinn blinked several times, his throat working as he finally swallowed. "Damn, lad, but I'm proud to call you my son."

"So you'll keep watch over her?"

"I give you my word."

Only then could Aiden relax. All the Warriors would have looked after Britt without having to be asked, but now he had made his feelings known. Britt would be carefully protected, just as any wife in the castle was.

Aiden watched the dark clouds in the sky, hating that after so many centuries, he'd finally found a woman he could love, a woman he wanted to go to bed with every night and wake up to every morning.

Could fate be so cruel as to give them only a few weeks together? Aiden knew all too clearly how harsh fate could be, especially when people least expected it.

"I'm going inside," he said, and turned on his heel.

"Nay," Galen said as he ran up with Phelan at his side.

Quinn was next to them in an instant. "What is it?"

"We leave," Phelan said as he looked around. "Now."

Aiden didn't have to be told twice. He ran into the cottage, banging open the door as he did. "Britt!"

She stood at the sound of her name, her eyes still heavy-lidded from sleep. Aiden grabbed her hand and dragged her out of the cottage behind him.

"We need to move fast," Galen said.

A muscle in Phelan's jaw jumped. "Wallace is here."

"Holy hell," Quinn mumbled. He then held out his hand to Britt. "Well, lass, it looks like I'll be carrying you."

Aiden saw the question in her lovely blue eyes, but there wasn't time for anything other than to give her a quick kiss and push her toward his father. "I'll be right behind you."

Once Quinn had Britt in his arms, Aiden met his father's eyes and knew Quinn would give his life to protect Britt.

"They've found us," Galen said as he looked across the field.

Phelan spread his legs as he took up a stance facing the direction Wallace would come. "I'll hold them off. Get moving."

Aiden started running in the direction his father went, but Quinn was already out of sight. It took no time for Galen to catch up with him.

"You run too slow," Galen said with a grin.

Aiden sidestepped before Galen could grab him. "I'll make it. You make sure Wallace doesna capture Phelan. Charon will never forgive us."

The grin fell from Galen's face. "Aye. But doona get caught either. I've no wish to face your father."

And then Aiden was alone, running as fast as he could toward Britt.

Toward the love that grew in his heart each time it beat.

Camdyn rolled over in the bed and reached out, only to find his wife's space empty. Instantly, Camdyn sat up and looked around the room.

He threw off the covers and rose from the bed. Just as he'd expected, he found Saffron in the doorway to their daughter's room.

"What is it?" he whispered as he came up behind Saffron

and wrapped his arms around her waist to drag her back against him.

Saffron shrugged. "I couldn't sleep."

"Are you worried about the others?"

"Of course." She turned in his arms and placed her hands on his chest. "I know we should be there helping them, but I can't risk Emma."

"Nay, we can no'," Camdyn agreed. "I've given most of my time as a Warrior in the pursuit of evil. But all that changed the moment we discovered you were carrying our child."

"I know," Saffron said.

"Then what is it?"

"I just feel . . ." She trailed off with a shrug. "I feel so selfish."

Camdyn placed a kiss upon her lips. "There's no need. Quinn and Marcail were able to raise Aiden without the threat of evil. If they were in our places, they'd be hiding their child as well."

"I know."

He took her hand in his and turned to pull her back to their bedroom when he felt a tremor run through her body. Camdyn jerked around in time to see Saffron's eyes turn milky white and began to swirl.

Her body crumpled, and he easily caught her in his arms, holding her tightly against him. "What do you see?" he asked.

"Dragons. There are dragons in the sky."

No matter how many times he witnessed her having a vision, he would never get used to hearing what sounded like thousands of voices added to Saffron's.

"Dragons? Are you sure?"

"So many colors," she whispered. "They're helping the others, but it won't be enough to stop Jason."

Camdyn ground his teeth together. Jason Wallace. How he couldn't wait to kill the *drough*.

Suddenly, Saffron blinked and her eyes returned to the

beautiful tawny color he loved so well. He smoothed back the walnut-colored strands of her hair from her face as she clung to him.

"Oh, God, Camdyn," she said in a shaky voice. "The Druids are going to try to help the Warriors against Jason, but it's only going to allow him to get free."

Camdyn glanced over Saffron's head to Emma, sleeping peacefully in her crib. He didn't want his daughter knee-deep in evil as he had been. She deserved better.

"I have to stop the Druids," Saffron said.

Camdyn looked down into her eyes. He knew what was coming next, but he wanted to put it off until he could try to think of a way to keep her and Emma away from the battle. "You said dragons."

"Yes," she said with a soft smile. "They're so lovely. I can't wait to see them."

Camdyn set her away from him. "Nay."

"Yes," she argued. "We have to go. Now. It's going to take me with the Druids, and your friends need you. The selmyr are there as well."

"Where is there?"

"Dreagan."

"Oh, hell."

"And send Malcolm a text!" she shouted over her shoulder as she ran into the bedroom to change.

Camdyn turned on his heel and hurried to get dressed. He should have known trying to keep his family away from the battle would be pointless.

But he'd be damned before he allowed his daughter or wife to be harmed. They would make sure Saffron's vision didn't come to pass, and then he was getting them the hell out of Dreagan.

Lucan strode wearily from the hospital to Cara, Broc, and Sonya, who waited for him across the street. He stopped in front of his wife, but couldn't get the words past his lips that the magic of the *mies* had failed again.

Cara's face crumpled, and Lucan pulled her into his arms, giving her the only comfort he could.

"I just knew it would work," Sonya said. "We're only missing Saffron, but that's because she and Camdyn are hiding Emma."

Emma. Every time Lucan thought of the baby, he felt a pang in his heart that demanded children of his own. Cara longed to hold her own baby, and it was a dream they had thought to have realized by now.

A dream that was fading as quickly as finding the spell that would bind their gods once more.

"Jason's magic is too strong," Broc said. "We're doing no good here."

"What else are we supposed to do?" Sonya asked her husband. "Do we continue to hide in the castle?"

Broc tucked a curl of red hair behind her ear. "Every second you're out here is a chance Wallace has of getting to you."

"Or to you," Sonya argued.

Cara sniffed and lifted her head from Lucan's chest. "Broc is right. We aren't helping here. Maybe we do need Saffron."

"What we need is more Druids," Lucan said.

"There is another," Fallon said as he appeared next to them.

Sonya jumped back with a gasp. "Dammit, Fallon. One day you're going to land on top of someone."

The pleased tilt of his lips that told Lucan his brother had good news. "What Druid do you mean?"

"Laura. She has her magic back," Fallon said. "As Charon explained, her mother and sister were syphoning it from her."

Cara's brow furrowed at his words. "How did she get it back?"

"The selmyr killed Laura's mother and sister, and all her magic was once more hers."

"Well," Sonya said as she blinked. "That's good as long as Laura isn't working with Jason."

Fallon scratched his chin and stepped into the shadows as a car drove by. "Charon assures me that she's on our side. He saved her seconds before the selmyr got to her. She went to her parents' house to confront her mother and get her magic back. It just happened to be when the selmyr attacked."

"Shit," Broc whispered.

Fallon motioned them closer. "You can hear the rest of it from Laura and Charon. We need to go."

"Go where?" Sonya demanded.

"Dreagan Industries."

Lucan chuckled. "This isna exactly a good time to drink, brother."

"It's where Charon and Laura are. As well as some new . . . allies."

"Allies?" Broc repeated, eyes narrowed. "How are they going to help?"

Fallon put his hand on Lucan's shoulder and waited for the others to touch. "You have to see it to believe it."

"Believe what?" Lucan asked.

His brother's sly smile only made him more curious. The fact Fallon was being so cryptic worried Lucan, but before he could ask more about it, Fallon teleported them out of Edinburgh.

And landed them in the middle of an open area with several parked cars and buildings all around them.

A man stepped forward with blond hair and black eyes. "Welcome to Dreagan," he said.

A loud roar got their attention, and they turned as one to see three dragons—green, amber, and blue—fly over the mountain and disappear from view.

Lucan looked at his brother to find Fallon's smile growing larger. "Dragons?"

"Dragons," Fallon replied with a nod, his eyes crinkled with excitement.

CHAPTER
THIRTY-EIGHT

Laura pulled her hair back and twisted the length of dark waves before wrapping it into a bun. She secured it with some pins before placing her hands on the sink and staring at her reflection.

The rain hadn't stopped for hours, and though she would have preferred to see the sun, Charon said the clouds helped to hide the dragons.

She looked into her green eyes that were exact replicas of her sister's and father's. There hadn't been time to mourn the loss of her mother and Lacy.

Laura still couldn't believe they were dead. After all they had done to her, she had wanted to confront them. How many times had she gone over in her head all she wanted to say to them?

Now she would never get that chance. The idea of not getting the anger and helplessness she'd felt at their hands off her chest hurt more than their deaths.

"What kind of person does that say I am?" she asked her reflection.

"You thinking of your mother and sister again?"

She saw Charon leaning against the bathroom doorway in the mirror and nodded. "I so wanted to tell them off."

"So do it."

Laura turned to face him. "What? They're dead, Charon."

He lifted one shoulder in a shrug and said, "I know, but telling them off was no' going to make them change their minds. It was about you healing. You willna be able to until you say everything you need to say."

"To the air?"

"Pretend they're in front of you."

She'd done it often enough while lying in bed at night. It just seemed so pointless if she couldn't say the words to their faces. "I'll think on it."

The skepticism covering his face told her he didn't believe a word she said. "Cassie is waiting to take you down to breakfast. She, Elena, and Jane want to talk to you."

"Are you coming?"

"Laith is going to show me around the nearby mountains so we can pick the best place of attack."

Laura pushed away from the sink and walked past Charon into the bedroom to grab her hiking boots. "The battle won't be out there?" she asked, and pointed out the window.

"It's best to keep the battle as far from the Kings' home as possible. It'll still be on their land, just no' close by."

"Jason will still know its Dreagan land."

"Perhaps," Charon said, a shrewd look in his eyes.

Laura finished putting on her shoes and chuckled. "Have you thought of everything?"

"I'm sure I have no'."

There was something in his voice that caught her attention. She walked to him and placed a hand on his cheek. "You're not doubting yourself now, are you?"

"Con assures me the only way a King can be killed is with another King."

"But?" she urged when he paused.

Charon took her hand and pulled it from his face to cradle before him. "Warriors and Druids can be killed. The selmyr have surrounded Dreagan. The odds of everyone living are slim."

"That's the way it is in every war. Why should it change now?"

"Because you're here."

Her heart missed a beat. She gazed into his chocolate-colored eyes and wished they had a few more hours alone. "You forget I watched you die. I don't ever want to see that again. Ever," she said over him when he tried to talk.

He kissed the hand he held, his mouth lifted in a half smile. "You're mortal, Laura. I'll heal from almost anything, but you willna."

"We can debate this for eternity. You don't want me to get hurt, and I don't want you to get hurt. Now that we have that hashed out, we need to realize both of us will be needed in this battle."

"Stubborn woman," he murmured before he pulled her into his arms for a slow kiss that set her body on fire and raging out of control.

Laura ended the kiss before she couldn't and stepped out of his arms. "Get moving, Warrior. You have a battle to plan."

He gave her a wink and walked out of the room. Only then did she sink onto the bed and drop her head into her hands. How could she help the Druids when she knew nothing about her magic?

She could call it up, and it answered readily enough. But what was she to do with it?

"Bloody hell," she said.

Charon was right. Sometimes things called for a harsh curse word.

All through the tour of the mountains and glens, Charon couldn't stop thinking of Laura and their parting words. He was miles away from the mansion, but still he could feel the threads of her magic.

It was as if they were tethered to him, stretching no matter how far he went. Knowing she was still on Dreagan land calmed him.

When they were on their way back to the mansion, he felt the first stirrings of her magic. It stopped him in his tracks, the desire so pure, so potent he was instantly, achingly hard for her.

If she had been with him, he'd have had her up against a tree and her clothes off, plunging inside her. He lengthened his strides, but not even Laith's shouts could slow him.

The closer he got to the mansion, the more he could feel Laura's magic. It came at him in waves. Her magic would crash into him, shattering him with the heady, intoxicating feel of it, only to have it ebb away.

Just as he got control of his body, another wave of magic would crash into him. Charon's body burned with a need so great, so intense that he had to find Laura immediately or explode from the desire.

He leaned a hand upon the outside of the mansion and shook off the water that coated him as he hurriedly kicked off his boots. He threw open the back door and stalked inside.

"Charon!" Laith called as he caught up with him.

Charon whirled around on the King as he reached the kitchen. "Leave me."

"What the fuck is wrong with you, mate?" Laith demanded.

Charon reached for the back of a chair as another wave of magic swallowed him. "Can you no' feel it?"

"What? Laura's magic? Is that what this is about?"

Only when her magic diminished was Charon able to lift his head. "Doona disturb us," he said and used his speed to get up the stairs and down the long corridor before more magic assaulted him.

He threw open the door to find Laura standing in the middle of the room. She lowered her hands, which had been raised before her, and frowned when she caught sight of him.

"Charon?"

"My God, woman. Do you have any idea what you do to me?" he asked as he stalked inside and slammed the door behind him.

He gave her no time to answer as he pushed her against the wall and slanted his mouth over hers. The kiss was almost cruel in his need, but she moaned into his mouth, which only sent his already heated body into a frenzy of fiery need.

Her hands tore at his soaked shirt as he cupped her breast. She had one leg wrapped around his hips while he rocked his arousal against her.

Their heated exchange came to a grinding halt at the knock on their door.

"I'm going to kill whoever it is," Charon said as he rested his forehead against hers.

Laura laughed and glanced at the door. "We had a few hours last night without being interrupted."

"I warned Laith no' to bother us now. I'm on fire for you." When she frowned, Charon lifted his head and said, "I could feel your magic. You were using it."

"Yes. I was trying to learn it. Is that why you came barging in here?"

"Aye."

She looked at him beneath her lashes, a look that made his rod ache for her. "I like knowing that. Now I know how to call you."

"Wench," he said as he nipped her ear.

The pounding on the door began again. Charon sighed and stalked to the door. He yanked it open to find Hal standing there with a grin upon his face.

"What the hell are you smiling at?" Charon demanded.

"We've got a bet going on how many times we can interrupt the two of you."

Charon leaned a hand on the doorway and growled. "You better have a good reason to be banging on the door, Dragon."

"I do, Warrior," he said, still grinning. "Your friends have arrived."

"How many?"

"Fallon deposited four before he left again. Lucan, Cara, Broc, and Sonya are waiting for you and Laura below."

Charon turned to Laura as Hal walked away. She was pale as she stood quietly by the window. Concern quickly washed away his desire. "They're good people."

"I know. You keep telling me that."

"What are you afraid of?"

She shrugged and nervously bit her lip. "You didn't trust me. What if they won't either?"

"They will."

"How can you be sure?"

"Because I told them they could."

Her green eyes grew round. "You did that for me?"

"Aye." He'd had a good reason to doubt her, and there was still a chance Jason had spelled her somehow. But Charon needed her beside him. Whatever else came, they would deal with it.

He held out his hand and waited for her to take it. Then he pulled her toward him and walked her to the door. "If there is one thing you can count on, it's that every Druid down there is going to stand with you."

"They're powerful."

He nodded as they left the room and started down the hallway. "Verra. Just as you are. You may no' know how to fully use your magic, Laura, but I know the feel of magic. Yours is verra potent."

She blinked up at him. "You think I need encouragement?"

"Nay, but I'm giving it to you anyway."

By the time they reached the stairs, she began to relax. Charon loved the feel of her hand in his, and he loved the way her eyes sparkled when she looked at him.

"Cara was the first of the Druids at MacLeod Castle," Charon explained. "Lucan saved her when she fell off the cliff. Sonya was the second, and came to the castle because the trees told her she was needed."

"The trees?" Laura whispered in awe. "She can talk to the trees?"

"Aye. She came to teach Cara her magic, since Cara didna know she was a Druid. Lucan is the middle MacLeod brother. You can pick him out because he still wears the small braids at either of his temples. And the MacLeods themselves still wear their torcs."

"So interesting. Who is Broc?"

"Ah, Broc," Charon said as he thought of the Warrior. "He is the Warrior with wings. He spied on Deirdre for centuries."

"What are their powers?"

"Lucan can call the darkness and shadows around him while Broc can find anyone, anywhere."

Laura came to a halt outside the parlor. Voices from within could be heard, and she peered around the edge of the door for a glimpse inside.

"They'll love you," he said.

She jerked her head to him, some deep emotion moving through her eyes. "Will they?"

"Aye." He pulled her into his arms and gazed into her eyes.

Charon gently placed his lips atop hers for a quick kiss. He knew their time alone had come to an end, and it tore at him. He wanted to roar his fury. There was no getting around leaving her.

There was evil to fight.

And his woman to protect.

He opened his mouth to tell her she was his when Fallon appeared in the foyer next to them.

Laura stepped out of Charon's arms with a soft smile. And for the first time in his very long life, he felt as if he could do anything.

CHAPTER
THIRTY-NINE

Aisley stopped short in the small grove of trees when Dale held up his hand to halt her. She waited, straining to listen to whatever he heard so effortlessly with his enhanced hearing.

A second later, Dale turned toward her, but he looked over her shoulder to Jason. "It's quiet."

"So?" Jason whispered impatiently. "They wouldna be making a lot of noise, would they?"

Aisley saw Dale curl his hands into tight fists until his knuckles turned white. It was a good thing Jason controlled Dale, or she imagined Dale would have already ripped his head off.

"Go have a look, Aisley," Jason said as he nudged her roughly from behind.

She ground her teeth together when she heard Mindy's grating giggle. Aisley turned and glared at the Druid, a thought taking root. "I think Mindy should take one side while I take the other. Surrounding them."

That silenced the bitch instantly. Aisley inwardly rejoiced when Mindy jerked her gaze to Jason and gasped in outrage when he gave a nod.

Dale gave Aisley a wink as she walked past, and hid his smile as he turned his back to Jason. It gave her some relief to know she wasn't completely alone. Dale was the closest thing she had to a friend. She just hoped he lived long enough so she could repay him for all the times he had saved her ass.

Aisley peered at the crumbling ruin of a cottage that stood three hundred yards in front of her. In order to reach the structure, she was going to have to leave the safety of the trees.

There were two Warriors with Britt, and then the Druid, Aiden. She'd seen Aiden fight in the alley in Edinburgh. He could hold his own, and shouldn't be taken lightly.

There had been an intensity to the Druid, a recklessness that told her he cared about Britt and would do whatever it took to protect her.

How different her life would have been had she had someone like Aiden to watch over her. Aisley mentally shook her head to clear it of such thoughts and concentrated on the cabin.

Who would attack her? A Warrior or Aiden? Aisley imagined both scenarios as she crept out of the trees to the cottage. She took the right side while Mindy went to the left.

Aisley bent at the waist and jogged the last few feet until she was able to put her back against the cottage near a window. She slowly peeked through the broken shutters to see Britt sleeping in a chair.

Galen and Quinn were cautious. They would be patrolling the area, and then there was the fact they could feel a Druid's magic. So the Warriors knew they were there. But where were the Warriors?

Something was off. Aisley knew it instantly. Whether it was a trap or not was still up in the air. She didn't want to be caught by the Warriors of MacLeod Castle, but then again, they could just kill her instead of taking her captive.

Aisley crept around the side of the cottage until she came to another window. There, she was able to make out another form. She couldn't see the man's face, but she suspected it was Aiden.

Her gaze surveyed the area before her, waiting for Quinn

or Galen to attack. Jason had told her Quinn's power was to communicate with animals, and Galen's was to read people's minds.

There was a lot the Warriors could learn of Jason if Galen got ahold of her. That's when Aisley realized Jason had no intention of letting her get captured. He planned to kill her the instant Quinn or Galen showed up.

The realization shouldn't have surprised Aisley, but it did. She was expendable to Jason. He doubted her, and in doing so it meant her death.

One way or another.

Aisley took a deep breath and slowly released it as her mind focused, sharpened. She felt the hum of her magic and let it fill her.

If she was going to die, she was going to go out in her own way. And it wouldn't be by Jason's hand, if she had any say in it.

She squared her shoulders and pushed away from the cottage to walk around the second corner to the front of the house. Mindy already stood there, her hand reaching for the doorknob. Before Aisley could stop her, Mindy opened the door and walked inside.

Aisley took a step toward her and stopped. Something touched her skin. It felt as soft as a caress, tender as a kiss. And as brilliant as a summer's day.

As swiftly as it had touched her, it was gone. Aisley had never experienced anything like it before. She didn't know what it was, but it had been something spectacular.

She was so absorbed in what had happened that she was taken unawares when there was a shout from Mindy as Aiden and Britt ran out of the cottage.

Aisley rushed after them, but Mindy blasted her with magic from behind that sent Aisley tumbling to the ground.

"They're mine," Mindy said between clenched teeth and took off after them.

Aisley climbed to her feet and hurried back to Jason. "Aiden and Britt ran," she told him between panting breaths.

Jason narrowed his cold blue eyes on her. "Why are you no' chasing them?"

"Mindy wanted to catch them. She's after them now."

Jason smiled, satisfied with her answer. "Where are Galen and Quinn? Quinn wouldna leave his son for long."

"I saw no Warriors in the cottage." Aisley looked around, noticing for the first time a few other Druids and Dale were missing. "Where's Dale?"

"Hunting," was Jason's reply.

Which meant Dale was hunting the Warriors.

"They're here," Jason whispered as he leaned a shoulder against one of the tall pines. "I know Galen and Quinn are near. Dale willna fail me. He'll bring me at least one of the Warriors."

"They're older than Dale," Aisley pointed out. "Which means they're stronger. Their power will be greater since they have full control over their god."

Jason's head slowly swiveled to her. "Are you doubting me, cousin?"

"Merely pointing out the facts. *Cousin.*"

"No' always a wise move."

She shrugged. "If you're looking for a reason to kill me, there's no need. Just do it."

"You're still useful," Jason said with a mocking grin. "But I doubt that'll last too much longer."

Aisley opened her mouth to reply when Mindy let loose a shrill scream that was cut short. Jason instantly took off running to where the sound had come from.

She was the only Druid of his coven that stayed behind. Aisley looked around and saw that she was alone. She could take a chance and run now. Jason would eventually find her, and what he'd do to her when he did would be horrendous.

"Now's your chance," Dale said as he walked from behind a tree.

Aisley jumped and turned to look up at him. There was a frown marring Dale's forehead, his mouth turning down at the corners in concern. "What are you doing? I thought you were looking for Galen and Quinn?"

"They are no' here. Something is, though."

"A Druid?"

Dale shook his head. "I suspect another Warrior. Doona concern yourself with that. You should leave. Jason will just get you killed."

"I know."

"Do you want to die?"

Aisley looked away from Dale's probing stare. "I chose this life. I'll live—and die—with what I've chosen."

"You deserve better. You deserve more."

She forced a grin, startled by the tears that suddenly filled her eyes. "You wouldn't say that if you knew the real me. The me before I became *drough*. I wasn't a good person."

"No one is ever a good person," he whispered.

A moment later there was a shout of pure fury.

A shudder of foreboding ran through Aisley. "That was Jason."

"I doona think you'll have to worry about Mindy anymore," Dale said. "Come. We need to get to Jason."

Laura stood by the door of the parlor as the Druids of MacLeod Castle gathered to recount their last few hours.

She learned a lot by just watching them. Not a one of them vied for power over the others. It was as if each Druid was comfortable with who she was.

A novel concept after the way Laura had been raised. Especially now that she knew her magic had been stolen from her. There was much laughter among the Druids, and lots of hugs.

Sadness weighed heavily in the room as talk of the innocents dying in Edinburgh reached Laura's ears. She leaned back against the door and watched as Marcail wrapped an arm around Cara in comfort.

Laura might not have been introduced to anyone yet, but she had caught their names as they greeted each other. She was waiting to learn the others' names when a woman with silvery blond hair and amazing emerald eyes turned to her.

"You must be Laura," the woman said with a welcoming smile as she walked to her. "I apologize for leaving you out. It's been a trying night. I'm Danielle Kerr, but everyone calls me Dani."

"Dani," Laura repeated. "It's nice to meet you."

A second woman with black hair and violet eyes held out her hand. "I'm Gwynn. We'd hoped to meet you while you were at the castle, but Charon wanted to keep you all to himself."

It was a nice way of saying she had been kept separated because Charon doubted her. Laura shook Gwynn's outstretched hand.

Suddenly she was surround by all nine Druids. Laura ran her gaze over the faces before her, unsure of how to proceed.

It was Cara with her wealth of chestnut curls who stepped forward next. "Charon has finally come to his senses, I see. Now, we're a loud bunch, so please forgive us. And with so many of us, we don't expect you to remember everyone's name. I'm Cara MacLeod. My husband is Lucan."

Laura was quickly introduced to Marcail, Isla, Reaghan, Sonya, Tara, and Ronnie.

"We're just missing Saffron and Larena," Tara told her. "Saffron has a baby she's keeping as far from the selmyr and Jason as she can."

Isla nodded her head of inky black hair pulled back in a French braid that hung to her waist. "And Camdyn is with them, of course."

"And Larena?" Laura asked.

Ronnie grinned, the corners of her hazel eyes crinkling. "I can't wait for you to meet her. She's the only female Warrior."

"Really?" Laura asked in surprise. She'd just assumed all the Warriors were male. But to have a female Warrior. It was exciting, and Laura couldn't wait to meet Larena.

"You realize she's our first English Druid," Marcail pointed out.

Laura looked into Marcail's unusual turquoise eyes before she glanced at the rows of tiny braids atop the crown her head. "The first?"

Tara took her hand and led her to one of the couches. "That's right. Gwynn was the first American. Dani is half American, and Saffron and Ronnie are both Americans as well."

"Cassie and Elena are from the States," Laura said as she thought of the Dragon Kings' wives.

Reaghan sat across from Laura. "Who?"

"Oh," Laura said, comprehending that they hadn't met any of the women at Dreagan yet. "Cassie is married to Hal, and Elena is married to Guy. They live here."

Isla leaned forward and lowered her voice. "You know Dreagan is the Gaelic term for dragon."

Laura looked away and bit her lip to keep from smiling. She couldn't believe the Druids didn't know about the Dragon Kings yet, but then again, when had the Warriors had time to tell them?

"Laura," Gwynn said with a knowing look. "What do you know?"

Laura parted her lips and glanced around. "I'm not sure it's for me to say."

"Spill," Dani urged with a grin. "Who knows when our men will tell us?"

The rest nodded their heads in agreement. Laura looked out one of the tall windows to find the rain coming down harder than ever. It was difficult to know when it was thunder she heard and when it was a dragon.

She stood and walked to the window. The storm had darkened the sky, and with the rain, it was almost impossible to make out the shapes of the dragons flying in and out of the clouds.

"I had to be shown," Laura said into the silence of the room.

A moment later and Reaghan stood beside her. "What did you have to be shown?"

Laura pointed to the sky and the amber dragon that dived

out of the clouds at that moment. "That. I had to be shown that."

There was an audible gasp from the room as each Druid caught sight of the dragon.

"They're real," Isla murmured, stunned.

"Very real," came a cultured voice from behind them.

Laura turned to see Jane. "I never get tired of looking at them."

"Me either," Jane said with a laugh. "And I'm married to one. I've made some tea, but since Con has sent everyone who isn't a Dragon King or mate away, I'm afraid I'm going to need some help bringing it in here."

Tara laid her hand on Jane's arm. "Dragon King? Is that what they are?"

"While you have your tea, I'll tell you everything," Jane promised.

Laura was the last to leave the parlor as Jane directed them to the kitchen. Charon had been right. The Druids weren't just kind, but welcoming as well.

"Are you all right?" Jane asked.

Laura nodded and walked beside Jane to the kitchen. "I wasn't sure what they would think of me."

"They'd be fools not to see what a wonderful person you are. You're a Druid, Laura. From what Charon told Banan, there are few of you left. I've a feeling they protect their own."

Laura paused inside the kitchen doorway. "Now I have something to protect. The Druids, Warriors, and the dragons."

Jane squeezed her hand before she pulled her into the kitchen and began her tale of the Dragon Kings.

CHAPTER
FORTY

Charon stood atop a mountain and dialed Phelan's mobile phone for the tenth time. Once more, it did nothing but ring and then go to voice mail. Charon shoved the phone into his pocket and let the drops of rain pelt him.

"He's fine," Arran said above the roar of the storm.

"He better be." Charon didn't want to think about Wallace getting his hands on Phelan.

Ian clamped a hand on Charon's shoulder. "Phelan is smart and cagey. He'll be here."

They had been standing in the rain for almost an hour surveying the landscape. Charon pointed out where he wanted to box Wallace in, and then showed them the two places in the valley that could be potential problems.

Charon was torn in his worry over his friend and his concern for Laura. She hadn't been in a battle before. She didn't know what it was like to face black magic. Or any magic, for that matter.

How could he concentrate on doing his part in the battle if he was fretting about her? Because if something happened to her, Charon would never forgive himself.

"It's hell," Logan said as he walked up.

Charon frowned as he looked at the Warrior. "What is?"

"Knowing you can no' protect your woman during a battle."

Charon looked away and swallowed past the growing lump of unease. "How do you do it?"

"With difficulty."

Charon met Logan's hazel eyes before they both began to chuckle.

"You have no choice but to trust her and the other Druids," Logan said once they had finished laughing. "The first time is the hardest."

"So it gets easier?"

"Nay," Logan confessed, his smile gone. "Every time feels as if you're walking through Hell. It's only after the battle is over and you can hold her in your arms again that you feel you've made it."

Charon pushed his wet hair back, the drops of rain falling from his eyelashes into his eyes. "I didna want to care for her as I do."

"I didna want to love Gwynn, but we doona get to choose when love finds us."

"Love hasna found me," Charon said sharply.

Logan merely grinned. "Has it no', my friend?"

Charon thought over Logan's words long after Logan walked away. Did he love Laura? Was it love that clawed at his insides when she was away from him?

Was it love that made him crave her touch?

Was it love that made him yearn to hold her in his arms?

Charon knew nothing of the emotion. But the thought of her no longer being in his life made him want to tear apart the world.

A dragon the color of midnight blue landed in the valley below and turned its great head toward Charon. Charon looked at the thick body and the long neck and tail with its gemlike scales of the darkest sapphires.

Charon could've sworn the dragon smiled at him while rows of massive teeth flashed. And in a blink, the dragon was gone as Banan shifted back to his human form, standing naked in the storm.

In two leaps, Charon was down the mountain and standing in front of Banan, eyeing the two intertwined dragons tattooed with an unusual mix of red and black ink. Or was it ink? Charon wasn't sure when it came to the Kings.

"What is it?"

"Quinn's group draws closer," Banan answered.

"And Wallace?"

Banan's lips turned down in a frown. "He's no' far behind."

"Any sign of Phelan?"

There was a moment's hesitation before Banan gave a slight shake of his head.

Charon ran a hand down his face. "How long until Wallace reaches us?"

"With the storm, I'd say two hours."

Without another word, Banan turned and shifted back into a dragon. He let out a roar and spread his midnight blue wings as he leaped into the air and flew away.

"I doona think I'll ever get used to that," Lucan said as he came up beside him.

Charon looked up to see several dragons above them. "They knew of us from the verra beginning."

"I know. Fallon told me."

"Is he angry? Are you, that they didna help us with Deirdre?"

Lucan sighed at the same time lightning forked across the sky. "In a way I am, and in others I'm no'. Fallon feels the same. I doona believe the Kings would've allowed Deirdre or Declan to take over."

"Jason must be a real threat for them to offer to help," Charon pointed out.

"Maybe." Lucan fingered the griffin head of his torc that he'd worn around his neck for seven hundred years. "With the dragons, Jason will be no more."

"And the selmyr?"

Lucan let out a string of curses. "That is another matter entirely."

Charon had seen what the selmyr could do. He knew in an instant they could take Laura's life. Or even his. It didn't matter how strong he was or what god he had inside him. The selmyr were too powerful.

They could disappear on the wind, looking like a gray mist until they suddenly reappeared. Arran had been bitten by them, and very nearly died.

Arran described their bites to feel like acid, and as the selmyr drank their victims' blood, the victims became so weak, they could barely move. And in a Warrior's case, that meant they couldn't call up their god or use their power.

Charon knew the chances of everyone coming out of the battle was slim, but he had put in a failsafe for the Druids. If the selmyr or Wallace got the upper hand, the Kings would ensure the Druids were kept safe.

The only problem was that while the Druids were away from the castle and Isla's magic shield, they were mortal.

Laura hadn't had the privilege of living under the shield, but Charon wanted her to. She deserved to have a long, happy life. And he wanted to be there with her.

Charon spotted Con as he walked down into the valley, Fallon by his side. He and Lucan walked to meet the two.

"Everything is in place," Con said.

"All the Kings are helping us?" Lucan asked.

There was a subtle shift in Con's demeanor that told Charon something was amiss.

"We have all we need," Con said.

A moment later, Fallon and Lucan walked off. Charon waited until they were out of earshot before he asked, "Is everything all right?"

"There are a couple of Kings that couldna be woken."

Charon was more than a little surprised Con told him such news, but even more worried about what that could mean for the dragons. "Does that happen often?"

"Sometimes a King will sleep for several thousand years. Some have been asleep since before the pyramids were constructed. Most realize we must get on with our lives, as difficult as it is without our dragons."

"Then they just wake up and find a new world around them?"

"It is the duty of those who remain awake to go in every century or so and share with those who sleep about the world."

"They're asleep."

Con chuckled. "Ah, but a dragon will always hear a dragon."

The rain slackened and Charon shook his head to displace the water running down his face. "Why tell me this? You could have told Fallon, but you chose no' to."

"You doona value your own worth," Con said as his black gaze came to rest on him. "As to why I didna tell Fallon, I didna want him to know."

"And me?"

Con shrugged and motioned to the mountains with his hand. "You seem a part of this. I can no' explain it. I know you are no' one of us. Yet I feel that you belong to us as much as you belong to the Warriors."

"I belong to no one."

A grin pulled at Con's lips. "There is one who would beg to differ."

Laura. Charon looked to the west, where he knew the mansion was.

"Aye," Con murmured. "A verra fine woman you have. Have you told her how you feel?"

"Everyone seems to think they know what I feel when I do no'," Charon ground out.

"There's no time to think of that now. Wallace will be here soon. The selmyr continue to test us, but we're holding them back."

"And Quinn's group? How will we get them here if Fallon can no' teleport them?"

Con grinned then. "Cassie and Elena have gone to get Britt. Quinn phoned Fallon's mobile about thirty minutes ago. They'll get Britt as close to the selmyr as they're able for the girls to bring her in."

"What about Aiden, Quinn, and Galen?"

Con's smile faded. "It's all up to my Kings to get them past the selmyr."

"I'll help."

"You're needed here," Con said as Charon began to turn away. "Wait. Tell me of Ian Kerr."

"Ian?" Charon repeated as he faced Con once more. "What do you want to know that you doona already?"

"We may know some Warriors better than others. For instance, we knew what Broc's power was. That doesna mean we know all of you personally. Now, tell me of Ian."

"He and his twin were taken by Deirdre. They were in Cairn Toul the same time as me. Deirdre then had Duncan killed."

"Duncan," Con mumbled. "So the twin is dead?"

"Aye. Ian now holds the full power of the god he and Duncan shared."

Con bowed his head. "That's all I need."

The rumble of thunder sounded around them. When the thunder died, the roar of several dragons drowned out the rain. The massive, majestic bodies of the dragons glistened with water. They cut a path through the downpour before disappearing over a mountain.

Con had said Charon belonged to them. Everyone—Kings, Warriors, Druids, and mortals—were counting on him and his plan. He had to stay the course.

"Phelan, you better make it here," he whispered.

Con began unbuttoned his shirt. He jerked it off and wadded up the wet material before tossing it aside. "He'll be here."

Charon caught sight of the tat on Con's back. It was the same mix of black and red ink, but this time the dragon was lying down, its wings opened to take up the entire span of Con's back while the dragon's tail wrapped around Con's hips.

"Where are you going?" Charon called out as Constantine began to walk off.

Con looked over his shoulder, a predatory look on his face. "To the skies, Charon. To the skies."

Charon watched Con until he disappeared over the top of the mountain. Then he turned to the Warriors who stood waiting for him.

He held out his hand and watched his skin turn copper while dark copper claws extended from his fingers. Ranmond bellowed inside him, impatient for blood and death.

Wallace had done enough damage. It was time for him to die, just as Deirdre and Declan had been killed. No longer would they fear *droughs*.

Then Charon would help the MacLeods in their search to find the spell that would bind the gods inside them once more. Though Charon hadn't decided if he would bind his god or not. That was a decision for another time.

Now . . . now it was time for battle.

The dark shape of a Warrior took to the skies. Broc spread his indigo wings and soared over Charon as he went to take his place for the battle.

Each Warrior knew what he had to do. Each was prepared to give their lives if it meant the end of Wallace.

Charon rubbed the spot on his chest where the blade had entered. It was a warning, of sorts, not that he needed it. He could detect the cloying feel of *drough* magic making its way toward them.

"Come on, Wallace. It's time to die," Charon said with a grin.

CHAPTER FORTY-ONE

"Slow down," Quinn directed from the backseat. "Pull over before you get to the river."

Aiden gripped the steering wheel tightly. He hadn't liked the plan. Actually, it wasn't the plan that was the problem. It was the fact that Britt would be going without him.

"Here, son," Quinn said.

Aiden put his foot on the brake and pulled the stolen car over before the bridge. Britt looked at him, fear in her soft blue eyes.

"You'll be fine," he promised her. He wasn't sure of all the details, but his father had told him everything would work out. His father had never lied to him before.

Britt leaned over and gave him a quick kiss. "I'll see you soon?"

"Aye." He forced a lightness into his voice he didn't feel as a car pulled up behind them.

Galen was out of the car before the other vehicle had been put in park. Aiden watched from the rearview mirror as Galen spoke to someone on the passenger side of the car.

A moment later, Galen looked up and nodded to Aiden. Aiden pulled Britt against him for another kiss. "It's time."

"Come, lass," Quinn said. "I'll walk you."

"No need," said a woman after she opened Britt's door and ducked her head inside.

She had the hood of her raincoat pulled up, but strands of her black hair poked out and stuck to her face. The woman looked to the backseat and Quinn before her gaze moved to Aiden, and then finally to Britt.

"I'm Elena. Constantine and Charon sent me to bring you to Dreagan, Britt."

Aiden leaned forward before Britt could get out and asked, "Are you sure you can get her to the mansion?"

Elena's deep green eyes softened. "We were able to get out. And my husband isn't far. He's watching as we speak. If there's trouble, he'll help. Britt will be in good hands. I promise."

"Be careful," Britt told him before she got out of the car and rushed to the SUV behind them.

Elena was quick to follow Britt, and Galen slid into the front seat.

"She's in good hands," Quinn said.

Aiden sighed, uncertainty weighing heavily upon him. "Really? Who are these people?"

"Dragons," Galen said.

Aiden's head jerked toward Galen before he turned in his seat to look at his father. "What?"

Quinn nodded. "They're dragons. I doona know the whole story. I'm sure we'll find out once we're there."

"If we can get past the selmyr, you mean," Aiden said.

Galen grinned. "Doona forget Jason is trailing us. It should be interesting."

That's when it occurred to Aiden. "We're bait. We're fucking bait!"

"Aye," Quinn said with a wry smile. "Someone has to lead Wallace to Dreagan. Who better than the people he's chasing?"

"And the selmyr?"

Galen rubbed his hands together. "I'm ready for those bastards. After what they did to Arran, I want some payback."

Aiden shook his head at his father and Galen and faced

front again. Their eagerness for battle had grown the closer they got to the meeting spot to drop off Britt.

Now that Britt was gone, Aiden was surprised the two Warriors hadn't jumped out of the vehicle to ambush Wallace. But it was always this way with Warriors before a battle. They didn't see it. It was part of who they were, part of the god inside them.

But Aiden saw it. It used to frighten him, but now he knew it was their way of preparing. He started the car and put it in drive before he pulled out onto the road, the wipers going as fast as they could and still not clearing the windshield of rain.

"How far until we're on Dreagan land?" he asked.

Galen laughed. "Lad, we've been on it for over an hour."

"One of these days I want to stop being treated as a child," he stated, and drove over the narrow bridge.

Quinn leaned forward and put his hand on Aiden's shoulder. "We thought it best no' to scare Britt more than we had to."

"You're right." Aiden slowed to take a narrow curve. "Where do I go now?"

"You need to drive slow. Verra slow."

Galen shifted in his seat, his gaze riveted on the side mirror on the car. "We need to give Wallace time to catch us."

"I'm going to kill them. Slowly. Painfully."

Aisley listened as Jason repeated his litany for the hundredth time since finding Mindy with her heart yanked from her chest.

There was only one creature who could have done such a thing. A Warrior. Aisley hated to admit she was overjoyed that Mindy was no longer around. Still, Aisley wouldn't wish that kind of death on anyone.

Aisley licked her lips and looked out the car window while trying to ignore the fact her cousin had the body of his dead lover in the backseat with him.

How close had Aisley come to dying? Why had it been

Mindy and not her? Was it just by chance that the Warrior hadn't chosen her?

Those thoughts had gone round and round in her mind for the last hour as they drove north, following whatever kind of trail Jason had found of Aiden and Britt.

The Warrior who had killed Mindy could've slain the rest of them. Why didn't he? Was he just toying with them?

"It had to have been Larena," Jason said. "She used her power to turn invisible and sneak up on Mindy. That's the only way Mindy would've been taken unawares."

"Mindy was always overconfident," Aisley said. "You don't know what happened."

Jason's hand slammed down on Aisley's seat from behind. "I know it was a Warrior. That's all I need to know."

Dale glanced at her before he took a sharp corner and stopped the car as they waited for another vehicle to cross the narrow bridge. Once the other car was clear, Dale put his foot on the accelerator.

"They're leading us into a trap," Dale said into the silence.

Jason snorted. "As if any kind of trap could stop me."

"And what about us?" Aisley asked as she turned in her seat to look at him.

Jason merely smirked. "You willna be harmed, cousin. As long as you prove beneficial."

"You wish you hadn't sent Mindy with me to scout the cottage, don't you?"

"You're bloody well right!" Jason took a deep breath, his face relaxing as he did. "Mindy had a great future ahead of her," he said calmly.

"And I don't?"

"Aisley," Dale muttered in warning.

Aisley glanced at Dale before turning her gaze back to Jason. "I'm right, aren't I?"

"You had potential, but you seem to have . . . lost it. You never could stay the course for anything. No' even your ba—"

"Enough!" Aisley shouted. Her magic rolled viciously

within her, urging her to use it on Jason. The impulse to harm him as he had done her was overwhelming.

And he knew it by the way he smiled at her.

He always did know how to strike to have the greatest impact. Aisley's chest heaved as she struggled to get ahold of herself while Jason's leer grew the longer he watched her.

"Did I hit a nerve, cousin?" he asked innocently.

"God, how I loathe you."

Jason laughed and reached over to run his hand down the side of Mindy's hair while her head lolled against the back of the seat. "If you ever grow the balls to take me on, let me know. I'd enjoy the brief entertainment."

Aisley turned back in her seat, her eyes dead ahead as she looked through the rain-drenched windshield. There was only one way she could take Jason on. That meant she would have to contact the Devil in order to get the power she needed.

But did she have the guts?

Then the words that had whispered so maliciously in her head after she performed the *drough* ceremony came again.

"Your soul is mine, Aisley. All mine."

She was going to Hell anyway. Why not go on her own terms? But she couldn't exactly call up Satan right then. She needed to be alone, which was going to be difficult, since they were trailing after Aiden and Britt into a trap.

There would be a battle. She had known it the instant Jason released his magic upon the unsuspecting people of Edinburgh.

He had taken the war to a new level, one that none of the Warriors or Druids of MacLeod Castle would stand by and allow to happen without some kind of retribution.

Aiden and Britt had been given no choice when Jason had then used more magic to prevent Fallon from teleporting them to safety. Their only option was to run.

Yet Aisley knew the Warriors of MacLeod Castle to be intelligent and crafty. They had given them too much time to formulate a plan. And once again, Jason was too confident in his abilities.

There would be death. So very much death.

Dale reached over and put his large, callused hand atop hers, which rested on her thigh, for a brief moment. She didn't dare look at him. If Jason suspected Dale's loyalties lay with her instead of with him, Jason would kill Dale immediately.

Aisley couldn't let that happen. She didn't want to feel responsible for him, but she did.

No other person would die because of her. No one.

"They're trying to hide in the glens," Jason said suddenly.

Almost instantly, the rain slamming against the car increased tenfold. Thunder boomed around them as lightning zigzagged through the sky.

Aisley leaned toward the window of her door and looked at the gray sky. Thick clouds, heavy with rain, blocked any light from the sun.

"Which Warrior is causing this storm?" Jason asked, curiosity in his voice.

A tremor raced down Aisley's spine. Jason enjoyed this cat and mouse game with those from MacLeod Castle entirely too much. It was lucky for them there was no other kind of magical creature that could choose sides, because she knew they would come up on the losing end.

CHAPTER FORTY-TWO

Laura stood alone in the parlor and stared out the window of the mansion, hoping to catch a glimpse of Charon through the dense rain.

"You won't see him," Dani said as she walked up to stand beside her. "They'll make sure to stay far away."

"I know."

Dani crossed her arms over her chest. "In the past, we Druids were in the thick of things. But not this time."

"Do you miss it?" Laura asked as she looked at Dani.

"Yes. And no," she answered. "It's scary being in the midst of battle, but I love to watch Ian. He's magnificent."

"Ramsey is ruthless," Tara said from behind them.

Laura and Dani turned to find her leaning against the doorway, a sad smile upon her lips.

"I nearly lost him once. I need to be with him."

Dani dropped her arms and quickly walked to Tara to put an arm around her in comfort. "Ramsey was most explicit in his instructions. Hell, all of them were. We're to stay here."

"Our magic can help," Tara raged.

Laura ran her hand along the back of the bridle-colored leather Chesterfield couch, her finger pausing at each tufted section. "Neither of you have seen what a selmyr can do."

Ronnie walked into the room and stopped, her face lined with anxiety. "No, but I have. They move so fast."

"As quick as the wind," Laura added.

Ronnie nodded. "And vicious. They were on Arran before he knew what happened. I could only stand there helpless as they bit him and drank his blood like a damned vampire."

"Charon wouldn't let me see my mother and what they did to her." Laura sank onto the rounded arm of the couch and wrapped her arms about herself. "By the way he and the Dragon Kings acted, I suspect the scene would've been a grisly one."

"It's good you didn't see it, then," Ronnie said. "Trust me, Laura, it's something I'll never get out of my head. Nor how they then turned to me. It was only Arran's quick thinking that got me out of there alive."

Dani blew out a harsh breath. "There has to be something we can do. It's not right that we're not beside our men."

"No," Laura said with a shake of her head. "The Kings made it clear. The selmyr feed on magic. If we go out there and try to use our magic, they'll come straight to us. The more magic we use, the more they'll feed. The Kings have been able to keep them at bay, but the Warriors are putting themselves in danger just to get a chance at killing Jason."

Tara looked down at her nails and scraped a bit of peeling gunmetal blue polish off. "Ramsey would have my ass if I were to leave the mansion."

There was something in her voice that caught Laura's attention. The way the other women looked at her with grins pulling at their lips told Laura something was definitely going on.

"Is Larena guarding us?" Ronnie asked.

Laura frowned as she recalled briefly meeting the beautiful female Warrior an hour before. "She left with the others. I heard something about them needing her invisibility."

"That's right," Tara said as she dropped her hands. "They couldn't get ahold of either Phelan or Malcolm, so they took Larena."

"Which means no one is guarding us," Dani said.

Laura looked over her shoulder as she heard a roar of a

dragon. Charon was out there, waiting to ambush Jason while trying to keep away from the selmyr.

It was an impossible task the Warriors had given themselves. Charon wouldn't have put the plan in to motion if he wasn't sure they could gain the advantage, but it was a dangerous chance they took.

"I can't sit here waiting to know if Ramsey is coming back to me," Tara said.

Dani caught Laura's eye. "Ian is my world. If he's in trouble, I want to be there for him.

"And if seeing you puts him in harm's way because you've taken his mind off the battle?" Laura asked.

Ronnie smiled sadly. "It's obvious you care for Charon, Laura, but maybe it's because you haven't seen how very close to death he's come."

"But I have," she argued. "He faced Jason and his group alone for me. I watched as magic was used against him and Jason put the *drough* blood in Charon's wounds. I watched Charon die. Don't tell me I don't know what it feels like."

Dani took Laura's hands and turned her to look into her eyes. "We know all of that. It's just . . . loving a Warrior is maddening, frustrating, and frightening. They're protective of the ones they care about, and sometimes that doesn't allow them to see we can help."

Laura knew they meant that in order to feel as they did, she had to love Charon, and because she didn't feel as they did, she obviously didn't love him.

How very wrong they were.

She loved him so much, it hurt. To know he was out there putting his life on the line once more made her want to scream. But she also knew he needed to be focused to carry out his intricate plan.

He couldn't do that with her there. Regardless of how much she thought she could help or wanted to be by his side.

Instead of arguing with the Druids, Laura pulled her hands out of Dani's grasp and faced the window once more. The silence that followed was drowned out only by the storm.

"You must love him very much indeed," Tara said.

Laura's chest tightened as she thought of Charon's teasing grin, of his beautiful dark eyes, of his amazing kisses. If she were honest with herself, she'd loved him from the moment she walked into his pub and he smiled at her.

"This battle isn't just about killing Jason," Laura said. "For Charon, it's about redeeming himself in his own eyes. If I go out there, I'll distract him. I can't chance ruining all of this just because I want to see him."

Laura turned around to see the rest of the Druids in the doorway. She wasn't sure how much they had heard, and it didn't matter. For too long, she had hidden her feelings from everyone, even herself.

"I've an idea," Isla said as she stepped forward, her ice blue eyes intelligent and kind as they focused on her. "It's going to take all of us."

Reaghan's amber eyes were alight with excitement. "We are going to help our men and the Dragon Kings. No one said we had to be near the battle in order to use our magic."

"I don't really know how to use my magic," Laura said when Isla pulled her into the large circle the Druids made. Laura wanted to help, but feared she'd be more of a hindrance than anything.

Isla tucked her long black hair behind her ear and winked. "We'll guide you to the ancients. From there, you'll learn quickly."

"The ancients?" Laura whispered as she sank onto the ground and crossed her legs as the others did.

Gwynn squeezed her other hand. "Close your eyes, Laura, and think of your magic."

Laura glanced up and caught sight of Jane, who stood off the side. Jane gave her an encouraging smile before Laura closed her eyes and her magic welled up inside her.

"Oh, shit," Elena said as the car slid on a patch of wet earth.

She glanced in the rearview mirror to see Britt go skidding in the backseat before Elena could straighten the car.

"Maybe I should've driven," Cassie said from beside her.

Elena rolled her eyes. "I remember all too well the story of your first day in Scotland. It's better for all if I drive."

"I've gotten better," Cassie said defensively, and then ruined it with a smile. "Well. A little."

"Wee bit," Elena said, mimicking the Highland brogue.

"Not that I'm not grateful for all you're doing," Britt said as she grabbed the handle above her and held on as the Range Rover soared into the air and came to a bone-jarring landing before it continued down the hill. "But how the hell can you joke at a time like this?"

Cassie looked over her shoulder and laughed. "Stick around for a while and you'll find out."

Elena caught sight of a dark shape coming toward them. "I think I see Hal."

"About time," Cassie said.

Britt looked out the window in the steel gray sky but saw nothing. She thought she'd be a lot safer with Cassie and Elena, but she was beginning to think it would have been better to stay with Aiden.

Suddenly, something huge came out of the clouds and straight toward them. Britt's mouth fell open when she saw the spread of large wings and the long body and tail.

"That's . . ." She couldn't get the words out.

Elena turned a sharp curve, the Range Rover jerking to the side before the tires found their grip and the SUV roared forward. "That's a dragon. Your eyes aren't deceiving you."

Britt couldn't take her eyes off the brilliant green scales of the dragon. How her two fellow Americans could be so nonchalant about it confounded her.

She turned as the dragon flew over them and straight into what looked like a massive gray ball of ash. The ball dispersed the instant the dragon flew through it.

"That's my Hal," Cassie said and let out a whoop.

Britt's head jerked to the women. "What just happened?"

"I suspect that's the selmyr Hal just saved us from," Elena said.

"Selmyr," Britt repeated, testing out the word.

"They feed off magic, but they're pretty pissed right now, so they'll attack anything," Cassie explained.

Britt rubbed her forehead, not sure if her head ached from hitting it on the roof of the SUV as they bounced their way over the land, or because of everything she was learning. "What's a selmyr?"

"Ancient creatures that were woken a short time ago by accident," Elena explained.

"But we don't have magic."

Cassie's smile was gone as her lips compressed tightly. "Like I said, they're pissed. And they'll attack those without magic when they get hungry enough."

"Great," Britt said right before she was thrown to the left and crashed up against the side of the SUV.

There were going to be bruises all over her. She really should have put on her seat beat. It was a mistake she hastened to correct, but it took several tries before she got the seat belt clicked in place.

A moment later and Elena slammed on the brakes. The seat belt locked, preventing Britt from being tossed forward. Before she could get her bearings, Elena had the Range Rover in park and the ignition turned off.

Britt fumbled with the seat belt. "If I'd have known," she mumbled.

Finally, she got it undone and quickly followed the girls out of the SUV and through a front door of a mansion. Where Britt came to a halt as she took in the grandeur before her.

"Welcome to Dreagan," Elena said with a wink.

Cassie took Britt's hand and pulled her forward as she began to walk. "Let's find the others."

They had gone through the foyer when a woman with short auburn hair and kind eyes came to meet them. She hugged Cassie and Elena before she turned to Britt.

"You must be Britt. I'm Jane," she said in a refined British accent. "There's a lot going on, so please let us know what we can do for you."

"Where are the Druids?" Elena asked.

Jane pointed to the right. "Since the Warriors wouldn't let them near the battle, they're doing what they can to help."

Britt quietly followed the three women as they spoke in hushed tones. She peeked around the door when they reached the parlor to see a group of women sitting on the floor in a circle with their eyes closed.

"Druids," Cassie whispered. "I never thought they could exist."

Neither had Britt a few weeks earlier. The same could be said for immortal Warriors and now dragons. What else was out there she didn't know about?

She found herself dragged into another room that looked like an office of sorts. It was very male, by all the dark wood and deep coloring. The large desk was another indication of masculinity, but its impeccable desktop showed it was for looks and not use.

Everywhere she looked there were dragons. They were carved in the wood of the legs on the chairs, a metal dragon came out of the wall, a light hanging from its front claw, and then there was the tapestry hanging on a wall featuring a gold dragon in flight.

Some of the dragons were easy to spot, others—now that she knew what to look for—were more difficult to find. Anyone who took notice of all the dragons would think the residents of Dreagan were more than a little obsessed with dragons.

Britt found herself standing in front of a cabinet where several crystal decanters sat filled with liquor. Jane poured three glasses of some dark amber liquid and held one of the glasses out to her.

"Drink. You look like you need it," Jane said.

Britt accepted the alcohol with hands that wouldn't stop shaking. "I'm usually just a wine drinker. Every once in a while I'll go nuts and drink a martini or margarita."

Elena smiled as she lowered her glass from her lips. "This has a bit more of a kick. But trust us, it'll make you feel better."

Britt shrugged and did as they suggested. The first touch of the liquid on her lips was a little spicy, and it burned a trail down her throat to her stomach.

After she was able to stop coughing, Britt found her hands had all but stopped shaking as warmth filled her.

"We told you," Cassie said as she lowered herself down on a chair, where she turned her gaze out the window.

Britt saw her reflection. The smiles from the women were gone, replaced with lines of worry. "This is worse than Aiden led me to believe, isn't it?"

Elena finished her whisky and gently set the glass down. "Yes."

Just one simple word, but Britt went from edgy to downright panicky. The women of Dreagan didn't pull any punches, that was for sure. "Aiden is still out there. Why is he still out there? Couldn't Hal or one of the other dragons get him in?"

The three women simply looked at her with sad, pitying expressions. Britt's stomach plummeted to her feet.

"Oh, God. Aiden's bait to get Wallace here. Why didn't I see that earlier?"

Jane was instantly at her side, an arm wrapped around her to steady her. "Banan won't let anything happen to Aiden, but Aiden was insistent that you be kept safe above all else. Your knowledge and findings are too valuable to his family."

"That stupid, idiotic man," Britt said, and blinked away the tears that filled her eyes. "He should've told me."

"He knew you wouldn't leave him," Elena said.

And Britt wouldn't have. "I feel so helpless. I'm not a Druid. I have no magic or anything to help them."

"Neither do we," Cassie said softly, and turned to look at her. "All we can do is pray. But you have something to do."

Jane nodded eagerly. "There's a space set up for you to continue your work. Aiden made a list of everything you might need and then some."

Britt wiped her eyes and squared her shoulders. Aiden was right. There was one way she could help. That was to find a way to not only combat the *drough* blood, but for the Warriors to have something to use against Wallace.

"Show me," she said.

CHAPTER
FORTY-THREE

Charon's gaze was locked on a group of five selmyr through the rain as they were kept at bay by a black dragon. He wished he knew who the Black was, but as forthcoming as the Kings had been about who they were, they were careful not to shift in front of him.

Except for Banan.

Charon would think about that later. For now, he had to stay focused on the selmyr. And Wallace.

By the way the selmyr occasionally glanced behind them, Charon knew Quinn, Galen, and Aiden were closing in. Which meant so were Wallace and his group.

Ranmond's roar filled Charon's head as his god lusted for death and battle. Charon wasn't sure where Ranmond's need ended and his began.

Deirdre had turned Charon into a monster, imprisoned and tortured him. Declan had dared to harm his friends. But it was Jason who had done the unthinkable by trying to get to Charon through Laura.

Charon peeled back his lips to show his fangs and growled as one of the selmyr lunged at him. It got no farther because the Black dived right at the ash-colored beast.

A smile pulled at Charon's lips when he saw the dragon's wings crash into one of the selmyr that didn't get out of the way fast enough. The force sent the creature tumbling to the ground.

An instant later, the selmyr was on its feet. It glanced down at its chest where the long gnash was healing quicker than anything Charon had ever seen.

"Ballocks," he whispered.

Every creature had a way to be defeated. The selmyr were no different. Finding a way to kill—or trap—them might be more difficult than Charon had first thought.

Suddenly, the five selmyr near Charon turned, and as one, began to run toward a large grove of trees. Charon glanced up at the Black to see the dragon had its eyes trained on the ash-skinned bastards.

Something had gotten their attention. But what? Quinn, Galen, and Aiden were due to drive on one of the back roads near there shortly. But it couldn't be them, because Charon didn't see the yellow dragon Con had said would herald their arrival.

The roar of a Warrior got Charon's attention. He ran after the selmyr into the trees and glimpsed the gold skin he recognized instantly. Charon launched himself at one of the creatures who had sunk his long, sharp teeth into Phelan's arm.

Charon severed the selmyr's head from its body with one swipe of his claws. Before he could turn to the next, the other four had latched on to Phelan, blood running past their lips as they drank.

Phelan's gold Warrior eyes caught his. Charon threw back his head and roared before he attacked again. This time he wasn't alone. The black dragon crashed into the trees and clamped its huge hand around two of the selmyr. A second later, the Black was once more in the air, its great wings beating against the wind and rain.

Charon knew the only way to stay alive was to make sure the selmyr didn't bite him. Somehow when they took a Warrior's blood, they took his power as well, leaving him too weak to combat them.

If they did that to a Warrior, what could they do to a Druid?

Charon ducked and rolled as a selmyr rushed him. He came up behind the seven-foot creature and put his hand through it, hoping its heart would be where a human's was.

He was wrong.

The selmyr jerked back his elbow, banging it into the side of Charon's head and his horn. Charon stumbled back, but regained his footing. He bent forward slightly before he jerked upward, spearing the selmyr in the back with the tip of his horn.

The beast screamed its fury. Charon used his other hand and sank his claws into the selmyr's back near its spinal column. And then wrapped his fingers around the bones.

With one yank, Charon jerked out the beast's spinal column. The selmyr fell lifeless to the ground.

Charon turned to attack the last one when something sharp and piercing sank into the top of his shoulder. Almost instantly, his blood began to burn as if acid had been injected into him. The pain was ten times what *drough* blood felt like.

And with the burn came the weakness. It became a chore just for Charon to stay upright. He could still feel the rain pelting him, but it was a distant sensation. Just as he couldn't focus on the world around him.

Laura.

The thought of never seeing her, touching her . . . kissing her again made him want to bellow his rage. But it took too much effort.

The more blood he lost, the weaker he became. Still, it wasn't in Charon to give up easily. He twisted and fell to his knees, hoping to dislodge the selmyr.

It caused the beast to loosen its hold. That was enough for Charon to focus once more, and he used that time to slam his elbow into the creature's side. The more he fought, the more blood the selmyr took.

Of a sudden, Charon found himself on his back, blinking through the torrential rain that fell upon his face. His blood still burned agonizingly, but the selmyr no longer drank from him.

Dimly, Charon heard something to his side. After two tries, he was able to turn his head and see Phelan fighting the creature. Charon knew it would take both of them to kill the beast.

Charon rolled to his stomach and pulled himself to his hands and knees. Phelan was struggling to hold off the selmyr's attack, the ash-skinned beast's large fangs getting closer and closer to Phelan's neck.

Charon was able to get a hold of a fallen tree and drag himself to his feet. He flexed his claws and slashed the back of the selmyr.

The creature turned its eerie black eyes to him, its stringy white hair plastered to its face. Charon reared back his hand, but just before he grabbed for the selmyr's spine, a shift in the rain caught his attention.

Charon glanced at Phelan, and they both knew more selmyr had arrived. He gritted his teeth and used the last of his strength to take hold of the selmyr's spine and jerk it out.

With the bloody spinal column still in his hands, Charon fell to one knee as it gave out. He nodded to Phelan as his friend tossed aside the dead selmyr and jumped to his feet.

Charon had no sooner dropped the spine than they were surrounded by dozens of selmyr.

"I think this is it!" Phelan shouted over the roar of the rain.

Charon once more pulled himself to his feet. It was getting more and more difficult just to stay upright. "It looks that way."

"I killed Wallace's lover," Phelan said with a tired grin.

Charon exchanged a smile with his friend, which soon turned into laughter.

"At least we're going out with style," Phelan said.

Charon wasn't sure how much strength he had left. It had never taken him this long to recover from a wound before, even *drough* blood. But whatever was in the selmyr's bite had done a lot of damage.

They stood back to back as the selmyr started to close in. Charon had seen a lot of ugly things in his life, but these new creatures were the ugliest he had ever laid eyes on. It wasn't just their ash-colored skin or the long, stringy hair. Nor was it their height or long limbs.

It was the skin pulled tight over their bones, as if their bones were part of their skin.

"Ugly buggers," Phelan murmured.

Charon took a deep breath and called to his god. He'd give Ranmond complete control if it meant he got out of this alive and was able to end Wallace.

"We take out as many as we can. If you get a chance, make a run for it up to the top of the mountain. It'll give you a vantage point to see Jason and attack," Charon said.

"Fuck you," Phelan snarled. "You take your place at the top of the mountain. Neither of us is going to die, so stop talking as if we are."

Leave it to Phelan to put things into perspective. Even though Charon knew they didn't have the full powers of their gods, they were Highlanders.

"Never surrender," he stated as a selmyr lunged at him.

Charon didn't know how long they battled the creatures. His body was riddled with bites, no matter how they tried to keep the selmyr at bay. They moved too quickly, and Charon was fading fast.

He ducked as a selmyr swung a hand at him. Charon's feet slipped on the grass and he fell. He dug his claws in the ground and shouted at himself to get up. There was a deafening roar that filled the air. Charon glanced up through the flailing limbs of the creatures and saw several dragons above him.

A moment later, and the selmyr were scattered to the wind as four dragons landed. It took three tries before Charon could get to his feet. He braced his hands on his knees and looked to the midnight blue dragon.

"Thank you," he told Banan, and then looked at the other three dragons.

Phelan turned from the blue dragon to the yellow, to the black, and then to the amber dragon. "I didna think anything could surprise me again. Dragons. Fuck me," he mumbled with a grin.

Charon nudged Phelan as the amber and black dragons took to the skies. "We need to get in place."

Together they hurried to the place Charon had left to help Phelan just as the yellow dragon flew over them and roared.

"It's time," Charon said.

Phelan's smile was deadly as he focused on the Jaguar XF following the small car that held Aiden, Galen, and Quinn. "Wallace dies today."

Aiden eased off the accelerator as the car began to fishtail. The road was nothing more than a trail, barely wide enough for the small Fiat they drove.

Just as Galen and Quinn had predicted, Jason Wallace caught up with them ten miles ago. Aiden would have preferred to keep a bit of distance between them, but his father had other ideas.

"Slow down, we're losing them," Quinn said as he kept a lookout through the back window.

Aiden clenched his jaw, wishing they had stolen a vehicle with newer tires. The car's engine whined as they went up a steep part of the road that would take them over a mountain.

"Soon," Galen said.

Aiden glanced at him to find the Warrior's eyes were still trained dead ahead. An hour past, both Galen and his father had shifted into their Warrior forms, as if they were eager for the battle.

In some ways, so was Aiden. Jason Wallace did nothing but cause trouble. But Aiden's hatred for all Wallaces went far deeper than just Jason's current spree of evil.

It was Delcan Wallace and his band of mercenaries who had killed Aiden's closest friend, Braden. They had grown up together at MacLeod Castle, learning who they were and their magic. For hundreds of years, they were inseparable.

But all that changed in one single night. Aiden knew how precious a life was. He'd taken it for granted before then because of the magic of Isla's shield.

He no longer took life for granted. With his thoughts on Britt, he pressed hard on the accelerator and gunned the car up the last few hundred yards of the mountain.

"Where the hell is everyone?" he asked. "I thought there was supposed to be a big battle and we were bait."

Quinn's head appeared between Aiden and Galen's seats. "They've been waiting for us."

Aiden was about to ask what he meant when they crested the hill and a line of ash-skinned creatures stood before them.

"Ram them!" Galen yelled.

Aiden didn't hesitate. He looked in his rearview mirror and saw Wallace's car skid to a halt and the selmyr surround them.

But Aiden wasn't in the clear yet. He winced when he barreled through the selmyr, but the creatures simply latched on to the car.

"Keep going!" Quinn shouted. "Doona stop, Aiden!"

Aiden locked his elbows and put the accelerator on the floor just as an arm busted through his window and an ash-skinned hand with unnaturally long fingers clamped around his throat.

CHAPTER
FORTY-FOUR

Laura was overwhelmed by the sheer magnitude of the chanting and drums that sounded as if they were all around her. She recognized them immediately. She'd only had a fleeting touch with the ancients, but they had left a mark upon her soul. One she knew she would never forget.

And now she was with them again. Laura breathed deeply, contentment filling her as her magic touched every fiber of her being.

It wasn't just the ancients she felt. Laura could sense the magic of the other Druids in the room. The sheer force of it all left her reeling.

There was no wonder why the *droughs* feared a group of *mies* gathering together. The amount of magic that was coming from them was more than Laura thought possible.

"Focus," Reaghan said. "Think of our men. All of them. We need to keep them protected from the selmyr."

Laura's mind instantly filled with visions of Charon. The voices of the ancients pulled her to them, protecting her from the war that waged just a few miles from them.

She didn't want to be protected though. She wanted to be out there with Charon.

"You are," the voices of thousands of ancients said at once. *"Your magic is with him, even now shielding him from being seen by the selmyr."*

It was as close as Laura could come to battling with Charon, and it would have to do. She poured every ounce of her magic into the room to mix with the others.

"Steady," Isla whispered.

Laura's breaths were coming in great heaving gasps from the effort it took to keep her magic focused. It never occurred to her to quit. Charon's life hung in the balance, as did every Warrior who fought against Jason Wallace.

She might not know a lot about her magic, but Laura knew she could do this much for Charon. She would do so much more if it meant he would come back to her.

He had to come back to her. There was no way she would lose him. Not now. Not after finally having him in her life.

With that thought, Laura dug deep for more magic. The drums and chanting became so loud they drowned out everything else. She didn't know how long she listened to them, and then it no longer mattered.

"There!" Charon shouted to Phelan, and pointed to the car just as it came over the mountain.

A second later, two other vehicles followed the first. And then dozens of selmyr were standing in the way.

"Shit," Charon said and took off running.

Phelan caught up with him as they used their incredible speed to race over the land. Out of the corner of his eye, Charon saw other Warriors come out of hiding and rush toward the car driven by Aiden.

Charon could see one of the selmyr had broken through the driver window and had a hand around Aiden's neck. But Aiden never slowed the car.

Quinn kicked out the passenger window and leaned out of it while he used his claws to slice the selmyr's face that had a hold of his son.

More of the ash-skinned creatures were attacking Jason's vehicles, because they had been fool enough to stop.

The car Aiden drove abruptly turned and slid to a rocking halt. Instantly, Galen and Quinn were out of the car. Charon was surprised when the selmyr that had a hold of

Aiden was thrown backwards. The car door was jerked open and Aiden stepped out, his face a mask of fury.

"Just like his father," Phelan said.

Charon didn't have time to agree as they reached the vehicle and selmyr surrounding their friends. "Pull out their spines!" he shouted as he fell to one knee and slid to the first selmyr.

He wasted no time in grabbing the spinal cord and ripping it out. The others were quick to follow his example. And it worked on the selmyr who had their back to them. It was another matter entirely when they faced the creatures one-on-one.

Charon and Phelan moved to either side of Aiden as they battled two of the creatures. Aiden used his magic while Charon and Phelan used their speed to confuse the selmyr.

It didn't take them long to kill both of the beasts. And when those bodies hit the ground, more took their places.

"Bloody hell!" Aiden yelled.

Charon silently agreed. At least the Kings would keep the rest of the selmyr away as they dealt with the ones nearest them.

"We can no' continue like this!" Quinn barked.

There was a blast of magic that knocked all of them to the ground. Charon's ears were ringing from the force of it. He shook his head and rose up on his hands to look around him.

The selmyr they had been fighting were either dead or knocked unconscious.

"Charon?" Phelan called from beside him.

He looked at his friend and shrugged. Then his gaze shifted to Wallace and his Druids.

"Let them finish him," Fallon said as he walked up.

Charon got to his feet and saw what looked like a bubble around Wallace. It was magic that kept the selmyr away from him, but it only drove them crazy to get in, which was evident by the way the selmyr kept throwing themselves at it.

"No' our worry," Aiden said as he climbed to his feet.

There was a pause, and then he said, "You've got to be fuck-ing kidding me."

Charon and the others turned to find dozens more selmyr coming right at them.

Aisley sat frozen in the car. Dale had pushed her onto the floorboard when he slammed on the brakes. For the rest of her life, she would hear the sounds of those creatures hitting and jumping on the car as they sought to get inside.

She'd had but a glimpse of the ash-skinned monsters, but that's all it took to scare her. They were evil. Evil knew evil, and there was no denying that's what they were.

Between their strange, eerie growls and bellows and Ja-son yelling at everyone, Dale leaned down and whispered for her to stay inside.

She met his gaze, and she saw the dread he couldn't hide. Whatever was attacking them was meant to be feared.

Aisley stayed hidden until she dared to peek her head above the dash. Her stomach dropped like lead as she saw the sheer number of the creatures. There had to be hundreds of them.

They didn't have the speed of a Warrior, but they could disappear and then reappear in a second.

She searched around the car until she found Dale. He was battling three of the creatures. They were tall, and their long arms were able to keep Dale at a distance while they in-flicted their damage.

Their talons looked to be twice as long as Dale's, but that's not how they attacked. They waited until he was fend-ing off one of them while the other two drew in behind him and sank their teeth into him like vampires.

Aisley gasped, her hand covering her mouth. She quickly looked at the other *droughs* and found most of them being fed off of by the creatures.

She swung her head back to Dale. He looked sad and re-signed, as if he were ready to die. Aisley slid to the driver's side and reached for the handle to open the door to help him when he mouthed "No."

A tear fell onto her cheek. She wiped at the condensation clouding the window and directed a blast of her magic at the monsters biting Dale.

They fell back, disoriented. It gave Dale time to get to his feet. Seeing him so unsteady had her sending another blast of magic at the three.

Dale had saved her so many times. By staying in the car, she hoped to confuse the creatures into not knowing where the magic was coming from.

But they zeroed in on her straightaway.

"Oh, damn," she murmured.

One moment the monsters were looking at her, and the next they were gone. Aisley blinked, and suddenly they were next to the car door.

The long, slim fingers of one of the creatures reached out and grasped the door handle. Aisley locked the door and looked up into the cold, sinister black eyes of the beast.

There was a loud roar she recognized as Dale's, and then he launched himself at the three again.

Almost in tandem, there was a blast of magic that hurled Aisley against the seat, knocking her head backwards. She opened her eyes to see Jason had done what Jason did best— look out for himself.

She sneered as she saw the large bubble of magic that surrounded him. Each time one of the monsters ran into it, it was killed instantly.

Yet, the bubble of magic did more than that. For every time they rushed the bubble, it seemed to take out more and more of Jason's magic.

"It's weakening him," she mused.

Aisley looked back at Dale to find him trying repeatedly to get to his feet. Bite marks covered his neck and arms, and she was sure there were more beneath his shirt she couldn't see.

She unlocked the door and opened it only to have him lean against it when he stood and block her exit.

"Let me help you," she said once the thunder passed.

Dale shook his bald head. "Get away from here, Aisley."

"I'm not leaving you."

He glanced at the creatures at his feet that were beginning to wake. "This is your chance to end Jason's hold over you. I willna survive this. Neither will he, by the looks of it. You can."

Aisley licked her lips. "You've helped me so many times. Get in, and let me help you."

"Nay, lass. I have to do this. Now, get out of here and live the rest of your life for the both of us."

She shook her head, but he pushed her back inside the car and shut the door before she could protest. Aisley screamed and ducked her head when one of the creatures' fists came through her window as it reached for Dale.

"Dale!" she screamed as he was once more fighting the monsters.

Aisley realized that some of the other beasts began to notice her. They couldn't get to Jason, the other Druids were dead, Dale was locked in battle, and she was an easy meal.

She started the car and jerked it into reverse. Aisley stomped on the accelerator and plowed into one of the monsters before she turned the wheel as she slammed on the brakes and then threw the car into drive.

CHAPTER
FORTY-FIVE

Malcolm stood over two dead selmyr as he watched his brethren from the forest. There were more of the damned creatures sneaking up on his friends, but he couldn't reach all of them.

A sudden gust of wind that had the rain falling sideways got his attention. He turned to glimpse a man running through the woods as naked as the day he was born.

Malcolm turned his attention to the man. Malcolm searched for a trace of magic, but it wasn't Druid magic he felt. It was something else entirely. Just as Malcolm went to search for the man, the air stirred around him.

"You're needed."

Malcolm spun around, his teeth bared and his legs bent, ready to attack. The man merely looked at him with his long dark hair plastered to his head and a brow raised.

"There is a Warrior and a Druid coming on to our land," the man said. "They have an infant. If the selmyr get to them—"

"Camdyn," Malcolm said and straightened. He looked at the man in front of him. "Who are you?"

"My name is Rhys, and I'm one of those," he said and pointed to the sky.

Malcolm lifted his eyes in time to see the sleek body of a dragon as blue as sapphires. He'd thought he saw something in the clouds earlier, but now he knew he most definitely had.

"Your friends are coming in through the main road," Rhys said.

When Malcolm looked back at him, Rhys was running out of the trees. And promptly shifted into a yellow dragon.

There was no time for Malcolm to stare in wonder. Camdyn and Saffron would need his help. He turned and raced through the trees as fast as his god would allow.

He came to the top of a mountain and spotted the dark green Audi Q7 barrel around a tight corner in the narrow road. Malcolm didn't bother with running down the mountain. He leaped instead.

Malcolm landed on the road, knees bent and one hand on the ground, as the lights of the Audi plowed toward him. He stood and met Camdyn's gaze through the windshield.

Camdyn stomped on the brakes as the SUV slid to a halt. It rocked against Malcolm before he jumped onto the roof.

"What in the name of all that is holy?" Camdyn yelled from the window he had rolled down.

"Drive!" Malcolm shouted. "And doona stop until we reach the house."

There was a pause, and three selmyr walked onto the road. Malcolm heard little Emma give a cry from inside the vehicle. There was no way he would allow Camdyn, Saffron, and especially Emma to be touched by the vile creatures.

"Drive!" Malcolm barked.

He barely had time to grab a hold of the SUV as Camdyn stomped on the accelerator. The vehicle rammed two of the selmyr, knocking them flat. But one managed to grab hold the side mirror and smash a hand through the window to make a grab at Saffron.

Malcolm leaned to the right and made a huge arching swipe of his hand. A satisfied smile tugged at his lips as his claws made a clean cut, beheading the creature.

He then kicked the body away. Malcolm looked straight ahead, the bite of the rain piercing his skin like shards of glass the faster Camdyn drove.

A few more selmyr dared to venture toward them. One even landed on top of the SUV with Malcolm. The selmyr peeled back its lips, showing elongated fangs.

The creature swiped a long arm at Malcolm, who managed to duck, but not without feeling the talons scrape his back. Malcolm lay across the top of the roof and rolled toward the selmyr, knocking the beast's legs out from under it.

Malcolm jumped up to land on the monster's back. But no matter how many times he plunged his claws into the selmyr, he couldn't kill it.

His only option was to try and find its heart. Before he could, however, the selmyr flipped them so that Malcolm was on his back staring up at the ash-skinned creature.

Malcolm swung his arm to try to cut off its head, but the creature caught his hand. Malcolm let out a bellow of fury as the selmyr's teeth sank into his skin.

No sooner had Malcolm begun to feel the biting inferno burn through him than a large, dark shape took form in the low hanging clouds. A second later he spotted Rhys dive toward them and clamp his monstrous dragon jaws around the selmyr before flying off with it.

Malcolm dropped his head back and just lay there for a second. They were nearing the mansion where he felt the magic of the other Druids. From his look at it an hour ago, he knew it was heavily guarded. He hadn't known by what at the time, but he knew all the Druids were safe.

He squatted atop the roof and turned as the mansion came into view. Malcolm anticipated Camdyn's braking, and when the SUV came to a halt, Malcolm tucked his body and flipped over the hood to land on his feet in front of the Audi.

Camdyn threw open his door and looked at the sky. "Dragons."

"You doona seem surprised," Malcolm said as he hurried to help Saffron out of the vehicle.

Saffron smiled at him, dark circles under her eyes. "I had a vision of the dragons, but more importantly, I saw how Jason would get away."

Malcolm escorted her into the mansion as Camdyn got

their daughter out of the SUV. Once inside, Malcolm pulled back the blanket shielding the carrier to find Emma's tawny eyes looking up at him.

"Thank you," Camdyn said, and held out his arm.

Malcolm clasped his forearm and nodded. "It wasna all me. Rhys, one of the dragons, told me you were coming."

"I know," Saffron told Camdyn when he turned to her and opened his mouth to speak. "Just come back to me. To us," she amended as she glanced at her daughter.

Camdyn pulled her into his arms for a kiss. "Always."

Malcolm and Camdyn walked back out into the rain. Camdyn released his god, the dark brown skin the color of earth covering him.

"There's no way I'm going to allow Wallace to get away this time."

Malcolm grinned, hearing the answering laughter of his god, Daal. "Then let's join the battle."

Laura's eyes flew open at the urging of the ancients. No longer could she hear them speaking, and the drums and chanting grew farther and farther away.

Yet she knew they weren't leaving her.

Laura squeezed Isla's hand to get her attention. When Isla's ice blue eyes met hers, Laura nodded to the doorway. Someone was in the house. Someone who hadn't been there before.

She stood with Isla as they silently made their way to the door. Laura looked around the corner to find a woman with walnut-colored hair removing her raincoat.

"Saffron," Isla said as she rushed past Laura.

The woman jerked her head to Isla and smiled, but it didn't quite reach her eyes.

"What are you doing here?" Isla asked as they hugged.

Laura slowly walked toward the two women as Saffron squatted down and unbuckled the baby from the carrier.

Saffron stood with the baby in her arms and looked at Laura. "Hello, Laura."

"You know her?" Isla asked with a frown.

"She was in my vision."

"Vision?" Laura repeated.

Saffron let Isla take the child from her and crossed her arms over her chest. "I'm a Seer."

"I thought you were staying away for the child's sake?"

"I was," Saffron said. She licked her lips and looked at Isla. "I saw how Jason would get away. We had to come."

Isla hugged the child to her. "For Emma's sake, you could have just called."

Saffron shook her head slowly. "You know Camdyn better than that. He wanted to leave me and Emma behind, but I refused."

"Come," Isla said as she turned and started back to the parlor. "The others need to know. What can we do?"

"Nothing."

Laura looked at Saffron, who still stood by the front door, and Isla who had stopped and faced her. "What do you mean nothing?"

"If we add our magic to try and halt Jason's departure, he'll use it to help him."

"He can do that?" Laura asked.

Saffron nodded. "Oh, yes."

Isla gave a slight wince when Emma grabbed hold of her long hair. "Then who can stop him?"

"The Warriors," Saffron answered. "I explained it all to Camdyn. He knows what to do."

"That's if he gets there in time," Laura added. "I hate to point out the obvious, but the battle could be over by now."

Saffron walked past Laura and Isla to the parlor and paused at the doorway. "He'll get there in time. After everything we've been through, none of the Warriors will let Jason walk away from this battle."

Laura waited for Saffron to enter the parlor before she looked at Isla to find the Druid's eyes trained on her. "We're Druids. We're meant to help."

"I know," Isla said. "That's the part that stings the most."

"Are Saffron's visions never wrong?"

Isla shook her head. "She only sees parts of visions.

When she isn't sure, she lets us know. I've never seen her so certain of something before."

"Why doesn't she just tell us the vision?"

"It must be bad enough that she's trying to spare us."

Laura turned to the window. "I won't accept the possibility of Charon not returning. I can't."

"And I can't think of Hayden being taken from me. They are Warriors, Laura. You need to trust in Charon's skill."

"I do," she admitted. "I've seen what he can do, but I've also seen Jason bring him down. With Jason and the selmyr attacking, will the dragons' aid be enough?"

"We just have to pray it is. And God help Jason Wallace if my Warrior doesn't walk through those doors."

Laura raised her hands in front of her as she felt her magic begin to tingle beneath her skin. She turned and rushed into the parlor to hear Saffron tell the others what was going on.

"You said Wallace would use our magic," she blurted out when Saffron paused.

Saffron frowned as she looked at her. "That's right. If we use our magic against him, he'll turn it to his advantage."

"So, let's not use our magic against him. Let's use our magic to heighten the storm or the forces of nature."

Sonya smiled widely. "Oh, I like that idea. Sitting by and doing nothing wasn't appealing to me at all."

"What do you think, Saffron?" Cara asked. "Can we do as Laura's suggested?"

Saffron sat there for a moment before a slow smile began to form. "Yes. I think we can."

Excitement pulsed through Laura, causing her magic to hum faster. The Druids resumed their circle on the floor, their hands linked and their eyes closed.

Laura's excitement grew as she once more heard the drums and chanting.

We're going to win, Charon, she thought to herself just before the ancients took her again.

CHAPTER
FORTY-SIX

There were too many selmyr. Charon realized it as soon as they were attacked. The dragons were holding hundreds more from getting to the others and joining in the attack.

He caught sight of two selmyr as they jumped on Hayden's back and bit him. Hayden let out a roar of rage, but couldn't get them off.

Charon rushed to the red-skinned Warrior and hastily jerked out the spine of one selmyr. The other turned to Charon with a hiss of indignation, Hayden's blood dripping from its lips.

"Come on, you ugly fuck," Charon taunted it.

Out of the corner of his eye, he spotted Hayden get to his knees and form a fireball in his hand. Charon dived to the side the same time Hayden launched the fire at the selmyr.

The creature was set ablaze instantly. It was Logan who gave a battle yell right before he beheaded the creature.

They only had time to get to their feet as more of the beasts rained down upon them. Charon glanced at Jason to see the bubble of magic he had surrounded himself with was diminishing quickly.

Something hurtled into Charon's back, knocking him face first into the ground. He bit back a yell when he felt a selmyr's bite.

Darkness, black as pitch, surrounded Charon. A heartbeat

later, the selmyr was lying dead beside him. Charon glanced up to find the shadows dissipating and Lucan leaning down to help him to his feet.

Charon pivoted as he caught sight of a creature and sank his claws into its back before he yanked out the spinal column. Around him, Fallon was teleporting all over the place, taking the beasts by surprise.

Broc was swooping down from the sky and beheading all he could reach, while Arran used his control over water to direct the rain into deadly blades.

Ramsey was using his ability as a half-Druid, half-Warrior to confuse the selmyr. Ian was absorbing any of the Warriors' power and directing it at the beasts to lethal precision.

Charon leaped over a creature as he searched for Phelan, only to find his friend surrounded by selmyr. Charon let out a battle cry and dived into the fray to come up and yank a selmyr off Phelan. There was a rumble beneath their feet, and suddenly the ground opened up around them to swallow the creatures.

"Duck!" shouted a female voice behind them.

Charon and Phelan didn't hesitate to do as Larena demanded. The only female Warrior was using her power of invisibility once again to her advantage.

There was a startled cry from a selmyr coming at them. Charon looked up to see its spine being yanked out by some unseen hand.

"There's more coming," Larena's disembodied voice said from somewhere in front of them. "Get moving."

Charon could see how weak Phelan was after all his blood loss. He wasn't feeling too frisky himself, but the battle was near to ending. How they would be able to sustain the battle, Charon wasn't sure.

And by the way Jason was now on his knees, the bubble around him thinning with each hit from the selmyr, it wouldn't be long before the creatures got to Wallace.

Then they would turn to the Warriors.

Charon got Phelan over to Quinn and Galen, who had set

up around Aiden. The Druid was using his magic against the creatures. Phelan dropped to his knees, his hands braced on his thighs as his head hung forward.

"I really hate these shits," Phelan said over the rain.

As if in answer, the storm strengthened. The rain came down at a punishing intensity while the wind howled and tried to knock them off their feet. The thunder rumbled constantly. Charon didn't know when one round of thunder ended and another began.

"Here they come!" Quinn yelled.

Charon looked up to see a cloud of ash approaching them. The selmyr abruptly appeared in front of them, their teeth bared as they went in for a bite.

Lightning forked viciously over the sky, lashing down upon them. The selmyr standing in front of Charon was fried to a crisp when a bolt zigzagged out of the sky and zapped him.

There was only one Warrior who could control lightning. Charon looked around and spotted Malcolm and Camdyn racing toward them.

"I'll be damned," Galen said with a grin when he spotted them.

Charon had never been so happy to see Malcolm or Camdyn. There wasn't time to welcome them since the selmyr had almost busted through Jason's magic.

"It's all about to end," Arran said, his white Warrior eyes trained on Wallace.

Charon wasn't ready to celebrate just yet. Deirdre and Declan had always managed to get out of tight spots. Even Jason had proved resourceful. It wouldn't be over until Charon was standing over Wallace's dead body.

The three MacLeod brothers lined up together as more selmyr appeared around them. Charon never got tired of watching Fallon, Lucan, and Quinn fight side by side. They were unstoppable.

But even they were soon overwhelmed by the sheer number of selmyr.

"Where are they coming from?" Ian asked.

Charon lunged forward the same time he dodged a creature's arm. He used his speed to get behind the selmyr and behead him. "Hell," he answered as the head fell to the ground.

There was no more time for talk as they fought to stay alive and struggled to keep the selmyr off them. There wasn't a one of them who hadn't been bitten at least a dozen times, and it was taking its toll.

Charon's usual speed wasn't there. It felt as if he didn't quite have control of his body. And he hurt. Everywhere, but especially the spots he'd been bitten.

He couldn't give up. He wouldn't give up. For Laura, for the Druids, for the innocents the world over who had no idea what was going on.

Or the costs it would have on the ones who fought the silent, unknown war.

Charon's knee buckled as he turned away from a selmyr. Phelan caught him before he hit the ground. He tried to smile at his friend, but it was Phelan's waxy complexion that made him anxious.

"I'm all right," Phelan said.

But Charon knew it for the lie it was, because he knew he looked just as bad as or worse than his friend.

Over the rumble of the torrential rain, Charon heard the roars of the dragons. He took a deep breath and got back on his feet. He managed to kill two more selmyr before he caught sight of Jason.

He wasn't the only one. The creatures around the Warriors had turned toward Wallace, their long strides eating up the ground as they hurried to him.

"Help!" Wallace cried to Charon.

Lucan walked up beside Charon and said, "This is going to be nice to watch."

"We should leave," Quinn cautioned.

Galen rotated his shoulders as his wounds healed. "I agree. Once the selmyr kill Wallace, they'll turn on us again."

"I'm no' leaving," Charon announced.

His words were accented by a fork of lightning that

landed close to them. He turned to Malcolm, thinking the Warrior had used his power.

"That wasna me," Malcolm said when everyone looked at him.

Phelan glanced up. "The storm. It's the storm."

"That recently strengthened," Aiden said.

Camdyn stepped forward. "Saffron had a vision on how Jason would escape. It's why I'm here. The Druids were going to use their magic to try and hold Wallace here, but somehow in Saffron's vision he turned it around and used their magic to his advantage."

"So they've strengthened the storm," Hayden said.

Charon could no longer see Jason, there were so many selmyr. After all the bastard had done to him and Laura, Charon was eager for Wallace's death. The only thing that could make it better was if Charon took his life himself.

Wallace's magic was fading quickly. No longer did the sticky feel of *drough* magic fill the area.

"He didna last as long as I thought he would," Phelan said.

Charon was about to agree with him when the sky opened and lightning hit Jason's magic bubble the same time a selmyr did. The *boom* was deafening as it spread, knocking everyone off their feet and onto their backs.

When Charon opened his eyes he blinked past the onslaught of rain, his ears ringing. He jerked as a face filled his vision. It was Phelan, and he was saying something, but Charon couldn't hear him.

The quick healing of his god made Charon's ears pop as Phelan pulled him on his feet. He looked to where Wallace had been, but found the spot empty.

All around it, in a huge circle, were the selmyr laid out unconscious. But they were beginning to stir.

"Shit," Charon said, and turned to the other Warriors.

"Larena!" Fallon shouted over and over for his wife.

Charon's gut clenched for Fallon. Larena's ability to turn invisible was a boon, but it came at a steep price when Fallon couldn't find her.

"Here!" came a shout farther up the mountain.

Charon turned back to the place Jason had almost been defeated. "He couldna have gotten away. No' when he was so close to dying."

"I guess there isna a chance the lightning got him, is there?" Arran asked.

Phelan snorted. "If only. We willna know for sure until we go looking for him."

"Until then, let's get out of here," Ramsey said.

Charon hung back with Phelan, Arran, and Ian as Fallon teleported the others to the mansion.

"We can no' leave these selmyr to live," he said.

Ian's lips flattened. "I want them dead as much as you do, but we're no' in fit shape to take them on again."

"We need to give ourselves at least a day to recover," Arran said.

Phelan caught Charon's gaze. "Then have a plan to take these buggers out in one fell swoop."

Charon nodded as the selmyr stood up one by one. He grinned at them, but before they could take another step, dragons dived from the sky, scattering the selmyr to the four winds.

"Until next time," Charon murmured.

He looked up to see a gold dragon. Somehow Charon knew it was Con. Charon lifted his hand to the King of Kings just as Fallon laid a hand on Charon's shoulder.

In a blink, Charon found himself in the foyer of Con's mansion. All around him, the Druids were fussing over their Warriors.

Charon, Phelan, and Malcolm stood alone, watching it all. The sea of bodies parted enough so that Charon spotted Laura at the base of the stairs staring at him.

"What are you waiting for?" Phelan leaned over and whispered. "She's meant to be yours, my friend."

Charon put one foot in front of the other as he walked to the one woman in the world who held his heart in her hands. He dodged people and ignored comments directed at him.

All he cared about, all he wanted was to get to Laura. Yet the closer he came, the more he doubted himself. She had been thrust into a world she wasn't prepared for.

He had questioned her and kept her separated from the other Druids. It had been done to protect the others, but in the process, he had hurt her.

By the time he reached Laura, he knew he wasn't good enough for her. But that didn't stop his love for her. It was love. He knew that now.

Laura's smile was bright as she threw her arms around his neck and hugged him. Charon held her as tight as he dared. The aches of his bite wounds fading with her nearness.

"I was so worried," she whispered.

Charon ran a hand down her hair and closed his eyes as he squeezed her. "I'm here, just where I told you I would be."

"It was close, wasn't it?"

He almost didn't answer her, but she deserved to know. "Aye."

"It killed me not knowing what was going on." She leaned back to look at him.

He gazed into her moss green eyes. Once more, he was drowning, sinking. Tumbling.

Into all that was Laura.

He'd never spoken words of love to a woman, and he wasn't even sure how to begin. Or what to say. Laura had been a coworker, and then a friend. She was now his lover, and the woman he loved above anything else.

"What is it?" she asked, a frown marking her forehead.

Charon cleared his throat.

Laura's gaze lowered and she saw all the bite marks that were healing, but gradually. "Oh, my God!"

"I'm all right," he assured her.

Her hands hovered over several of the bites, her eyes wide and her lips parted in horror. "You aren't healing."

"I am. Just slowly."

"Is that what's wrong?" she asked as her gaze jerked back to his. "Do you need to rest?"

Charon couldn't stop touching her, couldn't think of another minute without her beside him. "I'll be fine, Laura. I promise."

"Then what is it?" she asked hesitantly.

He saw the dread enter her eyes, and a knot of uncertainty coiled in his gut. "Laura . . . it's asking a lot, I know, but is there any way you could ever love a man like me?"

Laura's breath locked in her lungs. Of all the things she expected Charon to say, that hadn't been it. Her heart began to pound so loudly, she thought it might leap from her chest.

The uncertainty in his gaze and his disheveled, wet hair made her want to wrap her arms around him and hold him forever.

"No," she said.

Charon's dark gaze clouded as he visibly began to close himself off. He looked away. "I see."

"Because I already love you," she said as a tear fell from her eyes.

His gaze flew back up to hers, filled with hope and love. "You love me?"

"Yes, Charon Bruce. I love you."

He pulled her into his arms and held her tightly before he whispered, "I love you, Laura."

Her eyes closed as she smiled. They were words she had feared never to hear. But Charon had given them to her, and in doing so, she had given him her heart and her soul.

"I love you," he whispered again.

CHAPTER
FORTY-SEVEN

Aiden scanned the foyer twice, but still he couldn't find Britt. His gazed paused when he caught sight of Charon and Laura kissing. There was no doubt that another Warrior had found his mate.

Unable to stop himself, Aiden's eyes went to Malcolm, who stood silent and still beside Larena and Fallon while Aiden's parents were talking.

Malcolm's intense azure gaze met his for a moment before shifting away. There had been a flash of something—regret maybe—before the dead stare Aiden was used to returned.

Aiden was never sure what to say to the Warrior, but it would have to wait. He had to find Britt.

When he turned his head, he found Elena motioning him to come to her. Aiden hurried to her side, relief pouring through him at her kind smile.

"She's safe," Elena said before Aiden could ask.

Aiden let out a deep breath. "Thank you. Where is she?"

"Upstairs. We figured that would be the best place for her. She's been working there ever since she arrived. Third floor," she said as she gave him a push toward the stairs.

Aiden skirted around Charon and Laura, who were busy smiling at each other before he took the steps three at a time.

His heart was hammering wildly in his chest by the time he reached the third-floor landing.

He paused at the lone door that stood cracked open a few inches. There was a light coming from inside and a soft hum of music. A smile pulled up his lips when he heard Linkin Park.

With his hand upon the door, Aiden pushed it open and silently walked inside. His knees went weak when he finally laid eyes on Britt. She was slumped over, her head pillowed on her arm with her wealth of blond hair pulled back into a ponytail with several pencils sticking out near the holder.

Aiden hadn't realized just how tightly wound he'd been until he laid eyes on her again. Only then did the viselike clamps around his heart loosen.

He barely spared the pages of scribble on the table a glance as he smoothed a lock of hair away from her face. Unable to hold back, he ran the backs of his fingers down the silken skin of her cheek to her jaw.

Her eyes fluttered open. When her gaze caught sight of him, she slowly sat up. "You're alive."

"I am."

"Are you injured?"

"Nothing that can no' be healed," he said, and took a step closer to her. "Can you ever forgive me for dragging you into this world of mine?"

She raised a blond brow, a small smile playing about her lips. "As dangerous as it's been, I'd be more pissed had you not."

"My life is . . . complicated."

"Everyone's life is complicated. Are you going to try for another excuse, or are you finally going to kiss me?"

Aiden laughed as he moved between her legs as she sat on the stool. "My God, woman. You're a handful."

"But you like it."

"Oh, aye. I like it verra much," he whispered before he kissed her long and slow.

He was just deepening the kiss when she pulled back. "Wait," Britt said breathlessly, her lips already swollen.

"Doona tease me," he said before he nipped at her earlobe.

Her hands flattened on his chest before she gave a little push. "I've found something, Aiden. Something that could turn the tide of this war you're fighting."

All thoughts of kissing and laying her out on the table to strip her bare vanished. "Show me."

Con stood in the rain outside the mountain as he stared at the mansion that had been his home for centuries. It had felt so good to take to the skies and battle evil once more. But the battle was over. It was time to resume his role.

"Are you regretting it?" Rhys asked as he walked up, buttoning his jeans.

There were always clothes inside the mountain in case a King needed them.

"Nay. If we had no', they would've fallen, Wallace's evil would reign, and the selmyr would've slaughtered all the Druids. We'd have had to fight them anyway. Better to help the side of good in times like this."

Guy strode up and shoved his long wet hair out of his face. "Most of the Kings have returned to their sleep. A few others have decided to remain awake."

"Who?" Con asked.

"Ryder, Kiril, and Darius."

Con nodded. "They've all slept for many centuries. Who is getting them caught up on world events and technology for the last decade?"

"We drew straws," Guy said with a sly grin. "Hal and Laith lost."

For the first time in days, Con found himself grinning. He spotted Tristan still in dragon form flying through the skies. "How is Tristan?"

"He did good." Rhys frowned and shoved his hands in the front pockets of his jeans. "Too good. We all assumed he was battle-hardened, and he proved it today."

"Do we tell the Warriors?" Guy asked.

Con hesitated for just a moment. "No' yet."

"No' sure that's a good move," Rhys stated.

"It's my decision. Who put Tristan on patrol?"

Guy shrugged. "Tristan put himself. Said he wasna ready to come out of the sky."

Constantine's gaze lowered back to his mansion. "I doona know how long the Warriors and Druids will stay. They're welcome here from now on. Make sure everyone knows."

"They're going to have questions," Rhys said.

"Just as we would. I'll handle them," Con said, and started for the house.

He wasn't surprised when Rhys and Guy walked into the mansion with him. He'd given them an out, but as usual, they took their responsibility as Kings seriously.

As soon as Con was inside, every eye in the foyer turned to him. Fallon approached him first.

"Thank you," the leader of the Warriors said.

Con let his gaze roam slowly among their new allies. "Our home is yours. All of you are welcome to stay for a meal, warm shower, a change of clothes, and all the whisky you could want."

"I'm no' passing that up," Quinn said with a grin.

Con looked over Fallon's torn and bloodied shirt before he shifted his gaze to Larena standing in nothing but a blanket wrapped around her. "There have been rooms assigned to each of you and fresh clothes waiting."

"Sounds heavenly," Larena said.

Jane cleared her throat from the stairs. "If everyone will follow me, I'll direct you to your rooms."

They all started for the stairs. Everyone except Malcolm and Phelan. Con watched as Phelan scowled after lowering his gaze from Charon and Laura. He took a step backwards, trying to keep out of everyone's sight.

With a nudge to Rhys, Con gave a nod in Phelan's direction. Con's attention then turned to Malcolm. The scarred Warrior hadn't moved or spoken since Con arrived.

"Malcolm?" Larena asked, her brow furrowed.

Malcolm slowly released a breath. "It's time for me to leave."

"Stay this time," Fallon pleaded. "There's no reason no' to."

Con was startled when Malcolm's azure gaze landed on him. He waited, wondering what reason Malcolm would give for leaving the very people he needed. He might not know he needed them, but he did.

"There's every reason," Malcolm finally replied.

Without another word to Larena or Fallon, Malcolm turned on his heel and walked straight toward Con. Con stepped aside to allow Malcolm to pass, only to follow him back into the rain.

"What are you doing?" Malcolm asked, his back to him, when Con had shut the door behind them.

Con walked until he stood in front of Malcolm, ignoring the rain as he always did. "I doona want you to leave on our account. We're allies now, Malcolm."

"I'm leaving because it's what I need to do."

"You doona like being around your family? Do you know how much it pains Larena to see you leave each time?"

"I return," Malcolm replied without any emotion.

Con clasped his hands behind his back. "There may come a time when you need friends."

"I'll only hurt those near me. They think they want me around, but they doona. I doona want their pity or their kindness. I made my own decisions."

"Ah," Con said, understanding dawning. "You have no' been immortal for verra long. There will come a time you need someone. That time comes for all of us, no matter what we might tell ourselves in the long hours of the night."

Malcolm's dead expression didn't change.

Con stepped aside again. "I'll make the same offer to you that I made to Charon. If you ever find yourself in need of anything, you're always welcome here."

For a split second, Constantine thought he saw a flicker of something in Malcolm's blue eyes, but it was gone before Con could name what it was.

Malcolm didn't say a word as he walked away and faded into the forest.

* * *

"Leaving?"

Phelan growled his frustration as he turned to find one of the Dragon Kings behind him. Which of the dragons was this King? The Black perhaps?

"I doona think Charon would appreciate you sneaking off as you are," the man said, and followed Phelan into the conservatory. He paused to rub his fingers on the leaf of some plant and cut his aqua eyes to Phelan. "I'm Rhys."

"And like all the Kings, you know each of us?"

Rhys's grin widened. "Doona be so sour. You make it your business to learn about all the evil businessmen, wife-beaters, child molesters, and such in the world. We make it our business to know the Warriors and their women."

"I doona have a woman."

"Nay. No woman holds you for more than a few hours," Rhys said with a chuckle.

Phelan narrowed his gaze on the King. "What do you want?"

"I want you to consider staying for a wee bit. Charon was in a nasty mood when he couldna get a hold of you earlier."

"Charon is . . . indisposed right now."

"Jealous?" he sneered.

Phelan took the three steps separating them and got in Rhys's face, anger sizzling beneath his skin. Was it jealousy that Charon had found someone? Phelan didn't know, and didn't want to think about it. "He's my friend. I'm happy for him."

"Then stay," Rhys said, the taunting grin gone.

Phelan frowned and took a step back. There had to be a reason the Dragon wanted him to stay. "What are you after?"

"Nothing. Charon is a good man. He considers you a friend, a close friend. We're just looking out for him."

"Why did you no' look out for him when Deirdre took him? Where were you then?"

Rhys lowered his gaze to the ground for a moment before he looked back at Phelan. "Charon is the only man you've ever called friend. Is that truth or no'?"

"Truth," Phelan answered after a long hesitation, wondering where the hell all this was going.

"You Warriors are powerful. You've immense strength, speed, and other abilities added to each individual power given to you by your god. In times of great need, all of you will band together and fight." Rhys paused then. "Why is it when the battle is over, you're one of the first to run away?"

"I do better on my own."

Rhys shrugged one shoulder. "And now that Charon has found Laura?"

Phelan glanced over his shoulder into the foyer. He could no longer see Charon and Laura, but he didn't need to. He had caught sight of them heading up the stairs, their arms wrapped around each other seconds earlier.

He *was* happy for his friend, yet there was a part of Phelan that felt lost. Charon had been as alone as he was. Now things would return to what they had been before he met Charon.

"I'm happy for him," Phelan said. "He's wanted her for a long time. They look good together, do they no'?"

"They do. I know what it's like."

"What?"

"Not quite knowing what to do with the friends who've found their mates."

Phelan sighed, suddenly weary of hiding his feelings. "Is it difficult to cope?"

"Aye, but their happiness makes it easier."

"I'll worry about that once I know Wallace is really dead. Until then, I'm going looking for him. Now, sod off, Dragon, I've hunting to do."

He gave Rhys a friendly slap on the shoulder and strode out of the mansion. Phelan had no idea where he was going. Once he found his Ducati he had stashed in the forest, he'd set out on the roads and just drive.

It's what he had always done.

Con stood under the overhang of the stillhouse with Rhys and Guy. "What do you think?" he asked.

"Phelan willna admit it, but he's lonely," Rhys said.

Guy leaned a shoulder against the building. "Malcolm is difficult to get a read on."

"So you discovered nothing?" Con asked.

Guy snorted. "I didna say that. I said it was difficult."

"Well," Rhys urged when he didn't continue.

Guy looked out through the rain at Phelan. "As long as Larena is around, Malcolm will fight with the Warriors."

"And if she's no'?" Con asked.

"She's the only thing holding him to the Warriors or the Druids. I'd like to say he'd feel responsible to help them should the need arise, but I'm no' sure I can."

Con looked at the sky to see Tristan flying low. "Of all the Warriors, Malcolm spent the least amount of time with Deirdre. I didna think she'd get her hooks in him so quick or so deep."

"I think it stems from what happened to him before his god was unbound," Guy added.

Rhys nodded. "Could be. With all the time Phelan spent in Cairn Toul before—and after—his god was unbound, there isna a darkness in him like there is Malcolm."

"What is it about Charon that got you to change your mind about helping them, Con?" Guy asked.

Constantine looked at his fellow Kings and grinned. "He went back to the village he was raised in. He made sure they were safe, that they were never without jobs. Charon made a name for himself with his businesses all the while keeping what he is a secret."

"He did what we did," Rhys said with a nod of understanding.

"If Fallon or the MacLeod brothers had no' stepped up to lead the Warriors, I do believe Charon would've taken the challenge."

Con left Rhys and Guy to make his way to the hidden entrance into the mountain behind the mansion. He shook off the rain and walked to a cavern on the right.

There he paused beside the massive cage that held the four sleeping silver dragons. It was only the magic of the

Kings that kept the Silvers from waking and destroying man as they had been before being captured.

Male laughter filtered down to him from one of the corridors. He listened for a moment, then turned on his heel to find the Kings who had decided their time of resting was over.

CHAPTER
FORTY-EIGHT

Laura walked out of the bathroom and came to a halt. She smiled as she stared at the drop-dead gorgeous male who reclined on the bed with his eyes closed and nothing covering him.

She let her eyes run over every delectable inch of Charon's muscled form. The last of the bite marks from the selmyr were healing, and the fact he was lying there with his eyes closed told her how exhausted he was.

Though she was loath to disturb him, she wanted to be beside him. Laura quietly walked to the bed. The only sound was the wooden floor creaking beneath the rug.

She glanced at the bed to find Charon's chocolate gaze riveted on her. Her heart skipped a beat at the desire she saw.

Laura pulled at the belt holding her robe together. As soon as it parted, she heard Charon's growl of approval. She let the robe fall to the floor, and then stood while Charon's gaze raked over her.

He sat up and grabbed her hand to slowly pull her to him. Laura bent her knee to place it on the bed, and then found herself straddling Charon.

His thick arousal pressed against her stomach and made her blood run wild. She placed her hands on his chest and felt the hot, hard sinew beneath her palms.

In the next heartbeat, she was on her back, Charon kneeling between her opened thighs he held in his hands. Laura couldn't calm her breathing, not when the need was so great.

He released her legs and leisurely caressed from her neck, over her aching breasts, down her stomach until he reached her sex. With slow, measured caresses he teased the dark curls that hid her.

She gasped when his finger lightly grazed her clitoris. Again and again, he would draw near the swollen nub, but he wouldn't touch it.

The head of his arousal pushed at her entrance. Laura locked her eyes with his, and waited for him to fill her. With one thrust, he was seated to the hilt. Her body welcomed him, yearned for him.

Needed him.

He was all she ever wanted, all she would ever need. With him she felt as if she could conquer the world and stand against any evil.

With him she was complete.

"You're mine," he whispered as he stared into her eyes.

She placed her hand over his heart. "And you're mine."

"Forever."

"And always."

Laura's eyes slid closed when Charon bent and took her lips in a searing kiss as his hips began to move. She wrapped her arms around his neck and gave her body, her heart, and her soul to the immortal Warrior who had claimed it.

EPILOGUE

Ferness
Two days later

Charon smiled when Laura came up behind him on the bed and wrapped her arms around his neck. They stared out the window overlooking the forest for several quiet minutes.

"Any word?" she asked as she kissed his cheek.

"Nothing. There's no sign of Jason Wallace anywhere."

"He's probably dead."

"Could we get that lucky?"

She skimmed her nails through his hair. "The breadth and width of Scotland is being searched, my love. You spent all of yesterday looking for the bugger."

"We're missing something. I know it."

"What does Phelan think?"

Charon hated the frustration that wouldn't loosen its hold. "He says Wallace is dead."

"You don't believe him?"

"I can hear the lie in his voice. By the way Phelan is crisscrossing Scotland tells me he's doing some searching of his own."

"That's all we can do," Laura said and squeezed her arms around him. "Every Warrior from MacLeod Castle is searching. The fact Broc can't find Jason should say something."

"It should, but Declan was able to hide himself from Broc's power before. Jason could as well."

Laura rose from the bed and walked around to stand in front of him. He gripped her jean-clad hips as she stood between his legs. "To talk of happier things, Con sent over a truckload of whisky."

Charon took her left hand in his and pulled her down beside him.

"Why aren't you happy? You should be happy with that news," Laura said.

He grinned, but was too anxious to answer her. Instead, he flipped open his hand where the three-carat blue diamond in a filigree platinum band sat nestled in his palm.

"I know your world has been rocked, and there's a chance the war I've been raging will continue, but I couldn't go another day without asking if you'd be my wife. I want you to share my name as well as my bed, Laura. Will you marry me?"

Laura's hands shook as she covered her mouth and stared in shock at the stunning ring. She lowered her hands and nodded. "Yes. Of course!"

She smiled through the tears that filled her eyes as he placed the ring upon her finger.

"We can wait as long as you need," Charon said before he kissed her.

Laura had never been so happy, but there was one question she hadn't dared ask. "We don't live at MacLeod Castle. I'll age, Charon. I'll die."

"Then we'll move to the castle," he said matter-of-factly. "I'll do whatever it takes to keep you with me."

"Your life is here, not at the castle."

"My life is anywhere you are. Besides, I know the Mac-Leods are looking for the spell that would bind our gods."

She was so shocked that for a moment she couldn't speak. "You'd be mortal?"

"Aye," Charon answered with a wide smile. "We could grow old together."

"But you're a Warrior."

He shrugged and ran his thumb over her ring. "I know the Dragon Kings will watch over things. It's time for our life."

"Whatever that is. Be it you stay immortal or not. We are together. That's enough."

There was no more talking as he kissed her and pushed her back on the bed.

Glasgow

Aisley parked the car and got out, the steady beat of the nightclub filling the streets. How she had missed the music so loud that it drowned out her thoughts.

She walked through the back door to find Dan's surprised face. "Miss me?" she asked.

"More than you know," he said, and huffed on his cigar. "How long you staying this time, lass?"

She shrugged and walked through the curtain of beads into the small room that served as a dressing room. Aisley didn't even look in the mirror.

There had been a time she would have spent an hour sitting there making sure her hair and makeup were just right. But tonight she wasn't there to work. She was there to get lost in the music.

"Damn, girl!" Pam said when she caught sight of Aisley. "I didn't think I'd ever see you again once your cousin found you. All that money and all."

Aisley forced a smile. "Is my cage taken?"

Pam pointed up past the floor of crushed bodies moving to the music. "Stacy is up there now, but I can tell her to take a break."

Aisley pulled out a wad of pound notes. "Tell her to take the night off."

Pam whistled and then flicked the switch to lower the cage from the ceiling. Aisley impatiently waited. In the birdcage she could dance and let the music take away her worries without having to concern herself with anyone around her.

Once Stacy was out of the cage, Aisley stepped inside and held on as it was lifted back to the top. She closed her eyes, remembering a time when she had been hired to dress scantily and dance in the birdcage all night long.

That seemed like a lifetime ago. So much had happened since then. She wasn't the same naïve girl who had walked the streets of Glasgow with stars in her eyes and dreams as big as the sky.

The song faded, quickly replaced with "Where Have You Been" by Rihanna. Aisley felt the music drift around her. It called to her soul, and to her surprise, it was her magic that answered.

Music had always been her refuge, the place she would go to for everything. Tonight she needed the hard beats, loud drums, and long guitar solos like she'd never needed them before.

Her world was destroyed. She was both thankful and fearful. The selmyr could still find her, but until they did, she was going to revel in the music that let her drift away from the hell she lived in.

A surge of magic filled her, taking her breath. She gave in to the seductive beat of the music and her magic and left the world behind as she began to move to the haunting strings of the song.

Phelan shut off his Ducati and pushed the kickstand down as he removed his helmet. He was thirsty and hungry, and he needed a woman.

He'd been in need of a female for several days, but oddly, he had yet to find one who appealed to him. Which was just . . . strange.

Phelan had never been too particular when it came to his women. Many had flirted with him the past few days, and they had even offered themselves. For the first time, he was the one to walk away before he had sex with them.

He swung his leg over the motorbike and stood. On the side of the street he was on were two pubs. Both looked lively enough.

Yet it was the nightclub across the street that kept drawing his gaze. He could feel magic. For several minutes, he simply stood there trying to determine where the magic was coming from.

That wasn't the only weird thing. There were times he was sure it was *drough* magic, and others that it was *mie*.

"They're probably both here," he muttered to himself and crossed the street to the club.

He pushed through the front door and was instantly assaulted with blaring music, dimmed lights, and lasers. The feel of magic grew stronger inside the club, which intrigued him. After he paid the fee to enter, he walked through the thick throng of people to the even more crowded bar.

"What'll you have?" shouted a cute bartender with ebony skin and a blouse unbuttoned so she showed ample cleavage.

"Whisky."

She gave a wink and hurried away to get his order. Phelan slowly looked around the large club. He grinned as he spotted couples in corners—and some in the middle of the dance floor—kissing and grinding.

He turned to place both elbows on the bar when he noticed what looked like four human-size birdcages hanging over the dance floor. Inside each was a woman dancing.

All the women were beautiful, but it was the woman with long black hair, mini-skirt, and short shirt that ended after molding over her breasts who got his attention.

"Here you go," the bartender said.

Phelan paid her without taking his eyes from the woman dancing. "Who is that?" he asked over the music that seemed to grow even louder.

The bartender turned her head to look where he was pointing. "Oh, that's Aisley. She's not been here in a couple of years. Forget it. She doesn't talk to anyone. Though she always gets the blokes' flags to raise," she said with a knowing wink.

Phelan took his drink and moved to a different part of the club to get a better view of Aisley. She danced with her eyes closed, as if she were part of the music blaring around her.

He'd never seen anything like her before. Her body was pliant, her movements fluid. She was one with the music, as if she didn't exist without it, and it without her. Her dancing enthralled him, fascinated him.

Captivated him.

And that was nothing compared to what the magic was doing to him. It swarmed him, surrounding him in its persuasive, formidable tethers without him even knowing it.

His body was on fire, aching for a woman's touch—Aisley's touch.

Phelan had no idea how long he watched her or how many songs she danced to. He would stay there for eternity if it meant he could see her.

And then she opened her eyes to look right at him.

Something primal moved inside him. He had to know this woman. At all costs.

When he saw the cage being lowered, he hurried to her. She tried to evade him, but there was no way Phelan was going to lose sight of her.

He followed her down a long, narrow hallway that came to a dead end. She whirled around and glared at him with eyes as dark as her hair.

Phelan could hardly breathe. She was magnificent dancing, but up close he was stunned at her earthy beauty from her dark skin, speaking of Spanish heritage, to her incredible lips.

His hands itched to feel her mocha-colored skin beneath his. Even when he knew he should back away from her, he couldn't. He kept walking to her until he stood inches from her.

"Wh—?"

He placed a finger on her lips to silence her. "No' tonight, beauty. No words," he said as he leaned close and brushed his lips over hers.

Phelan felt her body jerk. Was it in surprise? Had she thought he would hurt her? Never. She was a woman to be protected and cherished, a woman to be loved and adored.

He placed his lips on hers. When she relaxed, he swept his

tongue inside her mouth and groaned at the smooth, honeyed taste of her.

Her soft moan was his undoing. He deepened the kiss, the need, the sheer, unadulterated hunger that assaulted him, left him reeling.

But he couldn't release her. She tasted too good.

Phelan lifted his hand and grazed his thumb over her bared waist. Longing shot through him, setting him on fire with the desire urging him on.

Her skin was as soft as down, and her kiss as heady as wine. The fact she was responding to his kisses only made his need grow.

He groaned when she placed her hand on his chest, and though he hated to stop it, he ended the kiss when she gave him a soft shove back.

Phelan glanced around, wondering if there was a place they could be alone. He had to have her, or explode from the desire heating his blood.

"You don't want to get mixed up with me," she whispered and moved around him.

It was only as he turned to watch her leave that he realized the magic he'd been feeling was hers.

"Go ahead and run, beauty. I'll find you again," Phelan said to himself.

Aisley shoved open the back door to the club and gulped in the cool night air. She reached out to grab hold of the side of the building as her world tilted haphazardly.

"My God," she murmured in shock and dismay. "I just kissed a Warrior."

How he hadn't realized what she was and killed her instantly, she didn't know. But it was time for her to get out of town.

Don't miss Donna Grant's sensational e-series

MIDNIGHT'S TEMPTATION

Available in Fall 2013

. . . and look for the full volume of
Midnight's Temptation in October 2013

FROM ST. MARTIN'S PAPERBACKS